SALEM'S GHOSTS

SALEM'S GHOSTS

by
Rose Earhart

Pendleton
Books

Copyright © 2000 by Harriet R. Tarr
All rights reserved

Published by Pendleton Books
666 Fifth Avenue Suite 365
New York, NY 10103

Printed in the United States of America

Library of Congress Catalog Card Number: 99-65851

Earhart, Rose/Salem's Ghosts

ISBN 1-893221-01-6

Without limiting the rights under copyright reserved above,
no part of this publication may be reproduced,
stored in or introduced into a retrieval system,
or transmitted in any form or by any means
(electronic, mechanical, photo-copying, recording or otherwise),
without the prior written permission of both the copyright
owner and the above publisher of this book.

FIRST EDITION

CONTENTS

PROLOGUE:	THE VOICES OF THE DEAD
PART ONE:	THE LOST SOUL
PART TWO:	SEDUCTION IN THE DARK
PART THREE:	INTERCOURSE WITH EVIL
PART FOUR:	THE DEVIL THIS WAY COMES
PART FIVE:	CROSSING THE RIVER STYX
PART SIX:	TOUCHING THROUGH THE VEIL
PART SEVEN:	THE BURNING MOON
EPILOGUE:	RESTLESS SOULS

For my mother,

Harriet Earhart Tarr

and

my father,

William Warren Tarr

ACKNOWLEDGMENTS

The living history of Philip and Mary English is true, a story that can be researched and read about as you walk the streets of Salem. There is also one ghost written about in this book who has quite a lively past. George Corwin, high sheriff of Salem during the Witch Trials of 1692, does indeed seem to have a restless soul. He abides in a magnificent brick house on Washington Street that now contains the Higginson Book Company. Many have seen and will testify to George's hauntings. There have also been sightings of a lovely woman with long dark hair in the same place. These phenomena have been well recorded, and have even been the subject of a documentary on the Arts and Entertainment Network.

I would like to thank the Higginson Book Company, the Peabody-Essex Museum, the Salem Athenaeum, the Salem Public Library, and the New England Pirate Museum of Salem, Massachusetts, for their help and continued support. I would also like to thank the Peabody Library of Danvers, Massachusetts, for valuable documentation of several events including the hanging of George Burroughs. In addition, I would like to acknowledge the debt I have to the actual victims of the witchcraft hysteria of 1692. Thank you for your courage and your love of the truth.

SALEM'S GHOSTS

"Wherever I go I hear voices of the dead."
Frank McCourt: *Angela's Ashes*.

PROLOGUE

STAVE ONE

"Oh Lord, here they come again!" I heard Bridget cry as she jumped atop the stone that bore her name.

"Keep calm Mistress Bishop," muttered old Rebecca who was almost deaf, but not deaf enough to ignore Bridget's shrill cries, "'twill only make matters worse."

"Calm yourself, you old biddy," said Bridget as she stepped onto the worn grass that grew beneath her memorial and stomped down five stones to where sweet Rebecca sat. "I can't understand how you of all people, Rebecca Nurse, can sit through this torture with such a straight face."

"But Bridget," I said, "if it weren't for those folks dripping their candles and shaking dying flowers at us you would still be a bit of dust lying in a rocky crevice up on Gallows Hill. Think of it, girl! You owe this whole miracle to the Temple of Nine Wells."

"Miracle indeed," snorted Bridget as she headed towards me. Much as I hated to be the object of her wrath it was a relief to see the fiery Bridget turn her anger away from dear Rebecca Nurse. At least I was free to escape from Salem's Witch Memorial and wander the streets of Salem as I pleased.

"Yes, miracle," I said as I carefully lured Bridget back to her stone. "Bridget, you must be in the proper position when the high priestess of the Temple of Nine Wells comes to chant and place her candles and flowers in your honor. Think how things have changed since they built this place. It seems to me that you have forgotten the terrible times when, for three hundred years, your soul lay trapped beneath the rocks up on Gallows Hill."

"It is but a cold, dark dream to me now, Mary," said Bridget sitting upon her stone and staring up at me with wild eyes. "But I suppose you're right. Stay I must on this stone while they drip their hot tallow on my breast and shake their flowers under my nose. But I tell you now that if I kick or sneeze I don't care who hears it. I will make no apology for scaring the wits out of a true believer. It's lucky you are, Mary English, that you have the run of the town."

"Aye, I am fortunate," I said with a smile. "But it's not luck, Bridget. It's the cleverness of my darling Philip that sets my soul free to wander where it may."

"And where is our fine Captain English this All Hallows Eve?" said gruff Giles Corey, who always brightened at the mention of my husband's name.

"Why strolling the candlelit halls of the place they call 'The House of Seven Gables,' down on Turner street. It makes him merry to think that our descendant, Nathaniel Hawthorne, rebuilt the family fortune on a tale about our home."

"But dearie," said Bridget with a giggle, "'twas the story before the 'Gables' one that was the greatest tale of all. You know, the one about your mother and old Cotton Mather. What was it called?"

"The Scarlet Letter," I said curtly, not feeling at all like getting into it with Bridget on this night above all nights.

"But 'twas a juicy time they had, wasn't it, Lady English?" said Bridget, determined to make me squirm.

"Well yes, I suppose it was," I said trying to give her enough satisfaction so that she would drop her eyes from me and set them upon the approaching witches. "Hush now Bridget, and do what you must to stay on this side of the mortal veil."

I put my hand upon Bridget's shoulder and squeezed it gently. Then I lifted my head and smiled to my other friends, each seated on a cold stone bench upon which was inscribed their name and the date of their execution. All were victims of the witchcraft hysteria that had gripped Salem, Massachusetts in the summer and fall of 1692. How joyous I had been when the worshipers of Wicca had finally triumphed over the town politicians and set up the memorial for my beloved friends.

It often seems hard to believe that we have all been dead over three hundred years. The men and woman I see neatly arranged on the semi-circle of stone benches look as alive as the Halloween revelers in the approaching crowd. But then, this is Salem, a place where the living and the dead spend their days together and the veil between the solid world and the spirit realm is always waiting to be torn through. And torn through it was, the moment the town council decided to celebrate the three hundredth anniversary of the hangings of Gallows Hill. As soon as chisel was set to stone and roots planted in earth for the memorial, things began to change. It was as if both Salems, the one that truly lives and the one that is eternally undead, had begun to grow together. It was my Philip who first noticed this as we stood together, choosing to be invisible to the living crowd around us. We watched in awe as first one old friend and then another appeared seated upon their stone benches. They looked at us in bemused wonder as the brothers and sisters of the Temple of Nine Wells dedicated the memorial in their honor. The condemned witches of Salem Town had at last been raised from their unhallowed graves and returned home. 'Twas the younger of the two high priestesses, Lillith March, who tolled out their names to the ringing of St. Peter's ancient bell.

>   Bridget Bishop-hanged June 10th. A lusty wench.
>   Sarah Good-hanged July 19th. The mother who lost her daughters.
>   Elizabeth Howe-hanged July 19th. A sweet woman who prayed.
>   Susannah Martin-hanged July 19th. A skeptic.
>   Rebecca Nurse-hanged July 19th. The sainted matriarch.
>   Sarah Wildes-hanged July 19th. A true witch.
>   George Burroughs-hanged August 19th. A man of God.
>   Martha Carrier-hanged August 19th. Mother of seven.
>   George Jacobs-hanged August 19th. He saved his granddaughter.
>   John Proctor-hanged August 19th. He loved his wife.
>   John Willard-hanged August 19th. He could not kill.
>   Giles Cory-pressed September 19th. His silence saved his children.
>   Martha Cory-hanged September 22nd. Pious and outspoken.

Mary Easty-hanged September 22nd. Her words ended the evil.

Alice Parker-hanged September 22nd. A lovely woman.

Ann Pudeator-hanged September 22nd. The rich widow.

Samuel Wardwell-hanged September 22nd. A fortuneteller.

Mary Parker-hanged September 22nd. Three loyal friends.

Margaret Scott-hanged September 22nd. Three loyal friends.

Wilmot Redd-hanged September 22nd. Three loyal friends.

These were, and now are again, my friends. That is why, even as we approach the new millennium, I feel it my duty to stand by them on All Hallows Eve. Let Philip run about town making merry with the others. I know what my duty is and would feel heartily ashamed if I were not here to quiet dear Bridget's fears and hold the hand of old George as they drop the tallow upon him. I can feel their fear as though it were my own, and well it might have been if Philip had not been a rich man and managed our escape when we too were accused witches.

I held Bridget close as the worshippers of the temple came near and began their chant. Perhaps this would be the year their love and power would be strong enough to free my friends from their stones as they had been freed from the unhallowed earth. I held my misty breath as first one priestess, and then the next, blessed our Bridget. At last they laid a flower that passed through Bridget's ghostly lap to the stone beneath her.

"Try it now, lovedy," I said to Bridget as she sat trancelike on the stone.

"Try what?" asked Bridget with a shake of her head.

"For God's sake, Bridget, see if you can walk past the memorial and into the graveyard beyond!"

"Oh yes," said Bridget, leaping to her feet and shaking her head. "I'm sorry, Mary. I'd quite forgotten that this was the time to try. You have no idea what the chanting and those incense smells do to us. It's like drinking a keg of bad rum. Give me your arm now and help me to the threshold."

As Bridget and I carefully made our way to the engraved stones that lay at the entrance, the oldest crone in the crowd raised her staff and gave a shout.

"Can you feel it!" she cried to the black clad followers of the temple.

"Feel what?" grumbled a man, dressed as the devil, who was part of the crowd of curiosity seekers and tourists who had followed the Wiccans to our sacred ground.

"Why the movement of the veil," said the crone as she lifted her staff above her head.

"All I feel is cold and damp," said a dripping female angel who was with the devil. "Let's get out of here, Pete, before we both get sick."

"I paid for this show and I'm staying to see it," said the devil, giving his angel a poke with his plastic trident.

"You've not paid for this," said the crone, looking at the tourist with blazing eyes. "This is our sacred time and this a sacred ceremony. I'll ask you to show some respect or go away."

"I've as much right as anyone else here, sister," said the devil as he began to make his way through the crowd to the high priestess. At the edge of the memorial he stopped and started to choke as the breath began to leave his body.

"What are you doing, Mary?" I heard Bridget cry as I placed my lips upon those of the hapless Pete and began to draw the air out of his lungs. There was no way I could answer Bridget with my lips pressed firmly against those of the man.

"Help him, please, somebody help him!" I heard a woman cry as my victim's unconscious body slipped from my arms and fell onto the cobblestones. I felt someone pass through me as I stepped back from Pete's dying body.

"Someone call an ambulance!" I heard from the crowd as I grabbed Bridget's arm and set her upon the entrance of the memorial.

"Hurry now, while it is still your time. Try to cross into the graveyard."

"But that man!" said Bridget looking down at the figure of the dying tourist.

"Never mind him, he was in our way, now he's not. Go on before it's too late."

"All right then, but I don't see why it always has to be me," grumbled Bridget as she placed one red heeled shoe on the words carved into the stone.

All became deathly quiet as Mistress Bridget Bishop walked through the dead man. No wind or rain or human voice could follow where Bridget and I now went. Not even the lifting of the dead devil's body by the paramedics disturbed our moment when the veil was torn through. I screamed with delight as I watched Bridget leap from the stones that had blocked her way to the graveyard beyond.

"We've done it Mary, look at me, I'm free!" cried Bridget as she ran from one old stone to another until at last she came to rest on the grave of Judge John Hathorne.

"Take this, you old bastard," I heard Bridget scream as she began to kick and pound on the grave of the judge who had sentenced her to death. At that moment a great wind began to rise from behind me and I watched in horror as Bridget was picked up from Hathorne's grave and blown back to her stone behind the witch memorial.

"What happened?" screamed Bridget as she began to cry angry tears.

"I don't know," I said as I sat next to her and tried to put my arms around her.

"Don't do that," sobbed Bridget as she pushed me away. "Just leave me alone. Can't you see it's hopeless."

"It is not hopeless. You've gotten farther than you ever have before. That means that there's a way out of here for you, for all of you," I said as I turned around to my other friends trapped inside the grassy enclosure. "I'll be damned if I'm going to give up on you, Bridget Bishop. It may take time, but what is time to us?"

"Never meant much to me," said old Giles as he shook off the hot wax that the temple worshippers had just dropped on him. "Why don't we give it another try, young lady. Oh, and by the way, you're already damned."

"Sit down, you old fool," said Martha Cory who sat beside Giles, desperately trying to fight off a sneezing fit.

"And since when have I ever let any wife of mine order me about!" said Giles as he leapt to his feet and hurried towards me.

"Come now lass," he said, "I've still got the tallow fresh upon me. Let's give it another try."

"You really want to?" I asked, looking at the hawk faced Cory and feeling strangely comforted. Here was another such as my Philip. Older to be sure, but a man true as steel.

"He just wants to play with his first wife, buried in yon graveyard," yelled Martha angrily as Giles made his way to the front of the memorial.

"Hush now, Martha," said Giles as he lifted my hand and kissed it as tenderly as a courtier. "Can't you see that I'm already surrounded by astounding beauty and yet am steadfastly at your side."

"That's only because you can't escape it," said Martha as she hurled her flowers and candle at Giles. It went right past the group of worshippers as they were blessing the final stone, that of Samuel Wardwell, the fortuneteller.

"Sisters and Brothers, it is time to leave these poor victims in peace," said the younger of the high priestesses, Lillith, as she eyed the flower and candle that had fallen at her feet. "It seems that some in this place are not having a good night."

"You can say that again," said her daughter, Lynn, as the girl eyed the tire marks left in the grass by the ambulance. "Mother, did that man really have a heart attack?"

"Who knows, dear, all I know is that it's time to go home."

"Now there's a wise woman," said old Giles as he took my hand and gave a merry laugh. "Come on now, what do you say we try again before it's too late."

"I know I must die... (May) the Lord in his infinite mercy direct... that no more innocent blood be shed."
Mary Easty on Gallows Hill. September 22nd, 1692.

STAVE TWO

Once again stillness filled the air as I took the hand of Giles Cory and stood upon the stones. Beneath our feet were carved the words of Mary Easty, begging mercy for all those suffering from injustice. In my mind I heard her whispers as I prayed to the powers that Philip had set in motion. I could feel my misty lips shaping the words, "free Giles Cory from the Witch Memorial," as I grasped him tightly. I know not to what I prayed, only that I prayed. I had long ago given up trying to figure out if there was a heaven or a hell, or who ruled what realm. I only knew that I, Mary Hollingsworth English, seemed to hold within me an odd sort of power for these sort of dealings. Perhaps it came from one of my parents, or perhaps it came from those powers beyond me that dear Philip had called into being at my death in 1694. Whatever the cause behind my strange quirks and fancies, they lay within me strong and true, and I gathered my strength as I stared into Master Giles large mournful eyes.

"Hold tightly, sir," I said to old Giles.

"With pleasure, my dear," answered the aging rogue, twinkling the sweetly youngish dimple that creased his right cheek.

I stared into his eyes and began to draw the night air into me in much the same manner as I had drawn the life's breath from the man in the devil's costume. How odd it was that I could not get that man out of my mind as I tried to spirit Giles away from his stony prison.

"Think not of what you have done this night," said Giles as he pressed his cheek against mine.

"And how do you know what I am thinking?" I asked, taking my face from his as if I had been singed by a flame.

"Because we can never really hide such things from each other and you know it, little Mary," said Giles in a strangely gentle manner. "I know that you did what you must. Never have I seen you able to draw breath from those who were not at heart wicked and full of evil deeds. But I know also, Mary English, that you still wish you were an innocent, whole and good, laying against the bosom of some comforting God. Not for you are the ways of this town and its undead. Tell me if that's not so?"

"It's not so," I said with a stubborn look in my eye. I set my jaw firmly and stared steadily at Giles as I grasped both his hands tightly. "Now, stop talking nonsense and concentrate on what we must do to get you out of this place. You, above all people, Giles Cory, know that one cannot always do as one wishes. Attend to the task at hand before we lose our chance for another full year."

"Right you are, Mistress Mary," said a sobered Giles. "But don't think you've heard the last of what I have to say on the matter. 'Tis scandalous, it is, you carrying on in such a manner...."

"All right then, all right," I said as the wind about us began to blow the leaves off the trees. I closed my eyes as a painful emptiness filled my soul. "Philip," I heard myself cry as Master Giles and I were lifted from the ground and thrown against the gates of the Charter Street graveyard, known to those of Salem Town as Old Burial Hill, or Point.

"There now, Mary English, it looks as if we've done it," I heard Giles cry with delight as I felt his hands unclasp from mine and watched him caper up the steps to the Wax Museum.

"Where are you going?" I cried as he passed through a group of tourists who had taken shelter from the wind underneath the colorful orange and black awning at the entrance to the museum.

"Why, to stare my wax likeness in the face. I've often wondered if it does me justice," said Giles. "Wait here for me and then we'll be off to find your Philip. Oh what a grand night this is, to be certain!" said Giles as he disappeared into the throng of the living to make his way to the glass case that held a larger than life replica of himself.

"Why, the conceited old fool," I heard Martha Cory snort from the memorial behind me. "He better watch his step or that idiot will find himself dragged back to his stone, just as Bridget was."

"I think not, Martha," said Bridget.

"And why is that, Mistress Bishop?" said Martha, obviously getting ready for a fight.

"Because the veil between this world and the otherworld has grown thick again," I said, moving to where Martha stood. I sat lightly upon her stone.

"So then, that's all there is to it? All we have to do is wait until the last moment when we can't be drawn back into the mist?"

"I think so, Martha," I said pulling her down next to me, "but there might be more to it than that. I believe that Bridget may have stirred up the spirit of old Hathorne enough to create some sort of wind devil that helped push her back into the memorial's grasp. Who's to know? We can only hope that Giles has escaped his prison once and for all."

"But what am I to do without him here beside me?" said an oddly tearful Martha. "I swear that as much as I hate that old man, I can't bear to think of being here without him."

"I heard that, Martha," said Giles reappearing at the edge of the memorial. "Take heart my dear, I'll be back for you, I swear."

"You swear, do you," said Martha, recovering some of her old fire, "swear on what?"

"Why.... I swear on the stone of my dear departed Mary Cory," said Giles heading towards the grave of his first wife that lay in Burial Hill.

"Don't do that, you old fool," cried Martha.

"Then you do care," said Giles turning around and making his way towards Martha.

"And don't do that either," said Martha sadly. "Stay away from both these places and keep what you've got, Giles Cory. 'Tis too long we've all been held here against our will. Let me at least take pleasure in knowing that you've escaped. Use your wits and work to free us all. That's what you can do for me."

"Spoken like my bright, brave Martha," said Giles, "but don't think you can keep me from standing here every single day and wishing you well, my love."

" 'Tis enough for now, if you honor your words, Giles Cory," said Martha with a sigh.

"Just you wait, Mistress Cory, it will be high times we'll have when I hold you again in my arms," said Giles with a shiver. "Why, in a way, it's almost worth the wait."

"Go along now, you old fool," said Martha, blushing as much as a spirit can and wrapping her arms around herself to ward off the night chill a spirit could not possibly feel.

"That I will, Martha, but it's I'll be seeing you on the morrow."

"Which is only fitting as it's to be All Saints Day," said Martha, brightening at the thought. "And Giles…"

"Yes Martha."

"Take care of yourself."

"That I will, old dame," said Giles as he took my hand and set his face towards the town.

"That I will," he murmured again as the tears ran down his cheeks.

"Philip English (Philippe L'Anglois), son of Jean L'Anglois,
was born on the Isle of Jersey, and baptized there June 30th, 1651;
and was in Salem in 1674, being first a mariner and afterwards a merchant."
Sidney Perley: *History of Salem*, 1928.

STAVE THREE

I gave a shudder as Giles and I stepped onto Liberty Street and made our way through Salem's "Haunted Happenings." If we had been mortal it would have been hard going because there was an ocean of tourists as far as the eye could see. It was as if the world had invaded Salem Town on this All Hallows Eve. The orange and gold trees above our heads were covered with small twinkling lights that cast their eerie glow on the costumed visitors below. As we moved silently through the throng, Giles and I heard not only English, but German, French, Spanish and Japanese as well. Salem, with its immense history, both sacred and profane, sounded as it had three hundred years ago when my husband, Philip English, had sent his ships around the world and back again. How strange it was that all had at last come full circle.

We stepped onto the crosswalk and held each other tightly as "Moby Duck," Salem's land and sea tour bus, passed directly through us and continued on its way towards Winter Island where it would take its land bound burden into the ocean.

"Imagine if Philip had been able to command such as that?" said Giles with a laugh, "he would have made a fortune."

"Aye, that he would have, Master Giles," I said as I grasped his arm and headed him past the Peabody-Essex Museum and towards the brightly painted tents that covered the usually tranquil expanse of Salem Common. "But then again, I think two fortunes were more than enough for our Philip, don't you?"

"How little you understand Philip," said Giles. "A man like Philip English can never rest easy while there is gold or power to be had. Especially not after what happened to you. Think you upon it my dear. If it had not been for Philip's first fortune, you and he would have been left to rot in those rocky crevices up on Gallows Hill with the rest of us. It was only his money that helped you escape from jail after you had lain there for more than five months."

"Ah, and don't forget the nine weeks Philip passed in that same place. 'Tis a mercy that he was forewarned by our dear friend, John Alden Junior, to flee so that he was not taken as I was."

"And how it broke his heart to leave you thus, alone and helpless," said Giles, looking at the moonlight sky overhead.

"But there was no hope for it, if Philip was ever to have a chance to free me. How brave he was to come back and let himself be caught so that he could help me escape. Remember, we had no true guarantee that all would turn out as Philip planned. There were many in this town betrayed by family and friends. And then, when our own friend John was betrayed and accused I thought we were headed for the gallows for sure. How true and loyal he was to risk his own capture to save our lives."

"'Twas a bravery made foolish by love, beautiful Mary," said Giles, tweaking my cheek in a playful manner.

"Whatever do you mean?" I asked as Giles and I stopped in front of the fried dough concession that sent its heavenly aroma of fried sugar and butter coursing through my body.

"Why, only what everyone in town already knew, Mary English," said Giles trying to avoid my eyes.

"And what is that?"

"Just that if things had been different, and Master Alden not been sent away by his parents old John and Priscilla, young Master Alden would have married Eleanor Hollingsworth's beautiful daughter Mary."

"What utter nonsense," I said.

"Call it nonsense if you will, but the truth is the truth, Mistress Mary. Deny to me that if your birth had been one those fools called honorable, you would be laying, even now, in a respectable grave in the Alden family plot."

"My birth was honorable, and you know it, Giles Cory. I am the only child of William and Eleanor Hollingsworth. My father was a merchant and my mother a tavern owner."

"Ah, yes, the Blue Anchor Tavern," mused Giles. "How blessed were the hours I spent beneath its roof tipping a pint or two. And how often I watched your mother show the honorable Reverend Cotton Mather to his rooms above. How often indeed."

"And what do you mean by that, Giles Cory?"

"Why, only that your mother and the Reverend Mather were the dearest of friends and that she often sought consolation in his company when your father was forced, by business, to be absent."

"Stop it right now, Giles Cory, before I slap you," I said, feeling the strange rage that had followed me through eternity now fill my spirit body and soul.

"Stop what?" asked Giles, backing a few feet away from me.

"Stop the words that are in your throat and threatening your tongue. Let me say them for you and then be done with it for the night. I am not the love child of Eleanor Hollingsworth and that witch hanging Reverend, Cotton Mather. And, the three of us were not the ones told about in Nathaniel Hawthorne's *Scarlet Letter*. I am also not of questionable birth. My father was William Hollingsworth and I was his heiress."

"Then why did the Aldens take you from young Johnny's arms and send him away in the dark of night?"

"I DON'T KNOW!" I screamed so loud that a small human "ghost" passing near me dropped his ice-cream cone and began to cry.

"There now, Mary, I didn't mean to upset you so. I was only having a bit of a tease. Forgive an old man who's too much of a gossip and a touch of the fool to boot. If you say that William is your father and Philip your one and only true love, than who am I to say different. And as for the rest, 'tis none of my business, to be sure. But you must admit that it is passing strange that only you and the moldering Mather seemed to have the same strange gifts when you both became spirits. I haven't seen his shade for many a fortnight now. Do you think the Devil finally dragged his shade to hell? Whatever his fate, I'm sure he earned it. Anyway, Mary, you know the drawing of the breath from the living is a power shared only by you and the Reverend. I beg you to accept an old man's humble apology for upsetting you this fine night." With that, old Giles got down on one creaky knee and reached for my white hand with his gnarled one.

"Get up now before someone sees you," I said as I looked past his head to see if any of our other ghostly companions were near. Blessedly they all seemed to have gone elsewhere for the moment.

"Then we are friends again, my love?" said Giles.

"For eternity, my dear," I said as I took the arm he offered me.

"And what is this I see?" I heard a deep voice growl from behind me.

"Philip," I cried as I whirled around to behold my beloved husband.

"Giles, you old rogue, you've finally done it I see!" said Philip, slapping old Giles upon the back with a force that sent the old man hurtling through two joggers and onto the nearby cinder path.

"Easy now, Philip," said Giles as he felt his misty bones for damage. "I know what it must look like, but I've no designs upon your lovely wife."

"Never thought you had, old friend," said Philip, with a laugh that lit my heart like a flame.

'Twas true that I'd had a youthful lust for young Johnny Alden, but nothing could compare with the consuming love that filled my soul at the sound of Philip English's voice. I watched as Philip helped Giles to his feet and wondered again how passion such as mine and Philip's could last so long.

"My darling, 'tis a fine thing you've done, freeing our friend," said Philip as he pressed his side against mine.

"Giles' courage did it all," I said as I watched the old man strut like a peacock at my praise.

"That and a bit of witchcraft from your lovely wife," said Giles, eager to pass the praise around.

"Yes, I heard about the dead tourist," said Philip, taking me by the shoulders and shaking me gently, the way he used to shake the children when they'd been naughty.

"How many times have I told you that such actions do us no good, Mary," said Philip sternly. "Don't you realize that somehow, someday such an evil deed may be the end of your immortal time? 'Tis a strange life we live, my Mary, but 'tis the only one we have. If you were taken from me I would have to once again go in search of you, and who's to say if we would ever find each other again."

"Oh Philip, I'm so sorry," I said fighting against the annoyance his words brought me, but touched to the heart by the lost look on his face. How he must have suffered those forty years when he walked the earth without me, only marking time until he could clasp his immortal soul to mine. 'Twas such a shame that I had become so weakened by imprisonment that I could not stand the burden of bearing our last babe, Ebenezer, born in the spring of 1694.

"Then you promise to stop doing such things?"

"I promise, Philip," I said solemnly, praying for the strength to keep my promise. We both knew that there was danger in such a promise. I had made it in the past only to break it when I felt a loved one in danger, or needed to use it to help someone as I had helped old Giles this night.

"Now then, my love," I said, anxious to change the subject, "what brings you here? I know how dearly you love haunting the candlelit tours at the House of Seven Gables on All Hallows Eve. It must be something truly important to draw you away from your yearly revels."

"That's what brings me here," said Philip. The look on his face made my blood run cold as he pointed toward Salem's old granite bandstand.

PART ONE

THE LOST SOUL

"Sometimes they come back."
Stephen King.

CHAPTER ONE

The twinkling lights that decorated the immense dome of the old bandstand shone down upon a mass of reddish curls that could only belong to our sixteen-year-old mortal niece, Eleanora English. She was seated with a group of people on a stone bench just inside the bandstand. Standing behind "Nora" was a tall boy holding a scissors in one hand and a battery powered razor in the other.

"What are they doing, Philip?" I asked, knowing that I would get no answer as I watched my husband's dark form move toward the group sheltered within the granite circle.

"Whatever it is, I don't think they're going to get a chance to finish," said Giles, holding me back as I started to run after Philip. "Don't you know who that boy is with your Nora?"

"I can't really see anything from here, Giles," I said as I tried to pull away from the surprisingly strong old man.

"The boy with your mortal niece is Jacob Corwin."

"Oh no," I whispered as the poison of black hatred and revenge filled my body. "Not Corwin. Giles, you must do something! Stop Philip before he does something terrible."

"We both know there is no stopping Philip English once his course is set," said Giles.

"But he might harm that boy," I said knowing that the poisonous rage that filled my husband's soul at the moment was more than enough to kill the young boy who stood near Nora. Corwin the lad's name might be, but this was a different time and place, one far removed from the Salem that Philip and I had known. It was no longer a forgivable thing to take a young boy's life in payment for the evil his kinsmen had done over three hundred years ago.

"Giles, my friend," I said as I gripped the old man's arm. "Go to Philip and try to stop him. This boy may be an innocent. If Philip harms him we will all be lost. You know that it is Philip's good deeds that have given the 'lost souls' of Salem the freedom to wander above ground. Philip must remain pure if we are to keep the safe harbor we have found."

"Right you are," said Giles Cory as he looked at me with panicked understanding. He knew as well as I that as forgivable it was for the rest of us have our little moments here and there with flying candles and breathless tourists, Philip English must be above reproach. He was our savior, the one who had wrought the miracle of "Salem's Ghosts."

How I would have loved to go to Philip at this moment and take him away from here and the danger he was placing us in, but I knew that reminding him of my presence would only make things worse. One look at my face might bring back that fateful day when this boy's ancestor, George Corwin, had almost parted me from my beloved Philip forever.

Never will I forget that cold, icy night in April of 1692 when Sheriff George Corwin burst into my bedchamber and demanded my arrest. How brave Philip had been to stand between the armed Sheriff and his sweet wife that night. We both knew from watching our friends and neighbors being dragged away to torture and death, that to defy Sheriff Corwin meant punishment. How desperate I was as I stuffed the coverlet in my mouth to still my screams of protest when Philip ordered Corwin and his men from the house. Alas it did no good. Corwin and his men surrounded the house and at daybreak demanded that I be turned over to the people of Salem Town. Both Philip and I knew that to resist further would have been the end of not only us, but out sweet children and loyal servants. I remember getting upon my knees amongst the children and servants for one final prayer before being taken to certain death.

Oh my children, my children! How lucky I had been to only lose one small boy and one baby girl. The rest had thrived and grown. My Mary, my firstborn, was a beautiful young woman of sixteen at the time of the terror. And dear little Philip, just eight years old, but a man just the same, with the look of his father about him. How my six year old Susanna and two year old

William had clung to my skirts as I opened the door to let the Sheriff in. Thank the Lord for my maid and companion, Sarah, who hid the children away and comforted my William at her own breast. And curse George Corwin for taking me away to that evil dungeon that broke my health and robbed me of seeing my children grown and happy with children of their own. True, I was rescued by my beloved Philip, but it was too late to undo what the hands and bodies of my evil jailers had done. It was a miracle that the instruments of torture that had been shoved inside me had not destroyed the child that lay within my body even as I was raped and beaten. Tiny John, whom I was already carrying during that cruel time, and the smallest, Ebenezer, whom I died for, were an added blessing, but one that was hollow for me. I suppose that is why, to this day, I cling to my children's children. They are balm to my soul and heal my saddened heart.

And now I watched my husband move with deadly determination towards Elenora, so like my Mary that I often thought of her as my own sweet daughter born again. The same red curls and bright green eyes flashed under the sparkling lights of the bandstand's dome as she turned her face towards the boy, Jacob Corwin.

To Philip English, the Corwins stood for all that was evil in this world. Bright, beautiful Philip, whose wife had been raped and tortured. Dear, wonderful Philip, who had risen from poor French mariner to fantastically rich merchant and seen the Corwin family, Justice John and his young nephew, Sheriff George, steal all that he had earned by honest labor. Trusting Philip English, who had watched as his children were torn from their mother's breast and been arrested himself, leaving our children orphaned and living upon the kindness of his former servants. My Philip would never rest easy until all the Corwins had been destroyed.

A man who has seen such things and lived to tell of it is a man to be feared. The Philip English who returned to Salem Town in 1694 was not the same young lover I had held in my arms. He was a man who saw himself as an avenging angel. Woe be it to any that stood in his way. Once he had put everything to rights and gathered our children about us once again, Philip set out to make those who had hurt us pay. And pay dearly. I often think it was just as well that I died before the worst of it, for it would have been too painful to watch my sweet Philip do what he must. First he saw to it that all our children were married and prosperous. Then he turned towards his good business and transformed it into a great shipping empire that sailed to the ends of the earth. Philip brought to Salem the riches of the world. These were the things that mattered to the small citizens of Salem Town and rebuilt our tainted name in their eyes.

It was with dark joy that Philip set about to destroy the Puritan stronghold that was Salem, and he succeeded most sweetly. He brought over his own folk from the Isle of Jersey, and later offered refuge to the Huguenots of La Rochelle. It was these brave Frenchmen who sailed the seas for Philip English and built his fortune. In return, Philip offered them shelter from persecution and built them a fine Anglican church, St. Peter's, on the very site of the dungeon that had killed his wife and where he himself had been held as an accused witch.

How surprised everyone in town would have been to learn that the foundation of St. Peter's held a blessed secret. It was a secret that Philip held close to his heart for the forty years he lived after my death. Beneath the very altar of St. Peter's lay the bodies of four men and one woman, all innocent victims of Salem's witchcraft hysteria.

Philip's passion for wandering the stony rocks of Gallows Hill began shortly before I died. It seemed to be the only thing that would soothe his mind and give his soul a bit of rest. I secretly believe that if he had not sought out the rocks and crevices where the bones of his friends lay rotting he might have gone mad. Philip blamed himself for my wasting body. I could see it in his eyes every time he looked at me.

The sadness in him was almost more than I could bear. I could not comfort him. His only comfort lay in those nocturnal strolls up on Gallows Hill. How his eyes glowed when he told me of his plan to find the bodies of all our lost friends and bury them in hallowed ground. I didn't have the heart to stop him even though I knew that he was putting himself in danger. For you see, to bury a condemned witch in hallowed ground was punishable by death. But I knew also that if Philip were to survive my death he must have something to live for.

Many months before the end of the witchcraft hysteria Philip had found the headless body of George Burroughs, along with four other bodies, and hidden them away. Philip patiently awaited the time when he could bury his dear friends properly. Philip found out that Cotton Mather had ordered Reverend Burroughs' head taken from his body after the unfortunate man's hanging. Cotton Mather wanted to study the head of a man of God who had sold his soul to the devil.

So, we had not just the headless body of George Burroughs concealed in our root cellar, but the bodies of John Proctor, Martha Carrier, George Jacobs and John Willard as well. It was soon after I died that Philip laid the foundation of his church, St. Peter's, upon the bones of his closest friends. He searched for the remains of the others his whole life through but never found them.

That is when things began to change for the restless dead of Salem Town. With each placing of stone and mortar over the newly sanctified bodies, we began to wake. Not as the living awake, but as only the dead can come to life. One by one I began to hear the voices of those who had gone before me and those who had followed soon after. We had nothing in common and yet much. Each of us had suffered some way through the cruelty of Salem and now that Philip English had tried to make amends, his ghostly loved ones were being given a second chance to live. We lived, not as we should, walking upon the earth breathing the fresh salt air, but as spirits, alive in a brand new way. And what of the souls of Gallows Hill? Their spirits still lay silent. It was only when other brave souls such as my husband defied Salem once again that the memorial was built and their souls at last journeyed above the surface.

The first few years of our undead life went quietly. Then, in 1697, Sheriff George Corwin died. At the time of his death he was in debt to my Philip, the very man whose property Corwin had seized only a few short years before. How Philip English managed this I can only imagine, but manage it he had. And that was when his plan for revenge began to come full circle.

Philip made plans to seize Corwin's body and hold it for ransom. It was only the Corwin family's quick action that stopped Philip from having his way. The Corwin family buried George's body beneath their home on Front Street. They had the house watched day and night until they were able to raise enough money to satisfy Philip's demands. I laughed heartily when I saw Philip use the Corwin money to buy the great bell for St. Peter's Church. How it must have galled them to hear it ring out every Sunday, reminding them of the foul deeds that George Corwin had done.

And that was not the last of it. George Corwin's ghost is carried back to the spot he was first buried in, now the site of the Higginson Book Company, whenever the bell of St. Peter's is rung. Many of the living have seen his ghost and many more have felt his icy soul as it passes through them. He is still a spirit of pure evil and I am glad that he is not always free to wander amongst the rest of the spirits of Salem. The times he is able to leave his haunting place are bad enough. It was with that thought that I suddenly let go of the past and stared at the scene in front of me. How could I have let my mind wander so! Perhaps this was one of those treacherous nights when George Corwin was wandering free!

"Forsake not an old friend; for the new is not comparable to him: a new friend is as new wine; when it is old thou shalt drink it with pleasure."
Ecclesiastics 9:10.

CHAPTER TWO

I looked up just in time to see the scissors fly from young Jacob Corwin's hand and the razor twist cruelly against his wrist.

"What the hell...!" I heard him scream as he dropped the angry razor and held his bleeding wrist against his chest.

Then I watched in horror as the razor screamed to life again and aimed itself towards the boy's other wrist. The force holding the razor was my husband, Philip English.

"Stop him," I screamed to Giles Cory, who stood as frozen as a granite statue a few inches from Philip. Then I saw another ghostly form move towards our beloved Eleanora. It was the spirit of George Corwin.

I picked up my skirts and began to run towards Nora. Pray God that I would get to her before George Corwin's ghost. As my feet reached the bottom step of the bandstand I slipped on the razor that Giles had knocked from Philip's grasp.

"Save Nora," I gasped as I stumbled onto the grass below.

"Mary," I heard Philip shout as my eyes fixed on the ghastly figure of George Corwin.

"Never mind me," I shouted back as Corwin's dark figure began to envelop Nora. "Save the girl. It's Corwin's ghost!"

It was with a mixture of pride and terror that I watched my husband turn with a dancer's grace and reach the side of our young kinswoman. Dead or alive, George Corwin was no match for Philip English, trained to climb a rigging before he was old enough to kiss a girl.

Philip placed himself between Nora and George Corwin's ghost, just in time to save her from being thrown off the bandstand and onto the granite below.

"Leave her be, you fiend," I heard Philip whisper with deadly quiet to the spirit of our enemy. It was then that I became aware of Giles Cory hovering next to me.

"So that's the spirit of the Corwin that did us to death. Is Philip strong enough to stop him?" Giles asked with a tremble in his voice.

"I'm not sure," I said as I saw the full moon come from behind the clouds and shine its shimmering light on the steeple of St. Peter's. "But I know something that is! To the bell! Hurry Master Cory."

With those words I got to my feet and flew across Salem Common towards the church. There was no time to look back and see what had happened, nor was there a moment to explain to Master Giles what my plan was. All I could do was run, praying with each step that my desperate plan would work. I could hear the footfalls of Giles Cory behind me and was amazed to see him pass me and make his way to the bell tower in half the time it would have taken me. The joy that filled my soul as I heard our old friend ring out the bell of St. Peter's was beyond belief.

"Giles, my friend, you did it!" I cried as I hugged the old man to me.

"'Twas a pleasure, to be sure," said Giles as he snuggled close to me.

"Stop that, you old devil," I said as I pushed him from me fondly.

"Now then, tell me exactly what I did?" said Giles, going to the edge of the bell tower and peering towards the Common.

From our eagles eye view we could make out the mortal and ghostly forms that filled the bandstand below. I could count five mortals, including Nora and the bleeding Jacob, as well as the beloved figure of my own Philip. The malevolent darkness that always swirled around Corwin's ghost was gone and the moonlight shone true and pure upon Philip's silvery curls.

"You, my dearest friend, have sent George Corwin back to Higginson's Book Company to scare the wits out of a ghost tour."

"Then the legend is true!" said Giles as he hopped from one foot to the other with glee. "Young Georgie is trapped by the sound of yon bell. How grand! That means we are at last free of his evil ways."

"Yes and no," I said to Giles as I took his hand and began to guide him down the old stone staircase that wove itself around St. Peter's.

"What do you mean, yes and no?" asked Giles.

"What I mean is that the ghost of George Corwin is free to roam, just as you and I are. The only time we can stop him is when the bell is rung. Then he must return to the site of his first burying. But sooner or later he manages to break free and wanders amongst us again. You know as well as I that the ghosts of Salem live under a strange set of rules, set up by God knows what, and as variable as the wind. There are times when I would just as soon be done with the whole confusing mess and gladly see us all resting peacefully under the ground."

"And what pleasure would there to be found in that?" said Giles as he pinched my cheek. "I say 'tis all worth it, Mary English, even with clanging bells, evil spirits and Witch Memorials holding you back, 'tis all worth it. Tell me truly, would you give back even one immortal moment spent with Philip?"

"No, I can't say as I would," I said as we approached the bandstand where a crowd of mortals and the ghost of Philip English now stood. I reached out my hand and gasped with pleasure as Philip took it and raised me to his side.

"She's safe for the moment, my dearest love," said Philip, as his misty form blended with mine.

> "If a man could mount to heaven and survey the mighty universe, his admiration of its beauties would be much diminished unless he had someone to share it with."
> Cicero.

CHAPTER THREE

But how could our Nora ever be safe? She carried within her the blood of Philip and Mary English, sworn enemies of George Corwin. Many was the time over the past three hundred years when I would have given up all that Philip and I had to see our children's children survive their cruel destiny. Philip and I had watched the sweet babes of the English clan be born, grow to adulthood and then be destroyed by what looked like random acts of fate. A fate brought about by the ghost, Corwin, and those who served him. What good was immortality if you could not protect those you loved?

There were times when I grew so saddened by my losses that I urged Philip to find a way to let us be nothing but dust under the ground. That was when he would hold me close and tell me that if we disappeared the forces that wished our family evil would still remain abroad. We must stay as we were and do what we could.

And now there was Nora, so startling in her resemblance to our own long gone daughter, Mary. Nora English, the last of our family. But it was not just the fact that she was the last of our blood to walk the earth as a living, breathing soul that made my love for her so great. There was something in this girl, this Nora English, that called out to my soul and told me that here was another, such as my Philip, such as Nathaniel Hawthorne, such as, if the tales were true, Cotton Mather. Within this girl lay the blood and bone of New England, old New England, my New England, come together and molded into a young woman who stood on the threshold of some greatness I could only guess at. The thought of it was almost beyond me at times. There were moments when I was tempted to take all the heads of the feuding families in this small town and knock them together. Why, oh why, couldn't we just forget our differences for a minute and see what we were doing? If Philip English and George Corwin kept it up much longer all would be lost. For if anything happened to our Nora and George's Jacob, that would be the end of it. They were the living, the hope for the future. We were but mere shadows of what might have been.

I smiled at Philip as he jumped from the bandstand to the ground below and urged me to do the same.

"Go on now," I said, not wanting my mood to spoil his fun. "Take Master Giles about the town while the revelers are still with us. 'Tis a rare treat to see them dancing and carrying on so. I'll join you in a bit, say at dawn, at St. Peter's gate."

"Come on now, Mary," said Philip with his lip stuck out like a small boy. "'Twill be no fun without you. Master Cory is a fine fellow, but he's not the shapely calf, or the soft bosom that sets my heart to singing."

"Hey there, Captain English," said Giles as he tugged upon his breeches and raised them to reveal a skinny leg. "I'll have ye know that this fine gam won me the heart of three ladies and it's not done yet, by the look of things. Do as he says, sweet Mary, and come along with us. This is a fine night just made for a bit of fun."

"No, let her be," said Philip, looking into my eyes full and clear. "I can see by the set of her chin that my wife means what she says."

"That I do, my brave fellow," I said as I tossed Philip the scissors that Jacob Corwin had dropped. "Here, throw this into the sea."

"Or bury it next to old Hathorne's stone," said Giles, tugging on Philip's sleeve.

"You stay away from Old Burial Hill until we learn what happened to Bridget, Giles Cory," I said. "And take care of each other, do you hear me?"

"Yes, Mary," said Giles skipping down the cinder path, anxious to get away from me before I spoiled his fun.

"Yes, my love," said Philip. "I better catch up with him before he gets us all into trouble, but tell me, darling Mary, what is it ye are up to this fine night."

"Just a bit of thinking, Philip," I said, knowing that if I said too much he would see into my soul and bedevil me with questions until the sun came up. "You know how it is with a lady sometimes. She needs to gather her strength about her."

"Then I'll see you at dawn, my lady," said Philip, blowing me a kiss.

"At dawn, my love," I said pretending to catch his love token.

> "...men may rise on stepping-stones of
> their dead selves to higher things."
> Tennyson: "In Memoriam."

CHAPTER FOUR

"At dawn, my love," I whispered to myself as I watched Philip and Giles disappear under the orange and gold canopy of trees that encircled Salem Common. Then I turned my attention to the two girls seated on the park bench near the entrance to the Common. One was my beloved Nora, the other girl was her best friend, Lynn March.

"But Nora, I don't want to," I heard Lynn say as I moved silently to the tree nearest the bench.

"Why not!" said Nora, turning her back on her friend as she rummaged in the brown canvas knapsack that never left her side

"Because Mom will kill both of us if she finds out, that's why not."

"So what could she do to us? Throw us out?" said Nora, looking at her friend in disgust. "She's too afraid of me running away again to do anything but yell. I'm just a poor confused orphan who needs understanding, remember? Come on. I only want to pay some old bum a couple of bucks to get us a bottle. What's the problem, Lynn?"

"The problem is that if you're caught again Mom might lose custody of you. You'll wind up in some foster home, idiot," said Lynn, getting to her feet. "I don't care, do what you want, just leave me out of it."

"Fine, I will," I heard Nora say as she grabbed her knapsack and pushed past Lynn.

"Come on, Nora," said Lynn as she grabbed her friend's arm. "You know you promised to help Mom with the crowd down at 'Crow Haven Corner.' No one is as good as you at selling stuff and telling people about Mom's books."

"I don't give a damn about your mother, or her books," shouted Nora with a wild look in her eyes, "and get your hands off me!" Tell your mother, the great Lillith March, that I've had enough of her, too!" With those words Nora ran past her friend and was soon lost in the crowd heading towards the Hawthorne Hotel.

My Nora, my Eleanora, was just as my own dear mother had been. Brilliant, beautiful and a lover of the grape. How could I tell Philip that the threat of George Corwin was nothing when compared to the destructive seed that lay within Nora, the seed of the Hollingsworth family. My seed and my shame. Many was the time over the past centuries that I had watched those of my family die by their own hand. Sometimes the end came swiftly through bad judgment and folly, but more often it came slowly as the drink ushered those I loved into the land of the living dead until at last, mercifully, their bodies succumbed to the poison that had already stolen their souls. And now I watched as the last and best of us hurried towards her own destiny of pain and death. How I wished I could wave my hand and remove this evil sickness from her. The ghost of George Corwin that rode upon Nora's shoulders was but a mere shadow of the dangers that coiled around her soul.

It was to my delight that I also saw Nora's constant friend, Lynn, dive into the smothering crowd in an attempt to follow her companion. How lucky Nora had been in her choice of Lynn March as a friend. It was because of Lynn that Nora had been surrounded with the love and caring of the woman, Lillith March, after Nora's parents had fallen out of the sky and burned in the wreckage of their small plane in the mountain snows of New Hampshire's ski country. And it was only because of Lynn that Nora had missed going with her parents. Lynn had nagged Nora into staying with her that weekend to study. It was a rare occupation for our Nora, but one that had been necessary if she was to have any hope of ever passing her winter classes at Salem High School.

And how had our darling girl mourned her parents passing? By going on a two week drunk and almost landing herself in state custody. It had only been by promising to watch Nora day and night that Lillith March and been able to take Nora into her own home. It was no wonder that Lynn was frantically swimming against the crowd in an attempt to drag Nora home. One more mark against my niece and she would be taken away from all who loved her and everything she knew.

"Oh dear Lord," I cried, as Lynn was almost run over by four men in a van. The driver, dressed as a dalmatian, stuck his hand out the window and tried to grab the girl's sweater. It was time to stop musing and start moving. I drew in a great sheath of air and blew out again, creating a gust of wind that pushed the people blocking Lynn's path to one side. To my delight, the slender girl took advantage of the momentary opening and slithered like a tiny snake to the entrance of the Hawthorne Hotel.

"Get your hands off me," I heard a girl's voice shriek as I watched Nora being pushed away from the hotel door and land in Lynn's arms. Both girls landed heavily on the brick sidewalk in front of the pumpkin festooned entranceway.

"Let's go home, I'm tired," said Lynn, rubbing a scraped elbow.

"Oh shut up!" screamed Nora as she shoved Lynn to one side and got to her feet. "Why don't you just leave me alone! Go home if you want to, just leave me alone."

"Why," screamed Lynn, even louder than Nora. "So that you can get yourself drunk or hurt, or worse? What's wrong with you? Why are you being so mean....and so stupid?"

"If I'm so mean and stupid you should get away from me, don't you think?" said Nora, secretly surprised by her friend's show of temper. Gentle Lynn never raised her voice, much less shouted.

"Because I love you, you jerk," said Lynn, bursting into tears as she buried her head in her arms. "And you don't care about anything. Not me, not you, not anything! What's wrong with you, Nora English?"

"I don't know," said Nora as she put her hands under Lynn's arms and dragged her to her feet, "but I'm sorry I made you cry. Let's go home."

I could feel the relief flooding my soul as I watched the two friends link arms and head for the old Victorian house on the corner of Washington Square and Forrester Street. If only I could have seen the dark shadow that walked between Nora English and Lynn March that night.

"Thou has not half the power to do me harm, as I have to be hurt."
William Shakespeare: *Othello*.

CHAPTER FIVE

"I thought you had the key," said Nora, with a sigh, "you always remember the key."

"That's because you always forget it," said Lynn. "I gave you my key this afternoon because you lost yours."

"I know," said Nora, "so where is it?" she asked as she took her knapsack and dumped its contents onto the massive stone steps that led up to the March home. Out tumbled an exotic collection of books, combs, lipsticks, matches, papers and keepsakes that could only belong to a teenage girl.

"It's not there," said Lynn with a resigned look at Nora as an empty nip bottle fell from the knapsack and hit the stones, shattering the quiet like a small bomb.

"I didn't think it was," said Nora, "you know that once I lose something it's gone forever."

"Not always," said Lynn with a laugh that made both girls feel better. "Remember how you lost three keys last winter and we found one in the backyard after the snow melted."

"I wish we had it now," said Nora. "I'm getting tired, and I don't feel like walking across the Common again. I've had enough of Halloween."

"Tell you what," said Lynn, grateful that her friend seemed to have calmed down. "You wait here while I run down Essex Street to 'Crow Haven Corner.'"

"You shouldn't go alone," said Nora.

"It will only take a minute, I promise," said Lynn as she squeezed Nora's hand and took off around the corner before Nora had a chance to change her mind.

I sat down next to my niece and waited in the glow of the full moon for her dearest friend to return. But she never did. The next morning the body of sixteen year old Lynn March was found in Old Burial Hill graveyard. She had been beaten, raped, and murdered.

".... Yea though I walk through the valley of the shadow of death,
I will fear no evil: for thou art with me...."
The Twenty Third Psalm.

CHAPTER SIX

"She's eaten nothing for three days," whispered Lillith March as she pressed a handkerchief against her face to stop the threatening tears.

"Neither have you," said Lillith's secretary, Hannah.

"But I know that I will, when I can. I have to keep going until I find out who did this to my child, my baby," said Lillith, shaking in body, but determined to stay steady in voice. "Poor Nora has nothing at all to live for. She thinks it's her fault that Lynn was murdered."

"I know, I've heard her crying up there," said Hannah with a shudder. "It's enough to make you afraid for her life. I've never heard anything so awful."

"I'm scared to leave her, even for this, but I have no choice," said Lillith as she pulled the hood of her black cloak around her face. "I never thought I'd be burying my own child," she said as she grabbed the edge of a nearby table and pressed her fingers into it until they became a bloodless white. "Call up to Nora one more time, Hannah. Maybe she'll change her mind about going with us."

I would have liked to do what I could to have comforted the witch, Lillith March, but I could only be in one place at one time, unlike some of my spirit friends who found themselves able to divide their souls from their spirits at will. How random are the rules of the ghostly world I live in. I longed to stay by Lillith's side and go to the graveyard where Philip would be, but I knew my place was here with Nora. If only I could do both. But stay I must, whatever desires I might have. The cold issuing from the rooms above gave me a feeling of foreboding that was impossible to shake. I felt my feelings were justified as I listened to Hannah's cries of "Nora, Nora," being met with a stony silence from above.

"That's enough," said Lillith, touching Hannah's arm. "Perhaps it's best that we leave the poor child alone to work things out for herself."

"And what if she doesn't?"

"We'll deal with that when the time comes," said Lillith as the shaking that had filled her body took away the strength in her legs. She grabbed at the table again and missed. Hannah made a leap at her employer-friend and managed, somehow, to keep Lillith from falling.

"I can't believe I've been worrying about some teenager's moods when I should have been taking care of you," said Hannah with a snort of self disgust as she steadied Lillith. "That's what comes from looking like you've got the whole world under control, Lillith March. For God's sake cry and be done with it. It's unnatural for you to be so steady about this terrible, terrible thing."

"I'll cry later," said Lillith, looking past Hannah and directly through me. The expression on her face was almost sardonic. "And don't worry too much about Nora. I believe for now that she will be quite safe."

With those words, Lillith March picked up her skirts and bravely opened the heavy wooden door. As the icy cold November wind hit her face she began to laugh, a laugh that would have frozen the devil in his tracks. It was to the echo of that laughter, cutting beyond words, that I climbed the stairs to Nora's room.

Upstairs I found our darling girl curled up on a rug and rocking from side to side. At first I thought she had become locked in silence until I crept quite close to her and heard a few low moans coming from between her dry lips. I willed with everything within me for her to feel my presence and to have it somehow comfort her, but it was useless. I sat beside the girl, stroking her soft, gleaming hair with my invisible hand, and listened as her moans became louder and soon turned into a meaningless babble. That is when I noticed her eyes.

There was nothing in those eyes, no joy, no pain, no life. I watched in horror as first one eye and then the other began to wander. It was if Nora's eyes were doing separate dances, each to its own macabre tune.

Then she began to make small choking noises that became louder as a whitish foam issued from her mouth. It was then that I realized that I was watching Nora English in the throes of death, a death that had been inspired by her own hand. I reached for her but watched in terror as my hand swept through the girl's chest and touched the rug underneath. I must save her, but what could I do! My gifts were only the ones of the air and moonlight. Then I remembered the look Lillith March had given me. Somehow she had known that I was here. I must go to her now and pray that she would heed my silent cries. It was Nora's only chance.

> "Zig, ziz, zig, death in grim cadence strikes with bony heel upon the tomb.
> Death at midnight hour plays a dance. Zig, ziz, zig upon his violin.
> The winter winds blow, the night is dark. Moans are heard through the linden trees.
> Through the gloom the white skeletons run. Leaping and dancing in their shrouds.
> Zig, ziz, zig, each one is gay. Their bones are cracking in rhythmic time.
> Then suddenly they cease the dance. The cock has crowed!
> The dawn has come."
> Henri Cazalis: "Danse Macabre."

CHAPTER SEVEN

It was a rare thing when I took to the air to travel through Salem Town, but now was no time to worry about the frightful emptiness that filled me as my feet left the earth and I began to glide swiftly down Essex street towards Old Burial Hill. The feeling was something akin to the one I had when I was dying, only worse. At that time I had experienced a moment of terrifying emptiness and then had embraced the oncoming quiet and peace. Now the emptiness just when on and on, sinking farther into me with a coldness beyond death. This is the coldness the mortals around us feel when they sense our presence. It is a feeling beyond the death of hope. It feels like the death of eternity. But now I tried to ignore the icy devils that surrounded me and focus on the face of my beloved Philip. In what seemed but an instant, I glanced his form standing behind the casket of Lynn March. He was shoulder to shoulder with Giles Cory, and each of them held something that looked like clumps of dirt in their hands. Then I watched in wonder as they tossed the earth upon the girl's casket. The air filled with a silvery darkness that surrounded the casket and made it shimmer. I locked eyes with Philip in understanding. Philip and Master Cory had given Lynn March the gift of the undead, the same gift that Philip had given me and the other chosen of Salem Town. That was Philip's power and Philip's gift. Only he could bestow it upon one of us, and only he could take it away. That was why he was respected and feared in Salem's underworld.

"Philip," I cried as I watched the delight of success spread across his face. "Philip, make haste before Nora is lost forever."

"What?" he said, shaking his head. The mist that he had conjured up always filled Philip's head with cobwebs after one of his miracles. I realized in that moment that it often took hours, if not days, for him to think clearly.

"What is it, Mary?" said Giles as I jumped upon the casket of Lynn March in a final attempt to rouse my husband from his lethargy.

"It's Nora, she's dying!" I screamed so loudly that the ancient double oak tree near Judge Hathorne's grave began to shake its leaves violently.

"Nora?" said Philip shaking his head as he tried to fight off the after-mist that filled him.

"Yes, Nora. She's taken something, and she's dying. Help her!"

"I can't," said Philip desperately. "You know what happens after I do this. My power is drained from me. I'm as helpless as a babe until it comes back. Listen to me, Mary, while I can still talk. You alone can help Nora. I don't know how, but you must. I had counted on you and Master Giles here to protect me from Corwin while I slept, but this is far more important. You must both go to the witch, Lillith, and make her see you. Do what you have to, but get her home."

"But how can I make her leave her own daughter's funeral?" I asked in a panic as I watched Philip's eyes glaze over.

"I don't know," said Philip, "just do it!"

"And what about you? We can't leave you here," said Giles looking over his shoulder. Both he and I could practically feel the evil delight issuing from St. Peter's churchyard at this moment. Corwin was trapped as long as the bells were ringing out the life of Lynn March, but once Corwin was able to free himself he would come for my Philip and try to destroy him while he slept.

"Oh Philip," I said sorrowfully as I took his hand.

"Don't worry, my love," he said, his lips brushing mine. "I'll never leave you."

"You promise?"

"I promise."

I held his hand as Philip lay down on the earth of Old Burial Hill and fell into a dreamless sleep.

"Mary," said Giles as he drew me away from my slumbering husband and towards the Witch Memorial. "I have an idea. Hurry!"

With those words Master Giles dragged me past Philip and stood upon Martha Cory's memorial stone.

"Martha, Martha, can you hear me!" he cried in a voice that almost dislodged the stone from the rocks that held it.

"What is it you old fool?" I heard the voice of Martha Cory whine as her spirit rose out of the stone.

"You see that woman over there?" said Giles with a wicked twinkle in is eye. "I've decided to lure her down to Collins Cove tonight. There I can see her drowned good and proper. Philip has promised to make her into a roaming spirit so that I can have some womanly company while I wait for you to be freed. You don't mind, do you my dear?"

"What? Who?" said Martha, trembling with rage as she set an evil eye upon the approaching Lillith March. "Why, I'll teach that harlot to take what is mine!" With that Martha Cory began to pick up the stones that lay about her and pelt poor Lillith March.

I ran to Lillith and began to blow the stones that Martha was tossing into a trail starting at Lillith's feet and leading back towards her home on Forrester Street.

"Come on Giles, help me!"

"With pleasure," said the nimble old man as he dodged a stony missile that Martha had aimed directly at his head.

"What's going on!" cried Hannah as she tried to shield Lillith from Martha Cory's fury.

"I'm not sure, but look there," said Lillith, pointing to the stone trail. "Someone wants us to follow the stones."

"But you can't leave now," said Reverend Hurlbert from the cover he had taken behind an old tombstone.

"Just keep the bells ringing for Lynn until I return," said Lillith, motioning for Hannah to follow. "I don't know what's happening, but I know better than to ignore it."

"The horror of that moment," the King said, "I shall never, never forget."
Lewis Carroll: *Through The Looking Glass.*

CHAPTER EIGHT

"She looks dead to me," said Giles Cory as he stared at Nora's motionless face. "I hate these modern hospitals with their tubes and beeping. All you really need is a good pail of leeches and someone to say the words over you if the leeches don't work. Of course, it's always handy to have a sin eater around too, in a case like this. What a large table of victuals we used to have to set for a suicide."

"My niece is not a suicide, Giles Cory," I said as I turned away from my fellow spirit. The very thought of what had almost happened to Nora was practically more than I could bear. I closed my eyes and tried to shut out the vision that Giles had placed before me of a snaggle toothed old woman eating off of Nora's corpse. What a hideous custom that had been. Only the truly starving would agree, for a few pence, to sit down at the side of a freshly dug grave and eat the food placed atop of a sinner's corpse. The superstition was that once the meal was complete, the sins of the dead transferred to the poor unfortunate beggar who had feasted upon the corpse. And what happened to the sin eater when it came her time to die? Surely she was too poor to leave behind what was needed to have someone eat her sins. To become a sin eater was to condemn yourself to the deepest pit of hell, that place where fire became ice and there was no hope of redemption.

All I had of hope lay in the hospital bed before me. Of course I loved Philip and would have thrown my immortality away in an instant for him, but the hope of our continued life on earth lay in this girl who was all that was left of the English and Hollingsworth families. One by one, Philip and I had watched our children, and our children's children, die. It was only through a miracle that we had not lost Nora too. I marveled as I watched Lillith March gently touch the face of my niece as she wiped Nora's forehead with a cold cloth. The kindness on Lillith's face was unmistakable.

"Are you sure she will be safe if I leave her for an hour?" said Lillith to the nurse who was attaching a fresh bag to the intravenous line that ran from a metal pole into Nora's hand.

"Don't you worry about a thing, Mrs. March," said the nurse. "Doctor Murray said that all Nora here needs is rest and time for her body to get over the shock of what she did to herself. What a shame! It makes you wonder what's wrong with this world when a child like that swallows a bottle of pills. You can stay here and watch Nora sleep if you like, but it looks like you need some sleep yourself."

"Thanks Joe," said Lillith, "but do you hear the bell outside? That's the bell that I asked Steve Hurlbert to ring for my Lynn. It's time for me to bury my daughter."

"But aren't you going to wait until tomorrow?" asked Hannah who had been sitting in the comforting quietness of the shadows.

"No, better to do it now and get it over with," said Lillith, setting her chin in the old familiar line that Hannah knew all too well. "Besides, Steve Hurlbert has been ringing that bell for hours. It's time I let my daughter begin her journey. It's cruel to keep her waiting any longer." With those words Lillith went over to the bed where Nora lay and took her hand.

"What's she talking about?" whispered Joe Fitzgerald to Hannah.

"She's talking about the veil that Lynn must pass through as she begins her journey to the otherworld."

"Then it's true, she really thinks she's a witch," said Joe as he backed away from the bed.

"Yes," said Hannah, with a smile, "the lady's a witch."

Joe quickly picked up the tray that held his instruments and mumbled something about another patient. I could hear the metal implements rattling against each other as his shaking hands carried the tray from the room. Lillith March often had that effect on people once they realized that her reverence for the Wiccan religion was real, and that she was not just another hustler trying to make money off the mystique that surrounded the Salem witch trial hysteria. Here and there in town you could find among the stuffed witch dolls and the tourists being shuttled about by horse drawn carriage and red trolley, a true believer. And Lillith March was a true believer and a true witch. She was one of a long line of witches whose family had been here a good fifty years before Salem had ever heard of a witch trial. Lillith March's family had been among the first settlers of Salem in 1629, and she came by her New England stoicism honestly. That, combined with her trust in the powers of Wicca, made her quite a formidable woman.

"Rest easy, my little love," I heard Lillith say to the sleeping Nora as the woman stroked the girl's hand. "It seems that we have been left in each other's care. Why, I don't understand, but I promise you that I will be as a mother to you and can only pray that you will someday find it in your heart to love me. But before you can do that you must learn to love yourself."

> "It is easy, terribly easy, to shake a man's faith in himself.
> To take advantage of that, to break a man's spirit,
> is the devil's work."
> George Bernard Shaw: *Candida*.

CHAPTER NINE

Lillith touched the light pad as she left Nora's hospital room, leaving us in gray darkness. The only light now came from the monitors hooked up to Nora. Giles and I stood in silence for a few moments and listened to the steady hum of the machines and the dripping of the liquid that flowed into Nora motionless body.

"Now what?" asked Giles.

"We wait," I said, taking the place beside Nora where Lillith had formerly stood.

"But what about Philip? Surely we must do something about him!"

"Not while this child lies here alone and defenseless," I said as I turned a heartsick face to my friend Giles.

"Go if you must, but I have to stay here, even if it means that George Corwin finds a way to part me from my beloved forever. How can I make you understand that this girl is more important than all the ghosts Salem has. She is of the living of Salem and if we let her come to harm we are nothing but meaningless dust."

"Since when have you thought so much of the living, Mary English?" said Giles Cory angrily. "Why 'twas less than a moon's turn ago that I watched you breathe the very life from a poor innocent tourist."

"He was hardly poor and far from innocent," I shot back at Giles in frustration, not understanding myself why my heart was changing. But changing it was. It seemed that my agonies over Nora had somehow touched a part of me that I had thought gone and dead forever. It was something that felt strangely human. Whatever happened to Nora seemed to have some sort of an effect on me as well. Like it or not I was powerless to change my wayward heart.

"I'm sorry Giles. I know that it seems to you that the child is safe, but there is a voice within me that tells me this night is far from over. Go to Philip, take him my love, and tell him what has happened. Guard him well and bring him safely back to my arms."

"You know I am new in the ways of this wandering life, Mary," said Giles sadly. "Even together, I fear that you and I might not be a match for Corwin. Alone, I know that I would be powerless."

"Then do what you can and try to reach the bell if all is lost. If I hear the bell I will try to come to you."

"And the child?"

"Just go, Master Giles, and do what you can. And Giles...thank you, thank you for everything you've done this night. Whatever happens, know that I will stand as your own true friend."

"Just help me explain to Martha that my lust for Lillith March was but a jest," said Giles, wiping his ghostly forehead with a rotted handkerchief. He gave me a wink and turned on his heel. The light tune he whistled as he strode down the hospital corridor echoed off the walls and made more than one mortal head turn as the whistling breeze brushed past them. So, that was Giles Cory's odd gift, the gift of merriment. I didn't know what it meant, but it seems all the spirits of the town had received something that could be of use in our strange world. Pray that Giles would use his wisely to keep Philip safe.

"Lynn, Lynn," came Nora's cries as she suddenly sat up in bed. "Lynn, Lynn," she cried again as she frantically clawed at the tube that ran into the front of her hand. I watched as the door opened and Joe Fitzgerald ran to the bed.

"Hey now," he said as he pressed Nora's hand against the sheet, "you can't do that. You'll hurt yourself."

"Who are you?" asked Lynn looking around wildly as she tried to push Joe away.

"I'm your night nurse and I'm not going to let you hurt yourself. Now sit back and let me see what you've done to this thing," said Joe as he examined Nora's hand.

"Just leave me alone," said Nora as the truth of where she was dawned on her. "Why can't you all just leave me alone?"

"Because you're not thinking right, that's why," said Joe, taping Nora's tube back in place with a double width of adhesive.

"It's you that's not thinking right," said Nora, turning her face to the wall. "Why can't you all just leave me alone and let me die? I'm sick of being in pain."

"Pain!" said Joe, sitting on Nora's bed and grabbing her shoulder. "What does a kid like you know about pain. Tell you what. How about tomorrow I give you a ride up to the kid's cancer ward so you can see some real pain. You don't have any idea what real pain is all about."

"I do too," said Nora as the tears began to flow down her cheeks. "What do you know about my kind of pain. Maybe there's something even worse than cancer pain, the kind you can't cut out of you, or have kill you. Maybe I know about a pain that just keeps going on and on and never stops. That's my kind of pain. It lives inside of me, screaming and screaming. It never shuts up."

"Well, anyway," said Joe, "it's time for you to rest. Just lie back like a good girl and maybe they'll get you someone to talk to in the morning. Someone who can fix the pain."

"Yeah, right," said Nora, closing her eyes and pretending to sleep so that Joe would go away. A few minutes later Nora heard the door close softly.

"Someone to talk to," Nora said as she tried to wrap her tube laden arms about her sobbing body. "What does anybody know about it. Why don't they just let me die."

"Because we love you," I said as I moved closer to Nora. "Please hear me child, oh God let her hear me."

It was at that moment that something strange began to happen. I felt my soul begin to leave my misty form. I watched with wonder as it rose above my unearthly body and swirled around Nora's head. Then I felt a great emptiness as my soul descended into Nora's body and molded itself to the tortured soul of Nora English.

What I found inside the girl was an agony beyond belief. Everywhere I turned was blackness and torture. I gasped as I was drawn into what looked like a series of floating rooms.

"This must be where our dreams come from," I whispered to myself as I was pushed by a warm current into a brownish foam.

"Mama," I heard a small voice whimper as I rose from the foam. In front of me was a small child, two or three at the most, reaching towards me with outstretched arms. I smiled at her as she began to run towards me, her whimpers turning to cries of joy. Then I watched in horror as a large, muscular arm snaked out of the mist and grabbed the girl. "Mama, Mama, make it stop!" screamed the little girl as the arm dragged her toward a boiling pit. I tried to run after the girl, but found my feet entangled in a mass of gnarled vines that held me fast. I watched helplessly as another arm reached out of the pit. This arm was different. It was a soft, feminine arm, complete with sparkling rings and polished pink nails. The little girl stop her panicked cries and began to coo as the man's arm made way for the woman's gentle caresses.

"Mama?" I heard the little girl ask as the woman's hand wrapped itself around the chubby arm of the child.

Then I felt the pain, a pain beyond any I had ever felt before. This was even worse than the agony that I had experienced in my death throes. I fought helplessly as my body was thrown into the muddy earth beneath me and covered with vines that held me tight. I screamed as the vines wrapped their tentacles around my head and mouth, leaving me to scream soundlessly from beneath their splintery fingers. But that was nothing when compared to what followed.

I fought with all I had in me to keep the vines from parting my legs, but it was no use. Then I was filled with panic. My heart beat against my chest and every nerve in my body screamed out for help, but there was none, only more panic, more helplessness as I felt the vines cutting my flesh and insulting my body.

This was more than the rape of my body. This was the taking away of all that was good and clean in me. It was as if everything I trusted and loved was being torn from me as the vines entered my nether regions and reached upwards towards my womb. I could feel the slithery tentacles searching, searching for something. The worst of it was I could hear their thoughts. They were angry at me, angry at something they thought I had done and this was my punishment. It would do me no good to plead for mercy or to beg to be freed from the vengeful vines. They would do to me what they wished until they were satisfied. Then I heard the cries of the child again and forgot my own desperation.

"Stop Mama, stop hurting me!" I heard the little girl cry as the tentacles shot their way even deeper into me.

"I'm not hurting you, darling," I heard a woman's voice say kindly. "I'm only making sure you're clean." These words were accompanied by the wordless screams of the little girl as she cried out inside my own body. Then suddenly the child began to chant a sweet prayer.

"Now I lay me down to sleep, I pray the Lord my soul to keep. If I should die before I wake, I pray the Lord my soul to take. There Mama, was I good now? Can I go to sleep?"

"Not yet, darling," I heard the woman's voice say as the vines suddenly loosed their grasp upon me. "Not until you take your medicine."

"Yes, Mama," I heard the little girl say sweetly. Suddenly I felt myself being lifted and placed before the mother and child. The child was sitting in a bathtub surrounded by black tiles and rosy pink walls. The mother was dressed in a pale green robe and was handing the little girl a glass of water and a handful of oddly shaped pills that were the same color as the mother's robe.

"Here now," said the mother, "take these and go to bed."

"Will teddy the bear be there?" asked the child as she swallowed the pills.

"Yes, teddy will be there."

"And green bunny, and Alice my doll? Will they all be there?"

"Yes darling, they will all be there."

I watched sadly as the little girl let the woman wrap her in a large pink towel and carry her off to bed. The woman stroked the child's forehead and kissed her goodnight. Then she turned off the light and shut the door, leaving the child in darkness.

The little girl lay motionless for a moment and then slid out of bed. I saw her kneel and listened to her repeat the sweet prayer she had said before and then make her way back to the bathroom. I heard the child turn on the water in the sink and then heard gulping sounds. A moment later I listened as the child vomited as quietly as she could. Then she opened the door to the bathroom and walked over to her bedroom window.

"Hello moon," I heard her say as she raised the shade and looked out. Then the child walked to her closet and turned on the light. She smiled as she adjusted the door so that only a slight glimmer of closet light shone into the room. Then the little girl got back into bed and put her arms around her bear.

"I love you Eddy-Teddy," she said as she hugged the toy tightly.

I closed my eyes and began to cry as I felt myself being returned to the harsh reality of Nora's hospital room.

"Someone to talk to," I heard Nora say again as her arms hugged her body in search of the long ago comfort of her lost toy.

> "Woe to him that is alone when he falleth,
> for he hath not another to help him."
> Solomon: *The Apocrypha.*

CHAPTER TEN

"Then talk to me, you jerk," I heard a girlish voice say as my mind fought to clear itself from the trance-like state I had been in. The voice was oddly familiar, but with more depth than I remembered.

"Is that you, Lynn March?" I asked the slight figure that stood next to me.

"Yes, it's me, but who are you?" asked the ghostly spirit of what had been the earthly girl, Lynn March.

"My name's Mary English. I am one of many who live in the otherworld of Salem," I replied, hoping that my words would not shock the new spirit.

"What are you talking about?" asked Lynn as she looked about her in confusion.

"What I'm trying to tell you," I said in as gentle a manner as I could, "is that you have died and been given the gift of the otherworld. You may be gone from the world as you know it, but you still exist in your ghostly body and true soul. All will seem strange to you for a time, but there will be a day when you will take comfort in the odd gift that is given to Salem's chosen."

"I don't want any gift!" said Lynn March's ghost frantically. "I want my life back, and my body too! What have you done with them!"

"Nothing, my dear," I said sadly. "'Tis not my fault that you find yourself thus. The fault lays with those who murdered you."

"Murdered me?" asked the girl.

"Yes, don't you remember?"

"All I remember is that I was crossing Essex Street, near Crow Haven Corner, when a car with some guy dressed as a dog came around the block. That's when the people inside started grabbing at me. I tried to run and then I remember falling, and then…"

"Then what, my dear?"

"Then," said Lynn, "I remember floating, just floating, as if I had become a cloud. And now I'm here. Wait, I do remember something else. There was a man, a man dressed in soft black who was calling me. And behind him was another man, he was old and had a wonderful smile. Then I heard the sound of bells and the next thing I knew I was here. Was I murdered by those two men?"

"No, my girl," I said to Lynn as I took her hand. "Those two men were my husband, Philip English, and our friend, Giles Cory. They were calling you back into the otherlife. You see, my husband has this strange power to call to those spirits who have died unjustly in Salem. All you had to do was heed his call and answer with your own pure spirit. I speak for all the ghosts of Salem when I say, welcome to our midst."

"But I don't want to be here," said Lynn as she touched her face and arms. "Why should I believe you. I feel strange, but there's nothing about me that feels like a ghost. Why, I'm as real as anyone else."

"That's true, you are real, as real as any living, breathing human, Lynn. The only difference is that you are a ghost."

"I am not!" said Lynn, running to Nora's side. "Nora, Nora, can you here me!" Lynn screamed."

"Of course I can," said Nora as she put her hands over her ears. "Do you think I'm deaf?"

"See," said Lynn, turning to me with a triumphant look on her face, "I knew you were lying."

"Who are you talking to?" asked Nora as she stared at Lynn with growing amazement, "and what are you doing here, YOU'RE DEAD!"

"I'm talking to that ghost lady right over there," said Lynn, "and do I look dead to you?"

"Actually, you do," said Nora. "I can see right through you. And, what ghost lady?"

"That lady there," said Lynn as her pointing hand passed through the heart monitor by the side of Lynn's bed. "Oh my God," she screamed as she grabbed her hand.

"Yeah, it's cool," said Nora. "Lynn you're a ghost."

"If I am then why can you see me and not her?" asked Lynn as she sat on the bed next to Nora.

"I don't know, but I'm glad you're here," said Nora as she wrapped her arms around Lynn and hugged the air. "Can you feel that?"

"Yes," said Lynn.

"I can too. How weird. I can't believe you came back to me. You know once I lose something it's gone forever."

"Not always," said Lynn.

"That's the last thing you ever said to me," said Nora with widening eyes. "Do you suppose that's why you came back?"

"I don't know," said Lynn as she looked at me for an answer. "Do you know, Mary English?"

"All I know," I said, "is that Nora tried to kill herself because she thought it was her fault you were murdered."

"Why did you think that?" Lynn asked Nora.

"Think what?" said Lynn looking from where Lynn sat to where I stood.

"That it was your fault I was murdered?" said Lynn. "That's the stupidest thing I ever heard."

"But don't you understand?" said Nora, bursting into tears. "I should have gone with you. If I had gone with you I could have saved you."

"That's not true," said Lynn as she put her arms around her sobbing friend. "There were five of them, I remember that now. They would have hurt you and killed you too. It would have been both of us, not just me."

"Really, you really believe that?" asked Nora.

"Yes, I do," said Lynn. "I just wish I could remember more. It all feels like a dream, a dream I can't remember."

"I know that feeling," said Nora. "It's like the feeling I had when I took those pills. I don't even know how they got there. All I remember is taking them and then waking up here."

"Well, here we are. Now what?" said Nora.

"Now," I said, "you must find out who did this to you, Lynn, and why those pills were in Nora's room."

"What did the ghost say?" asked Nora.

"That we have to find out who did this to us," said Lynn. "Why would anyone want to hurt us?"

"I don't know," said Nora, "but I do know that I tried to hurt myself. I was trying to get rid of that pain that's always in me. When you died it was too much to handle alone. Promise you'll never leave me Lynn."

"Can I promise that?" asked Lynn, turning to me with hopeful eyes.

"I don't know," I answered, thinking back to the odd things that had happened the last few days. "I do know that it seems you are closer than any mortal and spirit I have ever seen. Perhaps you can stay with her, Lynn, but I can't tell you to promise."

Lynn told Nora what I had said and then walked to the window. "Come on, Nora, let's say it."

"All right," said Nora.

"Hello moon," said both girls in unison as St. Peter's bell ceased its tolling.

"The Devil hath been raised amongst us and his rage is vehement and terrible, and when he shall be silenced the Lord only knows."
Samuel Parris, Pastor of Salem Village, 1692.

CHAPTER ELEVEN

I turned to leave quickly as I watched Nora snuggle into Lynn March's arm. Now that Nora had a guardian spirit, new in our ways, but wise beyond her years, my heart felt at peace. I must now hurry to Philip's side before he could come to harm. Besides, I needed Philip to begin to untangle the web that had been woven about us all. Lynn's murder and Nora's suicide had both been cleverly orchestrated, but by whom, and why? To blame everything on the Corwin curse might be a fatal mistake. The devil has many faces. I could understand that Corwin's revenge might fall upon Nora, but what of Lynn March? Why had she come to harm?

Then there was Nora's soul. What was I to make of her night terrors? I have learned through many centuries of strange revelations, that Nora's painful shadows were but a few of many in the pattern of human wonders and must be let to fly into the open air if the girl was ever to have peace. There were times that it seemed to me that the shadows of both the otherworld, and what mortals called the real world, were more than I could bear.

"Shadows, is it? 'Tis only shadows you fear?" I heard a growling voice say as I walked into the darkness of the hospital corridor.

I turned, and to my horror came face to face with the specter of George Corwin. Worse even than that, was the sight of the human boy, Jacob Corwin, making his way towards Nora's room.

"Hello George," I said to the ghost with the motionless eyes as I tried to keep my voice from shaking. "What brings you here this fine evening."

"Why you, my lovely lady," said George Corwin as he pressed me into the wall. I would have gladly passed through that wall, but felt myself blocked by something. That something, I realized too late, was George Corwin's tattered cloak, holding me fast. I was trapped much like a fly in a spider's web, powerless to move.

"Here now, Mary English," said George as he blew into my face with his foul breath, "'twill do you no good to struggle. You're mine now. And it's a fine bait you'll make. Just think, this day coming will see the end of the whole English clan, living and dead. Its enough to make me dance with joy!"

I watched in disgust as George Corwin began to dance about me in circles. It was then that I realized that he had finally gone truly mad. It took all my powers of reason not to go mad with him at that moment as I thought about Philip. What had happened to Philip?

"Then my niece Nora and I must be the only ones left," I said with a beguiling sadness.

"Aye, you two, and that pirate of a husband of yours that calls himself a merchant. Young Jake will take care of Nora and I've got you. Once Philip English learns we have his fine ladies he'll come a'running."

"Then Philip's still abroad?" I asked, fearing that I was being too bold, but desperate to know.

"That he is, damn Giles Cory for it. Who would have thought the old man had such strength."

"And Nora, what have you planned for her?" I asked as my heart filled with hope. As long as Philip was free there was hope.

"Why don't I let you see for yourself," said George Corwin as he wrapped his spidery cloak firmly about me and lifted me into his arms.

PART TWO

SEDUCTION IN THE DARK

"The warrant against her husband (Philip English) was issued April 30th, but the Sheriff could not find him."
Boyer and Nissenbaum: *The Salem Witchcraft Papers*.

CHAPTER TWELVE

George Corwin held me fast as we entered Nora's room. I was horrified to see young Jacob Corwin sitting on Nora's bed, holding her hand. I tried to signal to Lynn, but found that the cloak that I was wrapped in hid myself and George Corwin from her view. I was rendered both mute and invisible by Sheriff Corwin's spell and was helpless to do anything but watch and listen as Jake wove his own spell around my innocent niece.

"Trust me," he said in gentle tones. "I saw the dog costume you're talking about in that orange trash barrel at the 'House of Seven Gables.' Garbage pickup is tomorrow. We have to get the costume tonight or it will be gone."

"I don't know," I heard Nora say as she quickly glanced toward Lynn. "It's more dangerous than I thought out there."

"What are you talking about?" asked Jake as he stroked Nora's fingers.

"I'm talking about what happened to Lynn!" said Nora. "If something terrible like that could happen to Lynn, then it could happen to me."

"But she didn't have me to take care of you," said Jake, standing up and moving towards the window. "Besides, since when do you care if you live or die?"

"I do care, now that I'm here," said Nora.

"So all you care about now is your own skin," said Jake with disgust. "I think you're a pretty rotten friend if you lie there while the only evidence that can convict Lynn's murderers is burned at Salem dump. But if that's the way you want it...."

"That's not the way I want it and you know it," said Nora, jumping from the bed and heading towards the narrow closet that held her clothes. "Just give me a second to get dressed."

"Okay then, but hurry up before someone comes in here to check you out," said Jake as he crossed his arms across his chest and leaned against the window. Outside I could see the full moon glowing through the window. It cast an eerie light onto Jake Corwin's profile. It was then that I noticed several sores on the back of his neck.

"It's the sarcoma," I whispered to myself as I struggled in George Corwin's grasp. "The boy has AIDS!"

"That he does, Mary English," said George Corwin with a chuckle. "Its a pity that such a lad will soon be passing over to our side before he truly has a chance to make his mark, but perhaps we can see to it that he leaves something behind. What do you say, sweet Mary, to my Jacob and your Nora becoming the parents of a beautiful babe."

"That's insane!" I screamed as I tried to scratch at George's eyes with my nails.

"Aye, I know," said George with a sigh. "Dear Nora, and any babe of hers, would probably contract the deadly pox from Jacob. Then again, why shouldn't the boy have a bit of fun before he dies. Your Nora is a warm little wench and just right for my Jacob. I think I'll put the thought of it into his head."

"No!" I screamed again as I tried frantically to get the ghostly Lynn's attention. But I quickly realized it was no use as I watched Lynn shadow Nora to the window and whisper in her ear.

"You don't have to do this, you know," I heard the ghost girl say to Nora as she stroked her arm gently.

"Yes I do if I'm ever going to have any peace," said Nora to her dearest friend.

"What was that?" asked Jake as he took Nora's other arm and placed her hand on the window ledge.

"Oh nothing," said Nora. "I seem to be talking to myself a lot lately, don't pay any attention to it."

"You better watch that," said Jake with a strange smile. "People will think you're nuts."

"Maybe I am," said Nora as she looked out the window. "Come on, let's go."

I watched, helplessly, as first Jake and then Nora disappeared out the hospital window. A moment later, the shadowy form of Lynn March faded from view.

"Come now, Mary, it's time to watch the fun," said George Corwin as he once again wrapped his cloak tightly about me and filled my soul with darkness.

"More weight, more weight."

Giles Cory

(as he was crushed to death, 1692).

CHAPTER THIRTEEN

A moment later I found myself sitting beside George Corwin on Old Burial Hill.

"Now we wait for the two lovebirds, eh Mary? And speaking of lovebirds, isn't that your Philip over there?"

"Yes," I whispered, staring hopelessly at my husband. If only there was some way I could get word to Philip about what had happened. But how? What torture it was to see him so near to me. Next to him stood Giles Cory. They were watching somberly as the witch, Lillith March, lovingly placed daisies on her daughter's fresh grave. Philip moved gracefully towards Lillith and helped her to her feet with his invisible hands. How handsome and gallant he was.

"Whoever you are," I heard Lillith murmur," I thank you for your kindness."

Philip bowed to the grieving mother and then stepped back to where Giles was waiting.

"I wish we could let her know that her daughter's spirit lives on," said Philip to Giles as Lillith started to cry silent tears.

"Mayhap you can," said Giles as he studied Lillith March carefully. "There's something about that woman that is quite different from most of the modern fools that rush about this new Salem. She seems to see beyond their grasping and panting and back into something that she shares with us. There's something about Mistress March that I find quite intriguing."

"Aye, that there is," I heard Philip say as I watched him standing in the moonlight behind the lovely figure of Lillith March.

My husband and friend Giles were quite right. Lillith March did seem to have a special something in her that breached the mist between her world and ours. What a terrible pity that one such as she should have lost her only child, and to make it worse, that child was the only daughter of a powerful witch. Who would carry on after Mistress March?

"Well now, friend Philip," I heard Giles say, "there's still hope that she may yet find a life above ground that's worth living. Such a handsome woman would have little trouble snaring some yearning man in her net. By the look of her there's still time for one or two more babes if she steps lively."

"I don't think so," said Philip, looking at Lillith March in a way that almost made me jealous. "Yon woman is not one to take a lover lightly. The man who would win her must be full of strength and courage. 'Tis quite a prize she is."

"Don't let Mary hear you say such things," said Giles as he swatted the hat from Philip's head.

"Why not, you old goat?" said Philip as he picked up the hat Giles had knocked in the mud near the freshly dug earth of Lynn March's grave.

"Because the ladies never take kindly to such talk and you know it. Scratch the surface and they're all cats just waiting to claw each other apart at the mention of any rival."

"Not my Mary," said Philip as he hit Giles so hard on the back that the old man fell forward into the mud. "My Mary's the kindest, sweetest soul that ever lived and knows she has nothing to fear from me."

"Nothing?" said Giles with a leering smile at Lillith March as he watched the woman walk to where Judge John Hathorne was buried.

"Nothing," I heard Philip say.

But was that true? I too had seen the way Philip had looked at Lillith March. Kind and loving though I was, I was no fool. There was something about the witch, Lillith, that drew people to her. She poured her soul into her Wiccan religion and had made it her life's work to bring the message of the Goddess to any willing to listen. Her books were filled with wisdom and recipes for walking through life and into death as beautifully as one could possibly wish. She had the air of a saint about her, but there was also something else that troubled me deeply. Underneath the surface of this woman was an underlying current of sensuousness that seemed to emanate from her like a beacon. It was made all the more powerful by the overlay of religion and grieving motherhood that now enveloped her. I pitied any woman who had Lillith March for a rival. The battle would be over before it started. What man could resist her? What woman fight her?

"Friend Giles," I heard Philip say, "let's stop this foolish talk and look for Mary. I'm uneasy with George Corwin wandering about this night."

"Aye, he seems quite powerful," said Giles, "perhaps it's the moon, or just because we are still so close to All Hallows Eve. I had quite a time keeping him off you while you sat in your stupor."

"I thank you for that, old friend," said Philip as he put his arm around Giles and hugged him tightly. "There's no knowing what might have happened to me if you had not stood guard this night. What strength you have! No wonder it took so many stones to crush the life from your mortal body."

"Aye and it was eighty years old I was at the time, too. Imagine how long I might have lived if I had not been dragged out to my own farm and tortured by the town fathers? 'Tis indeed a sobering thought. But then again, why would I have wanted to live without my Martha. Shrew though she is, she suits me well. What a dance she leads me even now. It's two souls with evil tempers we are, and glad I am of it. How sweet it would have been to have just a few more mortal moments with her. But those bastards hanged her just three days after they murdered me. How could they have done that to my Martha, Philip?"

With those words Giles moved to where Lillith March was standing and stared down at the grave of John Hathorne.

"'Tis much ye have to answer for, Master Hathorne," said Giles as he shook his fist at the Judge's grave, "Oh what I would give to have you standing before me for just one moment so that I could have my revenge."

"Evil deeds are always repaid threefold," said Lillith March, turning to where Giles stood.

"Did she hear me?" said Giles, jumping away from the witch.

"I'm not sure," said Philip as he looked at Lillith in a worshipful manner that almost drove me mad.

"Let's get out of here and find Mary before anything else happens," said Giles, pulling at Philip's jacket as he stared toward the Witch Memorial where Martha lay sleeping. "I remember now that Bridget Bishop almost escaped until she taunted the Judge. She was wisked back for her teasing and is held as fast as any in the Memorial. I hate the Judge and lust for a bit of justice, but I'll be damned if I'll trade my freedom for it!"

"Calm down Giles, it's safe, at least for the moment," said Philip as he looked up at the moon. "But you're right. It's time to get out of here and find Mary. We'll find her near Nora, wherever that may be."

"Aye, let's leave this evil place," said Giles. "I've had enough of graves and death for one night.

I watched with two minds as the ghosts of my husband and Giles Cory drifted away through the graveyard and into the starry night. How dearly I would have liked to call out to them, but it was impossible. At least they were out of danger for the moment. I felt sick as George Corwin fondled the cloak and drew me closer to him.

"I felt your thoughts, Mistress Mary. You see now that you are as helpless as a babe. How sweet it is having you near me. For many years I've lingered alone and unhappy in this town. Perhaps, before I destroy you, we can have a bit of fun."

"Later, George," I said to my repulsive captor, knowing that if I showed an ounce of fear he would turn it against me. Pray God he could not read the terror that gripped my mind. "Wouldn't you rather have a willing lover than a reluctant prisoner?" I asked with a mock sweetness.

"I'm not so sure," said George Corwin, stroking my breast in a manner that made me glad that I was no longer capable of retching.

"Oh look," said George, clapping his hands together. "Here come the children."

> "An' the Gobble-uns 'at gits you,
> Ef you
> Don't
> Watch
> Out!"
>
> James Whitcomb Riley: *Little Orphan Annie.*

CHAPTER FOURTEEN

"Wouldn't it have been quicker to cut through the Common?" I heard Nora say as she panted after Jake Corwin. I could see her face in the moonlight and was alarmed by how pale she was.

Then I looked at Jake Corwin. How sweet and innocent he looked, standing there in the moonlight next to my beautiful niece. There was a confused tenderness on his face that was almost heartbreaking. It was then that I realized that not even Jacob Corwin was all bad. He was as lost a soul as those who had condemned my friends to death during the Witch Trials of 1692. I gasped silently as Jake took Nora's hands in his and turned towards her.

"Don't be afraid, little Nora," I heard him say with a tenderness that belied all I knew of young Jake. "I won't let anything hurt you, I promise."

"But Lynn's killers might still be around here," said Nora, turning away from Jake and glancing nervously about her.

"If they are, I know they won't bother you. Nothing can happen to you as long as you're with me," said Jake, laying Nora's head on his shoulder and drawing her close to him.

How could I hate the young Romeo who now held his Juliet with such loving tenderness? There was no mistaking the depth of Jake Corwin's words. He was hopelessly in love with Nora. A love he must know was doomed. For the first time in several centuries I felt an uncharacteristic moment of compassion for a Corwin. It was a great pity that Jacob Corwin was condemned to a life of pain and an early death. It was with even greater confusion that I heard myself whispering a prayer for the slender young man who stood in the moonlight with Nora.

"Please dear Gods and Goddesses," I heard myself murmur, "save this boy and help him to grow into a man that you would be proud of."

"What was that!" growled the voice of George Corwin.

"I was only praying," I said meekly, cursing myself for even a moments worth of tenderness towards any Corwin. Such thoughts could mean the end of us all!

"Then stop it, Mary!" said George as he threw his cloak, with me wrapped in it, to the ground. I trembled in horror as I felt the tatters of the cloak entwine themselves with the roots of the ancient holly tree that stood next to John Hathorne's grave. I screamed out as the filthy cloth of the old cloak pressed against my face and joined with the holly tree to create a shroud around me.

It was then that I realized that my screams had turned into senseless a babble and I was in danger of losing my mind. Anything but that! If I lost my mind than surely my soul would follow! I closed my eyes and tried to shut out the growing terror that filled me.

"Please, please," I whispered, "someone help me!" I tried to picture Philip, but found that all I could summon up was a form wearing a soft black cloak. Then the form turned towards me and I realized that the fantasy form was that of Lillith March. "How strange," I thought as the witch, Lillith, stretched her fingers towards mine and tried to grasp my hand. I found myself fighting to touch her, but it was impossible. The cobwebs of George Corwin's cloak held my hands tightly to my side. Somehow I knew that if I could only manage to touch Lillith March, the cloak's spell would be gone. I lay back against the cold stone of John Hathorne's grave and tried to remain calm as I listened to the voices about me. Now that I had the beginning of a plan to focus on, I felt almost hopeful.

Perhaps it was the tightness of the old cloak, or perhaps it was a bit of madness that filled me. Whatever the cause, I felt oddly at peace as I lay on Old Burial Hill much as I had over three hundred years ago when I had been put to, what I had thought at the time, was my final rest. I found myself listening with a strange detachment as George Corwin approached his poor, diseased nephew and began to whisper in his ear.

"Take her, lad. Take her now while all is dark and the moon is full. Take her like you did her little bitch of a friend," I heard the old devil mutter as clear a day.

"What? What do you want?" said Jake, shaking his head as he let go of Nora.

"I said take the little slut; now, here, before anyone can stop you. She's still weak, and suspects nothing but good from you. Throw her on yonder stone, rip the clothes from her, and choke the life out of her body while you're having her. Do it if you want to please me. Disobey my wishes and you will be a sinner in my eyes."

"Is that you?" I heard Jake say as he walked away from Nora and looked up at the sparkling late autumn sky.

"Of course it's me," said George in a beguiling voice. "Who else would come to you in such a way? 'Tis your oldest and only friend. Do as I say and I will always love you. I promise to care for you and remove the pox from your body. Disobey me and I will leave you forever."

"Jake, what is it?" asked Nora. "What's wrong? Your face, it scares me."

"There's nothing to be scared of," said Jake as he backed away from Nora and shook his head again. "I just have a headache. Sometimes I get them."

"Oh," said Nora as she put her hand on the boy's forehead and began to stroke it gently.

"Don't do that!" cried Jake in a tortured voice as he flung Nora's hand away. "Tell you what, why don't we just forget the whole thing? Go home Nora, get away from me."

"I don't understand," said Nora as she stood before Jake with tears in her eyes. "I thought you liked me. I thought we were friends. I thought that maybe you might even love me a little."

"I don't know what we are, Nora English, I only know that this whole idea is crazy. Get out of here. Get away from me."

"But it was your idea, Jake," said Nora. "And it was a good one, too. You were right when you said that we should get that costume out of the trash before its too late. We owe it to Lynn to find out who killed her. What's wrong with you? I know you're a lot of things that people around here don't like, but I never thought you were a coward!"

"I'm not a coward," said Jake, clenching his fists. "Do you hear me, I'm not a coward!"

"See boy," I heard George Corwin whimper in a plaintive voice, "what did I tell you? The little bitches are all alike. They just want what you can give them and then they call you names when they don't get their own way. Punish her lad, punish her now. Do it the way I taught you. Do it before I leave you forever."

"You can't leave me," Jake cried as he fell on his knees. "Please don't leave me. I'll do anything you want, but don't ask me to do that. Not that. I can't do it!"

"Jake, what's wrong?" asked Nora as she joined the boy on the ground and wrapped her arms around him. "I don't know what's going on, but I do know that something is hurting you. Let me help, please let me help! First you tell me to go away and then you tell me to stay. I'll do whatever you want, just stop acting this way. You're scaring me."

"Run, Nora, run!" said Jake as he stood up, dragging Nora with him. "Get out of here. Go to the 'House of Seven Gables,' get that dog costume, and then go home. Do what I say before it's too late."

"But I'm scared to be alone in the dark."

"There are worse things than being alone in the dark, Nora," said Jake as he took Nora by the shoulders and began to shake her. "Get away from me now. Go!"

"All right, Jake," said Nora, staring at Jake Corwin with terrified eyes. I'll go."

I watched with feelings of terror and relief as Nora turned away from Jake and ran down Liberty street. Jake was right. There are worse things than the dark.

"You fool," said George Corwin as his dark form surrounded his sobbing nephew. "You had her. You may never have another chance as good as this to kill her."

"I can't kill her, I love her," whispered Jake as he sank into the mud and began to cry.

"I can't kill her, I love her," repeated George Corwin as he cruelly mocked the boy. "That's not what you said when you tore the clothes off of Lynn March and raped her. What's happened to the Jake Corwin who laughed while he strangled little Lynn?"

"I was high. I didn't know what I was doing, you know that!" said Jake as he looked through Corwin with blazing eyes. "I've never been so high. It's like that junk I shot on Halloween had some sort of weird kick. I wish now I'd never done it. I wouldn't have hurt that poor girl if I'd known what I was doing. I swear I wouldn't."

"If that's how you feel, then you're on your own," said George as a wind devil began to swirl around young Jake. "I'm ashamed I ever bothered with a weakling like you now that I know how spineless you are."

"Who are you?" asked Jake. "Why do you want me to do these things?"

"I'm the only one who has ever loved you, or ever will, and you know it," said George Corwin in almost maternal tones. "You may think that girl likes you, but just wait a week, a month. She'll be like all the rest. She'll pat you on the back and kiss your cheek and then she'll kick you in the ass. Remember your loving mother? The fine lady who used to hold your hands under scalding water until you screamed? That's what all women are like. They should all be punished before they can hurt you, not after they've scarred and tortured you and left you to find your only happiness in some dirty needle. It's your mother's fault, Lynn March's fault, Nora English's fault, that you've got AIDS and are going to die a horrible death."

"What's happened to you boy? You had the guts to get rid of your Mama Corwin and baby Lynn. Finish off pretty Nora and be done with it. Finish her off before I change my mind about removing your sores and making you well. Or die. It's your choice. But one thing I can promise you, if you choose to die, you'll die alone. There'll be no Nora English beside you once she learns what you have. She's a fine lady and all you are is a poor diseased fool. A fool who's willing to cast your only friend away for a smile and a wink. And where will I be? I'll have found another friend, one with sense enough to listen to the truth. I love you boy, but I can't help you unless you do what I say."

"Just leave me alone," cried Jake as he curled into a ball in the mud.

"I will, for now, but there will be a day when you'll stand in the middle of this boneyard screaming out for me. If you're lucky I might hear you."

"The wrongdoing of one generation lives into the successive ones."
Nathaniel Hawthorne: *The House of Seven Gables*.

CHAPTER FIFTEEN

Imprisoned though I was by George Corwin's foul cloak, I was still able to follow Nora, with my mind's eye and the heart of a ghostly kinswoman, as the girl fled down Essex Street. I watched helplessly as Nora stumbled against the old bench that marked Turner Street, the unchanged eighteenth century lane that led to the "House of Seven Gables." She then made her way tearfully towards the massive wooden structure that stood by the restless sea.

My prayers went with her, even though my body could not. It was with reluctant relief that I watched Nora rummage through the garbage can and joyfully pull out the dog costume that had been worn by Lynn March's tormentor. Nora gave an exhausted sigh and stumbled to the old wooden steps of the "House of Seven Gables." Once there, she collapsed onto the wood and fell into an exhausted sleep. Then I saw the misty figure of Lynn March approach the sleeping Nora and wrap her arms about my helpless child. The mist that emanated from Lynn seem to cloud both girls from view. Somehow I knew that Nora would be safe while she slept on the old steps of, what most people thought was, the "House of Seven Gables."

How surprised the tourists who made their way through the old house would have been if they realized that the house their tour guide led them through was not the real house that Nathaniel Hawthorne had written about his legendary masterpiece. The real "House of Seven Gables" had been a few steps over, on the corner of English and Derby Streets. It had been my home, built for me with a loving heart by my sweet Philip.

My home, the real house with the seven gables, had been the finest in Salem. Built it was, in 1685, right after our small Philip was born. Baby Philip had been named after both his father and a sickly brother who had died a few years before. How strange it is that our son Philip was the child that grew to follow his father into business, and took on, with his other tasks, the running of my mother's tavern, the Blue Anchor. It was as if some essence of the great house had became part of our son and spurred him on to carry forward our legend.

I could feel the tears run down my eyes as I gathered to my bosom the vision of my beautiful home. It had stood until 1833, well over a hundred years, and had been the pride of my children and my children's children. I remember the day the great house was torn from its foundations. Philip held me as we watched, me sobbing, him silent and angry. He was but a specter even then, but felt that no one had the right to destroy what Philip English had built. I think he still holds the death of our home against the people of Salem and has added that deed to his list of grievances against Salem Town. Little Nate Hawthorne had grown up in the great house's shadow, and remembered it in his fine book many years later, but not even he was able to bring back Philip English's many gabled home.

It was a wonder! The cellars were completely finished and plastered, an unheard of thing in its day, and the stone wall that surrounded the house had been massive. Philip often laughed when he said those stones protected us from the sea, as if anything really could. There was an enormous hearth that could have sheltered twenty men, and the rooms were by far the largest of any house in town. The floors were laid of the widest plank that had been hewn from ancient trees taken from the forest that surrounded Salem at the time. I remember the day Philip and his men had gone to select those ancient timbers. How afraid I had been that the savages would harm them. But Philip insisted that only the largest and finest of Salem's trees was good enough for our home.

The upper part of our home was filled with many peaks and gave a feeling of space and light that was absent from any house I had ever known. The great house even had a shop and a counting house sheltered within its walls. They called it a mansion, and it was.

"And what of the secret tunnels that lay beneath your home, Mary English?"

"Who speaks to me?" I cried out. The forboding that filled me flooded my heart with terror.

"Well you know who it is, Witch English," said the deep, booming voice that shook the ground I lay on.

"It's you, isn't it, John Hathorne," I said steadily.

"It is I," answered the voice in quieter tones.

"What do you want of me, John," I asked trying to match the voice's mood.

"Only to speak to an old friend."

"And since when have you ever been the friend to any called English?" I blurted out before I could help myself.

"Since we all became trapped in this place by your husband's hand," laughed Hathorne in an almost merry manner. "You do remember your husband, don't you? He's that blaggard that even refused to forgive me when he thought I was dying."

"Yes, I remember," I said as I joined Judge Hathorne in his unholy laughter. "It was when Minister Higginson told Philip he must forgive all his enemies before he died."

"And Philip said 'all but Colonel Hathorne.'"

"And then the minister said Philip must forgive you too, John. But Philip said he would, only if he must. His exact words were; 'if I must, alas I will, that is if I'm going to die. If I get well, I'll be damned if I forgive him!' And damned you are, by the sound of you," I said, amazed at my tone. Here I was jesting with the most malevolent spirit that laid beneath the sod of Salem.

"It seems I'm not very well liked nowadays, am I Mary? Even my own kinsman, Nathaniel Hawthorne, added a 'w' to his name to keep his distance from my memory."

"And Bridget Bishop hops upon your grave with glee whenever she gets the chance," I answered, amazed by Hathorne's penitent tone.

"And what of you, Mary, do you forgive old John? After all our children did mix their blood."

"As far as I'm concerned there is really nothing to forgive, John," I said as I remembered all the old days I had shared with the Hathorne family. Forgiveness implies judgment, and I have tried never to judge anyone.

"The only thing that was ever the matter with you, Johnny Hathorne, was that you were far too proud to admit when you were wrong. You and my husband are more alike than different. Two male lions both fighting to rule the same jungle."

"It's amusing, don't you think, that two of my grandsons married two of your granddaughters," said John Hathorne in a faraway voice.

"And even more amusing that Nate Hawthorne always envied his rich cousins their money; money that was earned by my husband after he came back to Salem Town," I said, thinking as I had many times before that family feuds in Salem had always been rather silly. If you dug deep enough we were probably all related to each other in one way or another. That was the way of it back then. Why, one of John's other sons had even married a Corwin girl!

"I'll never forget that time Mistress Hathorne and I met you and Philip that Sunday afternoon after the trials were over," said John Hathorne with an uncharacteristic tremor in his voice. "It was the only time that I felt that perhaps my job was not quite done. Your husband looked like the devil himself that day."

"Aye, 'tis a wonder he didn't kill you with his bare hands in the warmth of that bright day, John. I remember hearing you whisper to your wife that 'only the devil could provide the fires which darted from the eyes of that man,' and then you added 'and that woman.' I guess I was more than a bit angry at you, John. If only I had known I had but a few months left I would have spent my time soaking up the beauty of that day rather than wasting my time hating you."

"And your Philip carried on that hate even after you were gone, Mary. He almost hounded me to death with his debt collectors and tax men. I never was that good with money and Philip knew it well. He drove two of my sons back to England with his endless harassing. 'Tis a pity it should have ended in such a way."

"If you'd had your way, John, both Philip and I would have been hanged on Gallows Hill and you know it," I said as I suddenly felt anger rising within me. What right did John Hathorne have to whine to me about his misfortunes when he would have gladly seen our children homeless and starving.

"Enough, Mary, enough," said John. "You're right, I'm right, we're all right. What does it matter? We're dead. What I can't understand is why Philip can't just let us all sleep. You have no idea how loud it is down here with all those ghosts over at yon Memorial moaning day and night. Why don't they just lie down and die like decent folk should?"

"Because their lives were stolen from them, John, and you held the noose," I said quietly, hoping that the ghost of John Hathorne had no power to hurt me.

"No more than any other who captured and condemned the witches," said Hathorne.

"But you were one of us, and an elder at that, Judge Hathorne. We trusted you as a child trusts his father. And you returned our trust with torture and death."

"I'm not the only one who ever did that in this town, Mary English," said John Hathorne. "What of your husband? What of his ships and his smuggling through the tunnels of this town? Many a starving family watched helpless as he refused jobs to the good citizens of Salem. He filled Salem with Frenchmen like himself and left his old friends to starve."

"Philip brought over those families from the Isle of Jersey and La Rochelle because he knew he could trust them. Besides they were fleeing from religious terror just like we did. The Huguenot's labor turned this town from a fishing village into a great city, Judge Hathorne, and everyone in Salem should be grateful that Philip brought them here."

"But the tunnels Mary, what of the blood that lines their walls?"

"Those tunnels were used to transport goods from our house to the sea during foul weather," I said, knowing that not even I would ever know if that was the full truth. As for the rumors about disloyal seamen being killed and buried down there, who really knew for sure, and Philip was not telling,

"There's far more to the story than that, Mistress English, and you know it. Do you take me for a child that can be bought off with a pretty story or a sweet in my hand? Everyone in our time knew that the tunnels under your house were used to smuggle goods. Your Philip ordered the tax collectors to crush me with one hand while he was bribing them with the other. I wish I had a shilling for every time Philip English paid a tax collector to look the other way while he ran silks and spices back and forth through those catacombs he dug under this town."

"I know very little about the things you speak of," I said, squirming under my bonds. "But I do know that not all those tunnels were dug by Philip. My own father, Will Hollingsworth started those tunnels long before the 1660's. They ran along Derby Street, under the old house we had. And then, when that house burned down in 1663, he continued the digging under our new home farther along down Derby Street."

"But," interrupted John, "he built another house on the land where your first home burned. Old Will must have been mightily afraid that someone would start digging in those blackened ruins and fall into one of his tunnels. I remember now that what you say is true. Philip didn't start the tunnels. 'Twas your own father that did the deed. How handy those caverns must have been when Will was laid low with the sinking of his ships in the seventies. It was then that your mother was given the license to draw beer and cider and keep a tavern in her own right. 'Tis said that she did a bit of black business herself with the pirates that ate at her table at the Blue Anchor Tavern."

"It was fortunate that my mother had been clever enough to get that tavern," I said, totally ignoring what Hathorne had said about pirates and any evil deeds my mother might have done. My mother, Eleanor Hollingsworth, had been a wonderful woman. She was a bright and lively lady that never let misfortune drag her down into the muck of daily living. "I remember, like it was yesterday, when they brought us the shocking news that my father had been lost at sea with the last of his ships. Mama said that it was just as well that he had drowned. There had been nothing left of the man she had loved and married after his first great losses. She said that Father would have surely died of a broken heart if he had somehow survived the wreak. 'God has been merciful to take him thus,' she had said as she held me in her arms." How I had loved her. "Speak no evil of my mother, John Hathorne. You know what a fine woman she was."

"And a beautiful one, too," said John Hathorne in a gentle voice. 'Tis no wonder that Cotton Mather lost his wits everytime he saw her. None of us ever found it in our hearts to really hold him to account for being caught in Eleanor Hollingsworth's spell. She bewitched him, for certain."

"She did not!" I yelled towards the earth that covered John Hathorne's dust.

"Then why do you have the look of Cotton Mather in the knit of you bones and the set of your eyes. Deny it all you like, Mary English, but those who knew Mather say you are his daughter and no one else's. You were your mother's only child, conceived after Will Hollingsworth became a dead man in a living body who forced your lovely mother to find her own way. You cannot escape the truth, Mary English. You are the daughter of Cotton Mather."

"Here now, what's all this blather," said George Corwin as he kicked my captured body with his heavy leather boot.

"Why," I said, almost grateful for the hulking George's interruption, "just a bit of pleasant conversation between me and the Judge."

"I'll be damned," said Corwin, peering at the ground with squinting eyes. "Is he still rolling about down there?"

"That I am, Georgie, that I am," said Hathorne with a chuckle. "And charming though the conversation might be, I'm a bit worn from Mistress

English's ramblings. What say you relieve me of her for a bit so I can take my rest."

"Anything you say Judge," said Corwin as he saluted the ground. "We always were a good team weren't we?"

"Aye, that we were, Georgie," said Hathorne as his deep voice faded into nothingness.

"Now then, Mistress, it's time for us to be a'catchin' up with our young ones."

With those words, Corwin picked me up and we vanished into the bright black night.

> "Everyone is a moon, and has a dark side
> which he never shows to anybody."
> Mark Twain: *Following the Equator.*

CHAPTER SIXTEEN

I was filled with a chilling dampness that made my ghostly bones ache as George set me down. I could hear the dripping of water and there was an odd smell, something akin to burning moss, that surrounded me. The darkness that filled the air was different from the evening mists I was used to. This darkness was all pervasive and seemed everlasting. Something within me rebelled against the terrible feelings that assaulted me as I sat, trapped by Corwin's evil spell.

"What's wrong with you, Mary English?" I asked to myself angrily as I watched George Corwin's ghostly shape move away from me and towards a small glowing ember. "Never have I seen you sit back and let someone take you without a fight," I continued to myself.

What was wrong with me? Why wasn't I using everything I had to get out of George Corwin's trap before it was too late. I realized, with horror, that I had wasted precious moments musing about this and that with John Hathorne when I should have been trying to think my way out of Corwin's trap. And where was Philip? He was wandering about town, totally unaware that Corwin was on a mission to destroy us all!

"Hush now my sweet," I heard from the folds of the filthy tatters that covered me. "If you just lay back and relax everything will be much easier. Haven't you always longed for that? Let me give you a moment of peace where nothing can disturb you but the grave. I can give it to you if you only let me. Sleep and wakefulness all in one breath, that's what my gift will be to you if you only let me have you."

"No!" I cried, realizing finally what was happening to me. Somehow, Corwin's cloak was infested with a spell of endless waking rest. Such a thing would doom me to an eternity of watching those around me be destroyed while I looked on helplessly. At last George Corwin's unbelievably hideous plan lay before me.

"But how can I fight it?" I said to myself, somehow knowing that each time I spoke aloud the spell seemed to pull away from me. "How can I remove these grasping tentacles that are filling my mind with dumb nothingness? "How can I stop it!" I screamed to myself as the silence around me tried to drag my body into the abyss.

"You can't," answered the spell within the cloak. "Sooner or later I'll have you and you will become a part of me. When that happens you will become one with the threads that make me up, just like the others who lay within my fabric."

"That will never happen," I said through clenched teeth as I felt the softness and grit of the cloak stroking my arm seductively.

"Yes it will, my love," answered the cloak. "There are many in my cloth just waiting for you to join them."

It was then, as my mind became filled with a deep blue fog, that I realized how cunning and insidious was the trap Corwin had laid for me. Every time I answered the voice I became weaker and more confused. I knew that no matter what the voice from the cloak said, I must not answer. To answer, even one more time, was to usher myself into a deadly life.

"Did I really speak to John Hathorne in his grave, or is his soul lying trapped within the folds of this evil thing?" I said to myself before I could help it.

"Listen and find out for yourself," answered the cloak with a chuckle.

"Speak not to me! Begone any spirits that lay within this place!" I spoke in a firm full voice as the cloak tried to enslave me within its babble.

"I hear no one, nothing but the sweet sounds of the night." As if in answer, I watched as a family of bats flew past me and perched on a high stone.

"Let me see now where might I be," I said to myself as the cloak's babble became an angry roar in my ears. "It looks to me as if this place is some sort of cave. Why yes, I do believe that's just what it is," I said cheerfully, trying to drown out the voices of despair that tried to fill me. And the miracle of it was that my desperate plan was working. The false happiness in my voice seemed to make the other voices back away into their tortured nothingness. I don't know what it was to this day that made me do what I did next. I only know that it was the miracle I asked for. I began to sing a sweet song that my small daughter Mary had always loved. It was the tune I had hummed to her as she lay dying in my arms. She had been but three years old and the joy that filled my days. Never will I forget her last smile as she closed her eyes for that final time to the words of the song I now uttered.

"Here we go up, up, up.
Up to the very top.
Then we go down, down, down.
Down where we never stop."

I began to repeat the song and was aware of a small, lisping voice singing along. How my children loved to sing. They all had their father's gift of a pure sweet voice. The memory of my long dead daughter joined me in song until the last of the cloak's evil voices wandered into silent nothingness. I sat there in the dark, afraid to move or even think, as my darling daughter's small voice faded away. It was clear that the voice of my small daughter had been heaven sent and bore no malice towards me as I felt a lightness of heart and new hope enter me. If Nora English were destroyed, the blood of my little Mary would cease to flow in the mortal world forever. Now I knew I could find the strength to fight the evil thing that wanted the souls of Philip English's family.

I sat quietly in the blessed silence and tried to gather my wits about me. It was indeed a miracle that I had been visited with a moment of clarity amidst my unbelievable confusion. To this day I have no way of explaining what happened to save me, I only take it as a gift.

The squeaking bats overhead and the glowing ember at the far end of the cave filled me with an unexpected coziness that was wonderful. Then I pulled myself up straight. Was I sinking yet again into the lethargy that had filled me? But no, this was different. This was the happiness that comes with renewed energy, much like the surge of wakefulness I used to get right before one of my babes was to be born.

Just what was that glowing ember, and why was George Corwin hovering about it so closely? I narrowed my eyes and tried to see through the blackness, but it was no use. The thick velvet darkness of the cave hid everything from view. Then a match was lit and I saw a mortal hand, the hand of young Jake Corwin, light another strangely shaped cigarette. The cigarette was more like the ones that Sir Walter Raleigh had brought into fashion than any that were known in late twentieth century Salem.

It was Jake Corwin who sat in the dark of the cave, smoking his cigarettes full of what I always think of as burning moss, but the Salemites call "pot." Again I felt a surge of sympathy for the boy as I watched the pain in his eyes being replaced with a dullness that reminded me of the foglike state I had been in just a few moments before. It was a shame that it should be thus with the boy, but that was the way of it, in my time as well as his. Many were the folk I had known who had become enslaved by rum or the odd herbs they found in Salem woods. It has even been said that some of these strange herbs might have caused the confusion that brought about the witchcraft trials of Salem, but I don't believe it. I don't believe it because there had been too many terrors against women in the Old World that we had left behind. More than one village had been wiped clean of its wise women because a group of foolish young girls had cried out against them in envy or just to relieve the tedium of their dull lives. The herbs that Jake Corwin now smoked had been around during my time, but they had been harder to find and thought of as medicine. How strange it is that something that can relieve pain and nausea should be used to dull the senses and escape from life.

"How is it with you, my boy," I heard George say to his nephew.

"It that you? I thought you hated me because I couldn't hurt Nora."

"You just don't understand, do you?" said George, casting an orange glow about the cave that brought both his spirit and the face of Jake into clear view.

"No, I guess I don't," said Jake. "But I do know that if you still want me to hurt her you can get the hell out of here."

"I thought it over," said George in a friendly tone, "and realized you were quite right not to want to hurt a second girl, Jacob. What sense is there in having you run the risk of getting caught. The police might stop looking for the murderer of one girl after a time, but two girls, never. You've become quite clever, lad. 'Tis a shame that her killing is what is demanded of you. You're damned if you do and damned if you don't. Of course then, with me around you just might get away with it."

"So the only reason I shouldn't kill her is that I might get caught," said Jake. "You make me sick. Why don't you just go away and never come back. I'm sorry I ever listened to you. Why, I might even go to the police and tell them what I did. Why not? I'm going to die anyways, I might as well die with a clear conscience. At least then they might put me somewhere like jail or maybe even Plummer Home for Boys out on Winter Island. It might be okay to die if I didn't have to die in a place like this. I'm sick of being alone and I'm sick of being cold and hungry all the time. And I'm sick of you. Get out of here, will you?"

"It's not that simple, boy," said George with a false sigh. "Have you thought about what your fine lady would say if she found out you had killed her little girlfriend. She'd hate you and curse you. And do you think the police would stow you away in some place sweet like Plummers? You're a murderer, boy, and a rapist too. Do you know what they do to pretty boys like you in prison?"

"No one would touch me. I've got AIDS and you know it."

"That's not what I've heard," said a laughing George. "I've heard that there's a special club for fellows just like you, you know, the ones with AIDS. Don't think you'd be safe from anyone who already has it, because you wouldn't be. You'd end your days praying for the comfort and peace of this place. Trust me, I know."

"How do you know so much?" said Jake as he lit a third cigarette and stretched out on the earth.

"Because several of my young friends have already traveled that road. Do you think you are my only disciple, Jake Corwin? There's many I have helped along the way. You're but one soldier in my legion."

"So, what you're telling me is that there are others like me and they've died just like I'm going to just because they didn't do what you say?"

"That's what I'm telling you, boy. But I'm also saying that you, young Jake, are a special case. I have an extra fondness for you that I can't explain. It takes a lot for this old heart to crack open a bit, but you seem to have done just that to me. Come on now boy, can't we put our heads together and try to figure out some way to save you from your own foolishness?"

"It's not foolishness, I love Nora. I can't kill her. Don't you see that.?"

"I know boy, I know," said George as he stroked Jake's head with his invisible hand. "It's just that I can't save you unless you do. Letting go of your love for this girl and holding her beating heart in you hand is what is demanded of you if you are to be free of the pox."

"But why? For God's sake why?" screamed Jake into the echoing caves. The bats, frightened by the noise, gathered their wings and took flight, creating a dry dusty wind in the damp place.

"God has nothing to do with it," said George Corwin.

> "And thus I clothe my naked villainy
> With odds old ends stol' forth of holy writ,
> And seem a saint when most I play the devil."
> William Shakespeare:
> *King Richard the Third*, act I, sc.iii.

CHAPTER SEVENTEEN

Lynn March watched in silence as the morning star began to rise in the sky. She stared down at the sleeping girl in her arms and wondered again at the strange circumstances that had brought her to this place.

"If only I could talk to Mama," she thought as she pictured the face of Lillith March in her spirit's mind. "Or even see that lady who stood by Nora's bed. She might be able to help us."

I was amazed that I could hear Lynn's thoughts so well as I sat watching George Corwin hover above poor Jake. Never before had I been able to read a ghost's mind the way I read Lynn's. Perhaps it was that the girl was from an unbroken line of witches, or perhaps I was still open to a daughter's voice after my moment with my little Mary. Whatever the reason, the channel between the ghost, Lynn March, and myself was crystal clear. Her thoughts rang through my mind unbidden.

"I wish you'd wake up," said Lynn to the sleeping Nora, as Nora rolled onto her right side and began to snore lightly. Lynn shook her friend, but it did no good.

"You and those stupid pills," said Lynn, putting her hands out and staring at them in fascination. They weren't quite transparent, but there was a luminescent quality to Lynn's hands that made them shimmer.

I smiled as I watched the girl familiarize herself with her new form. The fact was that Lynn March was far more beautiful as a ghost than she would ever have been as a mortal girl. Her hair, the hair that had been almost too fine and tended to fly away with any breeze, was now thick and full of the same shimmering quality that filled the rest of Lynn March's spirit. What had happened was simple. The inner goodness of the girl had infused her whole being when she became a ghost, much the way George Corwin's spirit had become rigid and warped. It seemed that whatever qualities you possessed in life followed you past the grave if you became one of Salem's ghosts. There was no hiding your true character when you rose from the dead in our small town.

I watched Lynn March touch her hair and then her arms. I remember doing the same thing when I first rose from the dankness of my grave. The thoughts that ran through the girl's mind mirrored the ones I had experienced on that long ago night when my husband's ghost had called me. It was very unsettling to be able to almost see through yourself and yet touch your limbs and have them feel as firm and solid as they had always been. That, coupled with the fact that most mortals could not see us while we walked amongst them, almost drove me mad at first.

More than once I had caught myself stopping to speak to someone in the street and been amazed when they looked right past me, or even worse, walked through me. Poor little Lynn! I didn't envy her the next twenty years or so. It took about that long for the customs and dress of the mortals around us to change enough so that we spirits could tell the difference between mortal and ghost. Until then the dear girl have to deal with the frustration of trying to link with the mortals she had left behind.

And oh, the longing we all have for a mortal to answer us, just once. It is like a thirst that can't be quenched. A spirit knows that such a thing is almost impossible, but we can't help trying. And then there are those rare moments when we do break through, much like Martha Cory did when she threw the Witch Memorial offerings at Giles. There is something about being seen or sensed by a real mortal that makes us feel real again ourselves. If only we could destroy the veil that separated the mortal from the spirit in Salem and travel freely between our two worlds! Certainly there were enough witches and warlocks gathered in our town who would be just as glad as the ghosts to be done with our separation forever. But I knew, as I watched Lynn March try to jostle her friend into wakefulness, that such a thing was impossible. I tried not to think of what would happen to our new little girl ghost when her murder was solved and Nora began to age and grow away from Lynn. There would be a day when the veil would come between the two friends and Lynn would disappear from Nora's thoughts forever. This never failed to happen once the departed spirit let go of its earthly conflicts and took his or her place amongst the spirits in full knowledge of what if meant to be one of Salem's ghosts. To remain an active spirit this must happen, or the ghost ran the risk of vanishing back into the grave and becoming a spirit trapped below ground. This is what I hoped might happen to George Corwin if his mind centered overlong in Jake's. Perhaps George would cross the line and be whisked underground forever.

"Nora, Nora, wake up. I'm getting scared," I heard Lynn say as she shook Nora with her whispy hands.

"What's there to be scared of? You're already dead," said Nora grumpily as she swatted at Lynn. Both girls stared as Nora's hand passed through Lynn's chest.

"That feels creepy," said Nora, sitting up and looking towards the sky.

"It's worse for me than for you, trust me," said Lynn, looking a little green.

"I bet it is," said Nora as she stood up. She picked up the dirty costume like it was a precious treasure. The two girls watched in silence as the moon escaped from behind the glowing clouds and shone down upon Salem Willows.

"I know where Jake went!" said Nora.

"Where?"

"To the caves, you know the ones that connect to the tunnels," said Nora trying to pull the ghostly Lynn towards Turner Street.

"But we can't go down there. It might be dangerous!" said Lynn. "Everyone says it's haunted."

"Duh," said Nora as the two girls broke into hysterical laughter. Then they put their arms around each other and started up the street to where the Blue Anchor Tavern had stood three hundred years ago.

'I am not afraid of death, but I am afraid of what follows.
I am condemned only upon circumstances, but
all should take care how they bring money into New England,
to be hanged for it."
Jack Quelch, the pirate:
spoken to Cotton Mather at Quelch's hanging, June 30th, 1704.

CHAPTER EIGHTEEN

"I always feel that I might run into the ghost of Jack Quelch when I'm down here," I heard a familiar voice say as my mind was suddenly turned from Nora and Lynn with a jolt. It was the voice of my own Philip, not ten paces from me. I struggled beneath my bonds, but it was no use. I was held as tight and as mute as I had ever been. "If I ever get out of this, you'll pay George Corwin, I swear you will."

"Be careful about throwing curses around, Mary," said George, looking first at me and then at the foggy specters of my husband and Giles Cory. I beat against the old tatters of that cloth like a moth beating against a flame. It was with shattering terror that I watched George Corwin approach Philip and Giles from behind.

"Can't you just feel it, friend Giles," said Philip as he touched the dripping walls of the ancient cave. "Quelch's treasure might still be hidden behind these stones."

"If it were here, Quelch would be sitting atop it." said Giles. "And right along with him would be old Cotton Mather, trying to take it away from

Quelch. I always thought it a great pity that Mather caught and hanged Quelch. Jackie was a good man. To think, Phil, the pirate was caught right in the Blue Anchor Tavern. 'Tis a pity you were away at sea at the time. If you'd been around I bet there would have been no hanging."

"Or maybe there might have been two," said Philip quietly. "There was nothing anyone could have done to save Quelch after he refused to give the Governor half the treasure. Not even Mather could have stopped the hanging once that happened."

"And Quelch died without telling his secret," said Giles. "But there was more than one about that said he left it with you and you founded your second fortune on the gold of Jack Quelch. Why else would he have been at the Blue Anchor that night? He was trying to find you. And when he learned you were at sea, 'twas said Quelch buried his treasure in the tunnels beneath the Blue Anchor. Did he really leave a message with your son, young Philip? I always thought it was strange that young Master Philip English chose to run a tavern rather than follow his father to sea."

"Someone had to do it, it was his mother's legacy, and I had the other boys with me aboard ship," said Philip as he shivered in the damp. "You know, it always annoys me that I can still feel hot and cold, Giles. You'd think that once I lost the need to eat or sleep, the rest would have gone as well."

"Just be grateful you can feel something, you old ghost," said Giles, giving a similar shiver as the night grew old.

"Can you feel that you're not alone," said George Corwin, laughing cruelly as he jumped forward. He stood in front of the stuperous Jake and waved to Philip and Giles in a playful manner.

"So that's where you went to, Corwin," said Philip.

"Aye, and here is where I mean to stay for a bit more," said George as he put his hand to his heart. "Tell me now, Philip English, what do you hold most dear in this afterworld."

"I don't know what you mean?" said Philip warily as he cast a side glance at Giles.

"Of course you do, old friend," said George, rubbing his hands under the flame of Jake's cigarette. "There's one thing in this world you would give your immortal soul to save. That old hag you call your 'precious Mary.' Tell me now, I bet you've searched this town over and under this night and have found nary a trace of her."

"Don't answer him, he's playing some sort of a game," said Giles.

"Shut up, old man," said George. "I'm talking to the Captain here. Come on now, English, surely you can't tell me your Mary is all safe and warm somewhere. We both know different."

"Where is she, you foul murderer!" I heard Philip shout so loudly that the massive rocks of the old cave began to tremble.

"Keep your hands off that slut Nora and maybe I'll tell you," said George Corwin with an almost feminine giggle. "But get in nature's way, or mine, and I can promise you that you'll never see Mistress Mary again. And by the way, I thought you might like to have this," said George as he tossed something small and shining into Philip's hand. I gasped when I realized what it was. Somehow, while I lay dreaming, George had stolen my most precious possession, the jade and gold wedding ring that Philip had brought me from the faraway Orient. It was that beloved token that Philip now stared at with horror. We both knew that I was never without it.

"Stand back, Philip English, or the dust you tread upon may be that of Mary."

"And if I do, what guarantee do I have that you'll give her back to me?"

"Why the word of a gentleman, my friend," said George Corwin as he turned to watch Nora English, shadowed by Lynn March, stumbling down the rocky tunnel's path.

"A pair of star-cross'd lovers."
William Shakespeare: *Romeo and Juliet.*

CHAPTER NINETEEN

"Jake, is that you?" I heard Nora call out as the ghosts of George Corwin and my husband faded from view. Philip whispered something to Giles, but I couldn't make out his words as Cory became but a faint shadow.

"Remember what I promised," was the last thing I heard Corwin say as the ghostly trio disappeared from view. I knew they were still there because there is an energy that always surrounds us, an energy that we can't hide from one another. As far as Nora and Jake were concerned there was no one left in the cave but them and the hovering shadow of the newly made ghost, Lynn March. Lynn, as a young spirit, had not yet acquired the powers that the older ghosts like Philip and I took for granted. A newly formed ghost was like a child who must be taught the skills that her elders took for granted. Lynn must remain visible to any who could see her until she learned our tricks.

"Nora, Nora!" cried Jake as he got to his unsteady feet and ran towards the girl. "I told you never to come here!"

"I know you did," said Nora as she put her arms around his neck. "But look what I've found," she said, picking the dog costume out of the dust mud where she had dropped it when she hugged Jake.

"You're a fool," he said, "but I'm glad you're here."

"So am I," she said as Jake kissed her. He held her close for several moments afterward and then guided the girl to the firm, dry earth where he had been sitting.

"You'd better watch it, you know," said Jake as he lit another cigarette and offered it to Nora.

"Why?" she asked, taking his offering and placing it to her lips. She inhaled deeply as she eased her body into Jake's waiting arms.

"Because you've been through a lot tonight. Are you sure you're all right? I remember being sick for a week when I had my stomach pumped."

"I don't remember that," said Nora. "What happened? Why'd you do it?"

"I don't really know," said Jake. "All I remember about it, is not wanting to live and wanting to get out of the pain I was in. Everyday was full of nothing, nothing at all. Every night I would pray to something to just let me die in my sleep, but I kept waking up. One day I woke up and I just couldn't stand living through another day. That's when I did it. I bought a couple of different bottles of pills down on Union street in Lynn and swallowed them. The next thing I knew I was up at the hospital. They were making me swallow something that tasted like charcoal and when that didn't work they slammed me down on this table and stuck a tube down my throat."

"Yeah, I know what that's like," said Nora, rubbing her stomach. "Why do they have to be so rough?"

"Because they hate us for doing it, you know, for trying to die," said Jake. "Old people are always running around spending lots of money to get back what we have and no matter what they do it doesn't work. They hate us because we're young and they're not."

"That's stupid," said Nora, giggling as she pulled out her blouse and looked down at her bare stomach. "Poor baby," she said to her stomach, " do you hurt weally bad? Widdle Nowa is sowwy that she hurtum oo." Nora rubbed her stomach and turned to Jake with a babyish smile. "Poor Jakey's tummy, they hurtum him too. Nowa wants to see Jakey's tummy."

"I don't think that's a good idea," said Jake as he inched away from Nora. "Here, give me that," he said taking the cigarette from Nora's hand and crushing it beneath his heel. "I'm a jerk for giving it to you. You're already hopped up on the stuff they gave you at the hospital."

"I am not," said Nora, pushing Jake onto the ground.

"Yes you are, and I'm not going to let you get any higher. You'll get sick."

"You're a wuss," said Nora as she crawled on all fours to where Jake lay, "but you're a cute wuss," she said, taking hold of Jake's wrists and holding him in mock captivity. "Now give widdle Nowa a kiss. If you don't she's gonna' beat her widdle wussy Jake up."

"Don't do that," said Jake with a groan.

"You see, boy," I heard George Corwin say as his dark oiliness crept towards the two young lovers. "What did I tell you? Look at her, she wants it bad. Take her, take her now before she runs off and couples with someone else. She's nothing but a bitch in heat. Send her away now and she'll find someone else before sunrise."

"No. Please," said Jake. "Please just get away from me."

"It's too late for that, Jake, my lad," said George Corwin as he became stronger, somehow more visible, despite the darkness.

Nora stared at Jake and was rocked into sobriety by the savage look that had suddenly appeared on her young lover's face. "Jake what's wrong?" she asked, backing away from him in terror. "I was only kidding. You know how I get when I smoke that stuff. I really didn't mean that you were a wuss. You're great, really!"

"Shut up, bitch!" commanded the voice that came out of Jake Corwin's mouth. But it was not the light baritone of Jake Corwin. The voice that came from the boy's chest was the booming bass of the long dead George Corwin. Somehow Corwin had managed to fuse his soul to Jake's body. I looked on in terror as I realized what was about to happen.

Jake/George grabbed Nora's wrist and dragged the screaming girl towards the back of the cave where the rocks joined the fine matted earth that led to the tunnels.

"Let me go, Jake," she screamed, "let me go!"

"Didn't I tell you to shut up!" he yelled as Jake/George ripped Nora's blouse in half.

"Lynn, help me!" she screamed as Jake/George crushed Nora's body into the earth and began to unzip her jeans.

"I can't," sobbed the helpless young spirit as she fluttered around Nora frantically.

"I can't," mocked Jake/George Corwin as he ripped the clothes from Nora's body. "There's no one in this world or any other who can help you now, cunt, so you might as well lie back and enjoy this."

It was then that I saw Philip break from the shadows and hurtle towards Corwin.

"Stay where you are," growled Corwin, "or your Mary will be screaming in the flames of hell this day."

In answer to his threat I suddenly became filled with an unholy warmth that quickly spread through my body and began to engulf my being. I was aware of my voice, the mortal one I had not heard in centuries, screaming in agony. It echoed through the cave.

"Stop it you bastard!" shouted Philip as he backed away from Corwin and the struggling girl. "I'll stand back if you stop it."

"That's better, Phil," said Corwin with a grin. "Now then little miss, let's see what those sweet legs feel like wrapped around old Corwin's back.

With those words the ghosts of Salem watched helplessly as George Corwin, using the body of his sick nephew Jake, plunged into Nora's virgin womb.

"There are people who eat the earth and eat all the people
on it like in the Bible with the locusts.
And other people who stand around and watch them eat it."
Lillian Hellman: *The Little Foxes*.

CHAPTER TWENTY

Something in the flames that had engulfed me left me almost mindless as the heat left my body. I lay beneath the tatters of Corwin's cloak and listened as Nora's screams shattered the thick silence. I remember thinking that it didn't really matter if she screamed or not because there was no hope of anyone hearing the girl through the thickness of those rocks. I kept waiting for the utter despair of the whole thing to engulf me, but I felt nothing. Then I began to be aware that the scene around me was changing. I could feel my soul floating above my ghostly form and taking to the early morning sky. Suddenly I became almost joyful as my soul melted through the yellow wood of Witch March's home. I felt myself come to rest on a soft pillow beside Lillith March. Whatever the reason for my strange journey, I was glad for a moment of calm.

There was an enormous black candle that must have been burning all night. It cast a comforting glow about the room that was decorated in shades of lilac. I smiled to myself when I realized that there were not one, but two women that lay beneath the soft velvety coverlet of Lillian's sleigh bed. I had long thought that Lillian March and her secretary, Hannah, were lovers, and now I saw with my own eyes that it was true. I watched with an odd comfort as the two women warmed to each other's embrace and began to murmur to each other. Something of their gentle motions seemed to make the horror of the past few hours a bit more bearable.

I felt Lillith's contented sigh run through me as she and Hannah ended their lovemaking. It was then that I realized that there still might be hope for us all, even Nora. The woman in the lilac room had lost her daughter, but not her love of life. Her mind and psyche were still intact. She was not about to throw away the gift of life that the immortals had given her. Lillith made me realize that there was still much that I had. I had seen my last living kinswoman beaten and raped by the dark force of George Corwin, but, as far I knew, she still lived. Whatever else happened, I must keep Nora alive.

PART THREE

INTERCOURSE WITH EVIL

"Farewell, Morning Star, herald of dawn,
and quickly come as the Evening Star,
bringing again in secret her whom thou takest away."
Meleager: First century B.C.

CHAPTER TWENTY ONE

It was a pleasant thing to eavesdrop on the two women as dark turned to dawn on that late autumn morning. All too soon the days would become as black as night itself when the Oak King presented his staff to the Holly King at the coming of the winter solstice. I'll never forget the first time I watched Lillith March present the ancient pagan ceremony on Salem Common. How amazing it was that what used to be a hanging offense in Salem Town was now celebrated out in the open with reverence and pride.

The witch, Lillith, was a rare woman, one who I would have been proud to call friend of we had both been mortals at the same time. There is no describing the gratitude I felt towards her for taking care of Nora. I could only pray that the sense that had first sent Lillith to Nora's rescue before was still strong within her.

The other thing I knew was that the fates were still with me or I would not be lying here now. By all rights I should still be trapped within George Corwin's bonds, but that was not so, at least not completely so. My ghostly body still lay within his grasp, but for some reason, my soul had been set free to fly to Lillith's haven. I had long ago stopped trying to figure out the vagaries of the spirit world that controlled our comings and goings in Salem. I now accepted them with an oddly childlike faith, a faith that I hoped would now stand me in good stead.

"Lillith, my sister," I whispered with my heart, "take your friend and go to Salem Willows. This is a dawn that must be shared. The ocean and what lies close to it call you this morn."

It was with thankfulness that I watched Lillith's eyes blink and her hand touch Hannah's.

"Come," I heard her say to Hannah. "For some reason I want to have our breakfast by the sea."

"Is this another one of your dreams?" asked Hannah as she turned lazily in the bed, obviously not wanting to move.

"It seems more like a command," said Lillith, throwing a long brown wool dress at Hannah. "I heard a voice telling me to go."

"Was it Lynn's?" asked Hannah.

"Perhaps," said Lillith as she pulled on her heavy walking boots, "perhaps not. "Whoever it was she was a spirit."

My soul joined the women as they prepared for the two mile walk down Collins Cove, past Winter Island, to Salem Willows. I felt that once we came near the spot where Nora was, my soul would be drawn back towards my entrapped spiritual body. But that mattered little if I could save Nora. And what's more, Philip was probably still there. At least he now knew that Corwin had me. After last night's despair. I saw even that as a cause for hope.

"Why do we have to walk?" asked Hannah as the sharp November air hit her face.

"I don't know," said Lillith, 'but we do. Why don't we take the way across 'Singing Horse Beach', the way that goes by the caves."

"I hate that way," said Hannah.

"So do I, but that's the way we have to go."

"Over the mountains and over the waves,
Under the fountains and under the graves;
Under floods that are deepest, which Neptune obey,
Over rocks that are steepest, Love will find out the way."
Anonymous: "Love Will Find Out the Way."

CHAPTER TWENTY TWO

"I can't believe all the stuff that's inside my boots," said Hannah as she shook her sand filled boot at Lillith. "Can we go home now?"

"Not yet," said Hannah, standing on the rocky beach that looked toward Danversport.

"What are we waiting for?" asked Hannah, kicking her foot in the sand.

"What's that?" cried Lillith as a small plastic band flew from Hannah's toe.

"It's some sort of name tag," said Hannah, picking up the band and shading her eyes from the bright morning sunlight.

"Let me see," said Lillith as she took the tag from Hannah and eyed it closely. "It's Nora's hospital band," said Lillith with deathly quiet.

As if in answer, there suddenly came a light groan from behind a stand of pine trees that linked the sand to the rocks on the beach.

"Nora?" called Lillith in a steady voice as she walked towards the sound.

"There it is again!" said Hannah.

"She's in a cave behind those trees," said Lillith as she began to run. "Nora! Where are you!" screamed Lillith over the sound of the crashing waves that ate mercilessly at the shoreline.

"Mama, is that you?" came the small whimper of a small girl's voice from right beneath Lillith's running feet.

"She's below us," cried Hannah as she began to make her way down the rocky incline that led towards the pines that sheltered the caves of Salem Willows.

"Be careful, Hannah," said Lillith, grabbing her friend's hand and following her down the treacherous incline.

"Hurry," was Hannah's answer to Lillith as she set her feet on the small ledge where the rocks touched the sea and helped guide Lillith to where the whimpers of Nora could be heard. Hannah took a deep breath, let go of Lillith's hand, and jumped from the ledge. She fell directly into the spiny pines and then disappeared. Lillith closed her eyes and did the same, praying that there was something beyond the pines to catch them. When she opened her eyes, Lillith saw that she and Hannah were standing in a massive cave.

"It must be older than time," said Hannah as she looked toward the cave's ceiling in reverence.

"Nora," cried Lillith, trying desperately to keep herself from being pulled in by the hypnotic force that clouded her mind as she and Hannah stood in the middle of the ancient cave.

"Help me, oh someone please help me," whispered a young girl's voice from the shadows.

"I'm here Nora," said Lillith, feeling strangely calm as she moved toward the girl's voice.

Nora let out another moan as Hannah stumbled over Nora's body and then smashed against the jagged walls of the old cave.

Lillith fell to her knees and cradled the bleeding girl in her arms. "Don't cry, sweet Nora," said Lillith as she tried to keep her tears from falling onto the torn girl's face, "everything will be all right. I promise you."

Lillith looked towards Hannah who was scanning the rape scene with a horrified look on her face. "Get help," was all Lillith had to say to Hannah to wake her companion from her shock and send Hannah running towards the opening of the cave and upwards out into the morning air.

"Hannah's gone for help, my love," said Lillith as she held Nora's torn body close and began to croon an ageless lullaby into the shattered girl's ear. Miraculously, Nora fell into a healing sleep as she cuddled against Lillith's breast.

"Who did this to you, child?" asked Lillith, more to herself than to the sleeping girl.

To Lillith's surprise, Nora sighed a name. "Jake."

> "Who ran to help me when I fell
> And would some pretty story tell,
> Or kiss the place to make it well?
> My Mother."
> Ann Taylor: "My Mother."

CHAPTER TWENTY THREE

It was with a mother's heart that I, Mary English whose soul found itself bonded to that of Lillith March, listened to the cries of the delirious Nora crying out for her long dead mother. It was in that moment that I knew that Lillith March and I would be fused together, forever, in foster motherhood, ever watching and crying over young Nora as if she were our own.

I could feel my soul trying to leave that of Lillith March's, called by George Corwin's evil spell to rejoin my ghostly body trapped beneath Corwin's magical cloak. But stronger than the call of dark magic was the white magic of womanly love that drew Lillith, Nora and myself into a trinity of pain and rage. It was truly rage I felt when I heard the name of Jake Corwin drop from Nora's bleeding lips. But what good was my rage as long as I remained powerless? Somehow I must find a way to once again become a free flowing spirit within my ghostly body. But until then I blessed the powers that had at least allowed me to join Lillith March's soul and give double comfort to the tortured mind and body of my lovely young niece.

"Was it Jake Corwin who did this to you, child?" I heard Lillith ask the confused young girl.

"Yes. No. I don't know!" sobbed Nora as she opened her eyes and looked at Lillith.

An incredible sadness filled me as I watched Nora. The confusion that filled our child made me want to weep dry, useless tears. Why had this happened to our dearest child? The senselessness of the whole thing threatened to fill me with a paralyzing despair. It was from this feeling of hopelessness that I was suddenly shaken by a searing light that traveled from Nora's eyes, through Lillith's, and into my heart.

"What is it Nora? What are you trying to show me?" I heard Lillith cry as she shook the girl.

"Dreams," was the only word that Nora could murmur before she fell into a death-like sleep.

"What are you dreaming, Nora?" said Lillith quietly as she held Nora in her arms.

The answer the girl gave was something I had never seen before, not even in Salem, where metaphysical wonders are an everyday occurrence. I watched in wonder as the eyes of Nora English truly became the windows of her soul.

Nora gave a small sigh as she turned her head toward the darkest wall of the cave and blinked. Suddenly, the cave was filled with a golden mist that was brightest around the damp stony wall. I was filled with peace as I watched the wall begin to glow and then take on the shimmer of the mist. In the center of the golden array I could make out three figures, that of a boy and a girl in tender embrace, and a larger figure looming behind them. The larger figure seemed to be wearing some kind of a cloak that was ragged at the edges. The effect of those tattered edges made the sinister presence look like some sort of bat.

I could feel the joy emanating from the two misty lovers as they held each other, totally oblivious to the dark presence that threatened behind them. Then, suddenly, I watched in horror as the lovers joy turned to terror when the dark presence filled the boy. That dusky spirit's twisted thoughts filled the entire cave with feelings of rage and murder. Lillith and I became one with that dark, all encompassing soul, as he took hold of the girl shadow and threw her to the ground in a brutal pantomime of the rape I had already witnessed. I felt Lillith March's mind trying to escape the madness that she had become a part of, but I knew from experience that it was no use. Once the dark forces of Salem had been set in motion there was no stopping them.

To my surprise, there appeared a fourth figure that stood behind the evil shadow. It was the form of a woman.

"Mama," I heard Nora moan as the woman lightly touched Nora's shadow self.

"Mama, don't," cried Nora as the woman shadow moved to the Nora's shadow's feet and savagely pulled the child's legs apart.

I felt the body of Lillith March began to shake as we were forced to repeat the rape of Nora English yet again. But this time it was worse, for somehow the horrors of Nora's past had merged into the terror of the present, making all one and the same. What hope was there for the girl if this is what filled her fevered thoughts?

"Stop!" I heard Lillith March scream as she dropped the sleeping girl on the earth and confronted the evil spirits. "No more! Do you hear me! Leave this child in peace!"

Miraculously, the power of the witch, Lillith, seemed to overcome the frenzy of the misty shadows as the cave retreated suddenly into darkness.

"Lillith, Lillith! Are you all right?" I heard Hannah shout as a rush of running footsteps came towards us.

"Yes," said Lillith weakly as she turned to face the crowd that suddenly filled the cave. "Help her," she said as she collapsed into Hannah's arms.

Hannah and Lillith clung to each other as they watched the Salem Police radio in the information needed to help Nora. Not once did the girl awake, not even when she was lifted into a sling and carried gently out of the cave.

The cave. The secret cave of Philip English was now filled with five hundred watt flood lights that illuminated the crime scene like the brightest daylight. Somehow the glare of those lights seemed an intrusion into the dark and gloomy place that held many of Salem's secrets. I felt myself trying to control a rising anger as the Salem Police photographed and dusted every square inch of our cave. My anger reached a pinnacle when Sergeant Jim Proctor reached right through my ghostly body and picked up a piece of Nora's torn blouse. Somehow, his touching my beloved girl's blouse with a plastic covered hand turned the stomach that I no longer possessed. It was as if my private world were being raped, much like Nora's body had been.

"Hey Sarge, look at this!" I heard Tom Riley shout as he picked up the dog costume that Nora had so proudly shown Jake.

"Careful with that," shouted Proctor from his stooped position under a rocky ledge. "That's evidence."

"Didn't the English girl say something about a dog costume when we questioned her about the murder of Lynn March?" asked Patrolman Riley as he carefully picked up the costume with a piece of plastic wrapped around his hand.

"That's right, she did!" said Proctor, dropping the clump of dirt he was sifting through as he stared at Riley with disgust.

"You know what this means, don't you?" said Tom as he dropped the dog costume into a bag and brought it over to his sergeant.

"Yeah," said Proctor standing up and taking the bag Riley offered. "It means that we've got a serious nut on our hands, one that buys into all the Salem Halloween shit. God, I wish we could just be like any other town."

"But we're not," said Riley as he pointed to his arm patch. On it was the Salem Police insignia, a black witch on a broomstick, flying across the moon.

"No, I guess we're not," said Proctor.

> "You are a liar."
> "I am no more a witch than you are a wizard,
> and if you take away my life,
> God will give you blood to drink."
> Sarah Good: Her last words,
> spoken from the scaffold to the
> High Sheriff, Nicholas Noyes, July 19th, 1692.

CHAPTER TWENTY FOUR

"All I know about it is that I had this feeling when I woke up," said Lillith to Sergeant Proctor.

"Oh come on," said Proctor, "I know that there's more to it than that. You can't believe that I'm dumb enough to fall for your 'I'm a witch so I get these funny feelings' line?"

"Yes I do, because that's the truth," said Lillith.

Somehow I found myself still journeying with Lillith March's body, even though my soul was beginning to long for its return to my spectral body. I was beginning to feel less of a shade than I already was and there had been a moment or two in the past few hours that I had begun to entirely forget that I was the spirit of Mary English. I was trying, as best I could, to control the rising panic within me.

"Please God," I whispered to myself inside Lillith's thoughts, "get me out of here and back to my essence. We must be rejoined soon or I may lose myself."

My thoughts must have been heard by Lillith, because her next words were ones of anger and frustration. "Why don't you stop wasting your time with me? It's time to get out here and do something about this," said Lillith with controlled rage. "The man who killed my daughter and almost did the same thing to Nora is still out there! What can I possibly tell you that I haven't already?"

"I don't know," said Proctor with a false smile. "I just know that every time something goes wrong in this town you seem to be there, Mrs. March. Can you tell me why?"

"You said it yourself, Sergeant," said Lillith with an equally false smile. "I'm a witch."

"All right, I give up," said Proctor as he took his foot off the table that separated him from Lillith. "You can go, for now. But don't try to leave Salem, I may need to talk to you again."

"Thank you, Sergeant," said Lillith, pushing herself away from the table and standing up. "You're most kind." Then Lillith offered her hand to the Sergeant.

"I take it we're still friends," said Proctor as he took Lillith's hand in his and touched her fingers gently.

"Eternally," said Lillith flashing a brilliant smile at the officer as she left the room.

"It must have been awful," said Hannah as she and Lillith made their way through Derby Square and started down Essex Street.

"Oh it was just the usual," said Lillith, putting her arm around Hannah. "Hurry now, let's go home and get the car. We've got to get to the hospital. I feel that Nora will be all right, but I want to be there when she wakes up."

Lillith's words were the last thing I was conscious of until I became aware of a steady dripping sound. I fought desperately to get past the fogginess that filled me and battle back into reality. I focused on that dripping sound until finally, Nora's face came into focus.

"Nora, can you hear me?" I heard Lillith say as we both gazed into the girl's bruised face. It was shocking to see how small Nora looked laying against the stark white sheets with tubes running from her arms and nose. As my thoughts cleared, I realized that the dripping sounds I had heard were the life giving liquids that flowed into Nora's veins.

"Nora," repeated Lillith as the girl stirred restlessly in the bed, "can you hear me!"

"Of course I can hear you, stop shouting!" said Nora as she pulled herself upright, almost tearing the tube that was attached to her left hand.

"Thank goodness you're awake, dear," said Hannah, touching the girl's hair and adjusting her pillows like some sort of mother hen.

"Will you stop that, it makes me nervous," said Nora, looking around the room angrily.

"Don't worry about that now," said Lillith. "Just try to tell us what happened to you after you left the hospital last night."

"Left the hospital?" What are you talking about?" said Nora.

"She's talking about how you went out the window and then walked to the Willows," said Hannah.

"What!"

"It's true, Nora," said Lillith. "You were found this morning, unconscious and bleeding in a cave underneath Singing Horse Beach. Darling, I know this may be hard to believe, but look for yourself." Lillith handed Nora her compact and watched sadly as the girl looked in the small mirror.

"What happened!" screamed Nora.

"We don't know," said Lillith. "Only you can tell us."

"But I don't remember a thing," said Nora as she tried to shift her body. Her face was suddenly covered with pain as she lifted the covers and looked at her pelvis and legs.

"What happened to me, Aunt Lillith?" asked the trembling girl. "Why am I so sore?"

"I don't want to tell you this, but I have to," said Lillith sadly. "Someone beat you, and then raped you, just like they did Lynn. If I could, I would give my own life to change things, but there is nothing I can do. At least you weren't killed. Try to think of that. It's very important that you remember what happened."

"You won't let him get me again?" screamed Nora, as the horror of what happened to her became a reality.

"No darling, I swear I won't. Sergeant Proctor said he would send over the police to guard you until you are well enough to go home. I promise that nothing like this will ever happen to you again. But I can't say that for the rest of the woman in town. Try to remember what happened, darling, it may save some other girl."

may save some other girl."

"I can't," said Nora as the tears ran down her cheeks. "I don't remember a thing. Help me, Aunt Lillith, you know you can. Tell me how to remember!"

"All I can tell you is that you said a name when I found you this morning."

"What was it?"

"Jake," said Lillith.

"No, it can't be!" said Nora, turning an ashen gray. "There's no way he would do this to me. He loves me!"

"But 'Jake' is what you said," said Lillith, "and then you said, 'yes, no, I don't know.' I have no idea what you meant by that, but that's all you said. Then you passed out and I held you while I waited for help."

"If Lillith hadn't had one of her feelings this morning you would have died," said Hannah. "I thought she was crazy, dragging me out in the cold, but you know how it is. When she says go, we go. Can't you get one of those feelings now to help Nora?"

"If only it were that simple," said Lillith sadly. "Don't you think I could have saved my own daughter if I could make these things come and go at will."

"Don't cry, Mama," I heard from the corner as Lillith covered her face. It was the spirit of Lillith's daughter, Lynn. I watched as the young spirit swept close to her mother's side and laid a misty hand on her shoulder.

"Don't cry," the ghost girl said again as she brushed her hand through Lillith's hair. "I will never leave you."

I could feel Lillith's heart and soul flood with peace as her daughter smiled down upon her. The energy with which the woman shook her head and squared her shoulders told me that somehow, in some way, she had heard her daughter. Lillith touched her own shoulder, melding her fingers with that of her ghostly daughter and looked directly at the spirit.

"We are one," I heard the woman whisper in her soul as she smiled. It was then that I knew that Lillith March held a power inside her that could break me out of my own prison. Her gifts were Goddess given and very powerful.

"So, you're awake," said Jim Proctor as he opened the door. Despite his size, Proctor moved with a strange grace as he moved to Nora's bedside.

"Do you think you feel good enough to talk to me for a minute?" said

"No," said Nora, turning her face to the wall.

"Maybe you'll feel like it when I tell you that we found Jake Corwin's fingerprints all over the crime scene. They were even on an old costume someone had left down there. We've got a call out for him now. It's only a matter of time before we catch him, Nora, so if you know anything you'd better tell me. He's not just a suspect in your assault. I have enough on him to charge him with the murder of Lynn March."

"That's not true, it can't be!" sobbed Nora.

"Sergeant, can't you see the girl's been through an awful time," said Lillith as she stood up and faced Proctor. "Get out of here before I throw you out!"

"OK, I'll leave for now, Mrs. March, but it seems pretty strange to me that you don't want to find your own daughter's killer."

"I want that more than anything in this world, you idiot," said Lillith, "but I won't stand by and see you torture Nora like this. Do what you have to about Jake Corwin, but leave her alone."

"I will, for now," said Proctor, "but don't think this is the end of it."

"Get out," said Lillith as she pushed Proctor out the door and slammed it behind him.

"Aunt Lillith," said Nora, "what are we going to do?"

"You're going to get some rest, young lady," said Lillith, "you've got your whole life ahead of you, starting now. I can't tell you why, but I believe that Jake is innocent. It might not be in the way you think, but somehow, I know he's not to blame for what has happened to you or to Lynn. You just concentrate on getting well and leave the rest to me. Can you do that, Nora. Can you trust me?"

"Yes," said Nora as she lay back on the pillow. "But what I don't understand is why you are so good to me."

"Because I love you, Nora," said Lillith as she kissed the girl gently.

> "The holiest of all holidays are those
> kept by ourselves in silence and apart,
> the secret anniversaries of the heart."
> Henry Wadsworth Longfellow.

CHAPTER TWENTY FIVE

Lillith waited until Nora fell asleep, and then left the hospital leaving Hannah by the girl's side. Sergeant Proctor's men were also nervously prowling the halls. I was surprised when she told Hannah that she would leave the car at the hospital. "I just feel like walking," was all Lillith said as she left.

Everything in me was willing Lillith to return me to the Singing Horse Beach cave, and I breathed an enormous ghostly sigh when I felt the woman's thoughts turning that way. Now I would be rejoined with my spectral body so that I could begin to work my way out of my prison. I had the key in Lillith March, and now I had to find a way to turn it.

Lillith was a woman of strange moods and great talent. She was known around Salem as someone who seldom did anything predictable. That is why, when she felt compelled to leave her own daughter's funeral, no one stopped her. No one ever questioned Lillith March. I could feel the storm of one of those unpredictable moods coming over her as we walked, and it didn't surprise me at all when she stopped at the gates of Old Burial Hill. What did surprise me was when Lillith went right past Lynn's grave. She strode all the way to the farthest most corner of the graveyard and stopped at a stone. Written upon it was the name "Dorothy Bishop."

I felt the love in Lillith as she knelt before the stone and traced the flowers that had been carved into the stone with a loving hand. Beneath the name was the inscription, "Beloved Mother-in-law and Friend."

So that was who Dorothy was! I remembered hearing the story about how Lillith March had been engaged to a young man many years ago. The man had died in a mysterious accident, leaving Lillith with the legacy of their love, the baby Lynn. Dorothy Bishop had been the mother of Lillith's first love and had taken care of Lillith and her baby. But the most important fact about Dorothy Bishop was that she was descended from Bridget Bishop, my dear friend, who had been the first victim of Salem's witchcraft hysteria in 1692.

Dorothy had taken Lillith March into her heart and home, much as Lillith had taken our Nora. Dorothy Bishop had also trained the youthful Lillith in the ancient ways of the Goddess and shown her the mysteries that could only be handed down from mother to daughter. It seemed that once Lillith carried the blood of Dorothy's grandchild in her womb she became one with the sisterhood that shared the secrets of the Goddess' universe.

"Oh Dori'," I heard Lillith say to the stone, "please help me through this, especially on this of all days. I want you to know that I will never forget that it was this day, years ago, when the police came to your door and told us Will was gone. How we cried. Then I told you about Lynn and your laughter filled the room! You said that as long as there was the baby you could stand anything, even the loss of Will. In a way I'm grateful you're not here now to see what's happened, but I still wish you were here for me. Now I understand what you must have gone through. What I don't understand is how you lived through it. Right now I just wish I could close my eyes and never have to open them again."

With those words, Lillith began to sob as if her heart were breaking. When she was done, she stood up and looked past Dorothy's stone towards that of her daughter, Lynn. What Lillith couldn't see was the shadowy figure of Lynn, standing above her marker, looking back at Lillith. All was deathly quiet as an unseen fog enveloped Lillith. I knew from experience that the mysterious fog was the essence of the Witch, Dorothy Bishop, filling Lillith with the power and strength that she needed to go on. Lynn's spirit walked towards her grandmother's grave and leaned toward it, sharing the healing essence with her mother. Soon, I felt both spirit child and mortal woman become quiet in the stillness.

"Thank you," said Lillith, turning her back on Dorothy's grave and walking to the iron gates at the entrance to Old Burial Hill. Lillith grasped the iron gates firmly with both hands and drew them together. She pushed the gates forward until they shut in the dead of Salem.

"It seems that my journey is not yet done," she said to the wind as Lillith set her face towards the caves of Salem Willows.

> "I'll come to thee by moonlight,
> though hell should bar the way."
> Alfred Noyes: "The Highwayman."

CHAPTER TWENTY SIX

The vision of Lillith March on her knees, deep in the muck of the damp cavern that lay below Singing Horse Beach, was a powerful one that will never leave me. She was praying to her Goddess, the sister sprit of my own benevolent God, in that dark place. As she prayed I felt myself beginning to part from her mortal body. My soul rose painfully above Lillith and began to drift back to my own ghostly form with torturous slowness. My melding into my own body was like being born into a hellish morass of stinging pain. At the last minute I tried to turn from my body and rejoin Lillith's, but it was too late. I was drawn, once again, into my own fate.

The tatters of George Corwin's cloak held me fast as I watched Lillith rise and leave the cavern. I don't know how she knew to pray for us in this dreadful place, I only know that when she did I was released from her body and transported back into my own. Painful though it may be, I knew that the only way out of this whole mess was for me to suffer through the process that would free me from Corwin's spell.

What force within Lillith told the witch that she was not alone within her own body? I don't think she knew who or what the presence was that had been enmeshed with her own soul, but I can tell you with certainty that the witch felt enough of my presence to turn to her Goddess for help.

What a comfort my thoughts of Lillith's powers were as I found myself once again enslaved by the evil of George Corwin.

I tried to call out to Lillith, but found myself as mute as ever. I felt a terrible helplessness as I watched the witch woman stand, look about her, and then leave my cold dark prison. Perhaps all the hope I had just felt was an illusion, some sort of teasing torture that would lead nowhere!

"Oh please," I cried to the nothingness about me, "release me from this before I go mad!"

In answer to my cry I sensed a ghostly presence right above me. It was my own beloved Philip, with Giles Cory by his side. I tried to quiet the pounding pulse of my spirit so that I could hear them.

"So, Master English, what are we going to do about all this?" said Giles, squinting as he peered around the cavern.

"We're going to get Mary back, that's what we're going to do about 'all this,'" boomed Philip with an angry voice.

"But what about the girl? What about Corwin?"

"To hell with them, I say," said Philip as he began to pace around the cavern. He barely missed the spot where I lay. It was maddening to be invisible to everyone but myself and that crazy ghost, George Corwin.

"But what about the legacy of the town? What of the girl's life?" asked Giles.

"What about them? I can't believe that you, of all people, would stand willingly by while Mary English is in danger. You'd be rotting up on the hill in that dank memorial if it weren't for Mary, and you know it. What's the matter with you Cory?"

"Nothing, nothing at all," said Giles, pulling at Philip's arm in an attempt to calm him. "I'm just trying to keep my head and think about this slowly. Don't you see that you're giving Corwin what he wants? Here you are stalking about like a caged lion while that madman has the run of the town!"

"But he's promised to destroy Mary if I make a move!" said Philip, sitting on the ground beside my invisible self.

"Do you really believe that?" said Giles with a snicker. "If you do than you're not the Philip English I know. The man I know would see through Corwin's threats to what lies beyond. Think of it Phil! Why would he want to settle for Mary when he could have you? His little plot to destroy the last of your line may work, what with that boy raping Nora and all, but even that's not good enough for George Corwin. There's only one thing he really wants, one thing he's always wanted, and that's you. Offer to trade your soul for Mary's and old Corwin will start foaming like a rabid dog."

"And then what, my friend? What happens if I trade myself for Mary? The whole town is left unprotected. He'd have her back under his spell before my wretched soul entered hell."

"Right you are, Philip," said Giles almost too quickly. "I thought 'twas a good plan until now, but if you feel for certain that Corwin's powers are that strong, then it's hopeless. There may be no choice but to let him have his way with your wife."

It was a blessing that Philip could not see Giles face at that moment. I could see the man as he turned away from Philip, unable to hide an impish grin that spread across his face. Why the old devil! He was playing my husband like a fiddle, cajoling and teasing Philip into finding an answer to the great tangled puzzle that George Corwin had handed us.

"I swear this to you, Master Giles Cory," said Philip, turning the old man round by the shoulders and staring into his watery blue eyes, "that not even hell shall keep me from my Mary!"

"Then you're betting on your God being stronger that Corwin's devil?"

"My God and if need be, anything else I can summon," said Philip strangely.

"Be careful, friend English, speak not the name of the unholy one in this place. I fear the evil has always been close to us here. Do you want to send all the spirits of Salem into the fiery pits of the dark master?"

"Of course not, you old fool, you know I can't do that," said Philip, "but there is one other force that I could try to call upon. The Goddess that the witches of Salem are always making such a fuss over."

"But how do you know she's not just another face of the dark one," said Giles.

"I don't, old friend. I can only pray that my God wouldn't have put the thought into my head unless it was a righteous one."

"But would she speak to you, Philip? You're a man of God who long ago denied such witchery in the woods. Magic is magic, be it white or black. The Goddess, even though she be good, might just feel that since you turned your back on her, she should do the same to you."

"Will you stop blathering and let me think?" said Philip as he walked to the mouth of the cave.

Over the water the moon was rising, full and fruitful. It was the symbol of the Goddess' power. Then I realized that there was a way for Philip to help me. If he could guide Lillith to my side and link our conscious thought together, I would be free. What's more, we would hold the power within our combined forces to destroy Corwin without destroying the town. Perhaps there might even be hope for Nora if the Goddess stood by her side. Miraculously, I heard Philip echo my thoughts.

"See yon moon, friend Giles," said Philip. "It is the place where Salem's Goddess hides her heart. And tell me, who wears the symbol of the moon at all times? The lovely witch, Lillith March."

> "A savage place! As holy and enchanted
> as e'er beneath a waning moon was haunted
> By woman wailing for her demon lover."
> Samuel Taylor Coleridge: *Kubla Khan*.

CHAPTER TWENTY SEVEN

It was with mixed feelings that I forced my "all seeing eye" to follow Philip as he made his way towards the home of Lillith March. Just how did Philip mean to persuade Lillith to join forces with him and his God? I knew Philip too well to think he would ever leave my side. I was his wife and his truly beloved. But there had been a few moments in our long time together when I had seen the lust in my husband overtake any sense he might have. He was a man, with all a man's virtues and faults, and not above falling into temptation now and then. And then there was Lillith, beautiful, curvaceous Lillith, with only the caress of her dearest friend to take away the chill of a winter's night. Who can say if she would be able to fend off Philip's charms once he turned them full upon her. And turn them he would. I knew my husband too well to think any different.

I know that Philip's motives were pure, but I couldn't help feeling very annoyed as he turned down Forrester Street, heading for Lillith's home. It was his lightness of step and the way he joked with old Giles that made me grit my teeth, trying as best I could stem the flow of molten jealousy that threatened to overtake me.

"How dare he be so cheerful at a time like this," I muttered to myself in my dark prison. "I'll just bet my husband is thrilled that the only way to save me is through that beautiful bitch."

My hands flew to my mouth in horror. It was rare that I ever resorted a coarseness like the one that had flown from my mouth. I realized just how bothered I had always been by Lillith's presence in Salem. She seemed to symbolize all the woman that had ever flashed an eye, or for that matter, a thigh, at my lovable, brilliant, and yes, sometimes wayward husband. What mattered my freedom if I lost Philip in the process! Better I should stay as I was and have Philip's undying love in the form of eternal mourning for my lost soul!

"That's ridiculous, you fool," I said to myself in anger. "Lillith March has been around a long time, and not once has Philip ever given you cause for worry."

But was that true? I had seen the way he looked at the beautiful witch with an admiration and respect that would have driven a lesser woman than myself to murder.

"Face it, old girl," I said as the tears of frustration began to run down my cheeks, "Philip has long looked for a chance to get closer to the lady. 'Tis a cruel joke that your own fate should bring them together! Oh Lord, what have I ever done to deserve such a thing!" I cried to the heavens as the darkness of despair and hopelessness engulfed me.

It was with a desperate eye that I turned myself back towards Philip as he crossed over to the street named after the wealthy privateer, Simon Forrester. Forrester had been quite a rover himself. What was there about Salem that bred such men, hard as the stone of New England, but ready to burst into a charming smile at the sight of a pretty face? Oh, these men were fascinating, there was little doubt of that, but they led their ladies a merry chase.

"Here now, Philip," I heard Giles say as they stopped in front of the massive double house that belonged to Lillith, "just how do you mean to connect with Mistress March?"

"'Twill be easy my friend, once she gets the cut of my jib."

The rascal!

"Oh Philip," I said as I was filled with an oddly cleansing fury, "you're going to pay for those words, my love."

I felt strangely better as my third eye floated through Lillith's heavy wooden doors with Giles and Philip. The thought of myself as a victim was not one I relished. Better nothingness than that!

"This house is quite a beauty," said Philip as he stood in the great hall and looked up at the dazzling crystal chandelier that cast its rich light on the cream, blue and rose of Lillith March's furnishings.

"'Tis indeed a palace when you compare it to what we thought fine," said Giles, smiling at Philip as he walked towards the living room. Inside the room, Giles took in the tasteful, yet eclectic furnishings that made up Lillith's home. Over the mantelpiece was an enormous gilt mirror that reflected the twinkling lights of yet another chandelier, this one of the finest polished brass. The mantle itself was of carved white marble, each ivory colored vine and leaf finely turned to create a breathtaking stone garden. The aubusson rug that Giles tread lightly upon was so deep that it caught the impression of Giles' ghostly footprints in its cream and blue nap. The furniture that was strewn about the room in a magically informal, yet comfortable manner, was a collection of Louis the Fourteenth drawing room pieces, early twentieth century art deco in rose and blue velvet, and modern keepsakes, each piece an individual in itself and yet forming a mystical whole.

The pictures on the wall were also an odd collection that would have driven an interior decorator to tears. Mixed along with old oil paintings of ships and ancient maps, were Chinese needlepoints. There were even French aqua tints adorning the walls. But most fascinating of all was a collection of scrimshaw that had been lovingly placed on top of what looked like an old captain's chest.

"Looky here," said Giles, almost running to the chest in his excitement. "Do you see what I see?"

"Why, that I do," said Philip, slapping his friend on the back. "It seems the lady is a collector of the fine arts of the sea."

Philip lovingly picked up a whale's tooth, carved with the likeness of three mermaids, and held it up to the waning light.

"'Tis like one I carved with young Philip on his maiden voyage. 'Twas sick he was, from the sea, and we sat together and fashioned one like this to take his mind off the storm. In fact," said Philip, stroking the ivory lovingly, "I think it might be the same piece! See here how the tail of the fishy lass curves about the anchor! 'Twas my own device, one that I taught only my sons. And here, Giles, see how the face of the most beautiful one looks like my Mary, fresh from her bed in sweet summer. Why it's one of mine all right. Think of it man, making its way down the years to this place. Why 'tis a miracle I say, a bloody miracle!"

"Aye, that it is," said Giles, caught up in Philip's excitement. "And look at how you caught Mary's likeness. I had no idea you were such an artist, Philip English."

"It's not hard when the lady is as lovely as my Mary," said Philip, sitting hard upon the floor next to the old sea chest. "What I wouldn't give for her to be standing in this very room right now."

As I listened to Philip's words, my heart began to melt a bit. It was as I thought. He did love me deeply, truly, as only a man like Philip could. The dear, brave man. But that still didn't change the fact that he was standing in Lillith March's home ready, able, and more than willing to seduce her into doing his will. If I didn't know him for a Godly man I would have sworn that Philip English had more than a little of the devil in him.

"I don't suppose that you knew the owner of yon chest?" asked Giles as he touched the satiny wood gently. There emanated from the fine piece of old rosewood an almost holy glow.

"Yes, I do," said Philip, lovingly stroking the rosy chest as he carefully removed each piece of scrimshaw with loving hands. "It was mine. See the hasps and the latch? No one but Joseph Collins, of this very cove, could have made it. And look you here, Giles, see the initials carved into the lock, 'tis my own."

"Why so 'tis," said Giles. "Such a pity, it is, that there is no key to open it with."

"You're wrong there," said Philip, giving a happy laugh as he pressed his thumbs into the side of the chest, right below one of the finely wrought brass handles. To Giles' amazement, a small drawer popped out. Philip gently put his hand into the drawer and pulled out a delicate brass key.

"Mary had this made for me for our tenth anniversary," said Philip, as eager as a young man. "Twas a wonder in its time, what with all its hidden drawers and secret compartments. Ah, how wise she was, knowing that I had need to hide from the world secrets that I could tell no one, not even her! And this key drawer was her way of showing me, that for all my fine ways, I was just a mortal man. I had a way of forgetting my keys, or belt, or whatever was not tied onto me, so Mary had this special drawer put in to make sure I would never lock myself out of my own sea chest. How we laughed when she showed me!"

Then Philip lovingly opened the beautiful chest that I had given him in the Salem of 1685, a full seven years before the witchcraft terrors. How it symbolized all we had been and still were to each other. It seemed oddly fitting that the chest would have survived and come to rest in this home on Forrester Street.

I watched with a loving heart as Philip searched first one, and then another drawer of his treasured sea chest. All were empty, except for the faint smell of tobacco and bay rum. How those smells brought the living Philip back to both of us. Then I felt the air about my gloomy prison begin to warm as Philip reached the last of the secret chambers, it lay at the very bottom of the chest, hidden by layers of wood and brass. I could feel Philip hold his misty breath as he deftly ran his fingers along the finely carved rosewood latch and released the slender opening beneath. The joy that filled his beloved face as he drew a small locket from its hiding place told my heart that I could forgive this man anything.

"It's here," breathed Philip as he struggled to open the ancient clasp that held the two halves of the golden oval together.

"Here, let me try," said Giles, taking the locket from Philip's shaking hands. The old man's ghostly hands pried the lovely thing apart and presented Philip the open locket that contained miniature portraits of Philip and Mary English as they had been on that bright September day back in 1685. The locket had been Philip's gift to me. He had commissioned the finest artist in France to form it. The locket had been sent over for our tenth anniversary day. It seemed but a moment ago, and yet, as I took stock of the year, I realized that our gifts to each other were over three centuries old.

"I take this as a sign that Mary will be returned to my arms," said Philip as he carefully undid the beautiful clasp and hung the locket around his neck.

Giles looked at Philip and gave him a wink. "'Tis like Mary herself were watching over us."

What Giles didn't see was Lillith March on the stairway, staring at the two men in horror.

> "The moon was a ghostly galleon tossed upon
> cloudy seas,
> The road was a purple ribbon of moonlight over the
> purple moor,
> And the highwayman came riding-
> Riding-riding-
> The highwayman came riding, up to the old inn door."
> Alfred Noyes: "The Highwayman."

CHAPTER TWENTY EIGHT

It was Lillith's strangled gasp that broke the spell of the locket. Philip turned round on his heel just in time to see the confused woman run up the stairs and into her bedroom.

"Stay here," said Philip to Giles as he took after Lillith, not bothering with the stairs, but choosing instead to rise from the hall. Philip moved rapidly upward until he reached Lillith's closed door. He knocked lightly.

"Go away, whoever you are," said Lillith.

"Come now, my dear, is that any way to treat an admirer?" said Philip. "I though such a woman as Lillith March would be beyond the silly vapors and tears of an ordinary woman."

"Go away, or I'll call the police!"

"The police!" laughed Philip with that beautiful deep rumble that had twisted my heart more than once.

"That's what I said, the police!"

"And what do you think they're going to do?" asked Philip, forced to raise his voice a bit as a blustering gust of wind shook the house. "Do you really think that anything mortal could stop me if I wanted to harm you, Mistress March?"

"No," said Lillith in a calmer voice, "but at least they can witness anything that happens to me. I promise you that I'll not go quietly to my grave. And I won't let you molest me like you did those poor innocent girls! You're dealing with a handmaiden of the Goddess. She protects her own. Woe be it to any man who violates me."

"If I swear to your Goddess that I'm an honorable man, will you open up to me?" asked Philip, unable to keep the frustration from creeping into his voice. I found it almost amusing that he stood thus, cooling his heels before Lillith March's closed door. Seldom had been the time in the past when such a thing happened to the great Captain and merchant, Philip English. His trouble was often quite the opposite, fending off love sick girls who waved their skirts at him with wanton abandon.

"I won't open my door until you can show me some proof that you are a good spirit," said Lillith stubbornly. "And I also want to know why you entered my house without being asked! All I know about you is that you went through my things and stole something that belonged to me!"

"I was only taking back what was my own," said Philip, putting his back to the door and sliding down to the floor. "If anyone's a thief, it's you, Lillith March. You hauled my handiwork and my own sea chest here with not so much as a by-your-leave. Those things belong to me. I've no use for any lady who thinks it's her just due to steal from the helpless dead."

"There doesn't seem to be anything helpless about you," said Lillith.

"And what do you know about it, Witch March? You spend your time worrying about you own little problems while the ghosts of Salem are fighting for their immortal souls! Look here, it's your decision to speak to me, or not. I'd rather you did because I need your help, but do what you want. Just remember that it was I, Captain Philip English, who gave you a chance to save you own daughter from losing her immortal soul."

"Oh you devil," I thought to myself as I listened to Philip begin to weave a tale, mixed with truth, untruth, and half truth about the goings on in Salem over the past week. George Corwin had been the author of many an unspeakable act, but I had seen little evidence that the soul of Lynn March was threatened. But then, as I listened to Philip drawing

Lillith to him much like the serpent coaxed Eve in the garden of Eden, it struck me. If Philip were destroyed, we all might perish. It was his deeds, good and bad, that had brought us this far. Our fate was forever entangled with his. If Philip English's soul ceased to exist, than the otherworld of Salem might cease to exist as well. I realized the painful truth as Philip pleaded with Lillith March to grant him entry. Philip must succeed or all those I loved might vanish forever. In his way, he was telling the truth.

"How dare you speak of my daughter's soul!" said Lillith furiously.

"I dare because I know of such things. You know, as well as I, that the souls of Salem are special to my God, your Goddess, and the Devil himself. We've always been the playground for their battles. For some strange reason we're a very special prize to the immortals. It would be a shame if the Devil claimed us all because Lillith March was nothing but a cowardly woman who refused to open her door to a harmless ghost."

"Prove to me you're harmless and I'll open the door."

"And what would you have me say, woman? You're of Salem and so am I and that should be good enough for you! Haven't I proved it over and over these three hundred years that I'm a man of my word? Why I even risked my own life to bury the dead of Gallows Hill underneath old St. Peter's stones up on Prison Lane."

"And just who is it who is buried there?" asked Lillith quietly, as the winds of a nor'easter began to batter the house.

"Why those who stood for this town when no one else would," said Philip. "It makes me sick to think of it, but if you insist I'll tell you their names."

"I insist," said Lillith.

"Very well," said Philip, "but only if you promise to open the door when I'm done."

"And who would I be opening my door to?" asked Lillith.

"Why to Captain Philip English of Salem Town," said Philip with a pride that was hardly humble, but well earned.

"I give you my word to open the door if your words ring true," said Lillith.

"The word of a lady is good enough for me," said Philip.

As I listened to Philip recounting the sad death's of his friends, Reverend George Burroughs, Master John Proctor, Constable John Willard, grandfatherly George Jacobs, and sweet but spicy Martha Carrier, I began to cry. Each one of our friends had died with the truth on their lips, and even now still lay trapped beneath the stones of Salem. Only Elizabeth Proctor had been spared because she was carrying a babe. The rest were hanged on a beautiful late summer's day in 1692.

I know that Philip must have nearly broken his body stealing the remains of our friends from the cold stones of Gallows Hill. I never lived to see the fine church that Philip built over their bones reach its full glory, but I was always proud of my husband for his act of mercy that night.

"'Twas a pity that I never was able to coax Cotton Mather into giving me back Burrough's head," said Philip as he finished his tale with the sad fact that George Burrough's head had been taken by Cotton Mather for scientific study, "but there was no help for it. If I said too much, the old goat would get suspicious of my doings. So there you have it, and that tale is just one of my deeds in this town. If you'd like to hear more I'd be glad to tell you, but not with a door between us."

"Please come in, Captain," said Lillith March as she opened the door to her bedroom.

> "Give me a spirit that on this life's rough sea
> Love's t'have his sail filled with a lusty wind,
> even though his sail-yards tremble, his mast cracks.
> And his rapt ship run on her side so low
> That she drinks water, and her keel plows air."
> George Chapman:
> 'The Conspiracy of Charles, Duke of Byron (1608), act III, sc.i.

CHAPTER TWENTY NINE

"'Tis many a year since I have entered a lady's chamber," said Philip as he looked around the lovely room. The pale pink walls contrasted with the creamy lace of the curtains and bed clothes to create the impression of being inside a curving pink conch shell. There was an old ivory dresser set that lay on a lace doily atop Lillith's mahogany vanity. Beside it were several pictures encased in silver frames. It was to her vanity that Lillith retreated as Philip came toward her. I had forgotten how tall he was until he stood next to the mortal woman as she brushed her hair nervously.

"What do you want of me, Captain?" said Lillith as she stared into the mirror. She looked into the mirror with intense curiosity as she realized that there was no reflection of the man in the old wavy glass.

"So, it's true," she said, not waiting for Philip's answer to her question, "you really are a ghost."

"And one who has no patience with childish tricks," said Philip as he turned Lillith around.

"I had to be sure," said Lillith, looking past Philip to the picture of her daughter, Lynn.

"I know, my lady," said Philip, taking Lillith's hand gently in his and kissing it with the merest whisper of his lips. "I would feel the same if it were my daughter's soul at stake."

"You said I could help you, Captain English," said Lillith, drawing her hand away from Philip as she cleared her throat nervously.

"Aye, that you can, that is, if you are as powerful a white witch as I believe you are," said Philip as he broke their touch and sat at Lillith's feet.

"What makes you think I'm a 'white witch?'" asked Lillith, looking down at Philip with the pursed lips of a school marm.

"How could a lady, sweet as you, be anything else?"

"Look, Captain, or Master English, or whatever you are, I think there's one thing we should get clear between us before we go any further. I don't like flattery, I never have. It always makes me feel that the one giving it just wants to take something from me."

"So be it," said Philip, rising from his place at Lillith's feet and striding over to her bed, "Why don't you just hop up here and we can get right to it. I certainly don't mind coupling like a couple of wild beasts if you don't. Look lively lass, get your clothes off!"

"What are you talking about!"

"I'm talking about what must be done if my God is going to join with your Goddess," said Philip. "You can't tell me that you, with your Midsummer's Night Eve and Beltane fires, don't see what must be done so that my God and your Goddess can fight the evil cloud that wants to destroy Salem and all the souls in it."

"I think you better get off my bed, out of my room, and my house right now, Philip English!" said Lillith as she grabbed Philip's jacket and tried to pull him from her bed. To her frustration, Lillith's hands went right through Philip, catching her off balance and landing her beside him on the bed.

"Here now, lass," said Philip with a look of amusement on his face, you don't have to be so eager about it! Take your time and have a bit of pleasure while you're at it."

"I don't care if you are a ghost," said Lillith as she glared at the laughing ghost, "I'm going to kill you if you touch me."

"And who says I have to touch you to have my way," said Philip, ginning widely. "Who's to say I might not just slither into your loveliness like a mist on a summer's morning. Mayhap I can do anything I please with you. It could be I already have!"

"You have?" gasped Lillith, sitting up in panic.

"Bless me, no!" said Philip, not able to stand the look that covered the good lady's face. "What do you take me for! If I did such a thing I would be as black as the worst of the devil's minions that roams this town. Here now," said Philip, turning to Lillith and stroking her cheek. "I'm sorry that I gave you such a scare, 'twas furious I was at you when you insulted my manhood. I'm afraid I wanted to give you blow for blow. But I'm that sorry, I am, that I did it. I want us to be friends, Witch Lillith."

"But was it true, what you said about us joining bodies so that Lynn's soul could be saved?"

"I don't know. I think it may be," said Philip trying to look sad about the whole state of affairs. I swear that if I'd had a broom in my hand and been able to break free of my damp prison, I might very well have beat my beloved to a second death at that moment. The rascal was enjoying his play acting at the expense of the beautiful Lillith, there was no doubt about that. Just wait until I was free of this place and had him in my arms. He would pay, by God, Philip English would pay for his bit of fun!

"I think you'd better tell me the whole story, beginning to end, Captain, before we go any further," said Lillith as she lay back on the lacy pillows of her bed.

"Right you are, lass, right you are," said Philip laying beside Lillith and turning toward her.

"Not from here, sir!" said Lillith, trying to push Philip from the bed and succeeding only in throwing herself off balance again. "Get off my bed and sit over there!" commanded Lillith in a voice that brooked no opposition.

"Yes ma'am," said Philip as he reluctantly moved from Lillith's inviting bed to an overstuffed chair that was covered in a rosy watered silk.

"Is this far enough away," said Philip, looking very out of place surrounded by the pink silk.

"No, but it will have to do," said Lillith, sitting up a bit as she plumped the pillows that lay behind her.

"Good for you, Mistress March," I cheered to myself as I listened to my uncomfortable husband begin to tell Lillith March of the secrets of Salem

Town and the ghosts that owned it. I felt myself become fascinated with Philip's tale as the lilt of his melodious voice and his gift of story telling wove together the two Salems, the living and the dead, into a wonderful tapestry. It was as if I were seeing all the beautiful times we had shared together come to life again.

It was only when Philip told of the evil times, the witchcraft hysteria, my tortures and death from weakness, and the present sadness about Lynn and Nora, that I closed my eyes and wished him to speak no more. What a tale ours was, one for the ages, and it was all true. Pray God that Lillith March would heed Philip's words and help us. I ached with every atom of my being to rejoin my beloved. To be denied that would be worse than any hellfire George Corwin could toss me into.

"So you see," said Philip quietly, "I'll never see Mary again unless you and I can find a way to defeat George Corwin's devil."

"And you say Lynn has crossed over the otherworld of Salem and become an immortal soul?" said Lillith with glowing happiness.

"Aye, but it is more than that," said Philip eagerly. "She is still the girl you know. Your daughter may yet have a chance to live and grow and find joy. Our realm is as real as yours."

"Unless George Corwin destroys it," said Lillith.

"And if that happens, all our souls will be taken to hell, never to return."

"I swear to you, Philip English, that I will do whatever I can to help you," said Lillith, closing her eyes and laying back on the pillows, "but right now I must sleep. Your words have made me very sleepy."

"That's the magic of Salem weaving its way into you," said Philip as he lay down beside Lillith and took her in his arms. "Sleep now, my Lady and keep this in your hand," he said, taking the locket from his neck.

"This will keep you safe from all harm, I promise," said Philip, placing the open locket in Lillith's hand.

"Your wife is quite beautiful," murmured Lillith as she fell asleep on Philip's shoulder.

"Aye, that she is, that she is," said Philip as a single tear ran down his cheek.

> "They are not long, the days of wine and roses;
> Out of a misty dream
> Our path emerges for a while, then closes
> Within a dream."
> Ernest Dowson: "Vitae Summa Brevis Spem
> Nos Vetat Incohare Longam" (taken from Horace).

CHAPTER THIRTY

I found myself irresistibly drawn to the slumbering figures of Lillith March and my husband as they lay dreaming in Lillith's bedchamber. My mind melded with theirs as Philip's spell took us all on a journey back to the Salem where he and I had lived and laughed.

Salem, my Salem of the 1690's! I opened my dreamy eyes to a beautiful September morning. From where I was I could see the figures of a man and a woman entering the small meeting hall that had stood in the middle of Salem Town long before the finer house of worship had been built. I could tell by the way the man stood and by the cut of the woman's dress, that the two people looking longingly into each other's eyes were Philip and me. It was our wedding day! Surrounding us were many beloved friends of so long ago, all dead and mostly forgotten now. Amongst the throng was my mother, the beautiful Eleanor Hollingsworth. How I longed to cry out to her. Oh, how wonderful it would be to be cradled within her arms just one more time and tell my Mama the troubles that filled me. I knew that if I could just feel her touch upon my brow, all the terrors of the past would be wiped away in one miraculous moment. But that was not to be.

The scene swiftly changed. One moment I was on the wharf, waving good-bye to Philip as he sailed to Barbados, the next moment I was giving birth to my children. It was all there, the sad times when we buried small Will and baby Susannah, and the happy ones when young Philip survived his fourth year, strong and healthy and we became convinced that we would at last see one of our children thrive and grow.

Then came the darkest times of all, when our home was surrounded and I was dragged away in chains to be tortured and accused by some of the very friends who had attended my wedding and stood fast during my joys and losses. At last there was that wondrous moment when Philip managed our escape. I'll never forget that thrilling night when he swung me upon his horse and carried me far away until it was safe to return to our home.

But it was never the same after that. The pictures in Lillith March's mind shifted to our return to Salem. The horror I felt as I walked through the rubble of our precious belongings is still with me. The theft and wanton destruction of my most treasured possessions was, perhaps, the worst thing of all. The people of Salem had abused me body and spirit, but until I saw the way they had pawed through the objects that made up my everyday life, I still believed I possessed my soul. But even that they had spit upon. It was then that I began to lose hope and start to die. Nothing Philip said or did was able to recall me from my agony, until at last, I gave up the ghost. I died not long after dear Ebenezer was born in the spring of '94.

The dreams of my death seemed to fill everything about us as we lay on Lillith March's bed. The darkness of it all had a choking quality that made me want to retch. Suddenly, the dark gloom began to glow and turn a rosy white as five souls lifted my body high in the air. I could make out the strong face of John Proctor and the kindly one of George Jacobs as they lifted me gently and placed me on the alter of St. Peter's, an alter that had been built long after I died. I watched as my own soul was resurrected into the form I now possessed.

Then the scene became larger, filling not just Lillith's mind, but the whole of Salem. We shared together the thoughts and dreams of all the ghosts who had passed through Salem's portals, until at last, the cacophony of souls jangled Lillith into wakefulness.

"So, that's what lays beneath our eyes," said Lillith, looking at Philip in wonder.

"Aye, my lady," said Philip.

"And now my daughter is a part of this great company that lives in the mists of Salem?"

"For the moment, yes," said Philip. "But if George Corwin has his way, that may soon change. He wants the evil he carried in life to return to Salem and rule as it once did. The only way he can have Salem is to destroy me, though Mary. Once I'm gone, Corwin will be the most powerful soul in Salem. If that happens he will convert the other souls into shades, like he has become, doomed to follow the dark master. They will be lost forever."

"And you think I can help you," said Lillith.

"I know you can," said Philip as he gently brushed the trembling lips of the white witch.

"Speak the truth and shame the Devil."
Francois Rabelais: author's prologue,
Gargantua and Pantagruel, bk. IV (1548)

CHAPTER THIRTY ONE

Lillith looked first at Philip's longing face, and then at the locket she held in her hand. She turned the small gold object over and over until, finally, Philip could stand no more. He had always been of an impatient nature and her actions were just the sort calculated to drive him quite mad.

"For the love of God will you stop that, woman!" he shouted as he jumped from the bed and began to pace around the room like a caged animal.

"Patience, Master Philip, patience," said Lillith with a smile. "If you wish to hear the voice of the Goddess, you must first show yourself worthy of her kindness. This is not the time for commanding words and fiery swords. That is the province of your God, not mine. Hush now, while I receive the essence of the 'Great Mother.'"

To my surprise, Philip took Lillith's rebuke and settled himself on the floor where he glowered like a spoiled child. I felt the room fill with peace as Lillith took on the glamour of her Goddess. Suddenly, she opened her eyes and smiled at Philip.

"Come my friend," she said as she took his hand in hers, "it's time to speak to your wife."

PART FOUR

THE DEVIL
THIS WAY COMES

"I shall curse you with book and bell and candle."
Sir Thomas Malory: *Le Morte d'Arthur*.

CHAPTER THIRTY TWO

I felt my spirit being carried back toward my cavernous prison as Lillith and Philip left the old house on Forrester Street. How I longed to follow them, but the dark force of George Corwin's spell was too powerful to fight forever. What could Lillith possibly do to bring me back into the blessed otherworld of Salem?

"Nothing," chucked a cruel voice behind me.

"How do you know that?" I asked George Corwin as he unwrapped the cloak he had buried me in.

"Because once I possess you, it will be too late."

"I don't understand," I said, trying to free myself from the tentacles of his grasp. "It's not possible for you to have me in that way and you know it. Our spirits would have had to been joined by God, before death, for you to share me in such a way."

"And what makes you think that the Devil isn't powerful enough to change the rules of God?" asked Corwin as his hands slid around and through me. His touch was terrifyingly cold and sweaty.

"Think you upon what happened to your little Nora, Mary English. What makes you any safer than she was from my desires? She was a lovely little thing, to be sure, but hardly the hearty meal you're going to be for my master."

"What is it you want from me!" I cried as I struggled to break free of the foul spirit's grasp.

"Why you, Mary English, body and soul. Once you become mine, I can do what I want with Philip. Think of it, my dear. You playing up to that puffed up pirate, making him believe that you are still 'his Mary,' while all along you'll be working for me and my master. There's nothing we two can't do in this town once we've joined forces."

It was then that the true horror of his plan began to dawn on me. George Corwin meant to use me, like some sort of soulless zombie, to control and destroy Philip!

"Come along now, pretty Mary, this can be simple or hard. It's up to you."

"Philip!" I screamed as George Corwin's filthy soul pressed itself close to mine.

"I'm right here, darling, you don't have to scream."

"Philip?" I said as I sat up.

"At your service, lovely maid," said my husband as he bent down and took me into his arms, holding me close in a fatherly hug.

"But how? What? Where are we?" I asked as he set me on my feet.

"I believe this emporium is called, the 'Derby Street Used Furniture Store,'" said Philip with a delicious laugh as he turned toward Lillith, who had her hands firmly grasped around a triangular disc.

"That's right," said Lillith, whose laugher matched Philip's in a way I found a trifle too intimate.

"It was the ouija board," said Lillith breathlessly, touching first my face and then my deep crimson gown with a look of disbelief. "The Goddess led me here, through this old board, to you. How like Nora you are! I would have known you anywhere."

"And you are the image of your daughter, Lynn," I said as I studied the woman's face carefully. "Really, it's quite a delight having her with us. She's so young and full of cleverness."

"Lynn, you know Lynn!" said Lillith as tears of joy flowed down her face.

"Of course I do," I said as I sat beside the witch.

"If only I could speak to her, see her once more," said Lillith.

"I don't see why you can't," I said as I looked at the battered ouija board on Lillith's lap. "It makes sense that if you can reach me with that thing, you can reach her."

"I wouldn't do that," said Philip.

"Why not? Surely we owe this lady something for taking me away from Corwin? You have no idea how close you came to losing not just me, but everything," I said, starting to shiver at the thought of Corwin's touch.

"I know exactly how close I came," said Philip, "and that's why I don't want you fooling with that thing. It's not of God. It's magic, so it must be evil. Who's to say we might not let the Devil in through its doors."

"That's nonsense, Philip," said Lillith turning towards my husband with a scowl. "I brought your wife back to you through white magic, good magic. There's no harm in it. Surely there must be some way to reach Lynn through it. Please help me, Mary. I know that if we join forces, as mothers, we can call Lynn to us."

"It's the least I can do for her, Philip," I said with a stubborn shrug of my shoulders as I placed my hand on the disc.

"No!" shouted Philip as a flash of light filled the deserted old store. He tried to pull my hand from the disc but only succeeded in having his ghostly flesh drawn towards it as well. I held my breath as the disc moved swiftly beneath our fingers.

"Mama," was the first word it spelled out as we heard the whisper of a child's voice echo from above us.

Lillith raised her head from the board and looked about her. All that was visible around us was the rubble of broken furniture and dust covered pictures and statues that filled the old store. Then our attention was drawn, once more, to the disc as it began to move again. The force that held our hands on the ouija board was very strong.

Once again the disc spelled 'Mama', but this time there was no voice. I could sense the spirit of a child near us, but something about the specter told me it was not the soul of Lynn March. Suddenly, a flash of lightning split the gloom of the room in two. One side looked as it had been a moment ago. The other side seemed strangely altered, as if the floor had tilted just slightly, and let in a different kind of light. I peered towards the light and realized what it was. The glow of a well tended hearth.

"What does it mean?" whispered Lillith as our fingers were once again forced to move upon the ouija board as the disc began to move swiftly towards the numbers that were etched in inky black at the top of the page.

"It's a window," said Philip quietly, never taking his eyes off the glowing firelight. "You keep watch of the words below. I've a feeling that they may tell us what manner of the Devil's handiwork yon light might be."

That was easier said than done as the flashing lightning, combined with the glow of the firelight, shadowed the letters from Lillith's and my watching eyes.

"Can you make it out?" asked Lillith as the disc moved from the numbers and returned to the letters. First it pointed out an "A" and then sped to the "N."

"Is it spelling 'and?' " I asked Lillith as the disc came to rest again on the "N" and moved no more.

"I don't know, I don't think so," said Lillith as she tried to remove her fingers from the disc. As she tapped the disc impatiently, a spark of flame came from the wood and shot up her arm. It barely missed Lillith's cheek as it sparked into the room and came to rest safely above an old wooden mirror with beveled glass. There the spark began to form into a ball and shimmer softly. As if in answer, the disc moved again. It repeated the motions it had before of "A" and then "N." But this time it remained on the "N" a shorter amount of time and then began to make its way towards the numbers again. The disc wandered first to the "1" and then the "6." Then it made it's way swiftly to the "9" and the "2."

"1,6,9,2," said Philip softly as he drew his eyes away from the glowing firelight long enough to look down at his hands. "And what of 1,6,9,2, you instrument of the Devil! Surely you're smarter than to try to lure us into your spell by giving us the numbers of the darkest year of our lives. Can't you see what's happening, Mary? This damnable thing is trying to remind us of our unhappiness by showing us such a thing. Tell it to be gone, now, before it's too late!"

I might have listened to Philip at that moment if it had not been for the voices that suddenly started to speak from the soft firelight beyond. Once again we heard a child cry 'Mama', and now I was certain it had nothing to do with Lynn March. The cry that came from the light could not have belonged to a child over ten.

"Will you stop that, Betty?" came the voice of an older girl as the room began to fill with the sound of beautiful humming. I couldn't really make out the words, but the flavor of the tune was not of New England.

" 'Tis the patois of the Caribbean," said Philip, staring at me in wonder, "and of the flavor of the times that I knew. It brings the sun of Barbados to mind. What manner of miracle is this?"

In answer to Philip's question, the dust and gloom of the used furniture store was suddenly swallowed up by the glow of the firelight, as Lillith, myself and Philip were enveloped into the ember's lure and into the room beyond. It was as if we were a part of what was going on, and yet onlookers too. It was then that I realized that we could see and hear what was happening, but there was no sense of touch or smell. We were in a new dimension, one created within the confines of the old used furniture store in the Salem of 1998. What lay beyond was the Salem of over three hundred years before.

Gathered around the firelight was an older black woman with a fantastically colored headdress. The hues of green and yellow and orange that shown above the black woman's face were in sharp contrast with the somber colors that made up the clothes of the young girls that huddled near the hearth, breathing in every word that fell from the colorful woman's lips.

"Ask her again, Ann," said a slight, redheaded girl as she pinched the smaller girl's arm. Something about the girl, "Ann," was terrifyingly familiar as Ann looked towards the firelight and then back at the black woman.

Ann drew in her breath and asked in a commanding voice that belied her size, "do the embers say that Betty's father will punish us for what we've done?"

"I can't tell, Missy Putnam," said the black woman in a terrified voice. "Please, missy, don't whip me again! I swear that I'm tellin' you all I know, I swear," said the woman as she ducked a blow from the girl's hand.

"Why 'tis the Devil's imp, Ann Putnam," said Philip as he drew me close to him. "Get us out of this place, now," said Philip to Lillith in a fearful voice. It was the sound of those tremors coming from Philip that scared me most of all. It was rare when my love was fearful of anything, but I understood his panic. Before us lay the scene that had caused the downfall of Salem. From the very fire that sparked before us, the Devil had emerged in all his lustful fury as he trampled Salem under his thunderous hoof.

"I'm not sure I can," said Lillith, closing her eyes and chanting something about the blue of the moon and the cool of the stars.

"Pray with her," I said to Philip as I felt the calm of Lillith's words begin to take hold.

"I'll not close my eyes with that Putnam brat so near," said Philip through gritted teeth.

"Do as she says," said Lillith, staring at us with sightless eyes. "Do as she says or all will be lost."

Reluctantly, Philip closed his eyes and began chanting with us as the lightning of 1998 mixed with the firelight of 1692. For a few moments a great wind arose as the forces of the Goddess battled those of the Devil for our souls, but soon, we felt the blessed coolness of the old shop, and smelled the lovely mix of dust and moldy fabric that filled the furniture store.

"Is it safe?" I heard Philip ask as he squeezed my hand.

"I think so," I said opening one eye and looking about.

"Where am I?" asked a girl's voice from behind Philip.

"In Salem, of course," came another voice near Lillith.

"My head hurts," said a third voice, so close to my shoulder that it made me jump.

Lillith, Philip and I all turned to see who spoke and then looked back at each other. Behind each of us stood a girl. Lynn, near Lillith, Nora's spectral self, faintly shimmering, behind me, and, close to Philip, the shade of Ann Putnam, the girl responsible for Salem's witchcraft hysteria.

"Fellow Citizens, we cannot escape history....
The fiery trial through which we pass will light us down
in honor or dishonor to the last generation."
Abraham Lincoln: December 1st, 1862.

CHAPTER THIRTY THREE

"Mama!" cried the ghost of Lynn March as she wrapped her misty arms around her mother.

"Lynnie," gasped an equally delighted Lillith, attempting to do the same to her daughter, but only succeeding in passing her hands through Lynn's chest.

"It's all right, Mama," laughed the girl ghost as she squeezed her mother tight.

"No, it's not 'all right,'" said Lillith with a sardonic laugh, "but I guess it's the best we can do under the circumstances."

The other two girls looked at Lynn in confusion. It was strange, but of the three ghosts, it was Lynn March who rightfully belonged in this place. She was a proper spirit of Salem, one that fit the mold and was welcome in our Salem Town of 1998. The other two girls were anomalies, things of the mind and air who belonged elsewhere. Somehow, some way, Ann Putnam had been torn from her rightful dimension in the Salem of 1692. Then, there was my own Nora's spirit was hovering near me, a spirit that should have been resting, however uncomfortably, in her bed at Salem hospital. Nora was still a living, breathing girl who should have been unified, body and soul.

"Why it's the 'three moments,'" gasped Lillith as she watched the three girls move toward each other.

"What do you mean?" asked Philip as he drew away from the mist as the ghost of Ann Putnam passed close by.

"What I mean is that the three girls stand for what has happened in Salem, what is happening now, and what will happen," said Lillith.

"I think I see what you mean," I said as we watched the three girls touch each other's hair and clothes. "Ann is the past, Lynn the present, and Nora, the future."

"Exactly," said Lillith as she turned toward where the three girls stood. It was then that I realized that Lillith March was the only mortal amongst us. How strange it must have felt for her to be in this world of shadow, peopled only by wandering spirits.

"It's not strange at all," said Lillith with a smile. "You see, I can read your thoughts, just as I always have. I've never been like other mortals. I've always seen the substance of shadows. What may terrify other mortals brings me a comfort that I cannot explain. I only know that I was born into this life just as I am. And thank the Goddess for it! Without my gift I might have lost my daughter forever."

"And Salem as well," said Philip, touching Lillith's shoulder. "Tell me, Lillith, what are they saying to each other?"

We turned towards the three girls and tried to make some sense out of their excited whispers, but it was no use.

"Lynn, Lynn March!" said Lillith in a commanding voice, "tell us why you are here."

"To learn, Mama," said Lynn as she turned toward her mother. "Surely you know that!"

"To learn what, darling?" asked Lillith.

"To learn of the Salem that lies covered with dust," said Ann Putnam as she pushed Lynn aside and walked resolutely towards Lillith March.

"I can see by the look of you, Goody March, that the Devil still walks in Salem Town!"

"Christ knows how many Devils there are in
His churches, and who they are."
Reverend Samuel Parris: from the pulpit, March, 1692.

CHAPTER THIRTY FOUR

Philip and I took a step back as Ann Putnam approached. She might have had the appearance of an innocent twelve year old child, but we knew that only evil lay beneath her smooth brow. We had seen her ruthless condemnations of innocent men, women and children. It was just as Philip had feared. We had led the Devil back to Salem.

To her credit, Lillith March stood her ground as Ann Putnam came towards her and stood directly in front of her. The girl tried to stare the woman down, but she soon found that intimidating Lillith March was a far harder task than she had thought.

"Have you no shame, witch!" screamed Ann Putnam as Lillith broke into a smile.

"None at all," said Lillith, beginning to laugh.

"I'll not have you doing that," cried Ann Putnam as she took a step back and looked about her in confusion. "Don't you know who I am and what I can do to you? One word from me and you'll find yourself rotting in the dungeons of Salem jail!"

"You poor child," said Lillith, falling into a battered overstuffed chair, "don't you realize what has happened? You're in my world now, not yours. This is the Salem of 1998! You can't hurt me, or any of my kind, anymore. Your type of evil is over, done with forever."

"I don't understand," said Ann Putnam quietly as she looked around the old shop in a confused manner.

"Of course you don't, dear," said Lillith, trying to touch the confused Ann.

"Don't do that!" screamed Ann falling to the floor and writhing about. "Look what the witch has done to me," screamed the girl in a terrified voice. "She has burned me with the embers of her fingers. See the marks here, and here, and even here!" said Ann, raising her skirts and showing us the reddish marks she had inflicted on herself when she fell.

"Get up, you jerk," said Lynn as she walked over to the younger Ann and pulled her to her feet. "That act may have worked three hundred years ago, but it looks pretty pitiful now. Get off it. We all know you were lying about the witches and the Devil to protect you and your friends. If anyone had found out that you and Mercy Lewis and Mary Walcott had been holding seances with Tituba the slave, you would have all been whipped in public. Whose to say that you might not have been accused as witches yourself and been sent to the gallows? You were evil and stupid, Ann Putnam, and no one believes in the games you play anymore. So why don't you just shut up! Or even better, go back where you came from."

"I would if I could," said Ann, rubbing her arm as she looked hatefully at Lynn, "but I don't know how. If you want me gone, get rid of me yourself, or ask that witch, your mother by the look of her, to do it. It's one and the same to me. Witch, or daughter of a witch, you all have danced with the Devil and shared his filthy bed."

"Would you stop yammering at each other!" boomed Philip as he made his way to Ann Putnam and grabbed both her arms.

"Tell me, young Ann Putnam, do you recall who I am?"

"To be sure, sir," said Ann, in new found tones of respect. "'Tis Captain Philip English you are. The very Captain English who married Eleanor Hollingsworth's bastard daughter and gathered her property to you after her death. 'Twas lucky it was that Mistress English died so timely and gave you a new fortune after the terrors."

"I should throw you into hell for that!" yelled Philip as he grasped Ann's neck firmly and began to squeeze. "'Tis you, you devil's imp, that spoke the words that condemned my Mary to arrest and torture. You are responsible for the weakness that caused her early death. Get on your knees before me, Ann Putnam, and beg my forgiveness. 'Tis the only way I swear that I will ever let you go. Deny me what I wish to hear and I will break every bone in your body, ghost or not."

"Please, somebody, make him let me go!" whispered Ann as Philip forced Ann to her knees.

"Uncle, stop! Please, for the love of God, stop," said the spectral presence of our own Nora, as Ann began to whimper in pain. "To hurt her like that is just as bad as what she did to you!"

"Yes, Philip," I said, amazed that Nora knew who Philip was! Had her journey into the mysterious spirit world opened her eyes to us? If that was the case, then maybe there was yet a way to save the girl. But, I realized, those thoughts would have to wait until later. Saving Philip from the blackness contained within his own soul was the work that lay before me now.

"Philip, let her go," I said as I drew near him. "There is no more this girl can do to me. Besides, the evil lies not in this poor twisted puppet. Look rather to those who pulled her strings and put the words in her mouth. She was only a child, after all."

"You speak of my mother, don't you?" said Ann as she backed away from Philip. "I'll not have you say anything against her."

Then Ann turned from us and tried to run back towards the glow of the firelight beyond. But there was no escape for her, something, or someone, blocked her way. It was heart breaking to see the way she beat her fragile hands against the invisible shield that now kept Ann Putnam from everything she knew.

"Let me pass!" she screamed hysterically at Lillith March.

"I can't do that just now," said Lillith, coming forward and making her way warily towards the sobbing girl.

"Yes you can! I know you're a witch, Mistress March. You have the look of it about you. And it's certain that if you were stripped naked before us you would have Satan's mark upon your body. Let me pass now, or I promise you will pay with your life for this!"

"Will you please stop making silly threats and calm down for a moment," said Lillith, stopping where Ann lay in a crumpled heap on the floor.

"Not until you let me go home," said Ann shrilly as the rest of us came forward and formed a three quarters circle around her. We would have completed the circle, but found it impossible. Whatever Lillith had done to block Ann's way into her Salem of 1692, blocked us as well. It was as if an invisible membrane had been stretched taut against the doorway that the old ouija board had opened into the past.

"If you won't let me go, than kill me," said Ann as she boldly got to her feet. She reminded me of a little girl chosen to be "it" in a child's circle game. The only difference was that this was no game. The only true mortal amongst us, Lillith March, held Ann Putnam's life in her hands at this moment. And she was not about to let the girl go.

"All I want to do is talk to you, dear," said Lillith, reaching towards Ann in a kindly manner.

"That's not 'all you want', and you know it, Goody March," said Ann with a poisonous look. "You want to beguile me with your sweet words and soft touch! Look at the spirits that surround you, trapped in hell, not even able to enter heaven's portals! If you think you can get me to join them, you're mistaken Witch!"

"I don't want you to join anything," said Lillith softly, "I just want you to help us, help us give my own daughter some peace, and lift the evil that threatens this town. Surely you must know by now that once evil is unleashed in this Salem, it's almost impossible to stop. If you'd just calm down and think about it for a moment, you'd realize that your own life was ruined by such a thing. You're not evil, Ann, but those around you were. They used you to get what they wanted. When they had it they gave no more thought to you than to the dust in the road. Surely you can see that you were as much a victim of the witchcraft horror as anyone who was hanged on Gallows Hill."

"How dare you say such a thing," said Ann, becoming calmer despite herself. "I'm a good Christian girl, Witch March. Everyone knows that if Philip English and his bastard wife had gotten what they wanted, the whole town would have turned papist, or at the very least that shameful half shadowed thing, Anglican. What would have happened in poor little Salem Village if the great heathen of Salem Town, Philip English, had changed our church for his? The King would have taken all our property away and given it to the wealthy merchants of the town. We would have starved while Philip and Mary English ate the food meant for our table."

"That's nothing but a fairy tale your crazy mother told you," said Philip, eyeing Ann with pity. "Can't you see how she used you, just as the other girls were used. Why, when I listen to you, I almost feel sorry for what they did to you. You had no chance at all to grow and become a proper woman with those fiends egging you on to spew their hate through your childish lips. Poor Ann, soon you were left alone to care for your younger sisters and brothers. And then it was you who made full confession in the church, begging the families of those you had killed to forgive you. I remember the day well, when you, as a young woman, spoke the words that would brand you for all times as the one who had caused the death of nineteen people up on Gallows Hill. 'Twas a brave thing you did, lass, and one that should have been rewarded with kindness. But what did your former friends do? They shunned you because you made them look guilty. They even let you make your way home alone from the meetinghouse. I have often thought that the sad death you died, well before your thirtieth year, was caused more by a broken heart than by a broken body. Poor Ann, to be used so and scorned thus."

"I don't know what you're talking about," said Ann, "I'm only twelve years old. How could you possibly know all that about me? I don't believe your evil words, either, You're just trying to get me to talk to you so that you can draw me into the enchantment of this horrible place. I want my mother and I want her now!"

"Your mother no longer exists, Ann," said Lillith, walking over to the crying girl. "She's been dead for three hundred years and may very well be in that hell you fear so much. I don't know why you came to us, but I do know that something, some force for good, understands that there was no evil in you. Perhaps it was the confession that you so bravely made that has saved your soul. Whatever the reason, I am glad you're here and I beg you to help us. Please, dear Ann, help us for your own sake."

"What do you want me to help you with?" asked Ann through her tears.

"First, I want you to help save the ghosts of Salem from oblivion. Then I want you to help lift the curse that lies upon this town. And last of all, I would like to see the soul of the living girl, Nora English, reunited with her healed body so that she can live a full and happy life."

"Is that all?" laughed Ann in a hysterically.

"No, there's one more thing," said Lillith as she bent to stoke the girl's golden hair. "I want you to do these three things so that, at last, your soul may be freed of this terrible thing and you can find peace, either amongst us, or in your beloved heaven.

"There is no such thing as 'peace,' Goody March, not in Salem Town," said Ann sadly as she got to her feet and put her hands into Lillith's, "but if you want me to try, I will. I don't know why, perhaps it is the madness of the moment, but I feel I can trust you."

"You can," said Lillith, as she put her arm around Ann Putnam.

"So we beat on, boats against the current,
borne back ceaselessly into the past."
F. Scott Fitzgerald: *The Great Gatsby*.

CHAPTER THIRTY FIVE

"What do we do first?" asked Ann, making her way towards the cracked window that gave a view of Derby Street. The girl gasped as two motorcycles roared by, drowning out any answer she might have gotten.

"We speak of the past so that we may understand what needs doing," said Lillith as she motioned for us to sit. "I just hope that no one bothers us before we're finished. 'Old Gil' is a friend of mine, but I'm not sure he would understand why I'm sitting in his locked shop without permission. The rest of you can vanish at will, but I'll have to explain what I'm doing here if I'm seen. Let's get away from the window."

Lillith motioned to the back of the shop where the gloomy light barely filtered.

"You'd be hard pressed to see anything back here," said Philip, sitting next to Lillith in a decidedly cozy manner.

"And what of that?" asked Ann, pointing to the gateway between her world and ours where the firelight glowed.

"I don't think anyone can see that but us," said Lillith. "It's something meant for only our eyes. "Now then, Ann, why do you think you were allowed to pass through to us?"

"Because you called me," said Ann.

"You're wrong," said Lillith, rubbing her hands together to keep warm, "no one called you, you just appeared. There must be another force at work that wants you here."

"Your Goddess," said Philip, "or perhaps, my God. Whatever the reason, some force wanted this girl here. Tell us, Ann, what was the last thing you said before you appeared to us?"

"I was asking Tituba to tell my future," said Ann. "But when she tried, Tituba began to moan and then she started to rock back and forth. It was as if she were scared of me."

"And well she might have been," I said, "considering what happened to her."

"What happened to her?" asked Ann with a look of genuine curiosity on her face.

"Don't you remember?" asked Lillith.

"No," said Ann, "the last thing I remember is standing in Reverend Parris' kitchen. Then, next thing I knew, I was here."

"Can you tell me the date," I asked, barely able to breath.

"It was late February, the twenty seventh, I think," said Ann.

"Then it was the beginning and end of everything," I said.

"Tell me, what happened?" said Ann, looking at me in wonder.

"We'll tell it together," I said, looking towards Philip for help. There was not strength enough within me to relive those dreadful days alone. I needed his help to get me through.

"And perhaps I can help," said Ann.

"Aye, perhaps you can," said Philip, drawing me close.

"'Twas on the eve of February twenty ninth, that odd day that falls but every four years, that the terrors began," said Philip solemnly as the firelight from the world of long ago lit his face. "Now that I look back upon it, it seems odd that none of us sensed the approaching danger. Perhaps it was the cold and the blowing snow of that terrible winter that blinded us to what had been happening in Salem Village. Whatever the reason, we were senseless as to what was taking place until it became too late."

"But it was not your fault for being blind to what was about to happen, Master English," said Ann with uncharacteristic compassion. "You folk of Salem Town always thought us Salem Villagers as little more than simple country folk."

"Aye, and that was our great mistake," said Philip, nodding his head in agreement to Ann's words. "Ours was the sin of pride. We of the town thought we were better than our neighbors to the west."

"But it was not your fault that you girls were dabbling in magic and spells in Reverend Parris' very kitchen," I said, not willing to take any blame for what had befallen us. "What you did was wrong, Ann Putnam, and you know it."

"'Twas Tituba's fault, hers and that heathen husband of hers, John Indian. They drew us towards the flame of evil," said Ann stubbornly, sticking out her lower lip in a childish pout. "They were the ones that pushed Betty and Susannah Parris, and their cousin Abigail towards the flames of unholiness. Those three visited our hearth fires with tales of Tituba's Caribbean magic until we could no longer resist. I well remember that first day when I journeyed to the Parris house with Mary Walcott, Elizabeth Hubbard and Mercy Lewis. We knew nothing of the Devil's magic until that day. Well I remember that cold winter's day when we first sat in Tituba's kitchen staring into the flames and asking our silly questions. Who was to know that little Betty Parris would be so upset by our games? 'Twas all Betty's fault that Dr. Griggs had to be called. If she had just remained calm, no one would have known of our doings."

"I remember that," I said, seeing again, the grizzled and bent figure of William Griggs as he made his way through town. It was Griggs who declared that there was the "Hand of the Evil" loose in the Parris' home that caused the girls afflictions. If not for his words, Reverend Parris might have never called together the elders of the church and issued those first warrants on that last day of February in 1692."

"Don't forget Mistress Silbey's witchcake," said Ann, nodding her head in agreement.

"I had forgotten that," I said, suddenly reliving the scene at Salem Village's meetinghouse as if it were yesterday.

"What's a witchcake?" asked the misty specter of Nora as she drew close to our circle.

"A witchcake is a foul thing made up of blood and human water and a few other things I'd rather not mention," I said. "I swear it was that foul thing that scared the good men of Salem into action. Until then, they were far too lazy to be roused from their comfortable fires in late winter. But once Mary Silbey forced Tituba into making the witchcake out of little Betty Parris' leavings, they had no choice. No one could possibly turn their backs on that. It was an act of witchcraft, made boldly in broad daylight for all to see, by the very servant of their own minister. What else could Reverend Parris do?"

"'Tis the truth you speak, Mary," said Philip solemnly, "Tituba forced their hand. It was as if the Devil himself was leading her towards her own destruction. It was the next day that Judge Hathorne and George Corwin's uncle, Jonathan, issued warrants for the arrest of Sarah Good, Sarah Osburn and poor Tituba for bewitching Betty Parris and Abigail Williams. They should have been ashamed of themselves for arresting a beggar, a demented old woman and a slave. Woe be it to those who condemn the innocent, less they condemn themselves."

"You sound like my father," said Ann, looking at Philip in disgust.

"By God, I do," said Philip, breaking into an embarrassed smile, "Mary, I do believe the telling of this tale is not a good thing. It brings to mind all the unhappiness and narrow mindedness of those times. Let's get beyond this thing and bring yon little girl into our midst here and now. I don't want to go on telling of those sad times."

"And what of the saving of Salem?" I said to Philip firmly. "You know as well as I that restoring Nora and saving the souls of this town can only happen if the curse against Corwin is lifted."

"And I want to go home, back to my own Salem," said Ann as she put her head on my shoulder in an almost daughterly fashion. "This place scares me."

"And well it should," muttered Lillith under her breath."

"What was that? What did you say?" said Ann, staring at Lillith in horror. "You were laying a spell upon me. You are a witch!"

"I was doing nothing of the sort," said Lillith wearily. "Look here, Ann Putnam, I want you away from here just as much as you do, maybe more. You make me sick! All I can think of when I look at you is what you did to my sisters and brothers. I don't care if it was a long time ago. And I also don't care that you think you were forgiven for you sins just because you asked. The fact still remains that nineteen people were 'officially' killed because you were weak enough to do your mother's bidding. And what's worse, hundreds of others either died, or wished they had died in Salem's dungeons. Children went mad or starved, fathers died so that their children and grandchildren could live, lovers were punished for protecting their mates, and innocent babes perished at their mother's breasts, just because you were a coward. Don't think that a few tears and your whining for home can win my sympathy now! Why, my own daughter has paid for your evil with her beautiful young life because you set into motion the wheel of fate that created the curse that swallowed her up in its very shadow. Shame on you, Ann Putnam. And shame on any that ever spoke to you with kindness or offered you shelter after your wickedness. If I didn't need you to help my daughter's shade find some kind of afterlife, I would lay a curse upon you, no matter what the cost to myself. But that's not the way it has to be, for now. You have a long way to go before you'll hear a civil word from my tongue or inspire a kindly thought in my head. So stop your babyish cries and stand before us, ready to pay the real price for your crimes against Salem. Help us to save the souls of this town and restore it to the purity of the Goddess. Then, and only then, will I grant you the kind of everlasting forgiveness that is real and will be honored by the otherworld you now inhabit!!!"

"Cry my friend, cry until you can cry no more," I said to Lillith as I held the grieving mother close. It was a blessing that, at last, Lillith had let go of her iron restraint and felt the pain of her loss.

"Oh, Mama," sobbed Lynn, running to her shaking mother. "It's all right. I don't really mind all that much!"

But there was no comforting Lillith as her grief washed over us all in dark waves.

"What have I done?" said the small voice of Ann Putnam as she stared at us in disbelief.

"You have become a fallen angel," said Philip, taking the girl by the hand and leading her towards the window of time that she had stepped through. "Your only hope for redemption is to help these poor souls find some peace. Are you willing to do that, no matter what it may cost you?"

"I am," said Ann Putnam, looking back at the grieving Lillith.

"The devil came to me and bid me serve him."
Tituba: March 1st, 1692.

CHAPTER THIRTY SIX

It was with pride in my sex that I looked at the three girls who stood before me, ready to take any risk to save our beloved Salem. My niece, Nora English, was the tallest, with a mature loveliness that made her seem older than her sixteen years. Beside her stood twelve year old Ann Putnam, small, but strong in her resolve to see this thing through. On the other side of Ann stood Lillith's daughter, Lynn. She was the most delicate of the three, with a piquant beauty that almost broke my heart when I thought what should have been for her. What a waste!

"Are you sure we're doing the right thing?" I asked Philip.

"I hope so," he said.

"I know we are," said Lillith, staring at her daughter through glassy eyes. "It's the only way. If we leave things the way they are now, our world will soon be shaded in complete darkness. What you fear is mere shadows when compared to that."

"She's right, Mary," said Philip.

"Yes, darling, I know she is," I said taking first my husband's left hand, and then Lillith's right into my own. "Let's just pray that our white magic can master the darkness that has surrounded us these three hundred years."

With those words I closed my eyes and began to move my lips in silent prayer. I could feel Philip and Lillith doing the same as the air began to move around us. The heat around me was so fierce that it penetrated my being. I had often found it hard, in the past, to experience sensations like those of the mortals about me, but that was before I had been held captive by George Corwin. For some reason many earthly sensations had returned. I found myself once again experiencing feelings I had thought were lost to me forever.

"What is it, Mary?" asked Philip as I put up my arms and tried to shield myself from the oncoming blaze of sweltering heat.

"Don't you feel it?" I asked, amazed that he was unconscious to the discomfort I was suffering.

"Feel what?" asked Lillith.

"Why the heat, the unbearable heat," I said, startled by Lillith's apparent lack of sensitivity. Was it just I who was aware of the steaming air about us that threatened to smother me by its closeness.

"Tell me everything you're feeling, Mary," said Lillith as she watched me intensely.

I tried my best to tell Lillith of the terrible heat that threatened to overcome me, but found it hard to speak. My very breath was becoming short.

"Mary, listen to me," said Lillith in alarm, "you must stay with us. If you let go the girls may be lost forever, doomed to wander in the shadowlands that lie beyond anything we know as a true dimension. I don't know what is happening, but I know you must fight it!"

"I know what it is," said Ann Putnam. I looked towards the girl, but all I could see was a wavering shadow.

"What? Tell us before it's too late," I said desperately.

"It's fear, I've felt the heat of this kind of fear before," said Ann sadly as she tried to make herself heard over the swirling air that had begun to engulf the old dirty shop. "It's the heat of fear flamed by the Devil! This is what I would feel right before I was able to throw fits in front of the magistrates and old Cotton Mather. This is the heat that I fed to the other girls so that they would act as I did and do what I wanted. It's the heat from the underworld that threw Salem to the Devil during the witch trials. You must do something, anything to get rid of it. If it follows us back, we are lost!"

"But why has it come to just me?" I asked, feeling the power of the evil force beginning to back off even as we spoke. Then it came to me. We had the answer in our hands! The heat of fear couldn't bear to be recognized and spoken of. It was happiest when attacking an innocent soul in isolation and trying to make it its own.

"Keep talking," I cried desperately. "Tell it that it no longer has a place amongst us. We wish it gone from this place forever."

"But how?" asked Ann. "It has been feeding on me for centuries. It won't let me go that easily."

"It must," said Lillith firmly as she took a limp flower from her pocket and tossed it to Ann. "Hold this before you, and believe that the love of this thing that once lived on earth, part of the Goddess' domain, will protect you. This rosebud, plucked from my daughter's funeral wreath, stands for all the love and goodness that now lives in Salem. Tell the evil spirit to be gone. Salem no longer welcomes it."

Philip, Lillith and I stood very still as we watched Ann eye the flower and speak to it in halting phrases. Suddenly, just as it had come, the dreadful fullness of the air lessened and I could once again taste the sweet cool air around me.

"You did it, child!" said Philip as he looked at the calm relief on my face. "Now hold on to one another as you journey."

"And remember, you are now sisters of the spirit," said Lillith.

"With three guardian angels," said Nora, laughing that beautiful laugh that reminded me of my own daughter, Mary.

"What did she say?" asked Philip.

"She said something about angels," said Lillith with a sigh as we watched the three girls fade from view. I opened my mind's eye full and willed it to journey with our Nora back into that place I had once called home, Salem in the high summer of 1692.

"Why did you call them angels?" I heard Ann Putnam ask Nora as the three girls sped through time.

"They have always been angels to me, at least Uncle Philip and Aunt Mary have. I never thought about Aunt Lillith as an angel until now."

"Oh, I know what you're talking about," said Lynn with a giggle, "those are the invisible people you used to talk to when we would play together down near Derby Wharf! I had no idea they were real!"

"Well, they were," said Nora. "They always have been, but I didn't really know who they were until I almost died at the Willows. It was only when my spirit left my body that I saw all of my past, including my ancestors, Mary and Philip English, standing near me. Who would have thought it would have taken so many people to make me!"

"And to think, you always thought of yourself as alone," said Lynn.

"Never again," said Nora with a smile.

"Well, that still doesn't make them angels," said Ann with a snort. "If you really knew them like I did, you wouldn't say such things."

"Oh, tell me! What were Aunt Mary and Uncle Philip really like?" asked Nora.

"They were just plain folk, just like all the other people of Salem, not that they ever thought of themselves as such. Master and Mistress English were always full of themselves. It serves them right that they were brought low by their betters. It was a true lesson in humility, it was, to see them bow before us."

"It sounds like you hated them," said Nora as she held tight to Lynn's hand. The three girls were suspended in an almost womblike state as they were carried gently back through the many years that Philip and I had passed through together. There was a smothering quality to the warmth and moistness that surrounded them bodily and me in spirit. If you held your breath you could hear the earthbeat echoing from inside the essence. It was like being encased inside a velvety heart, safe, but confining.

"I hate no one," said Ann almost angrily as she snatched her hand away from Nora and took a deep breath. "To hate someone is against God's teachings. Reverend Parris always said that we should love our neighbors as ourselves. It was just that Philip and Mary English put themselves above us. You see, if I really loved them it was my duty to correct their faults before they found themselves before their maker with the sin of pride staining them for all eternity."

"So you saw it as your duty to accuse them of witchcraft and see them hanged!" said Lynn incredulously.

"Of course not," said Ann with a self righteous tilt to her head. "But if that's what happened to them as a result of their insults against us, then so be it. It was out of my hands."

"You make me sick," said Lynn, trying to move as far away from Ann as she could despite the close softness that encased the three girls.

"You just don't understand anything about it," said Ann almost patiently.

"She's right," said Nora.

"How can you say such a thing," said Lynn.

"Because Ann grew up a lot differently than you or I did," said Nora. "She comes from a place where they could lock you up for kissing your own husband. Isn't that true, Ann?"

"Of course it's true," said Ann. "Good folk have no tolerance for public lewdness, it opens up the door for the Devil to enter. That's why a wench like Mary Hollingsworth English should have been on her knees daily, thanking her almighty God that we tolerated her in our town. We all knew that she was nothing but the bastard daughter of some passing tramp. She was no true daughter of the merchant, Hollingsworth. Baby Mary arrived but four months after William Hollingsworth returned from a two year journey at sea. What a fool he was to acknowledge the babe and parade her before the town for all to see. We knew the truth, we did, but we kept quiet for old Hollingsworth's sake. He was besotted with love for that harlot, Eleanor, and could not bear to see her convicted and hanged for adultery."

"I can't tell you how relieved we were when he died and we could all stop coddling Eleanor Hollingsworth and her bastard daughter. If we could, we would have taken that tavern license away from her, but it was too late. Cotton Mather, of all people, stood between us and the right way of things. It was a scandal to see that woman walking through town, bold as you please, claiming that her daughter had the right to marry any well born man in town. But we had our way. None of the right born men would have the girl, I can tell you that. That's why she had to turn to the French pirate you call Philip English. We all knew him as Philippe L'Anglois. He came from some little island stuck between England and France and was nothing more than a poor swabby when he hit our shores."

"How romantic," said Nora.

"Hardly," said Ann. "Give me an honest merchant with a good sailing vessel and a fine farm to the south, I say. Philip English was not as you think of him. My father said he was nothing but scum washed up from the sea that had the nerve to take bastard Mary as his wife. He married her so that he could use Eleanor Hollingsworth's Blue Anchor tavern as a meeting place for pirates and the like. It was a shame that the Reverend Mather never saw past Eleanor's bewitching smile to the black heart that beat beneath her bodice. He tried to give her the cloak of respectability by taking rooms in her tavern, but we all knew he was just taking pity on her and her family. But it still disgusted us. What was he thinking, spending his time in such a place, when he could have been respectably lodged in the Golden Ram down the street?"

"I've heard that Cotton Mather was in love with Eleanor Hollingsworth. I've also heard that he was Mary English's real father," said Nora with a teasing smile.

"Rubbish," said Ann. "That's just gossip and could not possibly be true! Reverend Mather told my mother that he took his rest at the Blue Anchor so that he could keep an eye out for any wrongdoing there. A woman like Eleanor Hollingsworth had to be watched over closely."

"Very closely," said Lynn, laughing, despite the pervasive quiet that enveloped us.

"Think what you like," said Ann with a snort. "I know what I know. You think that everyone is full of sin and lewdness like you, but it's not true. The only thing that we held against Mary and Philip English was the way in which they insisted on acting above their rightful station in life. If they had kept to themselves and lived in a proper shack up on the hill, we would have left them alone."

"Tell the truth. It was their money that bothered you, wasn't it?" said Nora. "You were all jealous. You stole their money, their property and my Aunt Mary's life because you were jealous! You make me sick!"

"You'll never understand," said Ann quietly as she cocked her head to one side. "Hush now, do you hear that?"

"Hear what?" said Nora.

"'Tis the sound of the King's pipers," said Ann.

"Deliver us from evil."
Reverend George Burroughs: at his hanging,
August 19th, 1692.

CHAPTER THIRTY SEVEN

The sound of bagpipes filled the air as the warmth that enshrouded us suddenly became filled with sunlight. As I watched, the three girls were transported from the safety of their time tunnel to a rocky ledge that overlooked my Salem of 1692. The intense heat told me it was indeed, high summer.

"Who's that?" asked Nora as she pointed to a crowd of people making their was up the hill.

"It's the people of Salem Town," said Ann, pulling Lynn and Nora down behind the rocks.

"Hey, let go!" said Nora, scraping her arm on the stone.

"Don't!" whispered Ann frantically as Nora tried to stand up again, an action that would have put her in full few of the townsfolk. "Are you mad!"

"Only at you," said Nora loudly. To her surprise, Lynn slapped her small hand over Nora's mouth.

"Shut up, Nora," she whispered as urgently as Ann had. "Can't you see who those people are? One more word out of you and we'll wind up in jail. I'll take my hand away only if you promise to keep still and out of sight." Nora nodded, but it was obvious from the angry look in her eyes that she was not happy about what Lynn had said.

"I still don't see what the problem is," said Nora.

"Maybe that man carrying those ropes will give you some idea," said Lynn pointing to a fat man who wore an elaborately embroidered vest. Over his shoulder were five heavy ropes that had been braided for strength. Behind the man walked four men and one woman. Their clothes were stained with the remains of rotten vegetables and eggshells.

"'Tis Preacher Burroughs they have," said Ann with a gasp. "Who would have thought that the hand of the Lord was so powerful. Praise to the Lord for his mercy!"

"Your 'Lord' doesn't look very merciful to me," said Nora, looking at the poor man trying to stumble up the rocky hill. It was an almost impossible feat, weighed down as he was with heavy leg irons. He was a small man of about forty, and it did seem almost miraculous that he was able to move forward at all considering his heavy load.

"Why does he have so many chains?" asked Lynn.

"Because he possesses the strength of ten men," said Ann with a nod. "See there how he can cover the ground faster than the other prisoners? It is said that Reverend Burroughs gets his strength from his master, the Devil. But look how we have triumphed over his evil master. Not even the Devil can break the chains we have forged with our prayers."

"What are they going to do to him?" asked Lynn, her face full of sympathy for the struggling man.

"Why hang him for witchcraft, of course," whispered Ann. She had a strange light in her eyes that was most disturbing. It was almost as if Ann were looking upon a scene that gave her sensual pleasure. The moistness of her parted lips and the curve of her body seemed to exude an animalistic message. She reminded me of a young female cat arching her back in the heat of her season. I thanked my lord that it was only my mind's eye, and not my soul's body, that accompanied the three girls as they hid behind the rocks watching the hanging party make its way up Gallows Hill. If I had been there in person, I doubt if I could have stopped myself from slapping Ann's disgustingly lustful face.

"Who are the other four people?" asked Nora, watching as the Reverend Burroughs passed by, making way for his fellow prisoners who lagged woefully behind.

The scene the girls looked upon was almost beyond belief by the standards that I had come to know in modern day Salem. It still amuses me to wander about the town and hear the scandalized whispers over some supposed horror that has happened in the town. What's an occasional bicycle theft or destruction of property when measured against the Salem of Puritan days? The Salem I had grown up in was a place capable of putting to death any who disagreed with what the town fathers thought was right. Struggling before us was the proof of that in the forms of five beaten and tortured souls whose only crime was to be different. And the irony of it was, not all were social outcasts! Look at poor George Burroughs, Harvard educated and a man of God, dragged before Cotton Mather and told that his life's work was for naught and that his soul belonged to the Devil.

"Oh look!" said Ann, panting with excitement," they've got that mean mouthed Martha Carrier, and John Proctor too. And behind them, can you see? Yonder comes John Willard, our 'ex' constable. He's the one helping old George Jacobs up the hill. 'Tis a pity the old man stepped in before we were able to cry out even more against his granddaughter. His lies saved his dear little Abby from the gallows, but perhaps once he's dead we can cry out against her again and see her hang too."

"I hate what you're saying. None of it makes any sense to me," said Lynn, slumping low behind the rocks as the townsfolk came near. The mood of the crowd was a mixture of merriment and mayhem. You could almost smell the bloodlust in the air.

"Here now," said Ann, sitting beside Lynn and motioning for Nora to join them. "Let me tell you of the five that just passed by. They are witches, accused and convicted, but once they were our neighbors."

"Then I don't see how you can do such things to them," said Nora, thinking of the old man who had stumbled by on the arm of the doomed constable.

"My mother says we must, at least we must if we are really Christian and believe in the holy book. To not do one's duty is a great sin, perhaps the greatest of all, and will be punished by the fiery pits of hell. The bible says that 'we should not suffer a witch to live,' and Reverend Parris has declared that 'the Devil hath been raised amongst us.' So, you see, we must cry out against those that don't agree with us and the Reverend's teachings. To ignore our duty would be cause for suspicion. Any who defends a witch might very well be a witch himself! You see before you proof of that. Rich John Proctor stood out in court and declared that his pregnant wife, Elizabeth, was no witch. Who but a witch himself would say such a thing when the evidence against Goody Proctor was there for the whole world to see. And how could a man as old as Proctor father a babe? And then there was old George Jacobs, defending that harlot of a granddaughter of his against us. She is known for roaming the woods at night and calling to the birds in their own tongue. If that's not a witch, I don't know what is! And perhaps the worst of the three is the constable there, John Willard. He was an officer of our courts until he refused to arrest any more witches. And you see where that has led him, to the foot of Gallows Hill."

"I think they're all fine, brave men," said Lynn. "Think of it. Those three are giving their lives because they love others. It makes me feel a little better about the whole 'witch thing' to know that there were people like that in Salem."

"Don't forget their Reverend," said Nora, "he must have done something to deserve his death."

"Aye he did," said Ann. "He buried his wife and babes in this town. They died, one after the other, despite all his prayers. That should be enough proof for you that he is a minion of the Devil. Why else would the Lord refuse his prayers?"

"And what of the woman? What did she do?" asked Lynn moving away from Ann.

"That is Martha Carrier," said Ann. "She has been convicted by the words of her own children. I was there when my father and Master Ingersoll examined the two boys. They tied their necks to their heels. It was only when the blood began to run from their noses that they betrayed their witch of a mother. You should have heard them screaming out her name! It was enough to make you want to drag her from her cell and see the woman hanged before sunset. But my father is a good man and insisted that all should be done the right way in a court of law. I remember Cotton Mather himself standing up at the end of her trial and saying 'this rampant hag, Martha Carrier, was the person of whom the confessions of the witches and of her own children among the rest agreed that the Devil had promised her she should be 'Queen of Hell.' That should be proof enough that wanting to rise above your station is the way to damnation."

"It just makes me sick," said Lynn as wail of the crowd and the bagpipes suddenly ceased. The only sound that could be heard was the shrieking of a hungry seagull.

"The hangings are about to begin," said Ann, pushing Nora to one side as she peeked from her hiding place behind the rocks.

George Burroughs was "dragged by the halter to a hole or grave between the rocks.... One of his hands and his chin could be seen sticking out."
Thomas Brattle: at the execution of
Reverend George Burroughs,
August 19th 1692.

CHAPTER THIRTY EIGHT

Lynn and Nora stood beside Ann, and the three girls watched in silence as the convicted witches were led to the hanging tree on Gallows Hill.

It was strange how still the air was on that hot August morning. Not even the bugs in the tall weeds nearby made a sound as George Burroughs stepped up to the ladder that was propped against the hanging tree. You could see the crowd take a collective step back as he turned to them and smiled benevolently.

"I remember many of you as my friends, almost my family," said the condemned man as he raised his manacled hands to the crowd in a sign of prayer, "and I bless all those in this place, whether they think me friend or foe, as does our maker who sees past our deeds and looks deep within our hearts for the truth of our spirit. I ask you all to listen as I repeat the words that the son of God spoke when he taught us how to pray. 'Our Father, who art in heaven....'"

"The boldness of the witch," hissed Ann, as George Burroughs preceded to repeat the Lord's prayer perfectly, beginning to end.

"He has said it just as it was written," cried a voice from the crowd.

"The man must be innocent," screamed a woman's voice, "everyone knows that a witch can't pray properly."

"Release him. Burroughs is innocent!" cried first one and then another of the crowd until the heat of the company threatened to overpower the heavy of the day.

"Oh look!" screamed the voice of a young girl as she pushed her way through the crowd, "I see him! I see the black man standing next to Burroughs and telling him what words to say. Can't you see him? He's standing next to the witch as plain as day! Hurry! Hang the witch before he loosens the Devil upon us."

Then a young man pushed poor George Burroughs from behind and roughly shoved him up the ladder. Another, larger man, steadied the ladder as the prisoner's neck was forced through the rope and he was pushed from the ladder. George Burroughs hung heavily from the hanging tree. Not even God's own words had been enough to save him from the terrible evil that surrounded Salem.

"Look not upon the witch's face!" commanded Cotton Mather. He made quite an imposing figure as he appeared before the crowd seated upon his fine black stallion.

"George Burroughs was no witch, and you know it Reverend Mather! He was a man of God, and a better one than you be," screamed a woman with her dirty hair hanging loosely about her shoulders. It was dear Goody Jacobs, soon to be widow Jacobs, who spoke. It must have been the madness of grief that made her scream so boldly in Cotton Mather's face. Everyone knew it was suicide to defend a condemned witch.

"The man you see before you was indeed a witch," said Cotton Mather, ignoring the distraught woman. "Think you not that he was a man of God. He had no proper ordination papers. The man you thought of as Reverend Burroughs, was merely Goodman Burroughs. He built his life upon a lie and has paid for it with his soul. The Devil has often appeared to me as an 'angel of light,' trying to lure me to his dark ways. It is the Devil's angelic form that stood before you just now, trying to compel you to take on his mantle. Look away from the witch before you are taken under the Devil's spell and find yourself beyond redemption!"

With those words, Cotton Mather motioned for the body of George Burroughs to be cut from the tree, stripped, and thrown upon a heap of rocks near the spot where Nora, Ann and Lynn huddled.

"Reverend Mather, Reverend Mather, would you pray with us!" cried the condemned Martha Carrier, falling upon her knees in terror. "I don't want to die, but if I must, at least pray that our deaths will be the last in this awful place," said Martha.

All but John Proctor knelt before the great Cotton Mather and received his prayers and blessings. The proud figure of John Proctor was one that made me think of my own husband, Philip, and how he would have held himself at such a moment. It was only fate that had kept us both from Gallows Hill. I was filled with a smothering panic as the crowd rose to its feet and watched as first, Martha Carrier, and then the three men, were led up the ladder to meet their death at the hands of the hangman. At the last possible moment John Proctor turned towards the crown and waved.

"You hang an innocent man," he said almost cheerfully, "one who leaves behind a beloved wife and an unborn child. Protect them, for my sake. Hangman, is there still no word from the courts about my innocence?" he said as he placed the noose around his own neck.

"None sir," said the fat hangman, Nicholas Noyes, as he brutally shoved the ladder out from under John Proctor.

After that, there was nothing for the crowd to do but leave. The heat of the noon day sun was beginning to beat down mercilessly on their heads, causing more than one of the less hardy townsman to wipe his brow. A few boys tried to stay and watch what the sheriff and his men were going to do with the bodies, but the boys found themselves shooed down the hill by their anxious mothers.

"Didn't you hear Reverend Mather?" I heard one woman say as she swatted at her child's ears, "he said the Devil might try to steal your soul if you look at those dead people."

"But Ma," said the whining boy, trying to break free of his mother's iron grip, "I want to see them stripped and their faces turn blue. Thomas said their tongues go all black. Come on, Ma!"

"Bring the Burroughs body over here," we heard Cotton Mather say as the last of the crowd disappeared from sight.

We watched in disgust as the sheriff's men dragged the naked preacher to the rocks where Cotton Mather stood. Mather placed George Burrough's head upon a stone.

"What's he going to do?" gasped Lynn as Mather drew his great sword from his scabbard and placed it against the neck of the dead Burroughs. With lightning speed, Cotton Mather raised his sword to the sky and swung it down upon George Burroughs neck, severing his head from his body.

"I think I'm going to be sick," said Lynn, turning away from us and throwing up as quietly as she could.

"Here now, what's this?" asked a voice from behind us. It was the young sheriff, George Corwin, flushed with the excitement of the hangings, and looking as much like his descendent Jake as a twin.

"I am innocent to a witch. I know not what a witch is."
Bridget Bishop, condemned witch:
Salem, Massachusetts, 1692.

CHAPTER THIRTY NINE

"'Tis none but Ann Putnam," said Ann curtseying before Sheriff Corwin with lowered eyes.

"Who is this wench who stares at me so boldly, and what manner of dress is this upon these two strange ones? Have you brought me more for the gallows, Ann Putnam? Surely none but a witch would be seen in man's breeches," asked George as he walked over to Nora and flicked her shirt with his sword.

"They are but poor orphans from the north, sir," said Ann, lying with such smoothness and quickness of mind that even I was astonished. I had known that she was clever, but her ability to dissemble under such pressure was absolutely amazing.

"Aye sir, that is what we are," said Lynn as she came forward and smiled sweetly at Sheriff George. "My sister and I were forced to flee from our home in the middle of the night. We took the clothing that hung on the nail by the door. 'Tis our poor dead brother's clothes you see upon us."

"'Twas savages that forced you here then, was it?" said Corwin, looking at Lynn almost too kindly. "Well then, there it is. See these two girls to your home, young Mistress Putnam, and cover then properly. It would be a scandal if the Reverend saw them this way."

"Yes sir," said Ann bobbing another curtsy to Corwin and turning to us with panic on her face.

"Come along now," she said steadily, "Mother will be glad to help you."

The three girls took off down Gallows Hill as if the Devil were truly following them. It was only when they reached the North River the Ann let them stop for breath.

"He looks just like Jake!" said Nora, gasping for breath.

"Well, he certainly doesn't act like him," said Lynn. "Did you see the way he was looking at me? It was creepy."

"The young Sheriff is one of the most eligible bachelors in town," said Ann an odd look on her face, "you should be flattered that he looked at you at all. I know many a girl who would leap at the chance to be noticed by him."

"What makes him so special?" asked Nora, trying not to giggle, "his way with a hangman's noose? Who would want to marry someone who runs around having people killed? I agree with Lynn. He gives me the creeps."

"If you knew about the property George Corwin held you wouldn't say that," said Ann, sounding much older than her twelve years. "He has a share in all the confiscated goods and deeds in the town. Why, I've even heard that he has a chest, full of jewels taken from the prisoners and their families."

"I've heard about that," said Nora, "it's said that a lot of it belonged to my Aunt Mary and Uncle Philip."

"And then there's what he stole from the poor," said Lynn with a faraway look in her eyes. "Nora, do you remember that lady, the one who said that Burroughs was innocent?"

"Yes."

"Well," said Lynn sadly, "that lady was old George Jacobs wife. We talked about her in school. I remember how Mrs. Harrington passed around these copies of what George Corwin did to her. Right after her husband was sentenced to die, Sheriff Corwin and his men went to her home and took everything away from poor Mrs. Jacobs. They even pulled the wedding ring off her finger. They left her with nothing, no home, no food and no husband. She had to go to her neighbors and beg for food so that her children wouldn't starve."

"That's even worse than what she did to my family," said Nora.

"I just don't understand you two at all," said Ann with disgust. "Everyone knows that it's right for criminals and their families to be stripped of their goods. How else can they be punished properly."

"Is it right for little children to starve because greedy sheriffs want to get rich?" said Lynn. "I think George Corwin is the worst criminal in Salem. It makes me sick just to think of it. He's the one who should be in jail, not those poor people who can't defend themselves."

"If it bothers you so much, why don't you tell him," said Ann, turning back towards Gallows Hill and pointing towards the horsemen who were making their way down the same path that the girls had taken. "I really don't care what happens to you now. I'm home, and I'm starting to think that all those stories that the witch, Lillith, told about my future were lies. I'm going home and I don't really care what happens to you. I do see that it might not be a good idea to be seen with either of you, you're already under suspicion, and a girl can't be too careful around Salem Town."

"But you told the Sheriff you knew us. You can't leave us now," said Lynn, suddenly filled with fear at the prospect of being abandoned in old Salem.

"That's easy," said Ann with an evil laugh, "I'll just say you bewitched me and made me believe your lies."

With those words Ann moved swiftly towards the woods. In an instant she was gone, leaving Nora and Lynn were alone and friendless in Salem Town.

Nora took Lynn's hand, squeezing it tightly. "Don't be scared, I'll do the talking," she said as George Corwin and his men overtook them.

The two girls watched in quiet terror as Corwin and his men encircled them. It was obvious that they had done such a thing before, because the way the horses blocked off any hope of escape was the most intimidating thing that either girl had ever experienced. I could almost feel the cold sweat that broke over them as George Corwin dismounted and stood in front of Lynn, almost touching her breast with his hand as he motioned towards the town.

"I thought you were under the protection of Ann Putnam," said Corwin as he looked Lynn directly in the face. His expression was one of a hunter who knows he might be on the scent of an innocent quarry.

"We are, sir," said Nora, trying to stand between Lynn and Corwin.

"I wasn't talking to you, girl," said Corwin, motioning for one of his men to take Nora away from him.

"Leave me alone," said Nora furiously as the man grabbed her by the arm and dragged her towards his horse.

"Look here, it's obvious the two of you are hiding something. Why are you really dressed in those strange clothes. Where do you really come from? Your speech in not that of our town, or even like any I have heard before. Most important of all, where is Ann Putnam? Have you done her some harm? I liked not your manner up there on the hill, or hers either, now that I think of it. Answer me, girl, and make it the truth."

"We're just what we said we are," said Lynn as sweetly as she could, looking directly into George Corwin's eyes. There was something about those eyes that was strangely familiar to her.

"I don't believe you," said Corwin, looking back at Lynn with undisguised lust.

Lynn turned to where Nora was being held and then back towards Corwin. "Oh please don't let me cry," she prayed to herself as she drew in a deep breath and tried again, knowing somewhere deep inside that she and Nora might never see home again if she failed to convince Corwin of their innocence.

"All I can tell you is the truth, for it's all I have sir," said Lynn, trying with all her might to imitate the manner of phrasing that both George Corwin and Ann Putnam had used. "My sister and I have had quite a shock. The Indians murdered our parents and brothers. We are fresh from burying them. It was only because we were hiding inside a secret closet that we were saved. Mother had always scolded Father for building it, she said it was a waste of good wood. I remember how Father would just laugh at her and tell her his family had always had such in the old England, to hide themselves when the King's men would come for them and try to stop their worship. You see, sir, our family fled to this country because they were Puritans, just as you are. 'Tis ashamed we are to find ourselves thus, practically naked before you and friendless to boot. We had heard my mother say she was distantly related to the Putnams of Salem, so my sister and I made our way here, hoping against hope that the Putnams would take us in. But alas, Ann does not believe our tale. She has refused to take us to her mother."

"I think it's because she's greedy and doesn't want to share what she has with us," said Nora, getting into the spirit of Lynn's story.

"Well, that does sound like Mistress Ann, and all the Putnams for that matter," said Corwin, looking Lynn up and down.

"It's God's own truth, I swear it," said Lynn, giving George a smile that would have melted a stone.

"Whatever the truth may or may not be is for me to say," said Corwin, putting his hands in his pockets and strutting back and forth like a proud cock.

"Take these two girls into custody," he said to the unmounted yeomen. "It will do them no harm to bide a bit in Salem prison while I visit the Putnam family."

PART FIVE

CROSSING THE RIVER STYX

"What other dungeon is so dark as one's own heart!
What jailer so inexorable as one's self?
God will give him blood to drink."
Nathaniel Hawthorne:
The House of Seven Gables.

CHAPTER FORTY

The dungeon that Lynn and Nora were thrown into was as dark as night. The clammy dampness and cold stone were in direct contrast with the bright summer sunshine that lay just beyond their prison door.

"Who be here?" came a voice from the corner. "I say now, who be here? Is it the black man come to take old Tituba for her badness?"

"It's me, Nora, and my friend, Lynn," said Nora, trying to make out the figure laying against the stone wall. Her body was at a peculiar angle.

"Be ye witches?" asked the woman's voice.

"No, we're just prisoners," said Nora, trying to keep from stumbling in the dark as she made her way over to the woman. It was then that she saw the cause of the woman's contorted figure. She was chained to the stone wall, by her hands, feet, and head. The cruel iron collar that surrounded her neck almost choked the woman as she spoke again.

"'Tis a pity it is that you're not real witches, but at least you're some company for this old body. Come near to me, girl," said the woman, Tituba, opening her eyes wide and nodding to Nora to join her friend. The glow of the woman's eyes was so bright that they almost served as a beacon to light Lynn's way.

"So you're Tituba," said Lynn, unable to hide the excitement in her voice.

"Aye," said the black woman, nodding her brightly turbaned head. "And who might you be?"

"I'm Nora, and this is Lynn," said Nora, reaching out to touch the shackled woman's hand.

"It's pleased I am to meet ye, young missies, even here," said Tituba almost cheerfully. "'Tis a rare day I have company now that they be hanging everyone. I thought for a moment ye might be old Mather come for Tituba's head like he came for Preacher Burroughs'. It's pay he will, will Mather, for the beheading of that saintly man. Even now the evil swirls around his shadow. He'll not know when or where, but pay for his meanness he will, in a way he never dreamed. We all have those we'd love beyond the grave, and Mather's beloved is young Increase, his gifted son. Little does old Cotton know that even now the lad is doomed because of his father's sins. 'Tis almost a pity young Increase will never see his twentieth year."

"How did you know that Cotton Mather has Reverend Burrough's head?" asked Lynn, backing away from Tituba. "And what do you know about Increase Mather? You're right, you know, I've seen his tombstone at Old Burial Hill graveyard. He died at nineteen. How do you know that?"

"Because I see things, child, I always have, even when I was just a little one running naked under the sun. 'Tis the way of it, it is, and always has been."

"My mother's like that," said a calmer Lynn. "She always seems to know what's happening to people around her. But she says it's more of a curse than a blessing, because she can never see what's going to happen to her, or the people she really loves, like me."

"Aye, that's the way of it," said Tituba nodding her head. "Do ye think that if I could have seen myself thus I would have ever let Annie Putnam and those bad girls warm themselves at my kitchen fire. 'Twould have been better for me to have thrown her and them to the flames and said that they stumbled. Think of all the innocent souls that would have been saved from Gallows Hill. And then there's this place. I'll warrant that it will kill far more than those that meets their maker up on the hill, kill them or drive the wits right out of them."

As if in answer to Tituba's words, the girls heard a strange keening from beyond their cell. It sounded more like a kitten than a human being, but the words that issued from the terror filled voice were all too clear.

"Mama, Mama! Can you come get me now?" cried the voice that Lynn and Nora realized belonged to a child. "I promise I'll be good now. Please come back and get me before the man hurts me again. Please Mama. I want to be with you. Mama, please!"

"Who's that?" asked Lynn, putting her ear to the wall, trying to hear more as the child's cries withered down to kittenish whispers.

"That be Dorcas Good, child of Sarah. Her mother was hanged a month ago, and she's been crying like that ever since. I suppose 'tis the fault of the fat guard, that Nicholas Noyes, that she's lost her reason, what with his fondling of her and sticking his manhood into anything she has that'll fit. But then again, I'm not so sure that the little one was right in the head before that. She saw her baby sister die right next to her and then lost her mama that way. Or, it might just be the chains that have driven her mad. It's certainly enough to do it," said Tituba, pulling on her own chains in frustration."

"That's horrible," said Lynn, sitting down on the damp floor of the dungeon.

"Aye, that it is," said Tituba sadly. "And it's all my fault. If I'd been strong enough to keep from screaming when that false preacher, Reverend Parris, put my feet in the fire, none of this would have happened."

Lynn and Nora looked to where Tituba pointed and saw that the woman's feet were bound in dirty rags. One foot looked much shorter than the other, and both of Tituba's legs were covered with angry red scars.

"They tortured you?" asked Lynn.

"Aye that they did. I told them, after it was over, that I only said what I said because of the pain, but no one would believe me."

"What did you tell them?" asked Lynn.

"That Goody Osburn and Goody Sarah Good were witches and flew with me at night upon their brooms. 'Twas all I could think of to say. Those were the first two names that came out of my mouth. How was I to know that they would drag old Osburn from her bed and put her in jail? Died she did, after but a few weeks in this treacherous place. Why, when she was arrested they had to have two constables hold her up, that's how sick she was. And poor Sarah Good. They took her with her newborn babe in her arms. I'll never forget how she cursed and screamed at the sheriff. The crowd thought she must be a witch for sure, what with all her carrying on. But it was hurting she was. You see, the constables waited outside her door while she gave birth. They took her as soon as the cord was cut."

"'Tis cursed I am to be sitting here alive, you see. Both Osburn and Good are dead, and I'm doomed to listen to Sarah's little Dorcas scream the night away, what with the raping and all. I don't have to sign any black man's book to enter hell, I've already found it."

"I had no idea it was this bad," said Lynn. "You read about the trials and you visit the places where it happened, but this is so different, so awful. What really makes me sick is that you tried to tell them they were wrong and they went ahead and hurt those poor people anyway. How could they do it?"

"Because Mistress Putnam, Ann's mother, is rotten inside," said Tituba. "She covets anything that anyone else has. That's why she's almost driven her own daughter to madness. The fits that young Ann has are real, all right, but they're none of the doing of any that lie within this place. Little Ann's faults come from her mother, direct and pure. 'Tis Mistress Putnam who is the real witch in this town. Mark my words, before this is over, the Putnams and their friends will have more land and riches than they ever dreamed of having. The only God they worship is gold, and they mean to be rolling in it no matter how much blood they have to spill to get it. What really makes me think they come from the devil is the way they wrap themselves in their holiness to get what they want. Imagine what evil must lay inside them to kill people in the name of God!"

"Lynn," said Nora, looking towards the wall where the sounds of Dorcas Good's crying could still be heard, "do you think it would do any good for Tituba to try one more time to tell Cotton Mather the truth?"

"No," said Lynn, "I don't. Why would anyone with power admit they're wrong now that people have already been hanged. You saw the faces of the people up on that hill. They looked crazy. They looked like they were enjoying what was going on. Let's just get out of here and go home. There's nothing we can do to help anyone here."

"What about that little girl?" asked Lynn, touching the wall between her and Dorcas Good.

"I don't know, I just don't know," said Lynn, bursting into tears. "She's dead now, at least dead in our time and space, and maybe that's the best thing for her. Dead is dead, I should know. Everything's just so awful and confusing. There's nothing we can do for anyone here. The best thing for us to do is to go home as fast as we can and try to help the lost souls in Salem that are still in pain."

"But I don't know how to get back," said Nora, suddenly realizing the truth of where they were. "Your mother sent us back here to lift the curse that lays over Salem's ghosts, but if what Tituba says is true, there's really no way to do it here. The accused are powerless, and the judges are happy with things the way they are. No wonder Salem lays under a curse. It deserves it!"

"But what about us? Are they going to hang us too?"

"Not if I can help it," said Nora. "There must be some way of sending a sign to your mother and getting us out of here."

"Then, ye are witches?" said Tituba in a hushed voice.

"Yes and no," said Lynn, looking up suddenly as the dungeon door began to open slowly.

"Now the fun begins," said George Corwin as he stood in the dimly lit entrance.

"Fun?" said Lynn.

"Aye, young Mistress, fun," said Corwin, stalking towards Lynn and grabbing her arm as he hauled her roughly to her feet. "It seems that ye have bewitched Ann Putnam. It's time for you and me to have a bit of a chat," said Corwin as he dragged Lynn from the room.

> "As I was going up the stair
> I met a man who wasn't there.
> He wasn't there again today.
> I wish, I wish he'd stay away."
> Hughes Mearns: "The Psychoed."

CHAPTER FORTY ONE

I became one with Nora as we listened to the anguished screams of Lynn March being dragged away. It was not the first time that I prayed to a nameless force to stop the horrors in Salem, but like before, my prayers were answered with nothing but silence. Why is it that I, Mary English, should be doomed never to hear an answer to my prayers? Such bliss seemed to be reserved for others. How I wished that I was strong enough to pull Nora and Lynn from that place and take them back with me to the safety of the old furniture store in modern day Salem. But I was indeed powerless, despite my ability to withdraw from my body and travel with only my mind. Such powers had never been mine. They were the province of such people as Lillith March and her kind. But there must be something I could do!

"What's he going to do to her?" screamed Nora wildly as she beat against the dungeon door until her fists bled.

"Oh, one of a thousand things," said Tituba, turning her face to the wall as she began to sing to herself.

"Tell me, oh please tell me!" said Nora, shaking Tituba.

But it was no use. The black woman would, or could, not answer. There was a faraway look in her eyes that seemed to look beyond the prison walls to some other place. Nora looked deeply into Tituba's eyes and soon found herself sitting beside the woman, holding her work roughened hand. Soon both girl and woman were in a place that was far away from the horrors of Salem dungeon. They journeyed past the moldy walls to a room above them, the room where Lynn March lay.

"I'm not a witch!" sobbed Lynn as she cowered on the earthen floor in front of George Corwin.

"If Ann Putnam says you be a witch, then a witch you are," said Corwin, kicking the defenseless girl. Lynn landed face down on the filthy floor. She put her hands over her head and began to wail like a small child.

"Leave me alone. Just leave me alone!"

"I can't do that, witch," said Corwin, kicking Lynn again in an attempt to turn her over. The girl wiggled away from his muddy boot and curled up in a ball on the floor. Corwin got down beside her and began to stroke her hair in an oddly compassionate manner.

"Come now, young missy, all you have to do is confess to your witchcraft and you can go back down below. I don't want to hurt you. It's them that is above me that tells me I have to if you stand firm. I know you're a witch. What else could you be, dressed thus and with such strange speech. Just say the words and I'll free you to return to your friend."

"And then you'll let us go?" asked Lynn, hope creeping into her voice.

"Let you go?" said George Corwin as he broke into a merry laugh. "Are you daft, or just simple? How could I let a confessed witch go. The whole town would be after my head if I did such a thing. No, there will be no freedom for you. You must be returned to the dungeon and chained to the wall with the other confessed witches. 'Tis the only way we can make sure that you're powerless to cast spells upon the innocent of the town."

"I'm not a witch, and you can't make me say I am," said Nora, getting to her feet and standing before George Corwin.

"What if I tell you that it's only those who swear they are innocent who find themselves up on Gallows Hill with a rope around their necks? In a way I hope you and your friend stand firm against us. This whole place is filling up with confessed witches. It makes me feel mightily uncomfortable to see them all chained up with their spells brewin' inside them. 'Tis beyond me why Cotton Mather has said that the unconfessed should hang and the confessed live, but that is the way of it. Confession is the only way to save your life, lass."

"You're all monsters, everyone of you. You should all be struck dead where you stand," said Lynn, staring into George Corwin's eyes. There was something about those eyes that the girl found fascinating and repellent at the same time.

"What are you looking at, wench," said Corwin, grabbing hold of Lynn's hair and dragging her across the room to a small table. He shoved her down on it and pressed his face into hers. "Stop that now, or I'll have to beat you. This is your last chance before I call in the others to make you tell us about how the Devil lifted your skirts and made you his. Confess to me now, or feel the whip."

"You'd like that wouldn't you," said Lynn, pushing Corwin off her with a strength born of desperation. "You'd like me to tell you some sick story about being handled and raped by the Devil. You're nothing but a sick pervert, you and everyone in this place. Get away from me, do you hear me! I swear that I will set some kind of a curse on you unless you take your hands off me!"

"Fine," said Corwin, rubbing his stomach in the place were Lynn had pushed him. "You've had your chance. I promise you, the next time you leave this place 'twill be for Gallows Hill."

With those words, Corwin grabbed Lynn roughly and pushed her back on the table. This time he was careful to secure her hands and feet with sturdy ropes. When he had finished, Lynn lay spread eagle, each hand and foot cruelly attached to a leg of the table.

"What are you going to do?" she whispered.

"I'm going to let you lie here in the dark to think about your crimes, witch," said Corwin, as he gently stroked Lynn's breast.

"But I'm innocent," said Lynn, trying not to vomit as Corwin carefully unbuttoned her blouse and fumbled with the front of her bra.

"What strange manner of dress is this?" he said to himself as he tried unsuccessfully to unlatch the bra from the front.

Lynn turned her head away from Corwin as he took a knife from his pocket and cut the bra from her body. "There now, that will make it much easier for the examiners to search for your witch's mark."

"The examiners?" asked Lynn, amazed as Corwin took his hands from her chest and began to remove her shoes.

"Aye, lass," said Corwin, removing Lynn's Reeboks and socks. "You have to be as naked as a babe for them to have a good look at you. You really are a strange one. Everyone knows that an unconfessed witch must be stripped naked and examined for her witch's mark!"

"Don't," cried Lynn, as Corwin took his knife and began cutting away her jeans. He did it so savagely that he nicked her in several places. Soon, all she had on was a pair of pink bikini panties.

"I know not where you come from, but I do know that you must be a harlot," said Corwin as he placed his knife between the satin of Lynn's panties and her delicate skin. "Only a woman who has no modesty before God would wear such things. 'Tis grateful you should be that we of Salem have taken it upon us to save your immortal soul!" With those words, George Corwin cut away Lynn's panties, leaving her naked before him. He stood for a minute, looking down at her with a wild lust in his eyes. His hands moved to the crotch of his breeches in an almost unconscious movement. Then they moved away again.

"'Tis a pity that I cannot have you now, before they poke and prod at you. Sometimes there's nothing left for me after they're done messing around inside a lass. See here, if you confess quickly you might just have enough for me to have a go at you. 'Twould be wise of you to think about that, lass, before I return with Putnam, Ingersoll and the rest."

With those words, George Corwin left the room, leaving Lynn naked and helpless on the rough wooden table.

"His eyes, his eyes," she murmured as she looked towards the door that closed after her jailer. "Where have I seen those eyes?"

> "The bell invites me,
> Hear it not, Duncan; for it is a knell
> That summons thee to heaven or to hell."
> William Shakespeare: *Macbeth*, II, i, 62'

CHAPTER FORTY TWO

"We can't let this happen," said Nora, suddenly awakening from her trancelike state.

"No we can't," said Tituba as she opened her eyes. Nora gasped as she turned towards the black woman. Her eyes had taken on a yellowish cast, almost like that of a cat.

"Can you help her?" asked Nora.

"Aye, that I can, if you promise not to forget old Tituba once you break free of this place. Come for me and your debt will be paid. Abandon me, and feel the weight of my curse upon you. The choice is yours, young missus, whatever you wish."

"But if you have the power to help us, why can't you free yourself?" asked Nora.

"I don't know," said Tituba sadly. "It's the same as being able to see what is to happen to others but not to me. 'Tis the curse of the gift I suppose. Quickly now, give your promise to me before it's too late."

"I promise," said Nora.

"Now then, let's see what a merry chase we can lead Master George." With those words, Tituba began to laugh madly.

It was a frustrated George Corwin that rode towards Ingersoll's tavern that hot August afternoon. How he would have liked to have the girl under him, fresh and unbroken. It was almost more than a man could stand, having Thomas Putnam and his rich friends have first go at all the pretty bits that by rights should have belonged to him, George Corwin, High Sheriff of Salem Town.

"Here now, what's this," he said to himself as a large black dog suddenly blocked his path. The dog was huge, with massive shoulders that measured a full three feet across. His muzzle was drawn back, and his grimacing lips showed teeth that were razor sharp. George Corwin was instantly on the alert as the dog approached his horse. Corwin kicked the horse in it's scrawny sides in an attempt to make a dash past the hulking dog that blocked his way, but it was too late. The terrified horse gave a desperate whinny and shied away from the black dog, then it froze in horror.

"Come on now," said Corwin, taking a softer tone with his horse, hoping against hope that gentleness could accomplish what roughness had not. But it was no use. The horse only gave a weak snort and bowed his head before the dog.

"Move, you damned beast!" cried Corwin as the panic of the steed between his legs began to spread to him, "move I said!" George Corwin dug his spurs into the poor horse, frightening him to the point that he reared up on his hind legs and dumped his master unceremoniously on the ground. Then the horse turned tail and fled down the path towards the center of Salem Town.

"Come back here, do you hear me!" screamed George as he shook his fists in the air. "I said come back here or I'll whip you to death!" The only answer Corwin received was the sounds of hoofs beating against the dusty path in the opposite direction.

"You really are a fool, if you think a dumb beast will come just because you call it," said a voice from behind Corwin. The Sheriff turned, relieved that he was not alone on the trail. It must be the voice of the dog's master he was hearing. But to his amazement, the only one who stood on the path before him was the huge dog, grinning widely as he revealed his sawblade teeth.

"Where are you?" screamed the frightened Corwin, not able to believe what his confused senses told him must be true. "Reveal yourself, sir, before I am forced to take a sword to your beast."

"I'm right here, you idiot," said the dog, almost smiling as he skewered the man's frightened gaze with his own.

"But this is impossible!" said Corwin, backing away as the dog took a few graceful steps toward him.

"Nothing is impossible for me," said the dog, in a deep, musical tone.

"What do you want from me?" asked Corwin, feeling something cold and wet run down his pants leg.

"I wish to feed on you," said the dog sweetly. "It's up to you how I do it. If you let me take your soul I'll leave you your body. But if you refuse me that, then I'll be forced to tear you apart. I like to leave the throat for last. It's really more pleasant that way. Then there's the heart. There's nothing like a warm beating heart taken from a man in the fullness of his prime."

"Who are you?" asked George Corwin, frozen by his fear.

"Lucifer," said the dog as his hot breath filled the air.

"I don't believe in you," said Corwin, trying unsuccessfully to tear his eyes away from the approaching dog.

"Of course you do," said the dog. "It's you, and your kind, that has long been doing my work for me in Salem. You've always believed in me, George."

"Don't touch me," screamed Corwin as the dog touched the man's hand with his muzzle.

"Come now, what do you say old friend," said the dog seductively, "this won't take but a moment if you grant me what is already mine. What have you got to lose? Your soul is already tainted by your deeds. I've seen the way you and that Nicholas Noyes torture that baby, Dorcas Good. It makes my wicked old soul tingle every time one of you lay a hand, or something else, upon her. Think you that your God would ever let you into paradise after such wonderful deeds? Why not come along with me instead? You're just the sort of man I'm looking for, young, bright, and talented. There's no telling how high you might rise in my ranks. All you have to do is let me give your left hand a small bite, just enough to draw a bit of blood. Then the world will be yours."

"I must be going mad," said Corwin, turning away from the dog and beginning to run down the path towards the prison.

"I wouldn't do that if I were you," said a booming voice, directly in front of the panic stricken man. The black dog appeared on the path, blocking George's escape.

"But how? What? That's impossible," said George turning and stumbling along the path, this time towards Ingersoll's tavern. Once again, he found the enormous black dog blocking his path.

"Let me pass!" the man screamed.

"Really," said the dog sternly, "I'm getting tired of this game. At first I though you might be amusing to have along, but I must say I dislike this independent streak you're showing, Georgie. What's it to be, your soul or your body? Tell me quick before I make up your mind for you."

"Go away, will you please just go away!" sobbed George Corwin as he fell in a heap in the dusty road. He curled into a ball and began to wail like an angry two year old.

"There now, that's better," said the dog, coming over to George and licking the man's tears of self pity. "There's nothing I like better that a sip of pain. Ah, that's good," said Lucifer as he sat on his haunches next to George.

The man continued to sob as the dog waited patiently beside him. Finally, George's tears stopped. The Sheriff looked up. The dog caught the man's gaze and spoke once more, in tones that froze George Corwin's heart.

"You're out of time, George old friend. Tell me what to do, now, before I shred your pretty skin from your body an inch at a time."

"Take what you want," screamed Corwin, holding his left hand out towards the dog.

The only sounds that filled the woods as the Devil made George Corwin his own were those of slurping wetness.

> "The magician Merlin had a strange laugh, and it
> was heard when nobody else was laughing...
> He laughed because he knew what was coming next."
> Robertson Davies: *A World of Wonders*.

CHAPTER FORTY THREE

The sounds of Tituba's laugher filled the small cell where Nora was imprisoned. The joyfulness of the sound filled Nora with the desire to join Tituba in her wildness. At the last moment, something in Nora's mind pulled her back. Almost at the same instant, Tituba stopped. The black woman breathed deeply several times as she wiped her eyes with her chain laden hand.

"Sometimes it's not so bad being old Tituba," said the woman, breaking into gleeful laughter again as she placed her hands in her lap. Then she moved them up and down several times making a turning motion with her closed fists. Magically, the heavy prison door swung open.

"How did you do that?" gasped Nora, looking first at the heavy wooden door and then at the seemingly helpless woman whose hands rested demurely on her tattered linen lap.

"I'm not sure I know," said Tituba, chuckling to herself as she whispered something under her breath. "But I do know that you better make haste to leave this place while you can. Once they winds the chains about you, you're lost."

"But what about Lynn! I can't leave without Lynn!" whispered Nora frantically, looking towards the door. She knew as well as Tituba that it was only a matter of time before someone passed by the open door.

"Your friend lies above you, up the stairs and first door to the left. She's frightened, but still unharmed. Make haste young missus, and take old Tituba's shawl with you. The girl will need a covering if she's to make it through the woods alive."

"Let me find a way to get you out of those chains, Tituba. There's no reason why you can't come with us."

"An old woman like Tituba would only slow you down," said Tituba, shaking her head sadly. "Hurry now, before it's too late. Do as you promised and come back for me another time. Sometime when it is safe. It would do us no good if we were all caught now. Return to me when you have your powers full and strong upon you, Nora English. Only then can Tituba leave this place for good."

"I'll never forget what you've done for us, I promise," said Nora, taking Tituba's large red shawl as she kissed the old woman softly.

"Go! Now!" said Tituba as she touched the girl on the cheeks with her chilblained hands. As Nora turned to go, a single tear ran down the old woman's face.

"'Tis a fool you are," Tituba muttered to herself as she watched Nora go. "And pay for this you will too. Ah well, what more can the Devil do to me!" laughed the woman madly as she consoled herself with thoughts of George Corwin burning in the eternal flames of hell.

Nora could feel the beating of her heart as she made her way as quietly as she could up the narrow stone steps. When she reached the top, Nora felt a moment of confusion as Tituba's words fled from her mind. Where was Lynn? What had Tituba told her? Then Nora heard a small groan and turned towards the sound.

"First door on the left," she said to herself as she made her way towards the sound. The corridor the girl walked through reminded Nora of a Salvador Dali painting she had once seen in one of her art teacher's books. The hall was filled with doors, some straight ahead, some at crazy angles above or below her. One seemed to be suspended in space, leading nowhere at all. It was only when Nora stumbled over a jagged rock that she realized the truth. The doors had been set into the jagged stones, wood giving way to rock.

Once again Nora heard Lynn's voice, moaning gently. She faced the first door on her left and turned the handle on her friend's prison door. Inside lay Lynn, naked but unharmed, miraculously unfettered by the cruel ropes that had held her to the rough wooden table.

"Here, put this on," said Nora, throwing Lynn Tituba's shawl.

"How did you get free?" asked Lynn, blinking as the light streaming through the open door filled the room.

"I'll tell you later," said Nora as she helped Lynn off the table. "Just hurry up!"

"OK, OK," said Lynn, wrapping the red shawl about her like a toga and following Nora to the entrance of the cell.

"Get your shoes, dummy," whispered Nora.

"Right!" said Lynn, padding back quickly and grabbing her shoes. She ran back to Nora and soon both girls were making their way up the winding prison stairs towards the afternoon sun.

"Ouch," said Lynn as she stubbed her bare toe on a rock. "Hold on while I put on my shoes."

"Not now," said Lynn, putting her finger to her lips, "listen."

From somewhere above, the two girls could hear the beating of horse's hoofs. Then the sound was gone as quickly as it had come.

"Come on," whispered Nora, pushing Lynn in front of her. Soon the two girls emerged at the top of the stairs. Luck, or something else, was with them because the main door to the prison stood open, just as Nora's cell door had been.

"Run," said Nora, pushing Lynn out into the open. About a hundred yards to their left was Salem woods, dark and forbidding.

Everything seemed to go in slow motion as the two girls made their way towards the thicket that lay across an expanse of open land. It was only luck that prevented Nora from smashing head long into the raised platform that held a set of three stocks, as she flung herself forward, fighting against both the physical and mental exhaustion that the past few hours and brought her. At the last possible moment she saw the heavy wooden beams in front of her and, with the agility of a ballerina, leaped to one side. She looked up towards the cloudless sky and then back to the earth, focusing her gaze on Lynn. She followed her running friend in desperation, secretly afraid that she would fail to reach the safety of the woods in time.

"Keep going, young mistress," whispered a voice in Nora's ear, just as she was about to fall to the earth in exhaustion.

"What? Who?" whispered Nora as the voice filled her with renewed energy. She burst past the first of the brush that marked the entrance to Salem woods and soon found herself following Lynn with an almost peaceful energy.

"All will be well, young mistress," said the voice within Nora, calming and energizing her as she followed Lynn at an even pace.

"Who are you?" asked Nora again, little expecting an answer. To the girl's surprise, the voice answered.

"'Tis I, Tituba," said the voice with the warm chuckle that Lynn remembered so clearly from her moments in the dark cell with Tituba.

"Why are you with us?" asked Lynn silently, finding it comforting to fill herself with the black woman's thoughts.

"Because your fate and mine are now woven together, young Lynn," said Tituba. "In order for you to escape I had to summon the dark man, the one you know as the Devil. Even now he walks abroad in Salem, more powerful than he has ever been before. 'Twas the only way I could think of to help you and Nora escape. But no matter. 'Tis only what the evil ones in this town deserve. 'Tis almost glad I am that I was forced to do it. Now, as Reverend Parris likes to say, 'the Devil hath been raised amongst us.' It's their own fault. Let them pay as they should for their wickedness against the innocent. I will soon be free of this place if you and your friend keep your promise."

"What promise?" asked Lynn.

"Why your promise to take me away from this place," said Tituba, gently. "Help your friend keep her word and I will be eternally grateful. Break it and you and all your kin will feel my power. Even now, that fiend George Corwin, is cursing the day he ever tried to hurt poor old Tituba. He's the Devil's own, and will remain such until the curse that I have laid upon Salem Town is broken."

"So there is a curse on Salem," said Lynn. "Mama always thought there was, but she said that she would never really know for sure until someone, or something, revealed how it happened. She said that it was only by knowing how the curse started that it could be broken."

"Aye, that's true," said Tituba, "and 'tis I that holds the secret. I'll tell you what it is if you promise never to tell another."

"Yes, please tell me," said Lynn, amazed at how she could run so swiftly without feeling any tiredness. "It must be more of Tituba's magic," thought Lynn.

"'Tis old George Corwin that holds the key," said Tituba, playfully, "him and Philip English. 'Tis the play of good and evil must come about to make the thing work. They must come together in a time far from this to join good and evil back together. Corwin must pay for his crimes as he has made others suffer for their innocence, high up on the Gallows of God's own choosing. And the instrument must be Philip English, he who has been given God's gifts many times over. Waste it, he will, in this life, chasing after fools gold. But there will come a time when he will discover the real treasure that forges together the souls of this world and the next."

"I don't understand," said Lynn.

"'Tis a riddle I've given you, Lynn March. Surely, you, daughter of a witch, have enough wits about you to hear its true song."

"I'll try," said Lynn, trying to focus herself on Nora's running figure as Tituba's voice faded into the air.

"All hope abandon ye who enter here."
Dante Alighieri : *Inferno*, canto III,1, 9.

CHAPTER FORTY FOUR

A strange mist enveloped the two girls as they burst forth from Salem woods.

"Look," said Nora, catching hold of Lynn's arm as the smaller girl stumbled from the woods.

"I don't see anything," said Lynn, squinting through the fog towards the spot where Nora pointed.

"It's a boat," whispered Nora.

"Listen," said Lynn, as a man's voice, hushed, but powerful drifted towards them.

"Speed bonnie boat, like a bird on the wing;
Onward, the sailors cry:
Carry the lad that's born to be king
Over the sea to Skye."

"How beautiful," said Nora, looking at Lynn with tears in her eyes. "There's something familiar about that song, I know I've heard it before."

"It's called the "Skye Boat Song," said Lynn. "I've heard it too, but never like that. He sounds like an angel."

How well I knew the song and the singer! It was my own beloved Philip who sang as he made his way down the North River in a small boat! What was he up to? I searched my mind frantically for an answer, and then it struck me as sure and clean as an arrow through my heart. This is where he had disappeared to during those hot August weeks while I had been left alone, frightened for my life and his.

I had been imprisoned in the early spring of 1692 and Philip in late May. Everyone had thought that he had run away, but what he really did was arrange for a way to rescue me from jail. That rescue called for his letting himself be taken. He soon arranged for more comfortable lodgings in the dungeon of Boston jail, and soon after, Philip and I found ourselves being spirited away by our friend, John Alden, to New York and safety. I never asked Philip what the cost of my freedom had been, but I could tell from the quiet moments when he would turn his face to the wall to hide the tears, that it had cost him dear. I now think that there may have been a blood boon asked of him, but I dared not ask by whom. That was only one of the many secrets that he hid deep within his stony and most generous soul. Not long after he had me safely tucked away in old New York, Philip had taken my hands and turned the palms upward, kissing first one and then the other, in a sign of ancient homage of a lord to his lady.

"Think not that I choose to leave you at such a time," said Philip, looking first at my face and then at my swelling body. "It's just that I must. I owe a debt, you see, one that I must pay."

"I don't understand." I had said, terrified to be left alone in a strange place, penniless and with child. What would happen to me and our babe if Philip were harmed or recaptured and taken back for trial? I knew that if he were caught they would torture him to find my whereabouts. I also knew that he would let himself be ripped apart slowly rather than to see me come to harm again. The magistrates of Salem were powerful and their reach was long. How else could they have taken George Burroughs from the safety of northern Maine and dragged him back for trial? They would do the same to Philip if he came out of hiding.

"Please don't go, my love," I said, taking his face in my hands and kissing him sweetly. "Whatever you may think you must do is not worth your life. It would surely kill me if you came to harm, I beg you not to abandon me." With those words I fell on my knees before my husband and pressed my face to his thighs.

"What is all this?" laughed Philip as he put his arms around me and brought me to my feet. "Do you think for a moment that I would leave you never to return? Impossible! Calm yourself, my Mary. I do what I must, but I promise you there is no danger in it. A man's word is a sacred thing, and as I have given mine in this matter, I must see it through. Think you on how it would be, for the rest of our lives, if it were learned that Philip English went against his honor and broke his word. Our days would be worthless. I must go, Mary, and that is the end of it. Now dry your tears and go lay down. I promise that before the leaves turn to gold, I will return."

"Make your promise not to me, but to our unborn child," I said to Philip, laying his right hand upon my belly and looking into his eyes. Surely if he were lying to me I would know it as he placed his large hand upon my trembling body and made his vow.

But he had lied to me, the blackguard! Here was my husband, my Philip, sailing down the North River of Salem, bold as you please, with a price on his head and a bounty on his body. He was rowing directly into the lion's mouth with little or no care of what happened to his wife and child. I was furious as I listened to him sing the song that he had once sung under my window as he wooed me. Then I caught a glimpse of his dear face, not as I had grown to know it in our afterlife, but the face of the real Philip English, firm and muscular, and in the prime of his manhood. What a magnificent figure he was as he stood with pike in hand, expertly maneuvering the small flatboat to shore.

"Quickly now, lads," I heard him say as he and his companions jumped lightly to the banks of the North River. They pulled the flatboat up after them and dragged it towards the woods. I watched as Lynn and Nora barely had time to hide behind a massive elm tree.

Then Philip and his friend expertly covered the boat with branches and leaves and turned their faces towards Gallows Hill. What were they up to? I could tell by the firm set of his jaw and the resolution in his eyes that it was no good. Whatever it was, I thanked God for the cover of the fog that made them almost invisible as the men made their way up the hill.

"What should we do now?" asked Lynn, looking after the men with a puzzled expression on her face.

"I'm not sure," said Nora sitting down beneath the shelter of the elm. "But I do know we can't stay here. According to everything I've read about Salem in 1692, the woods are even more dangerous than the town. There are Indians everywhere and they're not friendly. You saw how easily George Corwin believed Ann Putnam when she told him about our parents being killed in an Indian massacre. There was something called 'King Philip's war' back then, and many people around here were killed.

The Indians were mad at the Puritans for taking their land and destroying their hunting grounds. They didn't want to starve any more than the Puritans did. Besides, they thought that the Puritans of Salem were full of evil spirits. If I remember correctly, they even had a name for this river. It was something that really couldn't be pronounced or spelled by the Puritans, but it meant something pretty bad."

"How bad could it have been?" said Lynn, amused by the fact that her friend, who never admitted to being superstitious, was speaking of such things.

"It was really bad, now that I think of it," said Lynn. "This river was their gateway to hell, kind of like that river we learned about in mythology."

"The River Styx?" said Lynn.

"Yeah, that one," said Nora.

"Well, I think that's just silly," said Lynn. "They're always talking about gateways to hell in Salem. Why, my mother said there might even be one on Salem Common under some old tree. Who cares about old Indian superstitions, or superstitions of any kind. All I want to do is get out of here and back to our own Salem."

"Where you can take up your nice comfortable life as a ghost," said Nora, breaking into laughter.

"At least I know how I got that way. At least, I think I do," said Lynn, sitting next to Nora. "It's all too confusing to think about right now. All I know is that in our Salem I felt 'right,' and here I feel 'wrong.' I know I sound crazy, but I make sense to me... Nora," said Lynn, suddenly jumping to her feet, "do you know who that was? That man who was singing?"

"Who?" said Nora.

"That was the ghost lady's husband, you know, the one you call you Aunt Mary. That was her husband, Philip. I can't believe you didn't recognize him!"

"You're right," said Nora as she took her friend by the shoulders and began to jump up and down. "I don't know how I missed it. He looked different because he was alive, but you're right! That was Philip English. Do you think he can help us? I mean he doesn't know that he's a ghost yet, and might not understand what we're talking about, but he did seem like a nice guy. Besides, everyone says I look like Mary did when she was my age. Maybe he might recognize that I'm family."

"I don't know about that," said Lynn as her native caution began to return to her. "How do we know he's become nice yet? He might be like the rest of them around here and just want to hang us. I mean, what's he doing in that boat with those guys, going up to Gallows Hill. He might just be cleaning up the place for the next hanging or something."

"We have to do something," said Nora. "We can't just hang around the woods like this until we starve or get killed. Besides, look at the way you're dressed. I don't think you'll last long around here looking like that."

"You're right," said Lynn, pulling Tituba's shawl tightly about her. She would have never admitted it to Nora, but she was beginning to feel cold despite the warmth of the August day. The dampness of the woods and the darkness of the mist all combined to make the slender girl aware of the nakedness that the shawl barely protected. "I think I know what we could do."

"What?"

"We could hide under those blankets in their boat. No one would see us and we could get away from here. Think of it. The boat's really heavy, and we don't weigh that much. They might never notice that we're there. We could be stowaways!"

"You're nuts," said Nora, looking towards the boat, despite her scornful words, "but it might be our only chance to get out of here alive. Come on."

> "Oh Death, old Captain,
> it is time!
> Raise the anchor!"
> Charles Baudelaire:
> "Les Fleurs du Mal. Le Voyage, VIII."

CHAPTER FORTY FIVE

"I can't breath," said Lynn, pushing the wool blanket away from her face.

"Don't do that," said Nora, "they're coming!"

In answer to Nora's words, Lynn heard the heavy clumping of leather boots approaching the boat. Both girls stifled gasps as one end of the blanket was lifted and something cold and stiff was placed next to them. They hardly dare breath as the men repeated the action four more times until the blanket that covered the two girls now sheltered a far heavier load. Nora looked at Lynn as they felt the boat being pushed down the banks towards the North River. It wasn't until they felt the rocking motion of water under the boat, that either girl dared to look at what was with them under the blankets.

Nora felt her eyes widen in horror when she realized that they shared their close space with stiff, dead bodies.

"Don't scream," she hissed to Lynn as Nora put her hand over her friend's mouth. "Do you promise?"

Lynn gave Nora a wide eyed nod, and Nora removed her hand.

"Captain English, sir, I think one of them might still be alive," shouted a voice.

"Damn," said Nora, unable to keep back her frustration, "he heard me."

"That's not possible, Maurice," said the Captain. "They were as cold and as stiff as logs when we picked them up. Put your back to that oar, man, before we really have something to worry about. Dead is dead, and I'm sworn to see that these souls are given a proper burial. Let's not be adding any new bodies to the pile."

"Aye Captain," said the seaman. Both girls breathed a sigh of relief as they felt the flatboat take on the steady motion of the river. Once again they heard Philip English begin to sing the 'Skye Boat' song.

"It's almost like he wants someone to hear him," said Lynn, realizing that the man's song more than covered any sound she might make.

"You're right, it's kinda' weird isn't it?" said Nora, pushing the body next to her. "I don't care if he is dead, he's squishing me."

"I don't care what he's doing to you," said Lynn, trying to wiggle away from the body Nora was pushing towards her, "just keep him away from me! Yuck."

It was then that the body Nora had been shoving fell across Lynn's lap and both girls realized that it had no head. Lynn let out a bloody scream that echoed across the river in the still August twilight.

"Who in hell are you?" yelled Philip English as he tore the protecting blankets away from Nora and Lynn.

"We're nobody. Really," said Lynn, grabbing at Nora hand.

"That's right, nobody at all," said Nora, taking Lynn's shaking hand and squeezing it tightly.

"Whoever you are, I know you're not from around here," said Philip English, beginning to laugh. "Here now, don't look so afraid. Think you that I'm going to run you through with my sword? I can tell by the look of you that's there's no harm in you. Sit down upon the boards and explain yourselves. 'Tis only the adding of your weight that really makes me think of tossing you over the side."

"But we don't weigh that much, see?" said Lynn, pulling Tituba's shawl around her tightly to show how slender she really was.

"Aye, you don't," said Philip with a smile, "but every penny's weight makes a difference when you're trying to make speed down this river. She's a funny one, she is, and has always been a bit temperamental."

"Maybe that's because the Indians are right. Maybe this river really is a secret passageway to the underworld," said Nora.

"Look here, Captain, there's something funny about these two. Why, see the way that lass is dressed," said Maurice, pointing at Nora. "And that other one, she wears the shawl of that slave, you know the one they arrested as a witch! Slit their throats and throw them overboard before they get us all killed!"

"Aye Captain, he's right," said another of Philip English's scurvies, taking his hands from the oars and bending to touch Lynn's only covering.

"Keep rowing, you fool," said Philip, looking back towards the mouth of the river. "The only thing that's going to get us caught is lack of speed. Row, lad, before someone decides to find out what this girl was screaming about."

"Aye, Captain," said the mate, looking disappointed.

"Thomas always did enjoy a bit of throat cutting." said Philip, tickling Lynn's quivering chin. "Buck up now, lass, I know you mean no harm. I don't know why you picked our boat to hide on, but I think it's a fair bet that you want no more to do with the 'honest' folk of Salem than I do. Am I right?"

"Yes," said Lynn, smiling shyly at Philip.

"Well then, I'll give you what passage I can if you promise that you'll say none of what you've seen here," said Philip looking towards the east as he shielded his eyes from the merciless glare of the setting sun. "'Tis towards a cold dark place we're heading, a place that may be the home of these folk for many a year until I can return and give them a proper burial. 'Tis not as I would have it, but it's the best I can do for them for now."

"And then you'll go back to New York," said Nora, under her breath, not realizing she had spoke aloud.

"How did you know about that?" asked Philip roughly as he grabbed the girl by her collar.

"It was just a lucky guess," said Nora, realizing with horror that her words had been spoken aloud.

As I watched Philip with the two girls I knew I had to try to make my presence known. Besides, the lure of his earthly form was almost more than I could bear. How I had loved and still loved my husband, Philip English.

"Take your hands off that child, Philip!" I said. To my amazement, the force of my body encompassed my soul as I appeared before my husband in ghostly form.

"Is that you, Mary?" said Philip, dropping Nora to the wooden planks below.

"Aye my love, it is," I said reaching out to touch my husband's human hand with my misty fingertips.

"I love thee with the breath,
Smiles, tears, of all my life!-
And if God chooses,
I shall love thee better after death."
Elizabeth Barrett Browning:
Sonnets from the Portuguese, "No.43."

CHAPTER FORTY SIX

"Are you real?" asked Philip as his flesh touched me, sending tremors through the soul I had though of as dead for over three centuries.

"Yes," I whispered as I drew him away from watching eyes.

"Can anyone else see you?" he asked, looking back to see his men rowing towards Juniper Point, undisturbed by any ghostly vision.

"Only the girls," I said, "and they've seen me before."

"I don't understand, Mary. What's happened to you? Have you died?"

"Not as you know me in your time, my love," I said to him gently, touching his face, "but I am destined to die before you and take on the form you now see. It is only because of a chain of gracious acts, begun by you this very day, that we will be joined after death and for all eternity."

"Tell me. Tell me all, my Mary," said Philip, barely able to contain the sorrow in his voice as he looked towards the sunset.

"I will, if you promise not to be afraid of me," I said.

"I promise," said Philip.

It almost broke my heart to tell my beloved of what lay ahead, but I knew I must if I were to save us all. I know from experience that there is nothing more cruel than to know what is to come and be unable to alter even a moment of time.

"So then, the dead of Salem Town keep their promise, even beyond the grave," said Philip when I was finished.

"Aye."

"Then I will be afraid of nothing," he said, looking at me with a hunger that I knew well. "And what of those two?"

"Perhaps you and I can work a magic of our own," I said to him, putting his hand to my breast as I kissed him on the lips.

"How strange that even your ghostly form can make me feel thus," said Philip, returning my ardor in spite of himself, "are you sure you're not my own living Mary come to play a joke on me?"

"Look at me closely, love," I said to him. "The son I carried when you left me has been taken from this body for some time now. Feel you that there is naught here but my spirit?"

"Aye, it's true," said Philip, touching me with wonder. "Did you say we shall have a son?"

"Yes, a son he will be, and we named him John. He was such a beautiful baby. How I hated to leave him, so small and helpless without a mother's love. But you did a fine job in bringing him to manhood, my darling. Our Johnny sailed with you to the ports of the world, helping you to build your great fortune. His was a long and happy life, Philip, so I suppose I should not be sad, but somehow it still pains me that I missed so much."

"Mary, tell me that this is all a cruel joke, please!" said Philip, turning from me and wrapping his arms around his body like a small boy. "I don't think I could bear it if you left me. What good would anything be without you?"

"Did I say one word about leaving you?" I said putting my arms around his and turning Philip towards me. "There is only one destiny for either of us, and that is to spend all of time with each other. My body died before yours, Philip, but my soul has always been with you. There is no way we can ever be parted from one another unless the Devil rips you from my arms."

"And that is why you are here," said Philip, looking over my head to the two girls who had discovered a small sack of apples and were munching away at them as if they were on a Sunday afternoon outing.

"That is why I am here," I said echoing his words. "And we must act quickly before the curse that still lays upon Salem, three centuries hence, parts us forever. Help me, Philip, you were always so clever and could see many sides of a problem when the rest of us could see but one. Tell me what I must do and I will do it!"

"You're wrong there, Mary," said Philip, touching me again in a way that made me want to melt into his arms forever, "it was always you who could figure and cajole your way out of anything. By God, what a team we make. It's almost as if the heavens intended us to be one soul, not two."

"Philip, my love," I screamed, grabbing his face and kissing both his cheeks," that's it, that's the answer!"

"What's the answer?" asked Philip, looking about to see if anyone had heard me.

It seemed miraculous, but odd, that our traveling companions were totally oblivious to our conversation. Or was it something else? Was there some God or Goddess playing with us so that we carried out their plan?

"Don't you see?" I said, "you're the past and I'm the future. Perhaps if we join together we can take the girls back to the present!"

"But what about the curse that is upon us? I thought you brought them back here to break the curse. From what I can see nothing is any better than before you came here."

"You're wrong Philip, oh how wrong you are," I said laughing and dancing a merry jig around him. "Look at what the smaller girl has wrapped about her. 'Tis the shawl that the witch, Tituba, gave to protect her. Something tells me that fate's wheel has already been set in motion. All we have to do is give it a little push."

"And how do we do that?" asked Philip, smiling as he kissed my waiting lips.

"How else, my love, how else," I said as I sank into his waiting embrace and joined him, flesh to flesh, soul to soul.

"Eternity was in that moment."
William Congreve: *The Old Bachelor*, act IV, sc.vii.

CHAPTER FORTY SEVEN

I held onto Philip tightly as a great wind engulfed us. From somewhere far away I heard the barking and growling of a dog, and then suddenly I was ripped from his arms and swept up into a whirlwind. I heard myself screaming his name soundlessly within me, but there was no answer save for the rushing of the wind. I felt as if I had been torn from my mother's womb and left to wander alone and friendless in the winds of hell.

Then, just as I was beginning to lose hope, I heard the sounds of children laughing and turned my head to see Nora and Lynn running towards me. They were followed by a dark creature, I thought it might be the dog I had heard, but I wasn't sure. All I know is that everything went dark and when I opened my eyes again I was lying on the dusty floor of the old furniture store. Nora and Lynn were standing above me, each girl holding the apple she had been eating on Philip's boat.

"We're home, Aunt Mary," said Nora, staring at me as I began to cry. Both she and Lynn had reverted to their spiritual forms. Lynn's true body still lay in her grave and Nora's body rested in a coma in Salem hospital. Once again the room was peopled with ghosts, Philip and myself, Lynn and Nora, and old Giles snoring in the corner. The only mortal amongst us was Lillith, the witch.

"Philip, don't go," I sobbed as despair filled me.

"I'm not going anywhere, said my ghostly husband, kneeling by my side.

"But you did, you did!" I sobbed turning my head away from the specter that had once been my real husband. How could I tell him that I was crying for all we had lost, all we would never have again. I wanted the earthly Philip, the one who had held me only an instant ago, not this shadow man who haunted my existence. And yet, weren't they one in the same? I looked towards my Philip, the ghostly soul that was a match for my own, and suddenly realized that he had not really changed. The flesh was no more, but the strength and heart that made up what the real Philip English had been, remained intact. It was at that moment that I realized that I had been holding this Philip at arms length while I longed for the old one, the one who had walked Salem's streets with human feet. And how would I feel if he had turned from me just because I was a spirit and not a real woman? I would have been destroyed by his cruelty and lost in this world of shadows forever. It was strange, but in a way I had been longing for what had been standing before me all along.

"Everything's going to be all right, my love," said Philip, pressing his cheek to mine as he shared my tears.

"You're crying," I said in astonishment.

"Am I?" he said gruffly, wiping his face with his sleeve like a like a little boy.

"Why?"

"Because, when you disappeared I had the oddest feeling that I might never see you again. The same thing happened to me many years ago, during that terrible time when we were in hiding in New York. It was that time I had to leave you alone. Something happened that frightened me beyond life itself. I saw your spirit even though I was miles from the real you. I was afraid that you had left me forever."

"Then you've known all along that I was destined to go back to our Salem."

"Yes, but I was never sure where you went after you disappeared from the North River that day. I've always thought that we might never see each other again after that moment."

"And still you let me go."

"I had to," said Philip, holding me tighter than even his old living self could have done.

"It's all so strange Philip, it's like everything just goes round and round in a circle and we never really own the time we're standing in, no matter where we are."

"All I know is that you're here and so am I, and I'm never going to let you out of my sight again," said Philip, kissing me with a passion I hadn't felt in years.

"Oops," said Nora as she dropped the apple she had been eating. It rolled between Philip's feet as he held me close.

"What's this?" he asked as he picked the apple up and looked at it closely.

"Just an apple," said Nora, coming over to us and trying to take it from Philip's hand. "Lynn and I were starving and there was this sack of apples on your boat."

"Don't touch it!" said Philip, as Nora reached for the fruit. "And you," he said to Lynn, "give me your apple. It may be too late to do anything about this, but at least we can try."

"Here, let me take those," said Lillith with a horrified expression on her face. "I don't know how I could have been so stupid! I had forgotten that you girls would take on mortal forms once you went back to old Salem."

"What are you talking about?" asked Nora. "All we did was eat some apples. It felt wonderful to be hungry again."

"I know, darling," said Lillith gently, "but it's ancient knowledge that once a mortal eats of the fruit of a mystic land, he will be under that land's spell forever. You and Nora were mortals when you went back to the Salem of long ago, a Salem that is now a mystic land."

"But if it doesn't exist, it can't hurt us," said Nora firmly, taking both apples from Lillith's hands and throwing them towards a trash bin that stood at the front of the store. Unfortunately she missed and hit the large plate glass window that formed the front wall of the store, smashing the already cracked glass into a thousand pieces. To Lillith's astonishment, a dark man with glowing yellow eyes stepped right through the shattered glass and drew a gun on her.

"Put your hands in the air!" he yelled as he cocked the gun.

"What the devil was he doing in that galley?"
Moliere:
Les Fourberies de Scapin, act II, sc. xi.

CHAPTER FORTY EIGHT

"Jim, it's me, Lillith!" cried Lillith as she realized that the light had been playing tricks on her eyes. The dark man with glowing yellow eyes was just her old friend, Jim Proctor, highlighted by the sodium vapor lamp that stood outside the store.

"What in hell are you doing breaking into places and smashing windows, Lillith?" said Jim, putting his gun back in it's holster.

Lillith looked at Jim, and in that instant made a decision. She knew that once she shared her secrets with him there was no going back, but she had no choice.

"I didn't smash anything," she said quietly, looking back over her shoulder to where the ghosts and spirits hovered. "Nora English did it."

"Nora? How could Nora have done such a thing? She's in the hospital in a coma," said Jim as he peered into the dim, dusty store.

"She's standing right there," laughed Lillith with a decidedly disturbing edge to her voice. "I don't see why you can't see her. In fact I don't see why you can't see all of them. I always have. I don't want to see them, but I have no choice. What's wrong with you, Jim Proctor? You grew up in this town the same as I did. Why can't you see them too?"

"Maybe you should sit down and try to calm yourself, Lill," said Proctor as he put his arm around Lillith and tried to guide her towards a shabby wicker chair.

"You think I'm crazy, don't you, Jim?" laughed Lillith. "You all do. You let me roam around town, telling everyone I'm a witch, but you don't really believe me. But think, Jim, think for one minute. What if I really am a witch? What if everything I do is really sanctioned by the spirits in this town? What if my witchcraft is really as powerful as I pretend it is? What would you say if I told you this town was filled with real witches and spirits and ghosts, and that I see them all, everyday?"

"I would say that it's time for you to talk to someone who could help you," said Jim quietly. "You know as well as I do that the witchcraft you practice is a nice little religion based on nature and old ways of healing. It doesn't have anything to do with ghosts and spirits. You don't really see ghosts, Lillith, you're just tired and half mad from losing your daughter the way you did. Why, anyone would go crazy from such a thing. Let me take you home, Lillith. I'll just write up the window as vandalism and we can forget about it. But you have to promise me that you'll get some help."

"We do need some help," I said, "but it's not the kind of help you think we need, sir."

"Who's that!" yelled Jim, drawing his gun again.

"'Tis I, Mary English, I and my husband, and the two girls here, Nora and Lynn. We can hardly count old Giles in the corner. He's been asleep for hours now. I find that strange for a spirit, as we need no sleep, but sometimes we do it because it reminds us of our earthly ways. And we all know how curious Giles can be at times."

"What? Who?" muttered Jim, trying to point his gun at my voice.

"Don't look so troubled, sir," I said. "We won't hurt you. How could we ever hurt one of John Proctor's family? He that was so brave and gave his life so that his Elizabeth could live and bear her babe."

"Who are you?" demanded Jim Proctor, grabbing Lillith and making her stand behind him as he backed towards the door.

"I've already told you that, but you're trying your best not to listen. Perhaps it would be better if you could see us. What do you say, Witch Lillith, is it time to let this man in on our little secret?"

"I don't see how we can do anything else now," said Lillith. "It's just as well. I know I can't go on this way by myself any longer. Jim's not all wrong when he says I might be going a little crazy. It would help to have another living human in on this thing."

"Very well then. Here we are," I said, summoning the mist around me and wishing us all to appear before Jim Proctor.

> "Twinkle, twinkle, little bat!
> How I wonder where you're at!
> Up above the world you fly,
> Like a teatray in the sky."
> Lewis Carroll: *Alice's Adventures in Wonderland.*

CHAPTER FORTY NINE

It was Jim Proctor's turn to fall into the old wicker chair as we appeared before him, first myself, and then Philip, moving towards Proctor with the stately grace of a man welcoming an old friend's son home from the sea.

"There's really nothing to be afraid of," Philip said to Jim as he glided to the human man's side and removed the gun from his hand. "Here let me take charge of this before you blow your foot off. You look better than most when they see us for the first time, but you never know what might happen. These things are far more sensitive than the firearms I used."

Jim Proctor gave a helpless grunt as Philip moved away from him and Nora and Lynn's spirits came into few.

"Dear God," whispered Jim as he saw Lynn, still wrapped in Tituba's shawl. "She looks so alive, so real. It's like she never died."

"I didn't, not really," said Lynn, laughing at Jim's stunned expression. "It was Mister English here that made it all happen. I'm not sure how, but I don't really feel dead, whatever that feels like. I just feel kind of light."

"And has Nora died?" said Jim.

"No," said Nora. "My spirit was just pulled from my body to this place. I'm really still in a coma back at Salem hospital. I wouldn't be here at all if Lynn hadn't needed me. We're friends, you see, just like you and Aunt Lillith are."

"I don't believe this," said Jim, looking from one ghost to another.

"You don't have to believe in us," I said gently, "that will come in time. For now it would be enough if you could just help us. Lillith is right. She can't go on this way alone. She needs another mortal to help her."

"Help her do what, Ma'am?" said Jim, taking the first step across the line as he spoke to me. I knew that once a mortal started to talk to a ghost it was only a matter of time before we became friends.

"Find my killer," said Lynn sadly. "And we have to hurry, too. He wants to kill Nora."

"I couldn't agree more," said Jim, 'but it's only a matter of time before we find Jake. I wouldn't worry about Nora. I've a man guarding her."

"But you don't understand," said Lynn, pressing her hands against her sides in an effort to remain calm. "Jake's not the killer!"

"Of course he is," said Jim. "All the physical evidence says he is. The fingerprints we took from his cave down at the 'Willows' matched the ones that were at the crime scene where we found your body, Lynn. There's no doubt in my mind that he's the killer."

"Maybe his body killed me, but it wasn't Jake who killed me," insisted Lynn. "There was someone else inside of him making him do all those awful things. I saw him! Jake's eyes are not the ones that were staring at me, laughing at me, while I died. The eyes that killed me were the eyes of George Corwin, High Sheriff of Salem."

"What are you talking about?" asked Jim.

"The man who killed me was George Corwin, Jake's ancestor. You know, the one who arrested and help hang all those people back in 1692. I saw him myself. I'm sure it was him!"

"Perhaps I'd better explain what she's talking about," I said to Master Proctor as I sat down next to him and placed my hand on his knee. "Let me begin at the beginning and make quick work of it. That way we can leave this place and do what must be done to save Nora and the rest of us. My name is Mary English and I was born in this town in the year 1653...."

"I still don't believe I'm doing this," said Jim as he helped Lillith into his cruiser. In the back seat were five ghostly spirits, Nora, Lynn, myself, Philip, and old Giles, still blinking from his overlong nap.

"Just hurry up and get us to the hospital before something awful happens to Nora," said Lynn.

PART SIX

TOUCHING THROUGH THE VEIL

> "Fifteen men on the Dead Man's Chest-
> Yo-ho-ho and a bottle of rum!
> Drink and the devil had done for the rest-
> Yo-ho-ho, and a bottle of rum!"
> Robert Louis Stevenson: *Treasure Island*.

CHAPTER FIFTY

"That must be the new man, Gabe Brink," said Jim to Lillith as they walked quietly down the corridor towards Nora's room.

The patrolman nodded at Jim as he checked Jim's badge.

"Glad to have you with us," said Jim as Brink returned the badge and turned towards Lillith.

"This is Nora's guardian, Lillith March," said Jim as the new man looked at Lillith. Something in the way Gabriel Brink stared at Lillith made Jim uneasy. Perhaps it was just the way the light hit the man's yellowish gray eyes, or maybe it was just the shock of what Jim had been through in the past hour. Whatever the reason, Jim Proctor felt that the man was looking at Lillith as if he wanted to devour her on the spot. The expression on the man's face reminded Jim of a mean dog, waiting to rip apart his prey.

"Maybe that's not a bad thing in a man who's supposed to be guarding a girl from a murderer," thought Jim to himself as he pushed Lillith towards Nora's door.

"That man makes me nervous," said Lillith uneasily, picking up the same feelings Jim had.

"He's a policeman, trained to think everyone might be a criminal," said Jim.

"But the way he looked at me, it frightened me."

"Let's see how Nora is," said Jim, almost on overload. He made a mental note to make a thorough background check on Brink as soon as he got back to the station.

"Nora, Nora, can you hear me?" asked Lillith as she took the mortal girl's hand. Behind her stood the shadow of Nora's soul, wavering in the glow of the florescent lights.

"I think something's happening," said the spirit girl as she grabbed for Lynn.

"Then let it happen," said Lillith, stroking the unconscious girl's brow. Lillith closed her eyes and began to move her lips silently. Soon her silent prayers became a whisper as a gentle twilight breeze filled the room.

"Ah," said Philip as the cooling wind brought with it the smell of lilies, "the witch has her powers strong upon her now. Smell that perfume, Johnny Proctor? 'Tis the aura of the east wind that she brings forth."

"I don't understand," said Jim, shaking his head as the heady smell began to lull him into an unwelcome drowsiness.

"It's quite simple, really," said Philip, smiling at me gently as he attempted to give the mortal, Jim Proctor, his first lesson in the ancient lore of the Wiccan religion. "All of us belong to one of the four winds. They guard over us and protect us as we wander through the worlds of the spirit. There is the east wind that celebrates new adventures and protects those blessed with ambition and energy. It is called upon when you need courage, patience and clarity. Its fragrance is the lily, gentle and eternal. Then, there is the south wind. Its fragrance is that of the lilac. The south wind belongs to those filled with love and fantasy. They yearn for fulfillment. It is the perfume of enchantments and close comrades."

"This is ridiculous," said Jim as the twilight in the room took on the white glow of a fresh spring morning.

"Deny what you want, sir," said Philip, guiding the confused mortal man to a chair that had been placed next to Nora's bed. "The truth of it all will fill you soon enough. For now, your work is simply to listen and learn from what I have to say. I wouldn't be moved to tell you such things if there weren't a purpose to it. What it is, I don't know, but I've learned to trust my instincts in such things. I still have two winds left to tell you about."

"All right, all right," said Jim as a sudden, blinding headache caught him behind the eyes. "Just hurry up so I can get some aspirin."

"Right," said Philip, winking at me mischievously. Whatever Philip had done to Jim Proctor made him a docile slave to Philip's voice until my husband chose to release the poor man. Not for the first time, I wondered if Philip might not be the most powerful being in Salem. He had hidden powers that he revealed to no one, not even me.

"The other two winds are the west and the north. The west wind has the beloved fragrance of the rose. It belongs to those who are destined to erase doubt and prevail over fear, envy and hate. The west wind brings with it new confidence and the renewal of hope."

"And what about the north wind," said Jim.

"The north wind transcends all other winds and is the most powerful of all. It brings with it the fragrance of late summer, ripe apples, new mown hay, sweet corn and the crispness of the cooling nights. It is the golden wind that carries the fullness of life and the threat of death in its breath. The north wind is the source of all the strength that lies in the spirit. It can protect or kill. It grants upon those strong enough to withstand it the knowledge of what should be done to keep mankind well and the divine powers to carry out their task. It is the ancient wind of the Celtic Kings who offered themselves up for human sacrifice so that their people could live. It is filled with golden power and the blackness of death."

Jim Proctor blinked at Philip as the terrible pounding in his head magically disappeared. I could tell from his face that his pain had been replaced with a healing energy. That same energy began to fill us all as Lillith's chant became louder. Her words were so ancient that they lost all meaning in modern tongue, but there was something in them that called soul to soul and brought us all into her magic circle. I could feel our energy fusing together into a great whole, willing the spirit of Nora English to rejoin her body and bring about a healing that would remove all evil from her mortal frame. The healing power that filled the room was so powerful that it filled any who stood in its presence and removed any illness of mind or body. I could feel the darkness leave each one of us as we lay under the spell of the east wind.

I watched in wonder as Nora's spirit faded back into her living body. There was something deep within me that wanted to cry out to her at that last moment and keep Nora's ghostly self with me, but that would have been just the yearning of my own loneliness, calling out for a kinswoman to keep me company in my misty world. The goodness of the east wind quickly overcame my longing and I was able to watch Nora become whole once again.

"Her eyes are opening!" said Jim, jumping from the chair and leaning over Nora as Lillith took her foster daughter's hand.

"Is that you, Aunt Lillith?" said Nora, with eyes as alert and bright as the light that filled the room.

"The bell invites me.
Hear it not, Duncan; for it is a knell
That summons thee to heaven or to hell."
William Shakespeare: *Macbeth*, II, i, 62.

CHAPTER FIFTY ONE

"And you're still here too, Aunt Mary," were Nora's next words.

"You can see me?" I said with astonishment as Nora looked right at me.

"Of course I can. And I can see Uncle Philip, and Lynn and old Giles too!" Nora said laughing happily.

"What? What is that?" said Giles, coming towards the bed in astonishment. "You can see me too? I didn't think anyone could really see me but someone like her," he said nodding towards Lillith. "'Tis an odd thing."

"Not so odd," said Lillith. "Nora's been through the veil that divides this mortal world from all the others. It only makes sense that a little of her should remain behind, joining her yesterdays to her tomorrows. Isn't that true, Nora."

"I think so," said Nora, looking at Lynn with widened eyes. "But I do know one thing for sure. There's a promise I made when I was over on your side that I have to keep. If I don't, something awful might happen. I hope it's not too late. My promise was to the witch, Tituba. I swore I would come back and free her if she saved Lynn. But I don't know how I can do that now! See, look at Lynn. She's still wearing the shawl Tituba gave us."

"Calm yourself, Nora," I said as I looked first at Lynn and then at Lillith, "I think I know what must be done."

"Of course," said Lillith, grabbing two blue checked hospital 'johnies' from the hook attached to the back of Nora's door. "Go in the bathroom and put these on, Lynn, one front to back, the other back to front. Then come out and give us the shawl. I think that we just might be able to keep Nora's promise."

"I am getting real sick of having nothing to wear," muttered Lynn, taking the hospital gowns reluctantly and slamming the door of the bathroom after her.

"But it might be dangerous to bring Tituba into this time," said Giles, eyeing Lillith like an old pirate. "Remember the last time she came to Salem. Scores of people wound up either dead or in prison. I think the whole thing is a bad idea."

"We have no choice," said Lillith. "Nora gave her word. If we don't summon Tituba forth there may be consequences beyond our imagining."

"Well, do what you like," said Giles, "but don't say I didn't warn you." With those words, Giles crossed his arms across his chest and glared at us all.

"Here," said Lynn, emerging from the bathroom and handing the shawl to Lillith.

"Mary," said Lillith, "take this end of the shawl and hold it tightly while I twist this into it." Lillith took a small onyx ring from her finger and placed it inside the first twist she made in the shawl. I quickly grabbed the other end of the red wool as Lillith began to strike the shawl with her hand and chant an ancient rune.

"Upon this stone I knock a rag

To raise the wind in the Lady's name,

It shall not lie or cease or die

Until I please again."

Suddenly the while light that had filled the room turned lavender and the smell of lilies was replaced by the fragrance of lilacs.

"She comes from the south," said Philip.

"That I do, Master English," said the mocking voice of Tituba as she stepped from the mist. The dark woman was a splash of brilliant color standing in the dimness of Nora's drab hospital room. The many hued head scarf that was tied about Tituba's head crowned a face that was both round and sharp at the same time. In fact, the entire woman was a study in contrasts. Her skin was far more lustrous than Nora remembered it. There was even a shade of red under the slave's blackness that gave the impression of fine mahogany. For the first time, Nora realized that Tituba might be of mixed ancestry.

"That's quite true, missy," said Tituba, reading Nora's thoughts. "I be of more than any have ever thought I was. Do you think I was born and bred on this cold, god-forsaken rock, with no sunshine or passion flowing through my veins? I come from the land of Barbados. My father's people were from Africa, cruelly captured and chained to work the fields, but my mother was a Caribe Indian. She was a lovely, wild thing that was captured one night as she lay with my father. She was a Voodoo woman, she was, and couldn't stand the cage they placed her in for all to view. It was only the babe in her belly that kept her from taking her life those first few months. After I was born and safely in the arms of another slave who had milk in her breasts, but a dead babe in her arms, my own true mother threw herself upon a sharpened stick and bled to death before any could stop her. But that wasn't the end of it. She had her revenge upon them all. Every night her spirit would walk the sugar plantation where I was. She would come to me and teach me her ways. I can still hear her beautiful voice, singing to me as I fell to sleep in her arms. Then I would wake in the morning to the screams of someone from the big house. Sometimes my mother would take the breath of a slave who followed his master's bidding and was cruel to his fellow slaves, but at other times it would be the master's family that would feel her revenge."

"Then came the day when the young mistress came running from the house, screaming like a demon from hell. In her arms were the bodies of her twins, boys they were, and under a year old at the time. She came right for my hut and threw the bodies of those babes in my face. Then she took a knife from her bodice and fell upon me. I should have died right there, a girl of thirteen with my own womanhood newly upon me, but my mother's spirit was with me. It was the first time I had ever seen her in daylight, without the protection of the moon to guard her, and I knew that it cost her dearly. The knife twisted in the mistress' hand and turned upon her, slitting her white throat. I knew, as I looked at the bodies in my hut, that my own death would be long and terrible. Everyone would think that I had killed my mistress! It must have been the Voodoo gods that guided me that day, because I have never been that quick again. I took the knife that lay on the ground and placed it in my mistress' hand. Then I placed the two babes beside her. I will always remember running from that hut, screaming for my master to come quickly and see what the mistress had done to herself. I babbled on and on about how the mistress had gone mad, smothered her babes and then taken her own life. The wonder of it was that they believed me! Then the master decided that there was no more room on his plantation for the daughter of the Voodoo woman. I was bad luck. So I was sold away from my father and my home. I was bought by Reverend Parris. He made me couple with that worthless Indian John so that he could have a crop of babies that he could sell into slavery for a profit. I cried the first few times, but by the time they tore my fifth babe from my arms, my misery was so deep that it was beyond tears. Then the Reverend decided to go home."

"Home. What kind of a home is this, where they punish you for a few spells with torture and hanging? I'd rather be starving in a grass hut in Barbados than eat like a pig in this land of hell. It's grateful I am to you, young Miss, that ye've kept your promise, but I can tell you that now that I'm here I'll not be lingering long. 'Tis for my real home I'll be setting sail for as soon as I can."

"I'm afraid you'll find that impossible, Tituba," I said as I handed her the red shawl.

"You're Mistress English!" said Tituba, staring at me as if she'd seen a ghost. "What are you doing here? My power of the 'mind's eye' saw you dead and gone many a year now."

"As you are, my dear," I said gently, putting my arm around my old acquaintance. "This is not the Salem of your time, Tituba. Back then you were released from prison. You were sold to a man who paid your prison fees and he did take you back towards your home. There he worked you to death in under a year. You died under the lash, pleading for a drink of water. What we've done is give you a new life, here in Salem Town. It is closer to the year Two Thousand than to the year Seventeen Hundred. You've slept for over three hundred years and now we've brought you once again to our bosom. Only this time you're surrounded by friends who suffered as you did, from the cruelties of others. I welcome you as a sister and hope you have a long existence amongst us."

"Then, I am a spirit as my mother was before me?" said Tituba.

"Aye lass, that you are," said Giles, smacking Tituba on the back.

"Why, Master Cory, 'tis you indeed," said Tituba, putting her hands on her hips and giving a deep chuckle. "I remember the day you were crushed to death beneath those stones! Then they took Martha but two days later and hanged her on Gallows Hill. How she cried out for you as they dragged her off. Well then, this is a surprise. And you, young miss," said Tituba, turning towards Nora, "are you a ghost too?"

"Not anymore," said Nora. "I'm real, and so are my mother and Sergeant Proctor here. The rest of you are ghosts, at least now you are. I'm still trying to sort the whole thing out myself. You all seem pretty real to me."

"And what about her," said Tituba, nodding her head towards Lynn.

"I'm a ghost, but I've only been one a couple of days," said Lynn.

"Well now," said Tituba, "this place is still full of surprises."

"I hope you'll be happy here," said Philip holding his hand out to Tituba in a formal gesture of welcome.

"As happy as I can be anywhere, I suppose," said Tituba, taking Philip's hand and shaking it firmly. "And I thank you for your hospitality. But I still think I'll be making my way southward as soon as possible."

"That's not possible," said Philip.

"And why is that, Master English?" said Tituba. "Who's stopping me?"

"We're all trapped in this town until we break the curse George Corwin has laid upon us," said Philip. "He has made some sort of pact with the Devil, and we can't figure out how to undo it. That's why these two girls went back into your time. They were trying to figure out how to break the curse, but as you know, they had to flee for their lives."

"And whose to say we can't defeat the Devil," said Tituba, staring first at Lillith, and then at me and Philip. "I've summoned him once or twice myself when I've needed him. Why, I did it for that young one there. 'Twas the only way to get her free. It was Tituba that sent the Devil after George Corwin so that they had time to escape. I suppose that's where the knave met the dark man and sold his soul to him."

"It could be," I said, looking at Tituba suspiciously. Had Giles Cory been right? Had we only succeeded in bringing the Devil closer to us?

"It seems that this place is made up of circles within circles with the Devil in the center of it all," said Tituba, sitting on the floor with crossed legs. "Why, it would take the power of the four winds to blow it all away."

"What did you say?" said Lillith, looking at Tituba in wonder.

"I said it would take the power of the four winds to blow...."

"Don't you see? That's it!" said Lillith jumping from one foot to the other like an excited child. "If we could just gather together four witches with the four winds at their back, we might be able to blow away some of the evil, maybe the curse itself."

"What's she talking about, Philip?" I asked, moving back so that Lillith wouldn't step on my ghostly foot.

"I think I know," said Philip with a strange smirk on his face, "and I'm mad at myself for not thinking of it before. All we need is to join the four winds together. Not even the Devil could fight the combined forces of the universe. And we're already half way there."

"Maybe even more than halfway," said Lillith, turning towards Philip with a brilliant smile.

"There is something in the wind."
William Shakespeare: *King Richard III*, i, 69.'

CHAPTER FIFTY TWO

"Stand here, Lillith," said Philip, "and do a bit of what you did when you brought Nora back to us. And Tituba, you stand here and summon forth the power you felt inside as you traveled towards us," he said motioning Tituba to face Lillith.

The two woman did as he said, and almost immediately the room was filled with the fragrances of lilacs and lilies, intermingling deliciously.

"Now then, Mary. You stand in between them and think the thoughts you had when you called Lillith to save Nora."

"I don't understand," I said.

"You will," said Philip as he gently pushed me forward until I was shoulder to shoulder with Tituba and Lillith. I closed my eyes and almost immediately was filled with the familiar sensation I always felt when my soul left my body. The rosy glow inside my head suddenly moved away from me and filled the room with the scent of summer roses.

"I thought so!" said Philip triumphantly. "You're the west wind, Mary! We have almost everything we need to fight the devil."

"But what of the north wind?" said Lillith. "That is the rarest and hardest of all to find. Only one in a million possesses the north wind."

It was then I started to laugh. What Lillith had said echoed a pet phrase I had always used to describe Philip. He had always been my "one in a million." Philip heard my laugh and smiled firmly as he took his place in the center of our small circle. He closed his eyes and began to recite the "Lord's Prayer" as Tituba, Lillith and I held hands. The room began to glow with a golden light that engulfed the loveliness of our combined lilac, white and rose hues and soon all became one, fusing into a rainbow of color.

"Then we do have the power to break the curse," said Lillith, suddenly letting go of my hand and breaking our magic circle."

"Aye, we do," said Tituba, looking first at Lillith and then at me. "I never thought it was possible. I've heard of such things, but I only thought they were pretty tales you would tell a child."

"This is real, all right," said Philip quietly, "but it must be used very carefully. Too much magic has a way of coming back at you and asking for more than you can give."

"How true," said Lillith, looking at Lynn wistfully. "Do you think we could use our powers to bring someone back to life, someone who has only been dead a short time?"

"I'm afraid not," said Philip sadly, "that would be tampering with the otherworlds. Such a thing is the province of the Devil. If we used our powers that way, they would surely turn against us forever. No matter how bad something might be, I've learned it can always get worse. At least Lynn is still with us, even though she's a ghost."

"I suppose you're right," said Lillith, "but I can't help wishing it were different."

"It does no harm to wish, dearie," said Tituba kindly.

"And think of it, Mama!" said Lynn brightly. "Nora and I really did help. If we hadn't gone back to old Salem we would never have found Tituba and brought her back!"

"She's right," I said.

"Who's there," said Jim Proctor from the corner of the room where he had been quietly watching the going's on. We all turned to where he pointed and saw the face of a haggard young man peer through the hospital window.

"Jake," whispered Nora as Jake Corwin hoisted himself up on the sill and broke through the screen. We watched in silence as the wretched boy pulled himself through the ragged screen and collapsed on the floor.

"Someone help him!" said Nora, trying to get out of bed herself, but finding that she was too weak to stand. Jim Proctor rushed to the boy's side and gently lifted him to the bed, placing him beside Nora. Jake opened his eyes for a moment and then closed them again. His chest was barely moving as he struggled desperately for breath.

"What's wrong with him?" asked Nora.

"He has AIDS," I said, watching the slender boy warily. It seemed that all the evil energy that George Corwin had filled Jake with had left the boy. What lay before us was the shell of Jake Corwin. It was obvious that the boy had very little time left. "Philip, you said that it would be wrong to bring someone back to life after they died."

"Yes, it would be wrong because we would be interfering with the passage ways between this world and the otherworlds."

"But would there be anything wrong with saving someone from dying, especially someone who is young and who has been cruelly abused by the Devil's henchman?'

"Not a thing," said Philip, staring down at Jake. "It's hard to believe that this is the same body that hurt Nora and Lynn."

"It's not," said Lynn. "You saw his eyes. They were tired and sick, but they were innocent eyes. Jake Corwin is innocent. Please help him, Mama."

"Uncle Philip, can you save him?" asked Nora, holding Jake's unconscious body tightly against her own.

"Lillith," said Philip as he clutched the woman's hand, "it's up to you. You're the one with the greatest healing powers. Say what we should do for this boy."

"I don't know," said Lillith, eyeing Jake suspiciously. "It's hard for me to believe that he is entirely innocent. Lynn's dead, and it seems that nothing I can ever do will bring her back to life. She's been cheated of all the blessings a mortal woman can find on this earth. She'll never fall in love, marry, have children, or reach the fulfillment of old age. And most would say it's all that boy's fault. I know that you believe that it's George Corwin's fault, but there must have been something in this boy that Corwin saw. Something evil he could use. How else could Corwin have entered Jake and used him, body and soul?"

"That's not fair," said Nora, sitting up in bed and glaring at Lillith. "You don't know him the way I do. Jake may not be perfect, but there's nothing in him that's evil. I've known him all my life. It's not fair that he should die like this. Why, I bet that even the drug thing was caused by that evil ghost, that George Corwin. Jake used to hate taking anything that would make him feel different, he even told us so. Isn't that true, Lynn?"

"Yes."

"And then one day," continued Nora, "he comes up to us, slurring his words and with his pupils all dilated. There were track marks on his arms and he didn't care about anything anymore. It's like it happened overnight. I don't know a lot about how it's supposed to work, but it seems awful funny to me that he changed so quickly. It really was like he was possessed by something evil, something even greater than the stuff that he shot into himself. It's not fair that we should let him die! If we do, it's like we murdered him ourselves just because something evil used Jake to kill Lynn and hurt me. If we don't save him, we're no better than that murderer, George Corwin."

"She's right, Lillith," I said. "I've been a mother who has lost children, too. I think I know how you feel. But two murders can't make anything around here any better. It's time to turn this thing around and begin the healing in any way we can. And there's something else we need to think about. If Jake has AIDS then Nora might have it too. It's too early to tell with her, but the chances are pretty good that she may die the same way Jake is dying. She's come out of her coma and looks healthy now, but this AIDS, this plague, may yet claim her unless we do something to stop it. What we need is a miracle, and only you can give us that. I've seen what you can do and I know that you hold the power to vanish this thing in the palm of your hand."

Lillith looked first at Lynn and then at me. Then she walked over to the side of Nora's bed and touched Jake's almost motionless chest with the palms of both her hands. Silently she pressed firmly against him until he moaned with pain.

"Nora, take his hand," was all Lillith said as she closed her eyes and continued to press against Jake until his moans suddenly stopped. Then, from Lillith's own breast, a blinding white light flashed. It filled the room as it swirled around Lillith, Jake and Nora. It was as if they had become the light. Then, as suddenly as the light had appeared, it vanished, leaving us all in the gloom of the mortal world.

"What happened?" asked Jake as he sat up in the bed.

Nora, who was still holding his hand tightly, looked at Jake cautiously. "How do you feel?" she said as she took a deep breath.

"Like someone has been kicking me in the chest," said the boy, looking first at Nora and then at us in amazement. "But I feel good, too. In fact I feel better then I have for a long, long time. I feel like I've just woken up from some sort of bad dream, you know, like Dorothy in that storm."

"The Wizard of Oz," said Nora, laughing with delight.

"Unfortunately, your nightmare's not over yet, Jake," said Lillith, looking at Jake suspiciously. "There still lies within you the passageway that allowed the evil spirit to enter you. Until that's gone, nothing will ever be right for any of us. We're only halfway there."

"What's she talking about?" asked Jake.

"I'm talking about the spirit of George Corwin," said Lillith. "Once he discovers that you're well, he'll come back for you. The only reason he let you go in the first place was that you were no more use to him. He had what he wanted from you and was more than willing to let you die. But now that you're healthy and alert again, he can use you. We must exorcise George Corwin from you and fill you with a protective spell before he comes for you again."

"And then there's the matter of Lynn's murder and your assault on Nora," said Jim Proctor, fingering the handcuffs that hung from his belt.

"First things first," said Lillith, standing between Jake and Jim. "He's not going anywhere until we rid Jake of his evil demon. It may kill him, but we have to take that chance. Once George Corwin reenters him he's as good as dead anyway. Curing Nora and Jake of AIDS is only half the battle."

"What are you going to do to me?" asked Jake, looking around the room.

"Exorcise the Devil from you so that George Corwin can never use you to kill anyone again," said Lynn March, looking at Jake sadly.

"I'm sorry about everything I did," said Jake as the tears ran down his face, "but it wasn't really me, you have to believe that! I'd never hurt anyone. Please believe me!"

"We do," said Lillith, "but that doesn't change the fact that we must take the Devil from you, no matter the cost. Are you willing to let us try?"

"Yes," said Jake, staring into the eyes of Lynn March.

"O Death, old captain, it is time!
Raise the anchor!"
Charles Baudelaire: "Les Fleurs du Mal, Le Voyage, VIII."

CHAPTER FIFTY THREE

"Jim, could you handcuff Jake to the bed," said Lillith.

"Why?" asked Jim Proctor, feeling completely out of his depth. "What are you going to do to him?"

"It's not what I'm going to do to Jake, it's what the demons inside of him might try to do to him that scares me. You don't think they're going to leave without a fight, do you?"

"She's right, Sergeant Proctor," said Philip. "If you don't want to do it, I will. I've seen this once before, long ago when we founded Saint Peter's Church on the dead bodies of my friends. It's not pretty. We must protect the boy from himself, and us from him. I'm afraid it's the only way."

"All right," said Jim. "But I can tell you right now, this whole thing makes me really uncomfortable."

"Not as uncomfortable as having a murderer roaming around Salem," said Lillith. "There's no telling what George Corwin might do once he regains control of Jake's body."

"He wouldn't be able to do anything with Jake locked up," said Jim.

"There's no way you'd be able to keep the boy jailed," said Lillith. "George Corwin is more powerful than any mortal restraint. Only the supernatural can stop him now."

"I'm ready Sergeant Proctor," said Jake, holding his arms out to Jim. "I don't mind, really. Anything's better than what I've already been through."

"Put your wrists next to the headboard," said Jim gruffly, trying to hide the fact that he had been touched by the gentle submission in Jake's voice. Somehow there was nothing in the boy that reminded Jim of a murderer.

After Jim had secured Jake to the bed, Lillith, Tituba and I stood facing Jake. Tituba stood to the left, myself to the right and Lillith at the foot of the bed. Then Philip took his place in the center of the room, a little behind Lillith, and he began to chant. This time there was nothing of the Lord's Prayer in his utterances. The tongue he used was that of the ancients. There was something about the lilt of Philip's words that reminded me of a time forgotten, but what was it? I found my thoughts drifting away from the starkly white hospital room and wandering down a brightly lit corridor as Philip's voice droned on. It seemed as if Philip's voice was merging with the beloved voice of another, a deeper, rougher voice.

Then, in a moment of revelation, it came to me. I had heard Philip's words before from my own father's lips. How young I had been when he died. Too young to really remember his face. My recollections of my father, William Hollingsworth, were made up more of feelings of touch and sound than anything else. And here was Philip echoing my dearest father's very words, words that I had not understood at the time anymore than I did now, but words that brought to mind the season of winter and holly trees full of lovely red berries. It seemed that the sparkle of snow in the sun and the glistening of shiny green holly leaves filled my being as I desperately tried to focus my thoughts on the job at hand.

"Dreaming of the Holly King are ye?" asked Tituba as she stared into my face thoughtfully.

"What?" I asked.

"The Holly King, love," she said, nodding her head sagely. "'Twas said by some folks who lived about Salem that in old times there was two kings that ruled that ancient land, the Oak King, who made his way through the world at Midsummer's Eve, and the Holly King who took over at the Winter's Solstice. To me it was just more of the thing I knew as magic, but there were some hereabouts that really believed it had the greatest power of all."

"Yes, I suppose that was it," I murmured, reluctant to share my secret self with anyone, especially anyone as talkative as Tituba.

My mind cleared slowly as I concentrated on the familiar drone of Philip's words. Lillith reached for my hand and I reached for Tituba's as the room began to fill with a gentle fog. I felt Philip at my back, as he placed his hands on my shoulders. The four of us began to sway as one person as the light fog started to take on a darker hue. Soon the room was filled with an encompassing darkness.

Suddenly, Philip's voice was silent and the four of us stood in complete quiet, waiting. Waiting.

From out of the dark fog came the plaintive wail of a single bagpipe. The tone was both sad and heroic at the same time. A moment later the bagpipe was joined by the steady beating of a tight skinned drum sounding like the measured beat of a man walking towards the gallows to his death. Soon, the entire room seemed filled with an entire army of pipers and drummers spurring some unseen soul toward a gallant death. Then, the song of the pipers and drum was taken up by some sort of a large reed instrument. It sounded like the recorders I had heard the seamen playing on the docks of Salem, but this instrument was deeper, with a more masculine resonance. The instrument seemed to be ascending the scale as it took the now familiar melody into a new realm. I closed my eyes and could almost see the steady stream of men and women who had bravely made their way up Gallows Hill to defend the truth. It was at that moment that I felt a oneness with the linked spirits around me. Tituba, Lillith, Philip and myself became, in that instant, a single mind with four bodies. It was the music of our own souls, forged by the fires of Salem, that we were hearing. That music, oh that music! The very universe must have felt its shattered glory as it worked its magic into Jake Corwin, seductively drawing the evil from the lad, much as a snake charmer draws a snake from a basket.

I heard the boy cry out the timeless shriek of the Celtic warrior as the Devil's spirit left him. His cry was echoed by a chorus of other children's voices. Perhaps they were the dead children of Salem who had suffered so. A great wind filled the room, sucking the Devil's dark essence into its center. I could only pray that the thing that had tormented Jake Corwin was all the wind would claim as it howled around us, forming a miniature tornado. Then, as suddenly as it appeared, it left. I gathered my courage to me and began to count the heads of my friends and family. To my great relief, they were all there.

"Listen," whispered Nora quietly as she looked deeply into Jake's clear eyes. We turned as one body towards the open window that Jake had crawled through, and listened as the clear, angelic tones of Saint Peter's bells claimed the early morning air.

"The demon has returned to his liar," said Philip gleefully, grabbing me about the waist, humming a jig as he turned me round.

"And I'm well! I know I am! And so's Nora," said Jake, leaping from the bed with Nora in hand. I must say the boy did a fine job of imitating Philip's steps as he twirled our niece about the room.

"Too much joy too soon, means a sad end," said Tituba sourly, thumping down onto the abandoned bed.

"Ah Tituba, me lovedy," said Philip playfully, "don't be such an old grouse. Isn't this much better than moldering in your grave waiting around for the worms to eat your dust."

"And who's to say that still might not happen, Master English?" said Tituba, looking at Giles Cory, who had lit his ghostly pipe and was sitting in the corner pondering the voodoo woman's words.

"There's much to what she says, Phil," said Giles, looking out the open window to the town beyond. "All we've done is save these children here, and whose to say that's not just for this moment. The curse that holds this town, and Georgie Corwin's power are still with us. All we've done is 'plug up the hole in the dam,' so to speak. The Devil's curse is still loose on the town, and infects it layer by layer. We all know that sooner or later 'Old Nick' will find a way to free his henchman, George Corwin."

"I think he's right," said Lillith.

"I know he is," I said. "How could we have forgotten about the poor victims of the witch hysteria, doomed to live their afterlife cooped up in that stone memorial."

"But what can we do about it?" asked Lynn.

"We can take the power that we now know we have, and go to the source of the curse. Tell me, Lillith," asked Philip, "where is the greatest concentration of undead souls in this town?"

"Why Old Burial Hill, of course," said Lillith.

"Then," said Philip, "that's where we must go, now, before the Devil becomes powerful enough to unleash his fury against us. He must be downright angry at us for destroying his plans for Jake and Nora. There's no telling what he might do if we give him a chance to regroup and grow strong again. It's time to end this thing, once and for all. Something tells me we might never have another chance as good as the one we have now."

"Then, let's stop talking and go," said Giles, standing up and straightening his waistcoat over his ample stomach.

"Yes, Uncle Philip, let's hurry," said Nora, taking Jake and Lynn's hands and hurrying towards the door.

"Not so fast, young lady," said Philip, stepping between Nora and the door. "Where do you think you're going?"

"Why with you of course," said Nora.

"No you're not," said Philip firmly, turning towards Jim Proctor. "Sergeant, it's going to be dangerous out there, especially now. Can I rely on you to make sure that these three don't leave this room until after dawn?"

"Absolutely," said Jim, glaring at the angry young people. "It's time for you three to let the rest of us take over. Nora, get back into bed, and Jake, you just sit over there and keep out of sight until I can figure out a way to get your name cleared of the murder and assaults you've been charged with."

"You'd do that for me?" asked an incredulous Jake.

"Well, yes," said Jim, clearing his throat, "I've got no choice. It's clear that you're innocent, but I don't know how I'm going to prove that to anyone else. You've got to stay here, out of sight until I figure out what to do."

"And you, young lady," said Lillith, looking at her ghostly daughter who was tapping her foot impatiently. "I don't want to take any chance of losing what I've got left with you. If you had done what I said and come home to stay last Halloween, you'd still be a mortal. Ghost or not, you're going to mind me and stay put this time."

"Okay, okay, I get the point," said Lynn, stomping past Lillith and slumping on the bed next to Nora. "Go ahead. I was just trying to make sure that you'd be safe."

"I know darling," said Lillith, "but try to trust me. Worrying about the three of you will just make what we have to do that much harder."

"Don't worry, Lillith," said Jim. "I'll stay here with them until it's safe."

"Thank you, sir," said Philip, as he motioned for the rest of us to leave. We formed a traveling mist to take us quickly to the graveyard and were soon speeding on the dew of the early morning towards Old Burial Hill.

"Why does the air feel so heavy?" I asked Philip as we touched ground near Judge Hathorne's stone.

"'Tis the Devil's breath," said Tituba.

> "Reach me a gentian, give me a torch!
> Let me guide myself with blue, forked torch of a flower
> down the darker and darker stairs, where blue is darkened on blueness
> even where Persephone goes, just now, from the frosted September
> to the sightless realm where darkness is awake
> upon the dark"
> David Herbert Lawrence: *Bavarian Genetians*.

CHAPTER FIFTY FOUR

"Can you keep quiet?" asked Jim as he started towards the door.

"I suppose so," said Lynn, still not happy about being left behind. What good was being a ghost if your mother still treated you like a kid?

Jim nodded his head and shut the door quietly behind him. He made his way down the corridor to dismiss the new man, Gabe Brink. The last thing he needed was a curious novice hanging around. To his surprise, the man was gone.

"Well, I'll be", muttered Jim, looking around for some sign of his new patrolman. In a way it was a relief to find him gone, but it was also disturbing. It was a firing offense for a man to leave his post without giving notice to his commanding officer. But to bring the man up on charges would mean there would be an inquiry over all the circumstances that surrounded Gabe Brink's abandonment of duty. The last thing Jim wanted right now was people asking questions about this strange night.

"Better to let the whole thing go, for now," thought Jim, "and keep an eye on the guy. If that's the way he acts the first night on the job, it should be easy to find something else to fire him for." With those thoughts, Jim turned on his heel and made his way back towards Nora's room and his reluctant charges.

Gabe Brink closed his glowing eyes quickly as the heavy mist began transforming itself into the forms of Lillith March, Philip, myself, Tituba and Giles Cory. I felt an evil presence in my mind as my feet touched the earth.

"Curse you bitch," he swore to himself as I suddenly turned towards the great oak tree that seemed to house the presence.

"What's wrong, Mary?" asked Philip.

"I'm not sure," I said, "but I think there's someone else in here with us."

"Of course there is, Missus," said Tituba merrily, "there be most of our old friends and neighbors gathered somewhere about this place. It gives me a bit of a peculiar feeling too, if that's any comfort."

"That's not what I'm talking about," I said, reviewing the scene that I had seen in my mind as we passed through the night air. I had watched Jim Proctor wander down the hospital corridor and then back up again, reentering Nora's room with a puzzled look on his face. I knew from experience that when I saw something there was always a reason, something I should learn from it, but I couldn't figure out what. I'm sure that it would come to me, hopefully sooner than later. What I was to learn, later, was that the Devil was with us that night, in the form of Gabriel Brink, watching and learning what he could about us so that he would be able to destroy us later on.

"Come on now," said Philip urgently, "it's time to begin the ceremony."

We followed him quickly as the first redness of dawn began to shimmer through the trees. The light pointed our way as it made a blood red stain upon the gravestone of John Hathorne. Philip stood directly on the center of the grave and directed us to form a circle around him.

It was only when I looked at Philip that I began to feel fear. His normally beautiful countenance was glowing bright red in the early morning dawn, and his hair had taken on a strange blackness that made his teeth gleam a stark white. Then I glanced at my other two companions and saw that the same thing had happened to them. I could tell, by the way that they were looking at me, that I looked equally as strange. I could feel the laughter bubbling up in all of us as Tituba made a horrible face.

"Stop that!" hissed Philip as he tried to regain his composure.

We all tried to look suitably serious as the heat of the sun bore down upon us.

Then, without warning, the heat turned to a gentle, late fall whisper of coolness as Philip gave three long whistles, summoning our essences into him. The three of us pressed tightly against him as Philip, the north wind, swallowed our gifts of the east, west and south.

The winds of the earth seem to swirl around us, as once again, Philip summoned their forces by taking his right hand and giving three long whistles blown between his first and forth fingers. Contained within that wind were all the souls who had trod upon the earth where we were now standing. I could hear their voices calling to us, for the third and last time, as Philip let forth the three long whistles that summoned the winds. Then, all was quiet, as if the earth were waiting in silence for some far away piper to start the tune for the final dance.

The first soul to whisper by us in the quietness of that red dawn was Judge Hathorne himself, judge of us all, and forbearer, along with Philip and myself, of that wonderful boy, Nathaniel Hawthorne, who wrote of the wonders and terrors of Salem as if he had truly lived with us in that long ago time. Then came the soul of Richard More, waving his plumed hat merrily as he strode past us, hardly looking like a spirit at all. He had been one of the first to lay down the foundations of Salem, and had come over on that small wooden boat, the Mayflower. Behind More came the shade of Samuel Shattock, he who testified against Bridget Bishop, sending her to Gallows Hill because of his tales of how she used voodoo dolls to cause his son's death.

There were so many that danced in the red dawn that morning that it is hard to remember them all, but each and every one called to me as they passed, blithely unaware that they were in deadly peril of sinking below the earth of Salem to the Devil's own hell that lay below. I could feel the Devil's breath surrounding us, just waiting for me and my friends to fail. There were many who deserved the fiery pits, such as Chief Justice John Lynde, who was responsible for condemning many including the men of the great Boston Massacre, and the son of Cotton Mather, Nathaniel. Nathaniel had been a strong willed young man who had been caught with his hand up many a skirt in our fair town. Strange to consider, if the rumors were true, that dissipated young man was my very own brother.

The last to pass by us, with a gentle smile and a winking eye, was Giles Cory's first wife, Mary. Giles had been standing outside our circle, but he too was enmeshed with the heavy red mist that flowed through Burial Hill like sparkling lava. I could see the tears streaming down his face as young Mary reached her hands towards him in a beckoning gesture. I could tell that it took all the self will he had to resist her longing looks.

As the misty fog became even thicker, the air before us filled with the symbols of the living and dead that had been etched lovingly on the stones of Old Burial Hill. Anchors and angels merged with crowns and death's heads as the mist lifted us towards the heavens. I looked down to the earth below and was surprised to see Philip still standing atop John Hathorne's grave.

"Farewell for now, my Mary," I heard him call. "'Twill be but an instant until you see me again. I must live through the months that you are traveling through in an instant. 'Tis the only way to guard the gate."

"But why Philip," I cried, terrified at the thought of traveling through time without him. What if something should happen to him!

"Because we have left our two girls and that boy unprotected. The Devil still wanders Salem's streets. Someone has to stay to protect them, and someone has to go to save their future. Don't be afraid for me. Giles here will take care of me. Won't you friend?"

"Aye, that I will, Mistress Mary," cried Giles above the wind's fury as the two men disappeared from sight.

"But you promised never to leave me again," I whispered to myself as I grabbed for Tituba's and Lillith's hands. Somehow their touch brought me new courage. What Philip had said was true, if our plan worked it would be just a few minutes more before I saw him again, but those minutes would seem like an eternity.

Once again the symbols of Puritan death began to pass by us, this time in rapid succession. Pyramids and serpents, urns and vultures all flew at us, missing us or going right through us with breathtaking speed. I saw my own stone, a dead tree with six limbs cut off to symbolize the children I had left behind. Finally there appeared above us a winged hourglass, pouring its sands upon us in a shower of gold.

The four winds, children of change, the most enduring thing of all and the very essence of witchcraft, had delivered us safely to our destination, Salem on Halloween day, 1999.

"While from a proud tower in the town
Death looks gigantically down."
Edgar Allen Poe: "The City in the Sea," st. 3.

CHAPTER FIFTY FIVE

It was as if nothing, and yet everything had changed as the three of us, Tituba, Lillith and myself, Mary English, materialized atop John Hathorne's grave on that cool, brilliantly sunny October morning. It was early yet, so the tourists had not begun to invade the graveyard. From experience I knew that by noontime the place would be mobbed with curiosity seekers, hoping to spy a real ghost or witch on this, "All Hallows Eve."

There was an energy about the place that you could almost reach out and grasp. The food vendors displaying soft pretzels, sausages and ice cream were already in place, and there were four different vans displaying the call letters of three radio stations and one television station. These were perched just outside the graveyard gates waiting to catch the first imprison of locals and visitors from far away as they wandered towards this Mecca of Halloween, Old Burial Hill. Who knows, if they were lucky enough, one of the reporters waiting out the frostiness of that cool morning in their plush lined vans, might even be lucky enough to interview a real witch!

"Can anyone see us?" asked Tituba as she looked around the graveyard at the scattered early morning visitors.

"No," said Lillith, "not right now. But it's only a matter of time before the spell that hides us from view dissolves. I think we better get off this stone and try to look 'normal.'"

"That's going to be a little hard," I said looking at Tituba's brightly colored turban and dourly colored puritan dress, not to mention my own crimson satin gown, with its lace color and embroidered bodice. The only one who looked slightly normal was Lillith, dressed in a long denim dress and high heeled brown leather boots.

We stepped away from John Hathorne's stone and made our way towards the witch memorial, being very careful not to step on the resting place of any of our friends. I started to laugh as I realized my concern about how we looked was groundless! After all, this was Salem, and it was Halloween. If either Tituba or I materialized, we would look downright normal when compared to some of the figures I had seen wandering around the graveyard last year. I transmitted my thoughts to my companions as we stood at the entrance of the Witch Memorial, and they both turned towards me and smiled.

There was a pretty woman placing three flowers on the stone of Sarah Good. She spoke quietly as she laid first a bright red rose in full bloom, and then two pink rosebuds upon the poor woman's stone.

"What's she doing?' asked Lillith as the mortal pilgrim looked once more around the tree lined memorial and then walked off.

"I'm not sure," said Tituba, "but I think she left those flowers for Sarah and her two daughters, you know, the babe that died at Sarah's breast while she was in prison, and the four year old girl who was accused as a witch herself and chained up in Salem dungeon until she went mad."

"It seems I'm not the only one who's lost a daughter to this horrible curse, am I?" said Lillith, looking thoughtfully at the retreating figure of the pilgrim as she disappeared into the morning's mist.

"Look," I said as we looked into the grassy enclosure of the memorial, "there's Jim's new patrolman, Gabe Brink!"

Sure enough, there was officer Brink, sitting on top of John Proctor's stone, looking as if he owned the town. I'm not sure why, but it made me angry to see Brink sitting on John Proctor's memorial stone, swinging his legs absently as he lit a cigarette. Lord knows there had been thousands of people who had done the same thing, but there was something about the man, an attitude of insolence or irreverence, that mad me want to knock him from that stone and kick him to the ground. My anger increased as I watched Gabe Brink toss his still lighted match on top of Rebecca Nurse's stone as he made his way towards the entrance of the memorial. But that was nothing compared to his words.

"You should have been burned, you old bitch," he said to Rebecca's stone as he stubbed his freshly lit cigarette out on the dear woman's remembrance. Then he laughed cruelly as he dug his heels into the soft ground and walked past us. I raised my hand to slap Gabe Brink's face, but Lillith grabbed me just as I was about to land the blow.

Lillith put her finger to her lips and motioned for us to stand to one side as Brink walked towards the intersection of Charter and Essex Streets. There, he walked over to the parked patrol car and took out a bright orange traffic belt. I watched, furiously, as the man adjusted his belt and took his place at the intersection, obviously waiting for the rush of traffic. Then I heard Lillith sigh as Jim Proctor appeared, carrying two cups of coffee in styrofoam cups. He saw Gabe and waved one cup towards him as the two men met. Gabe Brink took the cup and gingerly lifted its cover, releasing the steam of the hot coffee into the early morning air.

"Why'd he do that? What's wrong with him?" I asked Lillith furiously. "And why did you stop me? That fool deserves to be hit."

"I remember last Halloween," said Lillith looking at me sternly. "Your powers are very strong on this day, in this place, Mary. Remember the tourist who died when you sucked the wind from his body?"

"Oh yes," I said sarcastically, looking towards Gabriel Brink and Jim Proctor. "It would have been a pity, wouldn't it, to have seen that man collapse and die."

"Now, Mistress English," said Tituba, "you're beginning to sound a bit like me. Hold your temper for later. 'Tis a good thing that ye be in a high temper, but save it for the greater battle. It would be a shame, wouldn't it, if ye wasted it on little things and had nothing left to send the Devil back to hell."

"I'm not so sure that the Devil isn't already with us," I said as I looked towards Gabriel Brink. To my surprise, he looked back at me. Then he took off his traffic belt and handed it to Jim. Jim Proctor replaced Brink in the intersection and Brink made his way back towards the memorial and took up a watchful position in front of it.

"Please don't step on the gravestones," he warned a passersby as he touched his hat in an early morning greeting.

I backed away warily as once again he looked towards the three of us and smiled. I don't know how it was possible, but I was sure Gabe Brink knew we were there, even though we were invisible to the rest of the mortals who had begun to wander the graveyard.

I saw Lillith give a backwards glance at Jim Proctor, looking as if she wanted to run over and say something to him.

"What is it Lillith?" I asked my mortal friend, as tears appeared in her eyes.

"Nothing," said Lillith.

"It must be something," I said.

"Well, if you must know, there's something about Jim Proctor I like," said Lillith with a shy smile. "I've had nothing to do with men for a long time. To me they've all seemed the same, full of empty promises and childish behavior, but Jim is different. He seems like someone who would really love and honor a woman in the way she deserves, someone who would be a friend and a lover, not a bother."

"I think there's a bit of romance in the air if I'm not mistaken," said Tituba with a mischevious leer. "But I'd move quickly if I were you, dearie," she continued giving a grunt in Jim's direction. "A prize like that doesn't stay around for long. See, some other likely lass is already buzzing around your pot of honey, Lillith March."

"Oh, that's nothing," said Lillith as she turned to see her good friend Hannah approaching Jim Proctor and put a friendly hand on his arm.

"Never be too sure about things like that," said Tituba, nodding her head wisely. "Many a friendship's ended in marriage when a man gets tired of waiting for something he can't get. Yon lass has had over half a year to get him to warm up to her smiles. Don't forget, Lillith, ye've been gone, traveling the sky, while he's been attending to that one. And she's a pretty thing too!"

"But you don't understand," said Lillith, watching Jim and Hannah start to laugh as they shared a familiar moment. "Hannah not interested in men, especially one like Jim Proctor."

"Really?" said Tituba as she raised one eyebrow sarcastically and closed her lips in a sardonic grin.

"Look! There's Jake and Nora," I cried, pointing past Jim and Hannah towards the two happy figures as they ran across the street holding hands.

"Why aren't they in school?" asked Lillith.

"I think it's Sunday," I said, suddenly aware of the fact that I had heard several sets of church bells ring since we had arrived at Old Burial Hill.

"You're right, Mary," said Lillith. "Last year Halloween was on a Saturday, so it must be Sunday. Look at how happy those two look. I wonder if they still remember that we were going to finish our work, here, on this day."

Lillith's question was answered as she saw Nora wave to someone inside the gates of the Witch Memorial. We turned, and to my delight, saw Philip and Giles sitting on the grass, listening intently to Martha Cory hold forth against something or someone. I could tell by the ghostly woman's animated movements that Martha had lost none of her temper or passion in the last year. Then I saw Lynn March step shyly from behind a tree and join the other spirits gathered around Martha Cory.

"It seems as if we're all here," I said mentally counting off my friends and family as a schoolteacher might count off pupils. There were the ghosts of Salem; myself, Tituba, Philip, Lynn, Giles and Martha, and then there were the mortal players, Lillith, who was still spiritual in form but soon to be returned to the mortal side, Nora, and Jim. Not a single one of us was missing. Why, even my friend Hannah, and Jim's man, Gabe Brink, were here in this place on Halloween morning. In a way it was rather strange that we had all appeared in this place at the same moment, as if some great magnetic force had called us forth. The only one who was missing was the cause of all our troubles, George Corwin, and for that I was truly grateful. My wits were scattered enough, what with my moments out of time and all that had happened in the past few months. Perhaps this was a gift from the gods, a moment of peace to gather our strength to us before the battle began. Then I heard the church bells of Salem again and realized that, indeed, we had been given a moment's respite. As long as the bells of St. Peter's rang out, George Corwin was forced to stay within the bell tower. How lucky we were that the last Halloween of the old millennium should fall on a Sunday!

I watched in delight as Nora and Jake made their way towards Philip and Giles. I motioned to Lillith and Tituba to follow me and soon all of us, mortal and spirit alike were gathered around Martha's stone.

"Oh! Here I go," said Lillith as her spiritual form began to flesh out and make the journey back towards the other side, the mortal side. There was a sudden gust of wind from the east as she became a true mortal woman again. She fell forward and landed on the soft grass.

"Careful Mrs. March," said Jake as he helped her to her feet. Nora gave Lillith a great hug as the woman struggled with the sudden transformation back into her mortal form.

"I never realized how cumbersome our bodies felt," said Lillith, feeling her arms and shoulders.

"It's a funny feeling, isn't it?" said Nora, watching Lillith sympathetically. "It took me a month to get used to the real me again."

"Did anyone see me appear?" asked Lillith.

"I don't think so," said Jake, looking around casually, trying hard not to seem suspicious. "The only one near us is Officer Brink, and he was talking to that guy in the black robe with the death head's mask on."

I looked towards Gabe Brink and saw that Jake was right. The only one close enough to notice Lillith's sudden reappearance was Brink, and he seemed absorbed in his conversation with the tourist dressed as death. Then the two men turned and looked directly at us.

"Mrs. March," yelled Brink as he left his companion and hurried over to us. "It's great to see you! Hannah and Nora said you'd been holed up in your house writing a book, but we were beginning to believe someone had murdered you and buried you in the basement. If Sergeant Proctor hadn't told me over and over again that you really were at home, writing, I would have broken down the door looking for you. But here you are, safe and sound. I hope the book was worth it. What's it about? Nora and Hannah said it was a secret, and you wouldn't come out until it was finished. But now... don't you think it's time you shared it with the rest of us?"

"I'll be glad to, very soon," said Lillith, looking over Brink's shoulder as Jim Proctor and Hannah joined the party of real Salemites standing inside the Witch Memorial.

"Take the traffic, Gabe," said Jim as he took off the orange belt and handed it back to Brink. "Lillith and I have a lot of catching up to do." With those words, Jim Proctor put his arms around Lillith and kissed her, slowly at first, and then with the passion of a lover.

Philip drew me close as we watched the two embrace, knowing, as all lovers do, that it should be only a matter of time before Jim Proctor and Lillith March became one forever. Then, suddenly, a cold chill ran through me as I watched Gabe Brink turn back towards us. The look he gave Lillith was one of evil, naked lust, followed by a murderous glance at Jim.

"There's something wrong with him," said Lynn as she moved in front of Lillith and Jim in an effort to block the two lovers from Gabe Brink's view. "I've known it for months. I'm not sure what it is, but I don't think he's really mortal. He's not one of us, either, so I don't know what he his."

"Lynn's right," said Philip, sitting down on the grass and drawing me upon his knees. "But there's enough time for that later. First let me tell you what's gone on in Salem since we saw you last."

"Mirror, mirror on the wall,
who's the fairest of them all?"
The Evil Queen: *Snow White*.

CHAPTER FIFTY SIX

"I can't believe that all that evidence just 'disappeared,'" laughed Lillith as Jim finished his tale about Jake.

"Everyone said it was kind of strange, Aunt Lillith," said Nora merrily, "but they couldn't hold Jake over for trial without any evidence."

"Even though Officer Brink tried," said Jake, looking at Brink who was busy showing two heavy women, dressed up in pink 'good fairy' costumes, the way to the pirate museum.

"No evidence, no trial,," sighed Jim in mock sorrow.

"I don't know how to thank you, Jim," said Lillith. "I know how hard it must have been for you to help Jake."

"It wasn't hard at all," said Jim as he put his arm around Lillith. "The boy's not guilty. I did what I had to do. What we have to do now, is catch and punish the real criminal, George Corwin."

"He knows we're on his trail," said Philip. "Why else would he have laid low these past few months? He's had plenty of chance to bother Jake and Nora, and he hasn't. It seems that old George has been content to leave them alone, for the moment. But I don't trust him. I know Corwin's just gathering strength for his next adventure."

"And you can bet that he's going to come out tonight," said Giles gazing up at the sun. It was now heading towards the midday mark.

"Well, I think all your fine talk is just that, talk," said Martha Cory, glaring at Giles. "Are you, or aren't you going to let us loose of this place tonight?"

"Can't you see we're trying, my dear," said Giles, backing away from Martha as her face began to turn red.

"You better do something fast, before it's too late," continued Martha, "or all of us in here will go mad. It's the price a ghost pays, you know, for being cooped up in one place so long. That's why all those ghosts who haunt the houses hereabouts are so mean and mischievous. They've all gone a bit mad. I'd hate to see that happen to the good folks here. They've been through enough, seems to me."

"Yes, my dear, quite right," said Giles.

"Then, let's get to it," said Philip, stepping in between Martha and Giles as he had so many times before.

"And let's get out of this graveyard," said Nora. "I don't think anything's going to happen until after dark. Besides, I'm getting hungry."

"Why, so am I!" said Lillith, "I'd entirely forgotten about eating. Let's go to my house and see what's left of it. I can just imagine what it must look like by now."

"It looks the same as it always did, Lillith," said Hannah linking her arm around Lillith's. "Come and see for yourself."

"I'll be back for you soon, lovey," called Giles to Martha as he hurried after his friends.

"Just see that you do, you old fool," said Martha as she sat down upon her stone and viewed the onslaught of Halloween tourists as they made their way into the graveyard.

"But you can't leave now," said Lillith as she and Lynn stood in front of the great wooden doors of her home on Forrester Street.

"I have to, Mama. There's something I forgot back at the graveyard. I'll only be a moment, I promise." With those words, Lynn disappeared before Lillith could say anything.

"I wonder what that was all about?" said Lillith, looking intently at the spot where her daughter had disappeared.

"Yes, I wonder?" I said taking Philip's hand as he guided me up the steps and into Lillith's home. I sat down on the rose velvet couch in

Lillith's living room and closed my eyes. The misty form of Lynn March came into view as she retraced her steps towards Old Burial Hill. I watched as the girl silently approached Gabriel Brink.

"So, you're back again," the man whispered to the ghostly girl as he motioned a black car to turn right.

"Where else did you think I'd be after what I saw?" said Lynn March, floating intimately close to Gabriel Brink.

"I don't know what you're talking about," said the patrolman, smiling and waving as three ten year old girls crossed the street in front of him.

"I think you do," said Lynn. "From the very beginning there was something about you that bothered me. At first I thought it was the fact that you could see me, you, a stranger in town who had never known me while I was alive. Then, about a month ago, I began to realize who you really were. You tried to make me believe that you were my friend and that Sergeant Proctor had assigned you to my case. But why would he have you working on my case when he already knew who my real killer was? You were lying to me and I knew it, but why? And then today, when you looked at my mother, I figured it out."

"I'm sure I don't know what you're talking about, young lady," said Brink, taking off his hat and smoothing back his jet black hair.

"Yes you do," said Lynn quietly. "We both know you're not really what you say you are. Your eyes, they're just like the eyes of George Corwin when he raped and murdered me. He looked at me the same way you looked at my mother today. For some reason you can change shape, but your eyes always stay the same. I've come to tell you to stay away from her."

"And who's going to stop me? You?" laughed Brink as he took off his traffic belt and threw it in the patrol car. "If you really want to do something about me you better find out just who I am and how powerful I can be. Say now, why don't we walk down the street and talk about this a little more privately."

"I don't trust you," said Lynn backing away from Brink as she felt an odd pulling around her breast. The air about her began to shimmer as Brink started to walk towards the Peabody-Essex Museum. Lynn found herself being dragged helplessly after him.

"Let me go," she cried as he pushed the door of the museum open and stepped inside. Brink showed his badge to the volunteer at the desk and she waved him inside with a smile.

"Where are we going?" asked Lynn, her voice filled with terror.

"Does it really matter, my dear," said Brink, leering back at the helpless spirit of Lynn March as he dragged her forward towards the great hall of the museum. Inside the enormous room were actual parts of the old trading and whaling ships that had set sail from Salem's Derby wharf. At the end of the hall stood an exquisite collection of mirrors, large and small, brought back from all over the world. Gabriel Brink stopped before a tiny gold and cloisonné mirror.

"Philip English brought this back from China, my dear. Don't you think it's quite beautiful," said Brink as he took the mirror off the wall and turned it over in his hand.

"Let me go, please," begged Lynn, in the deserted hall, as an implacable force drew her closer and closer to the mirror.

"Let you go?" laughed Gabriel Brink. "Why my lovely little girl, I've just begun to have my fun with you. Now then, get in here like a good girl and I promise that I'll think about leaving your mother alone. Fight me, and I'll take her soul along with yours."

"No! No!" screamed Lynn as she desperately fought against the pull of the tiny mirror. But it was no use. In her last free moment she screamed out Lillith's name. I heard it rush through my own soul as Lynn dissolved into the mirror. Then, there was something else I saw. Inside Lynn's mind flashed a picture of George Corwin, hanging from a high tower as five tortured souls danced at his feet. Then I saw Tituba's face in front of me. The old witch woman was shaking me.

"Mistress English, come back. Come back now before it's too late," I heard her call as the white and pale pink living room of Lillith March came back into focus.

"What happened?" asked Lillith as she dropped to her knees in front of me.

"Your daughter, your daughter Lynn," I gasped. "The Devil has stolen her soul!"

PART SEVEN

THE BURNING MOON

> "Keeping time, time, time,
> In a sort of Runic rhyme,
> To the tintinnabulation that so musically wells
> From the bells, bells, bells, bells,
> Bells, bells, bells."
> Edgar Allen Poe: "The Bells."

CHAPTER FIFTY SEVEN

"So the dance of death begins," said Philip, looking at me grimly.

"I'm afraid so, my love," I said.

"I should have never let her go," cried Lillith as she laid her head in her hands.

"There was no way you could have stopped her," said Tituba. "Mistress English told you what she saw and heard. The only thing that would have happened is that you would have been trapped along with your daughter. Looky here, hasn't anyone realized how important this all is? The Devil has followed us through time and eternity to this place, this Salem. There must be something here he wants that he can't have. Why else would he be playing games like this? It used to be he could do anything he wanted, have anything he wished with a snap of his fingers, but now, for some reason, he's hanging around Salem in disguise, watching and waiting for his chance to do us harm. Maybe he's weak, so weak that he has to do something to recover his strength. For some reason he can only do it here, through us."

"I think she's right," said Philip. "Don't you see? When the four of us joined forces, we created something that crippled his power. Why else would he resort to taking Lynn hostage. I know what Tituba's talking about. In the good old days the Devil would have just waved his hand and destroyed us all. This means that there must be some way we can beat him at his own game. But how?"

"By letting him think we want to play," I said. "Philip, I told you about Lynn sending me the vision of Corwin hanging from a high tower with the five souls dancing at his feet? Think Philip, think. What does that mean?"

"That we are not alone on our quest," said Philip, smiling at me in an almost evil way. "And I think it's time we became the hunters rather than the hunted," he said, heading towards the door. "Come on!"

Lillith, Tituba and I ran after Philip as he swiftly reached the bottom of the granite steps and headed towards Salem Common, where the bright lights of the carnival rides and games of chance filled the encroaching twilight.

"There's our man," said Philip, almost gleefully, as Gabriel Brink approached my husband and offered him his outstretched hand.

"Good evening to you, Captain English," said the Devil. "I've been waiting a long time to meet you face to face."

"But I thought we had already met, sir," said Philip, merrily, ignoring Brink's outstretched hand.

"I have no idea what you're talking about," said Brink, taking his hand back and placing it in his pocket. It made me uneasy to watch him as he gently fondled a small object beneath the cloth.

"I think it's time for both of us to stop waiting for the other to act like a fool, Officer Brink," said Philip, looking the man straight in his yellow eyes. "There's more to both of us than that, as you well know. You want something, and I want something, so let's stop wasting time and get to it."

I watched quietly as a charming smile came to Brink's face. It was a smile that was capable of melting the heart of any woman, and many a man. I do believe it was the most beguiling smile I had ever seen.

"Don't look at him," hissed Tituba, nudging me harshly as she pointed towards Lillith softening gaze. "See what he's trying to do? He's trying to seduce us, just like he always has."

"Ah, do I hear the voice of an old friend?" said Brink, turning his attention from Philip and Lillith and aiming it in our direction.

"Hardly a 'friend,'" said Tituba, standing nose to nose with the demon. "You're nothing but a lying cheating imp," said Tituba, pointing towards Brink's pocket, "and your time in this town is almost through. Hand over that girl to us, right now, or I swear that you'll find all the evil you ever unleashed in this town turned back against you threefold."

"Oh, that's really rich!" laughed Brink as he took the small mirror out of his pocket and flashed it in our eyes. "You really think you have enough power to command me to do your bidding! Who do you think created you, all of you? You're nothing but a group of lost souls wandering on or above the earth at my pleasure. Why, I can turn anyone of you to dust anytime I please. Just look in here if you doubt my power!"

With those words, Brink held the small mirror high so that we could see the shadowy form of Lynn, beating her tiny fists against the wavy glass in a futile attempt to break free.

"Lynn, Lynn!" cried Lillith, running towards Brink in desperation.

"Not so fast, my lady," said Brink, slipping the mirror into his sleeve as he made a grab for Lillith, catching her around the waist. "If you want this little girl, you'll have to pay for her. And I think what I want might not be so hard for you to give me," said Brink, plunging his hand under Lillith's skirt as he held her tight.

It was then that I saw something that truly amazed me. Suddenly, the tearful Lillith was left standing alone as the demon, Brink, found himself thrown across the grass. He landed at the edge of the pebble strewn playground. He lay there stunned, for a minute, and then slowly got to his feet. I held my breath as I watched him brush the dirt and stones from his uniform and then walk slowly towards Philip.

"It's time to stop playing games, or rather, it's time we started playing the right games, Master English," said Brink softly.

"I quite agree," said Philip, looking over Brink's head towards the bright lights of the tiny carnival that covered the busier half of the Common.

"I had no idea your power had grown so. Why, now that I think of it, no one has ever been able to do such a thing to me before," said Brink, taking a step towards the tiny midway.

"You flatter me," said Philip, with a sardonic grin, "but, as we all know, the Devil's flattery is just another way he has of spinning his web around a soul until it is hopelessly trapped. Leave off your false words, Brink, and let's get to it."

"As you wish, Philip," said Brink, taking the mirror from his sleeve and holding it towards the twinkling lights of the fair. "What say, you and I have a bit of fun!"

> "Come Watson, come!
> The game is afoot."
> Sir Arthur Conan Doyle:
> *The Return of Sherlock Holmes.*

CHAPTER FIFTY EIGHT

"What are you going to do?" I asked Philip as I frantically grabbed at his arm. The idea of my husband dealing with the Devil face to face terrified me. If he failed, I knew that Philip, and my heart, would be lost forever.

"Only what I must," said Philip, gently taking my hand from his arm.

"Oh Philip," I sighed as he outdistanced me and strode side by side with the Devil.

"Don't lose sight of them," said Giles as he motioned for me and Tituba to hurry our pace. Lillith followed a bit behind, still slightly bemused by the Devil's onslaught.

We moved in silence across the velvety green of Salem Common. I tried to see us as the Halloween revelers, who filled the Common, saw us. To them there were only two figures making their way under the magical spread of trees that ringed the Common and formed a soft dark canopy over all the spirits within its confines. The patrolman, Gabe Brink, went first, followed at a distance by Lillith March, one of the most well known witches in Salem. What the living didn't see was that beside Gabe Brink walked my husband, Philip English, a giant among men of any age, and the greatest power in the town. It made me smile to think that all the curious had flocked to Salem hoping to view a real ghost, or witch, and here we were, the Devil himself up ahead accompanied by the spirit of the great privateer, Philip English, while following behind were Lillith March, a living witch, the spirit of Tituba, the instigator of the witchcraft hysteria in Salem, along with myself, a Goodwoman of the town, and Giles Cory, well known because of the legend that had grown up around his bravery and stubborn refusal to be labeled as a witch. So here we were, living and dead, man and woman, witch, devil, pirate and saint, gliding past the gullible tourists just hungering for a taste of the supernatural. Was it any wonder that I sometimes found it all ironically amusing? Despite myself, I started to laugh.

"What's so funny" asked Giles as he puffed beside me, still not quite used to moving about as a spirit.

"It's all funny, in a way, old friend," I said to him.

"Watch out," cried Giles as Tituba leaped to one side to avoid being passed through by a fried dough vendor and his pushcart.

"I thought they couldn't harm us," said Tituba as she looked at Giles with a confused look on her face.

"They can't, at least not really," I said to Tituba, "but it feels very odd when something that large shares the same space with us."

"What I really hate are the horse drawn carriages," said Giles, nodding his head towards the pretty white and gold carriage that made its way slowly around the Common. It was pulled by two large, coal black horses with swishing tails.

"So do I," I said. "I think it's because they move so slowly. It's almost like being a piece of thread drawn through a needle. I suppose a mortal would call it agony."

"You've not known agony until ye've seen what I've seen," said Tituba. "You have no idea what its like to be owned by another human being, never knowing from one minute to the next if you're going to be allowed to live or die."

"You're right, Tituba, I don't know of such things," I said as I caught a glimpse of my husband and Gabe Brink heading towards a dark blue tent covered with blinking neon stars. It sounds strange, but for some reason Tituba was trying to be quarrelsome. In fact, I felt rather quarrelsome myself.

"Here now," said Giles, "I'll not have you making Mistress English feel bad for something that was naught of her doing. She's a fine woman and always did what she could to help others. Why, we wouldn't be here now if she, and her brave lad up ahead, were cowards. Pity yourself if ye feel ye must, old woman, but when ye've done with it, let go and get on with what we must do. I find it odd that we're talking of such things when we should be thinkin' of a way to help Master English. Say, now that I think of it, my head feels like it's full of buzzing bees. It's like there's something in me that wants to start a ruckus with one of you."

"I feel the same way," said Lillith as we watched Philip and Gabe Brink duck beneath the folds of the midnight blue tent.

"Can't you see what's happening," I realized as I lost sight of Philip. "The Devil's trying to divide us! He's trying to get in our minds and come between us!"

"You're right, that's just his way!" said Lillith, coming to a standstill in front of the blue tent. "The Devil is cunning and insidious. It's just like him to try to separate us and make us think its our own fault. Mary, Tituba, take my hands. No matter what, don't let go. And no matter what evil or nagging thought fills your mind, let it flow through you like a river. Keep nothing within you except the thought that we love one another. It's the only way we can give Philip the strength he needs to defeat the devil!"

Lillith stood before the entrance to the tent and looked up at the full moon as we each took one of her hands and melted into one being. I was conscious of Giles standing a few feet to my right, but knew that for some reason, he was not a part of our power. His fate lay elsewhere.

"Hey lady, do you want to buy a ticket or not," said the young boy who stood in front of the tent, guarding his post behind a slanted old card table.

"What's the ticket for?" asked Lillith.

"It's for the 'Las Vegas' style gamblin' inside," said the boy. "We're givin' part of the winnin's to the 'Boys and Girls Club' here in town."

"And what do you do with the rest?" asked Lillith.

"Why, that's for operatin' expenses, a' course," said the boy with a wink.

"Of course," said Lillith as she handed the boy the five dollar entrance fee that the sign on the table asked for.

"You're sure all the games are honest?" asked Lillith.

"Trust me," said the boy with a grin that revealed two missing front teeth.

"There's something familiar about that boy,'" muttered Giles as the three witches and the old man entered the gaming tent.

"Too familiar," I said as I caught sight of Gabriel Brink and my husband standing in front of a black roulette wheel. My husband had allowed his form to take on flesh and now stood as visible as any other man.

"Then it's agreed," I heard Philip say, "one spin decides it all."

"Agreed," said Brink as he shook my husband's hand.

"It is double pleasure to deceive the deceiver."
Jean de La Fontaine:
Fables, bk.II, Fable 15.

CHAPTER FIFTY NINE

"What are you doing, my love?" I asked Philip as he and Gabriel Brink stood before the roulette wheel.

"Just playing a bit of a game, my sweet," he said to me as he flashed me an innocent smile.

"But, that's a game of chance, Philip. And I heard you say something. You said, 'one spin decides all.' What did you mean?"

"How many times have I told you not to worry, Mary," said Philip with a slight edge to his voice. It was so unusual for Philip to use such a tone with me that I was taken aback. I pressed my lips together and stared at my husband. He tried to turn his eyes from mine, but found it impossible.

"Excuse me a moment," he said to Brink as he moved to the side of the tent. It must have looked as if the tall man, costumed from the late sixteen hundreds, was talking to himself in the dark corner of the tent, but I didn't care. I knew my husband! And I knew that if he were trying to keep me from knowing what he was doing, there was something wrong about it. Philip had always acted exactly the same way when he used to try and tell me he was 'just going for a night stroll', when in reality I knew he was secretly sneaking down to the caves under Salem Willows down at Juniper Point.

"Now then, just what are you up to, Philip English?" I said to my husband.

"Why nothing much, Mary," said Philip. "Why don't you and the others go on ahead to the monument up on Burial Hill. Mr. Brink and I will only be a moment here. It seems that he wants to try his hand at the wheel. He hasn't seen one for a long time, he says."

"You're lying to me, Philip, and you know it," I said, feeling the air around me begin to crackle. It was the same as it always was on Halloween night. I could begin to feel the extra power of 'All Hallows Eve' begin to move about me as I faced Philip. Try as I might I could not control it. Even Philip's almost mortal cheeks began to blush as the heat from my energy field began to fill the tent.

"Stop that, Mary," said Philip, backing away from me as a few tiny sparks began to flash from my toes.

"I can't," I said helplessly. "I don't know how it works. I just know that no one should upset me on this night. Remember what happened to that poor man last year? Do you think I really wanted to go that far?"

"I know, I know," said Philip, shaking his head as he looked over his shoulder to the waiting Gabriel Brink.

"Look Philip, just tell me what you're up to and get on with it," I said kindly, realizing that he was just trying to do what he thought was right, just like in the good old days when my husband pillaged far and wide to keep his family in comfort.

"Do you really mean that, Mary?"

"Of course I do, my love," I said, taking his strangely solid hand into my misty one. "All I want to know is what you're planning. Don't you think I have the right, after all we've been through?"

"Of course you do," said Philip. "It's just that I wanted to keep you from worrying too much. You see, I'm going to have to take a terrible risk, one that might mean the end of me. I was afraid that if you knew about it you might try to talk me out of it. And I have to go through with my plan. If I don't, all of us, you, me, our friends trapped in the memorial, and the living of Salem, will find themselves under the Devil's thumb, now and forever. Do you really know what that would mean, here in Salem?"

"It would mean that what happened over three hundred years ago, in this very place, would be but a prelude of what was to come," I said quietly.

"It would mean Armageddon," said Philip as he held me close. I knew that when he let me go and turned towards Gabriel Brink, that I might never be held by my beloved again. But then, that is how I had always felt as I had watched Philip sail away from Salem harbor. I was a sailor's wife and used to such things.

"Are you through with your lover's spat," I heard Brink say as he motioned Philip towards the roulette wheel.

"'Twas nothing of any consequence," said Philip, pulling himself up straight and setting his jaw.

"It never is if it involves a woman, eh, my friend," said Brink, slapping Philip on the back and offering him a small black cigar.

"Hey, no smoking in here," said a carny, who sat like a fat spider, at the far edge of the tent.

"Sorry," said Brink, crushing the flaming weed beneath his foot. "We wouldn't want to go up in flames, now would we, my friend.

"On with the game," said Philip as he placed his hands in his pockets and studied the wheel.

I motioned for Lillith and Tituba to join me in my darkened corner as I watched Philip face Gabriel Brink at the gaming table. It almost made me laugh to see the way Giles Cory remained glued to my husband's side. He made a most unlikely guardian angel, what with his large frame and mane of generous white hair. He looked more like Santa Clause than Saint Michael.

"Choose your color, sir," said Brink stretching his frame upward until he seemed several inches taller than he had before. I watched as the man/devil began to change, subtly, before my very eyes. It was not so much an outer change as it was something from within that made Gabriel Brink gradually take on the glamour of a powerful, dark spirit. Then, to my amazement, I watched as my husband also began to change.

"Why," said Tituba with a low toned chuckle, "those two look like a couple of male birds at mating season. Do you see the way they're strutting and preening! 'Tis a funny thing to see. A man in heat."

"They look more like dancers to me," said Lillith as we watched Gabe Brink extend his hand towards Philip and grasp it tightly.

"But most of all, like lovers," I said as Philip touched Gabe's hand with an almost gentle caress. He smiled at Brink and took a deep breath.

"Then it's black I'll take, friend Brink," I heard Philip say as he looked towards the gambling master who stood poised to spin the wheel, "and remember, if I win, the mirror and the girl's soul belong to me."

"And if you lose, we go to Saint Peter's so that I can send your soul to hell," said the Devil, giving Philip a playful wink.

"No!" I screamed as Philip looked at the dealer and said....

"Spin."

"Nobuddy ever fergits where he buried a hatchet."
Kin Hubbard:
"Abe Martin's Broadcast."

CHAPTER SIXTY

It seemed as if the world that swam before my eyes had slowed a hundred fold as we watched the red and black roulette wheel begin to spin. A haze of reddish black filled my head and merged into one dark bloody cloud in my thoughts. All I could see was the agony of an eternity before me, an eternity with no Philip.

"Please God, if Philip loses, let the Devil take me too."

"What utter nonsense," said Tituba as she jabbed me in the side. "Why would God give you to the Devil?"

"I'll not be separated from Philip," I said stubbornly.

"You may have no say in the matter, Mary," said Lillith. "I would have traded my own soul for Lynn's, but that was not in destiny's plan."

"Then to hell with destiny!" I cried as the roulette wheel ground to an agonizing halt.

"Red!" shouted the dealer as he took the token Philip handed him.

"Too bad," said Gabriel Brink, leering at my husband. "I almost wish the game had gone on a bit longer. It's rare I have such a lively prey."

"Let's just get this over with, shall we," said Philip steadily.

Despite the hopelessness that welled through me I couldn't help but feel a bit bemused. There was nothing about Philip that made me think of a defeated man. He squared his shoulders and waved his hand towards me with an almost jaunty smile.

"You won't mind if my dear wife and her friends come with us to St. Peter's, will you? After all, we should be allowed to say our farewells."

"By all means, Master English, invite the ladies," said Brink.

Then Philip looked at me as he touched his hands to his heart and gave me a slight bow. Over his head I could see Giles Cory's face, as stormy as thunder on a hot, gray summer afternoon.

"And what of friend Giles?" said Philip.

"Just the ladies," said Brink.

"I'll not be told what to do," bristled Giles as he took a swat at Brink.

"Get ye gone before I decide to take you too!" cried Brink as he jumped out of the angry spirit's way.

It was a lucky thing that the tent had been abandoned by everyone except the roulette dealer who stood with his back to us drinking wine from a bottle hidden in a paper bag. The last thing I felt like right now was dealing with interfering mortals. If this was to be the last time I was with my husband then let it be a moment shared only by those who lived in my shadow world, a world that had become home to me. I looked towards dear old Giles, he who had always loved my husband so, and couldn't help but feel the rage welling within me. How dare Brink deny Giles Cory such a small thing after all the man had suffered! Then I remembered. Giles had cheated the Devil out of his final victory when he had chosen death over hell. No wonder Brink wanted nothing to do with Giles Cory. In a way, he had won where my husband had failed. Giles had beaten the Devil at his own game.

"Go to the Witch Memorial, friend Giles," said Philip. "Guard the ones we love and help Mary to someday find a way of bringing their souls into the light of Salem."

"Who's to say there will be any light left once I'm through with you?" said Brink.

"Just wishful thinking," said Philip meekly.

How strange that Philip should be acting so meekly. Meek! My husband had never had a meek moment in his life! It was then that I knew he was up to something. And Giles Cory knew it too. I could tell by the way his eyes burned up at Philip's as the old man backed away from

Brink and floated towards the entrance to the tent. Whatever Philip was up to did not include surrender to the Devil.

Soon we were making our way up Brown Street, past the "Witch Museum." We could hear the horrified cries of the frightened tourists as they were led through the story of the witchcraft hysteria. Their cries echoed my own thoughts as we walked along the brick sidewalk that led to St. Peter's.

Saint Peter, the patron saint of fishermen, pirates, and all those who chose the sea as their earthy saint. Philip had always had an almost human relationship with Saint Peter. Many the time it was that I had seen Philip with a small sharp knife, whittling yet another exquisitely turned statue of his favorite saint. Sometimes I think those small statues, along with the great figureheads that adorned Philip's ships, were the reason that George Corwin was able to accuse us of witchcraft. To the Puritan's, any doll-like figure reeked of the Devil. To the people of Salem there was no difference between Philip's statues of Saint Peter and Tituba's voodoo dolls filled with pins. And in a way there wasn't. Both figures were part of a religion held dearly. Just because they were different didn't make them any less precious to the believer. Our greatest crime, besides prospering and rising above our station, had been to be two Anglicans surrounded by close minded, unbending Puritan's.

Well, Philip had solved that problem with one great bag filled with gold. He had turned his back on the Salem that had betrayed and hurt him so, and had built a new Salem within the old. And his finest achievement was the beautiful church he had built and dedicated to his own beloved Saint Peter, a man of the people who had risen to be the leader of Christ's people here on earth. No wonder Philip seemed to feel no fear. He was walking with the Devil, to be sure, but their feet were heading straight towards Philip's holy of holy, his temple dedicated to his friend and patron, Saint Peter.

I always felt a moment of awe when I beheld the fine stone structure that Philip had built. Even now it towered above the other buildings in Salem. The beautiful stained glass windows and fine bronze trim had been regarded by the Puritan's as a sinful vanity. They had sworn that Philip would yet come to an evil end because of his vanity. But those small bits of elegance had been nothing to what lay ahead for the wonderful church. I had been a spirit, yet to be raised from the ground, when the first church bell had arrived to take its place in the magnificent bell tower, but I have heard stories and listened to Philip tell me of the wonder of that bell. How proud he was of it. And what a symbol to his rebirth in Salem it had been! Every Sunday, without fail, that bell had rung to gather together the refugees from La Rochelle and the Isle of Jersey. Each Sunday, the souls that Philip had saved from destruction gathered together and gave thanks for their new life in a new world. And they still did. The descendants of the French Huguenots, Philip's own people, still came here. And every Sunday they passed by the varnished wooden plaque that told of Philip English and his founding of Saint Peter's. There was even an ancient glass and wood case that held the original documents, in Philip's own handwriting, granting the land and the monies for this haven.

"It's really quite nice, for a church," I heard Gabe Brink say as he motioned for Philip to enter St. Peter's.

"No, after you, I insist," said Philip with a regal wave of his hand. I had been right, the closer he got to St. Peter's the braver my husband felt. I could almost smell the courage that welled up inside him.

"Oh no," laughed the Devil, "I'm not falling for that one. How do I know what's in there? After all, this is your 'lair' is it not, Master English?"

"I have no idea what you're talking about," said Philip, "I was just trying to be polite. It's a shame that first thing to go when one is under strain is manners, is it not."

"Are you saying I have no manners?" bristled Gabe Brink.

"No, I'm just saying...."

"Never mind, let's just do this, shall we?" said Brink, impatiently pushing at the heavy wood and iron doors. They swung open far more easily than even I expected. It was almost as if unseen hands were welcoming the Devil into what he called, Philip's "lair."

Philip and Gabe Brink stood at the back of the church, poised for the walk down the aisle. The midnight black of Brink's police uniform contrasted sharply with the blue velvet breeches and blousing white linen of Philip's shirt. It was pure coincidence, I know, but the long cream satin vest that Philip wore over his shirt, and stock wrapped about his neck, were the very ones that he had worn on our wedding day. My own mother, Eleanor, had embroidered the fine pale blue forget-me-nots and yellow buttercups that were scattered elegantly across my husband's broad chest. Philip took a deep breath and took off his dark blue hat with the white feathered plume. Then, hat in hand, he bent a knee in respect to the alter and his saint.

"You'll not be doing that much longer," laughed the Devil. His laughter echoed hollowly in the great expanse of the old church, and then, suddenly, was picked up by another, deeper voice, that seemed to issue from the altar.

"What's that? Who's there?" yelled Brink.

"'Tis nothing but the wind," said Philip calmly as he got to his feet. "Now, as you said, 'let's just do it.'"

Philip took Gabe Brink's arm and began to lead him down the aisle towards the altar. Tituba, Lillith and I followed behind, like three bridesmaids trailing an unholy wedding. From behind, I heard the old doors open again and was aware of another presence, a human presence. I glanced back to see Jim Proctor and Lillith's friend Hannah staring at the figures of Gabe Brink and Philip English as they made their way towards the great alter of St. Peter's. To my surprise, they quietly slipped into a pew at the rear of the church and sat down. I heard Hannah whispering something to Jim, but was unable to make out her words. Then I turned my attention back towards the altar where the Devil and my husband now stood.

"Would you allow me a few moments to pray," asked Philip as he got to his knees.

"It would hardly be polite for me to refuse such a request," said Brink.

"I can see I was wrong about you, sir," said Philip with a brilliant smile. "You are a gentleman."

With those words, Philip closed his eyes and began to pray:

"Dear Lord of us all, protect me as I walk this night into hell. Know that even thought I take the Devil into my heart, of my own free will, I do it through the teachings that you have given me. I ask only that you guard and care for those I leave behind."

It was strange, but as I listened to Philip's voice, I seemed to hear the humming of another being issuing from somewhere beneath my feet. The voice was light and deep at the same time, like that of a large woman or a smallish man. Then the sound stopped as suddenly as it started.

"It must be some madness contained within this place," I whispered to myself as Philip began his final prayer, the one that no true witch could repeat without stumbling:

"Our Father, who art in heaven, hallowed be thy name.
They kingdom come, thy will be done, on earth as it is in heaven.
Give us this day our daily bread, and forgive us our trespasses,
as we forgive those who trespass against us.
And lead us not into temptation, but deliver us from evil.
For thine is the kingdom and the power and the glory, for ever and ever.
Amen."

As Philip finished, I felt a strange, snakelike movement beneath my feet. I steeled myself to take a last look at my husband before Gabriel Brink dragged him into the molten filth of hell, but as I looked towards Philip I saw that he was pressing his face against the altar cloth in a desperate attempt to disguise the intense joy that shone from his face. It was then that I heard, once again, the voice beneath the altar.

"Forgive us our trespasses, as we forgive those who trespass against us!" shouted the fiercely angry voice in a mad parody of Philip's prayer. Then the voice continued, rearranging the 'Lord's Prayer' to suit its own whims. "Tempt us not into evil," it shouted madly, "for we may create a kingdom more powerful and glorious on this earth as in heaven, a kingdom that will last forever and ever! For we are the hallowed and we do have names!"

The screaming voice surrounded all the watchers in the church as a swirling force began to engulf us. The doors of St. Peter's slammed shut violently, shaking the very glass in the windows. I looked at Philip again and saw that he was standing with his feet wide apart and his hands on his hips. He was laughing like a madman.

"Philip!" I screamed as the whirlwind knocked Lillith, Tituba and myself against the ancient wooden tablets that had been decorated with the finest gilt and emblazoned with the Ten Commandments.

Philip looked directly towards us as we cowered under the shelter of the tablets. We were confused but unhurt. I waved to him to let him know we were safe, and he blew me a kiss. I caught it with my hands, as I had always done when we played our happy lovegames, and smiled at him triumphantly. I tried to let him know, without words, that I loved and believed in him. I knew that, whatever happened, our love was an eternal thing that not even the Devil could take away from us. Somehow, in some way, I know Philip heard my thoughts, because I saw him turn back towards Gabriel Brink, ready to fight to the death for what he believed in. This was the Philip English that I had first believed in as a ragged scurvy, hanging around Derby Wharf as he told the laughing sailors about how he would someday own the greatest fleet of sailing ships the world had ever seen. This was the Philip English of legend that had awed the world with his cunning and bravery.

And, I saw that he was no longer alone. Standing upon the altar were four men and one woman. They were broken and bloody, with remnants of sackcloth hanging from their frames. The smallest, most powerfully built of the men, leaped from the altar and stood between Philip and the Devil.

"Do I still look like an angel of light, friend Philip?" asked the laughing wraith.

Upon hearing the Reverend George Burroughs perfectly recite the 'Lord's Prayer' on the Gallows, Cotton Mather declared that the Devil was capable of transforming himself "into an angel of light." The restless crowd found comfort in Mather's words as they allowed the hangings to continue.
The Reverend Cotton Mather:
August 19th, 1692.

CHAPTER SIXTY ONE

"More than ever," said Philip as he stretched his right hand towards George Burroughs, former pastor of Salem Village, and victim of the witch trials. The incredible strength that was housed in Burroughs' small but powerful body was evident still, even though he had spent over three hundred years buried beneath the altar of St. Peter's.

I looked towards the altar and was delighted to see four more old friends, friends that Philip had honored in death by taking their earthly remains from the rockpile on Gallows Hill and burying them here, in hallowed ground. Their death and reburial beneath the holy stone had set in motion the wheels of fate for the ghosts of Salem. These five were the charter members of our misty community, its founding fathers and mother, so to speak.

"Who are they?" I heard Lillith ask Tituba, as one by one our old friends leaped from St. Peter's altar and stood next to each other. They formed a barrier between Philip and the Devil.

"They're the folk that was hanged up on the hill in August of 1692," said Tituba with a merry cackle. "It seems that the longer I 'hang' about this new Salem, the more it feels like home. That woman there is Martha Carrier, whose two boys were tortured into betraying their mother. Then, there's that small gent who was the best Reverend this town ever had, George Burroughs, himself. The others be Johnny Proctor, that's him with the fine hat, Constable Willard, who died 'cause he wouldn't hang his neighbors, and old George Jacobs. He saved his granddaughter, you know. The Putnam's wanted to see some Jacobs' blood spilled and had to settle for old George. He's a sly one, he is, getting the girl to confess and then accuse him so that they couldn't hang her."

"George Jacobs?" said Lillith, "I though his body had been stolen away by his family and buried on old Rebecca Nurse's farm."

"'Twas a body, to be sure, that the Jacobs' family took from under the rocks. No one knew whose, so eaten it was by the dogs and crows. They thought it was George, at first, but soon learned different," said Tituba. "Master English beat even the Jacobs family up the hill that day. We all soon learned that Master English stole these five away to be hidden and buried decently later. I've often wondered who's buried up in Rebecca's apple orchard."

"She's right, Lillith," I said to the confused mortal, "That's old George, I'd know him anywhere."

"Look," whispered Lillith as a dark cloud began to form in the aisle behind Gabriel Brink. At first it seemed to take on the qualities of muddy steam, hissing and boiling as it swarmed around Brink, and then it gathered itself together and became more solid. The Devil backed towards the cloud as the five hanging victims crowded him away from the altar where Philip stood. The varnished wooden floor beneath the old oriental runner began to sway and ripple under the heat of the hissing form as it walked backwards behind Brink. The Devil began to inch his way slowly towards the closed doors of St. Peter's.

From somewhere far above the chanting of the five souls was taken up by a ghostly pipe and drum. It was a slow cadence, the pipe sang mournfully as the drum beat a slow tattoo.

"I remember that sound," said Tituba as the drone of a single bagpipe joined the reed pipe and the tightly stretched drum. "'Tis what the King's men played when they came for the condemned. It's one sound I'll never forget. I lay in the cold mud, night after night, hearing that sound in my dreams. But they never came for me. One by one I watched the others go, while I stayed chained to that cursed wall. It would have been much easier for me if they had hanged me too. To see the innocent go so bravely to their death because of something I did almost drove me mad. 'Tis hell I deserve, and hell I'll get."

"Hush now, don't say such things," I said as I watched the swirling cloud behind Gabriel Brink begin to take shape. "There's no fault in you, Tituba. What happened was the same thing that had happened to women in Europe, long before you were ever born. Everyone knew that over and over again, groups of young girls and lust filled men had wandered through the villages of Germany, France and England, accusing and burning the old, the sick and the poor. At least here, the Puritans only hanged us."

"What is that thing?" said Lillith, grabbing my arm in panic as the dark cloud behind Brink began to take form. There was an almost oily look to the spirit thing as it began to gel. Suddenly, I knew who. There was only one soul in Salem so disgusting. Never again would I be able to gaze upon that shape with anything but revulsion.

"It's the shade of George Corwin," I said in terror as I watched Gabe Brink stop halfway down the aisle. The music from the rafters had become louder as Corwin's shape became more firm. Philip stood at the altar with only the poor tortured souls of our five friends protecting him from the Devil and his hideous imp.

"Oh my love," I said as I stretched out my arms to my Philip. I began to rise from the protection of the wooden tablets and float towards him.

"No Mary!" he screamed as I alighted by his side.

"I have no choice, my darling," I said, touching Philip's dear face. "Win or lose, we're doing this together. You never left me in my time of need. How could leave you?"

"But you're wrong, Mary," said Philip. "I did leave you. When they came for me, I left you to your fate in Salem dungeon. It was only when I was caught that I was with you again."

"You're lying Philip, and you know it. You just want me to go away so I'll be safe. A man like you never lets himself be caught unless he wants to. You and young Johnny Alden made up a plan. And getting caught was part of that plan. But you had no guarantee that it would work. You were ready to die for me, Philip, and I know it. How could you ever think that I would do any less for you!"

"I would never leave you, my beloved," said Philip as he put his arm around my waist and tilted my face towards his. He kissed me softly, with a passion beyond the flesh.

"Nor I you, my darling," I said as I beheld his dear face, scarred from the sea, and beautiful beyond belief. We joined hands and stepped from the altar, moving slowly towards the five souls that stood between us and hell.

"Oh beat the drum slowly and play the fife lowly,
Play the Dead March as you carry me along."
Anonymous: "A Cowboy Song."

CHAPTER SIXTY TWO

There were seven souls that faced the Devil and his minion on that All Hallows Eve. The Church that my husband had founded upon the blood and bones of the victims of the Salem Witch Trials was to be the final battleground between the Devil and the ghosts of Salem.

John Proctor, George Burroughs, John Willard, Martha Carrier, George Jacobs, and Philip and Mary English were determined to have done with the Devil, once and for all. The souls of the five men and two women that advanced on Gabriel Brink and George Corwin had a dreadful secret, a secret shared by only the most desperate. It was simply this. We had nothing left to lose, therefore we had no fear. Each one of us had loved and lost that which we held most dear, as had all those who had suffered at the hands of the demonic creatures that now blocked our way.

George Burroughs turned to us as our feet touched the carpet below the altar. "Welcome to the battle, my friends."

"So now it's a battle, is it?" hissed Brink as he tore the shirt from his body, revealing what lay below. He was built like a man and yet not like a man. The muscles beneath his skin undulated in an oddly sensuous way. They were almost like an entity to themselves as they knotted and flexed in the soft candlelight of the church.

Then the Devil smiled at Martha Carrier. "Come my dear, why would you want to spend eternity in this place when I can offer you the beauties of my world? All you have to do is take my hand. I can offer you so much more than this cold, ghostly existence. My way is one of the earth, the flesh and desire. Take my hand and all that I have can be yours."

I watched in horror as a bemused expression came over the Martha's face. Who could blame her for being tempted? She had been torn from her hearth and home in the fullness of womanhood. The warmth of Brink's smile must have been heart warming after the coldness of her three hundred year sleep under the stones of St. Peter's.

"Don't," I screamed as I hurtled forward and grabbed Martha's outstretched hand. The moment I did so, a feeling of power rushed through me. "Philip, take my other hand again," I said to him as I struggled to hold onto Martha.

Even the combined force of the two of us was not enough to keep Martha from the almost magnetic force of the Devil. One by one the seven of us joined hands until, at last, Martha's eyes opened wide with horror.

"Get thee behind me Satan," she screamed, echoing the scriptures she had chanted since childhood. In a blinding flash of light, Brink disappeared, leaving the shade of George Corwin to face us alone. The five souls of St. Peter's fell on Corwin and lifted him high.

I had a vision of the last thought Lynn March had sent through my head before the Devil had carried her off. It was a scene of George Corwin in the bell tower of St. Peter's.

"So now, the prophecy is fulfilled," laughed Tituba as she ran madly after Corwin and the vengeful souls.

"Hurry, they're heading towards the tower," yelled Lillith as she followed Tituba towards the small door next to the baptismal font. I was dimly aware of Jim Proctor and Hannah watching in horror as Philip and I flew past the end pews, but there was no time to do anything but follow the grotesque mummers parade as it made its way up the narrow staircase towards the bells of St. Peter's.

Then, the "Gallows" band struck up its tune again, this time with a more lively cadence. First the tight headed drum quickened its pace, followed by the reed and then the bagpipe's droning wail.

"Philip, do you recognize that tune?" I asked as we quickly but carefully made our way up the narrow winding staircase.

"'Tis the same one I used to sing to our children when they woke in the middle of the night afraid of the dark."

"Aye," I laughed hollowly, "that's the very one. I always meant to ask you the name of it, but I kept forgetting."

"My own mother sang it to me when I was but a babe in arms," said Philip with glowing eyes. "It's called, 'La Mist' En L'aire:'"

"Bon homme, bon homme,

que savez vous faire?

Savez vous jouer de la mist' en l'aire?

L'aire, l'aire, l'aire, de la mist' en l'aire?

L'aire, l'aire, l'aire, de la mist' en l'aire?

Ah! Ah! Ah! Que savez vous faire?"

Philip's beautiful voice filled the stairway as we made the last turn towards the bell tower. Suddenly, his voice was joined by others, sweeter and higher than Philip's, but of the same quality and richness. The sound brought tears to my eyes as I struggled to keep my mind on what lay ahead. It was a miracle! How could a mother ignore such a beautiful choir, one made up of her own children's voices?

"My little loves," I cried out to the unforgiving stones, "are you with us at last?"

"We always have been, Mama," said the voice of my daughter Mary, not a woman grown, but as I remembered her at five.

"And I'm here too, Mama," said a boy with a slight lisp. It could only be our small William who had died so young and tender, long before his baby sounds had become a man's.

"We're all here, Papa," said Susannah, who had always been Philip's special darling. "There's me and baby Susannah, Mary, big and little William, Philip, who's still trying to tell us all what to do, John, and baby Ebenezer. We've always been here. Our singing fills St. Peter's every Sunday when the choir sings."

"And it's you who make the merry music now?" asked Philip, trying to understand this happy thing.

"Aye, Father, 'tis us," said young Philip in the cracking voice of a thirteen year old. "We're together and happy, as happy as we were on earth with you and Mama."

"Thank the Lord," I breathed.

"And the Goddess, Mama, don't forget her. She's here tonight too, you know. She knows that the evil spirit who lives here must be sent from this place," said Susannah. "Hurry Mama, before it's too late. He grows in power daily and has threatened to harm us. We're tired of his stink and his evil ways. He frightens baby Ebenezer."

"Yes Mama, make him go away," lisped little William, "he tries to pinch us in the dark. I don't like Master Corwin."

"Will you still be here if we do this thing? Banishing one spirit may banish all" I said to my children, overwhelmed at the prospect of losing them again.

"Only those who have chosen the Devil will banish with Corwin. We will be here, in this place forever if you drive away the evil this night," said steady John. "It was Corwin that kept us from singing for you, but once he is gone we shall be free to fill St. Peter's with music forever."

"Then it shall be done," said Philip, taking my hand and pulling me forward. "Come, Mary, let's finish what we have started."

"But the children!" I cried, reluctant to leave my babies, the little souls that had been the living symbol of our love. Six living, two dead, all dead now because of the heartlessness of time.

"We will be here waiting, Mama," said William.

Now I knew how Lillith March must have felt when she first saw and heard her own ghostly child. How terrible it must have been to lose Lynn not once, but twice. Even as we struggled up the last few steps to the bell tower, I was overwhelmed with grief for the mortal woman. The Devil had disappeared with Lynn's soul tucked away in his pocket. My mother's heart bled for the witch, Lillith March.

As we made the final turn into the bell tower I was overwhelmed by a yellowish fog and an incredible smell.

"It's sulfur," said Lillith, turning towards me. She and Tituba were standing before the great leaded glass window that made up the rear of the tower wall. Quickly, Philip and I joined them, being careful to stay out of the way of the "Gallows Five" as they held Corwin aloft in their arms.

"The rope, friend English," said John Proctor as he nodded with his head towards an ancient length of rope that lay abandoned on the stone floor.

"What do you want me to do with it?" asked Philip, for once deferring his command to another.

"Loop the rope around yon bell and tie it tight," said Proctor.

Philip did as he was told with a sailor's skill. The rope neatly snagged the top of the bell and rounded it handily.

"Now, tie it off there," said Proctor, pointing to an enormous metal rod that ran through the wall and down into the church. It was plain to see how this tower had withstood many a hurricane and nor'easter. It was built like a fortress. Philip's fortress against any storm.

"What are they going to do?" I asked Tituba as I waved the yellow cloud away from my face. Ghost that I was, I could tell that this essence came straight from hell.

"They're going to hang the fiend," said Tituba.

George Corwin struggled in the arms of his victims, but it was no use. Every time he tried to scream, the yellowish filth issued from his mouth making the whole scene look like a ghastly parody of a bright August day, a day like that of August 19th, 1692.

We watched as John Proctor, John Willard, George Jacobs, Martha Carrier, and the Reverend George Jacobs solemnly tied the noose around the silently screaming Corwin. The only sound that could be heard was the innocent voices of my children, chanting their childhood tune as they played on their instruments.

"Are there any last words you have to share with us," asked Burroughs.

"You can't do this!" screamed Corwin. "I've had no trial, no judge, no jury. I'm not ready to die!"

"Your own words condemn you, Corwin!" shouted John Proctor. "Those were my last words, spoken as you pushed the ladder from beneath me and watched me die. So be it, you have stood as your own judge and jury. Let me have the pleasure of being your hangman!"

The muscles in John Proctor's arms strained as he gave George Corwin a great push, sending Corwin out into midair. The Sheriff of Salem struggled helplessly from the bell. We watched with feelings of delight and horror as his face turned red and then black. George Corwin struggled for a few moments and then became motionless. Then, he opened his eyes and began to cry.

"Someone help me, help me, for God's sake, help me!" he screamed in raspy tones as the noose held his neck fast.

"Pray to your Devil for that," yelled Burroughs.

"But ye say ye are of heaven! Isn't it right and proper to forgive me?" pleaded Corwin.

"I think I've had enough of holiness if it means helping you!" yelled Martha Carrier like a banshee.

"You'll die if you have to stay there for a millennium," said John Willard the Constable. "'Tis the law of man and God that has decreed it. We do no foul deed, only justice here. If you had ten thousand eyes we could not pluck them out fast enough to bring everything about even. 'An eye for an eye,' you know. 'Tis the heaven's own law!"

Echoing Willard's words was a sound from outside. It was a great rumble that turned into a magnificent clap of thunder. Suddenly the tower was engulfed in an all consuming thunderstorm that shook St. Peter's to its foundations. I could hear footsteps from below hurrying up the stairs. Jim Proctor and Hannah appeared under the arched stones that formed the bell tower.

"Lillith," yelled Jim, "get away from that!"

We turned to where Jim pointed and saw that the heavy metal rod that held Corwin's rope was beginning to vibrate. Lillith ran towards Jim and Hannah and the three mortals huddled under the safety of the arched stones just as the whole bell tower was struck by a tremendous bolt of lightning.

When the air cleared there was nothing left of George Corwin but his tattered black cloak, fluttering towards the ground like a dead bat.

"Never send for whom the bell tolls;
it tolls for thee."
John Donne:
"Devotions Upon Emergent Occasions, No. 17."

CHAPTER SIXTY THREE

Giles, what's that sound?" asked Martha Cory as she took her husband's arm.

"'Tis the bells of St. Peter's, lovedy," he said pinching her on the cheek.

"Then they've done it," laughed Bridget Bishop as she jumped from stone to stone, upsetting her emerging neighbors as they floated above their monuments. Of the nineteen, there were fourteen who now stood above the carefully placed markers that the faithful of Salem had carved out in remembrance of the terrible year, 1692. Giles looked around the grassy expanse and took careful count.

"Bridget Bishop, Sarah Good, Elizabeth Howe, Susannah Martin, Rebecca Nurse, Sarah Wildes, Martha Cory, Mary Easty, Alice Parker, Mary Parker, Ann Pudeator, Margaret Scott, Wilmot Redd, Samuel Wardwell...."

"And Giles Cory," said Martha, looking up at Giles. "But where are the other five? Where are George Burroughs, Martha Carrier, George Jacobs, John Proctor, and our friend, John Willard?"

"They're at St. Peter's," said Giles. "'Tis they who have wrought this miracle. They and Mary and Philip English."

"Well, shouldn't we all be together at a time like this?" said Martha, giving Giles a little push.

"Still nagging me, eh, Martha," said Giles lovingly, as he closed his eyes and made a wish upon the Goddess' moon that appeared bright and full in the clearing sky. When he opened them, Giles and the rest of the monument ghosts stood in the great bell tower of St. Peter's. The shining bell moved back and forth slowly as it tolled but once.

"It's All Saint's Day," said Mary English as she came towards them.

EPILOGUE

RESTLESS SOULS

"This is very midsummer madness."
William Shakespeare: *Twelfth Night*, III, iv, 62.'

CHAPTER SIXTY FOUR

Midsummer's Night Eve,
The New Millennium.

"Do I look as stupid as I feel?" asked Nora English as she straightened the wreath of pink and white roses that Lillith had placed on her head.

"I think you look beautiful," said Jake, staring at Nora in awe.

"So do I," I said as Philip gave me a happy hug.

"Come on, Nora," said Lillith, "we had to ask someone to be our 'maiden.'"

"I'm hardly a maiden after what I've been through," said Nora, staring out the living room window towards Salem Common. Gathered in the beautiful evening sun were all the faithful of the Goddess, the worshipers of Wicca, awaiting the feast of midsummer.

"How many times have I told you that nothing was your fault, or Jake's either for that matter. You have to let go of the past. It's the only way you're ever going to leave this thing behind you. Think of tonight as a new beginning," said Lillith firmly.

"Sure, just like you have," said Nora. "You don't think I hear you crying for Lynn, but I do. You haven't been able to let go of her."

"That's different," said Lillith, looking towards me sadly. "I hope you never understand the pain of losing a child. But what's done is done. Whether we like it or not, we have to go on living."

"I'm sorry, Aunt Lillith," said Nora. "It's just that this whole 'Midsummer Night's Eve' thing makes me nervous. We never did find out what happened to Gabriel Brink. What if he's out there waiting for us. I know I'm not the one that sees into the future around here, but I've had a funny feeling all day that something strange is going to happen."

"We'll probably never find out where Brink went," said Philip, standing up and straightening his vest. "He wasn't real, you know. Brink was just a form the Devil concocted to gain our trust."

"Well," said Nora, "if he did it once can't he do it again? Especially on a night like this when the veil is thin between our world and his."

"That's why we're here, my love," I said to Nora. "It's much easier for us to spot the Devil that it is for you. Don't be afraid. Philip beat the Devil at his own game. I doubt if he'd show his face around here again. The Devil hates to look foolish."

"So do I," laughed Nora, fluffing out her white linen dress. "Come on Jake, I'm not walking out of here alone."

"Delighted to escort you, ma'am," said Jake in his best "Rhett Butler" imitation.

We crossed the street and entered Salem Common. On the bandstand stood the high priests and priestesses of many temples. Halloween was for the tourists. Midsummer Night's Eve was for the faithful followers of the Goddess who had come to Salem to live under her protection. Long before the witch trials, Salem had possessed an aura of the supernatural. Even the natives who had lived on this land for thousands of years had known that Salem was built upon the earthly home of the otherworlds. They had always regarded it as hallowed ground.

"I've never seen him before. Who is he?" asked Nora, pointing towards a tall man with flowing golden curls. He was dressed as a high priest of Wicca and held out a branch of linden leaves as green as his own sparkling eyes.

"I don't know," said Lillith, adjusting the sleeves of her willow green gown as she moved gracefully towards the bandstand. The man with the linden branch came slowly towards Lillith. He greeted her more like a familiar dance partner than a stranger.

"You're Lillith March, aren't you," he said as he held his arms towards her and enclosed Lillith in a warm embrace.

"Why yes, I am," said Lillith, laughing like a young girl as the man kissed her on both cheeks.

"Michael Paradise, at your service, oh beloved of the Goddess," said the man, taking Lillith's hand and kissing it reverently.

There was something about the man's smoothness that made me uneasy, but I was reluctant to interrupt the faithful of the Goddess as they ascended to their place of worship. I watched warily as Michael Paradise took Lillith's hand and escorted her to the stone pillared platform covered with a massive granite canopy. What Salem called a bandstand actually looked more like a small castle. It had been constructed under an arch of lush elm trees and was surrounded by a moat of emerald green grass. The grass had been freshly cut and gave off a magical fragrance.

I turned my head as Lillith's happy laughter floated towards me. It was a long time since any of us had heard Lillith laugh. The glow of the setting sun cast it's rosy beauty on the stunning man and woman standing above me. They looked like a great lord and lady surveying their estates.

"Do you think he's the one Lillith has been waiting for?" asked Philip as he put his arms around me, twinning the actions of the high priest and priestess.

"I don't know," I said, "but it's wonderful to see Lillith happy for a change."

We watched in delighted silence as Nora and Jake joined Lillith and Michael Paradise at the altar of the Goddess. The evening star came out and shown down upon the new found lovers as they separated from the two younger worshipers and descended the steps.

Lillith and Michael Paradise moved down the path towards the largest tree on Salem Common. It was a giant ash tree that loomed above all others. The tree was what the ancients had called Yggdrasil, the tree that held the world together. It was said to be the home of the goddess, Hel, who made her home in its roots. It was the door to the underworld.

"Aunt Mary, stop them!" screamed Nora as Michael Paradise pressed a small shiny object into Lillith's hand. "It's the mirror!"

But it was too late, the ecstasy on Lillith's face told me that the high priestess of Salem had become the devil's consort. Lillith had given her soul to the devil to save her daughter from eternal damnation.

"They do make a lovely couple," I said to Philip as Michael and Lillith walked towards the house on Forrester Street.

"And now I know where the Devil lives," said Philip, raising his face to the full moon of the Goddess. "Mary, I hate to admit this, but things were really getting a little too quiet around here for my taste."

"I know my love," I said, turning my lips towards my lover, my husband. "It should be quite an interesting millennium."